PRAISE FOR
SO HAPPY TOGETHER

"*So Happy Together* exposes disturbance beneath the surface of innocence and desire amid a group of college students during the tumultuous '60s. Twenty years later and with grit, humor, and compassion, a spirited Caro unpacks a past shadowed by secrets, unrequited passion, and the consequences of settling. This is a page-turning road trip story of a human heart coming to terms with brokenness and regret, not just once, but finally, and where the map gets drawn as we go."
—JODI PALONI, author of *They Could Live with Themselves*

"Spoiler alert: no one is really happy together in *So Happy Together*. That's because the road trip we join herein is about busting through such fantasies to get to self-actualization. And although perfect happiness may be elusive, along the way we do get candid, carnal exploration, as our exuberant narrator takers her "journey to parts unknown"—geographic and metaphoric. Bouncing back and forth between love beads and yuppie '80s trappings, loveless sex and sexless love, Shepherd's novel is like sharing late-night gossip with a good friend."
—ARIELLE GREENBERG, author of *I Live in the Country & Other Dirty Poems*

"Shepherd takes us on a literal ride into the not-so-distant past, remembering how naïve we were before we understood there are things you just can't change—even if you're destined, even if you're soulmates, even if you're willing to risk everything . . . some calls are louder than love . . . The reader will ache at the forced (and quite salty) sass of the young narrator, desperate to show it doesn't hurt. And highly enjoy the ironic wit of the mature voice who knows better and goes for it all the same. A story for anyone who can relate to how we cling to a fantasy of the past to avoid committing to the present."

—RITA DRAGONETTE, author of *The Fourteenth of September*

"Shepherd's novel carries us on a journey many of us think of taking when we reach mid-life, when family responsibilities threaten to drown our creative selves. Who were we back in our vibrant youth? Can we recapture some part of that? I was captivated as the protagonist, Caro, sets off to find both her lost love and her identity as a youthful playwright and finds self-knowledge and joy in the process."

—ELAYNE KLASSON, award-winning author of *Love is a Rebellious Bird*

SO
HAPPY
TOGETHER

SO HAPPY TOGETHER

A Novel

DEBORAH K. SHEPHERD

SHE WRITES PRESS

Published 2021
Printed in the United States of America
Print ISBN: 978-1-64742-026-0
E-ISBN: 978-1-64742-027-7
Library of Congress Control Number: 2020916344

For information, address:
She Writes Press
1569 Solano Ave #546
Berkeley, CA 94707

Interior design by Tabitha Lahr

She Writes Press is a division of SparkPoint Studio, LLC.

All company and/or product names may be trade names, logos, trademarks, and/or registered trademarks and are the property of their respective owners.

This is a work of fiction. Names, characters, places, and incidents either are the product of the author's imagination or are used fictitiously. Any resemblance to actual persons, living or dead, is entirely coincidental.

"Love in the Middle of the Air" and excerpt from "Love-Lust Poem" from *Collected Poems of Lenore Kandel*, published by North Atlantic Books, copyright 2012 by The Estate of Lenore Kandel. Originally appeared in *Word Alchemy*, Grove Press, 1967. Reprinted by permission of North Atlantic Books.

"Most Like An Arch This Marriage," from *I Marry You*, by John Ciardi, published by Rutgers University Press, copyright 1958. Reprinted with permission from Ciardi Family Publishing Trust.

For Henry

PROLOGUE

Tucson, Arizona, 1967

P eter never stuttered when he was on stage. Framed by a proscenium, he was as eloquent as Sirs Richard Burton, Laurence Olivier, and Alec Guinness put together, and could vanquish those plosives and fricatives and bilabials like Hamlet dispatching his duplicitous mother and murderous stepfather with a thrust of his sword.

Offstage, Peter MacKinley (first name starting with a plosive, last name with a bilabial) couldn't even introduce himself without grimacing and grunting and repeatedly pursing his lips. At first, it was painful to watch, but I got used to it. Except for that stuttering and his surprisingly wry sense of humor, you might not even notice he was there. He was a sweet, shy, soft-spoken, self-effacing, church-going college boy who blushed easily, was good to his mother, and rescued stray cats.

But somewhere between the green room and the wings, he transformed. It wasn't just the makeup or the costume or the lights or all the theatrical abracadabra that I knew was just an illusion. It happened every time he stepped on stage. To me, he seemed broader and taller and more at home in his own skin. And did I mention brave? He didn't just *play* the part, he was *alive* in it.

That blossom in my heart, I'll fling to you—
Armfuls of loose bloom! Love, I love beyond
Breath, beyond reason, beyond love's own power
Of loving! Your name is like a golden bell
Hung in my heart; and when I think of you,
I tremble, and the bell swings and rings—
'Roxanne! Roxanne!' . . . Along my veins, 'Roxanne. . .'

Each night, I hovered in the wings and held my breath as he declaimed these words to my stage rival. Each night, he could have had me right then and there, on those floorboards, curtain up or down, audience be damned.

And then, after the bows and the adulation, the cold-creamed makeup removal and the costume change, swashbuckling Cyrano de Bergerac became sweet, shy, stuttering Peter MacKinley again.

I loved him in both his personas.

CHAPTER ONE

Westport, Connecticut, 1987

I don't remember exactly when it started—it had been awhile since I'd given Peter much thought—but then, there he was, dropping by with increasing frequency and always at the most inconvenient moments, distracting me from one chore or another, until I had to shoo him away so I could get the kids to basketball practice or take my husband's suits to the cleaners or put dinner on the table. I took his visitations as a sign of my unhappiness, until the nightmare, and after that, I knew there was more to it. I just knew he was in trouble. And so was I.

It was right out of the awful last scene of that Stephen King movie, *Carrie*, when Sissy Spacek's bloody arm reaches up from under the ground to grab Amy Irving. Only this arm was skeletal, and it was Peter's. I woke up screaming my head off, just like Amy, but I was in our bedroom and it was Jack who reached out to comfort me.

"Honey, what is it? Bad dream? Shh, shh. It's alright. Everything's alright."

He wrapped his arms around me, still making those "shh, shh" sounds, and then started rubbing my back. And, against my better judgment, I snuggled into him for comfort. And he kept rubbing. "Shh, shh." Rub. Rub. Rub.

And then, because my back is my second most erogenous zone, and despite the fact that I had not desired my husband for months, and he had pretty much given up on trying, we were there.

I knew Jack's contours as well as I knew my own, maybe better, and we were moving to our bodies' shared memory of so many years, so many couplings.

But it was Peter who made me come.

And once I had committed adultery in my heart, in my husband's embrace, I knew it would only be a matter of time.

But the next morning, I started doubting myself. Maybe the bad dream was just another manifestation of the spring, summer, fall, and winter of my discontent? There was a simple way to find out. Peter's number was indelibly printed on my brain. I could just pick up the phone and call him and ask him if everything was okay. Wait, no, I couldn't, not after the life-altering debacle of our last time together in Tucson, not to mention it had been twenty years since I had laid eyes on him. He was probably fine, and I would look like some kind of idiot, still connected to him after all these years, despite everything I had learned. It would be humiliating and so painfully awkward. I wouldn't know what to say. Neither would he. I would beat myself up for months afterwards (maybe forever), and I would still be stuck in my stultifying marriage and I just couldn't bear it.

I put it out of my head and filled the empty space with plans for my father-in-law's surprise sixty-fifth birthday party. But it was Peter who reminded me to order both a chocolate and a carrot cake, because my mother-in-law is allergic to chocolate. Uh uh, not taking dessert orders from someone who separated his Oreos and licked the icing before dunking the plain wafers in milk. And I rejected his ideas for redecorating my daughter's bedroom. Pretty nervy of him, suggesting color schemes and telling me what kind of wallpaper to buy. Yeah, as *if* I would take the advice of someone whose apartment looked like it came straight from the pages of

"Trends in Tacky Motel Décor, circa 1958." I found Peter looking over my shoulder while I was leafing through garden catalogs for next spring's perennials. He told me not to buy the rose bushes I was coveting because they attracted Japanese beetles, and pointed out some stunning orange dahlias, instead. I had to tell him that here in the Northeast, dahlias were not technically perennials, that the tubers had to be dug up in the fall, stored through the winter, and then replanted in the spring, and stunning though they were, I didn't have time for such labor-intensive flowers. He insisted that their beauty made them worth it. Easy for him to say.

And yet, and yet . . . I'd have given anything to have him here in the flesh, my partner in crime, just like he used to be.

I couldn't call him, and I couldn't live with his phantasma-goric presence. But I could call Ernesto. He would know. Once upon a time, Ernesto, his boyfriend Scott, Peter, and I were The Fabulous Foursome (not a rock group, but the best of friends). I had a hunch Ernesto would still be in contact with Peter.

"Hey, Caro, it's been ages. How are you?"

"Fine, Ernesto. How about you?"

"All good here."

And then there was a pause. He knew I hadn't called six years after we'd last run into each other, on Manhattan's Upper West Side, to inquire about his health.

"Listen, I know this sounds weird, but I just have this feeling about Peter . . . I don't know, Ernesto, I think he might be in some kind of trouble . . ."

There was a beat, and then another, before he answered.

"You know, I always thought you two had this deep, other-worldly connection, like you could read each other's minds . . ."

"Oh, God, Ernesto, is he dead?"

"No, no, no, he's not dead, Caro. Something did happen, but he's okay now, or as okay as Peter ever was. I'm not being judg-mental, we just all know Peter can't be really okay until he . . ."

"Ernesto . . ."

"Oh, sorry. Look, I'm not sure he'd want me to tell you, but . . . he had a breakdown. Remember I told you when I saw you that I could see that coming? Anyway, a couple of weeks ago, he took pills, but then changed his mind. They pumped his stomach and then he signed himself into the hospital until they could stabilize him."

"Oh my God!" My hands, which had been trembling since I'd picked up the phone, started shaking so hard I was sure Ernesto could hear my bracelets rattling, and I nearly dropped the receiver.

"Don't worry, he's out now and he's on Wellbutrin and lithium, I think he said. Anyway, that's allowed him to go back to work and everything. He certainly sounded better than the last time I talked to him a few months ago. But he's not a happy camper, kiddo. You know, he's still alone, still living in the middle of Nowheresville . . ."

I was crying and wiping my dripping nose on my sleeve so he wouldn't hear me sniff, and then biting my lip so hard to keep myself from dissolving into big, heaving sobs.

"But, hey, we should get together sometime, Caro. Next time you're going to be in the city, let me know."

After we hung up, I remembered that I hadn't asked about Peter's mother. Well, Ernesto did say he was alone, so she must've died. But I couldn't call him back to verify. I didn't want him to know what I was thinking. He already pitied me for loving Peter so desperately back then. But he did give me the answer I was and wasn't looking for: Peter still needed me.

So now I had the why. I just didn't have the how. How could I come to Peter's rescue when my life was here? Mothers don't walk out on their children, no matter how loudly the siren song of a past love calls to them. Peter might need me, but my kids needed me more. Mothers don't leave.

CHAPTER TWO

Patience is a virtue, but not one of mine. A couple of times over the next few months—no, more than a couple of times—I dialed Peter's number, only to hang up as soon as the receiver was lifted at the other end, before he even had a chance to speak. It was creepy, I know, but I just wanted to make sure he was still alive. I don't know what I would have done if the phone had rung on and on or if that message had come on that said the number was no longer in service. I am so antsy these days, like I just want to jump out of my skin and teleport myself somewhere else. I don't know where. Just not here.

So, lately, in an attempt to self-soothe, I've taken to playing solitaire on the antique farmhouse table (lovingly refinished by a man I no longer love): endless rounds of meaningless games, cards turned over and over, well into the night. Sometimes, too tired to shuffle and set up the cards again, I cheat, turning over one or two cards instead of three.

The solitaire is a new distraction. I play to keep myself from fantasizing about Peter. Sometimes it works, sometimes it doesn't.

Once in a while, when I want to feel productive, I do needlework. As I plot to leave my husband, I am pulling peach-colored thread through the canvas, cross-stitching a sampler that bears the legend:

Contentment is not the fulfillment of what you want,
but the realization of how much you already have.

But usually it's solitaire, my drug of choice. And then, long after the children have finally turned out their lights, and hours after Jack has fallen asleep, I reluctantly tuck the worn blue deck into its vinyl slipcase and squirrel it away under the dishtowels in the kitchen drawer that no one ever opens but me.

Then I check the doors to make sure all is secure, flip the porch light on and off to scare away possible intruders, check (twice) that the burglar alarm is activated, unplug the TV and the toaster, lest an electrical fire consume the house and all its inhabitants while we sleep, hover over the children until I'm sure they're breathing. I do all this to ward off some kind of divine retribution for what I am about to do, even though I don't believe in God. Just hedging my bets. And then I check my hairline to see if my roots are showing.

Exhausted beyond the point of sleepiness, I crawl quietly into my marriage bed, as if I don't belong there, fearful that the shifting of the mattress, the pulling up of covers could awaken Jack, who, forgetting we have not touched each other in months, might reach out to me.

Ever since that nightmare business last winter, I've thought of myself as a woman who deserves to be cheated on. I am always looking for clues. Each time Jack returns from a business trip and I'm sorting his dirty laundry, I bury my nose in his shirts, hoping I will sniff out Chanel Nº5, or Obsession, or even Jean Naté, that my nose will find the evidence I can't see. But all I find are traces of his aftershave. It smells of bergamot and orange and rosemary, no girly notes of lilac or lily-of-the-valley or rose at all. I go through his pockets and fish out his credit card receipts: always dinners for one, with a glass or two of wine, never evidence of an expensive bauble purchased for a mistress. The truth is, I want him to hurt me in this way. If I did find something, I don't think I would confront him. I'd just sit with my abject pain. And then maybe I could embrace the role of betrayed wife and justify my unannounced flight from domesticity. It won't play out that way, though. I can't be 100 percent sure, because God knows spouses have been known to stray, but Jack is such a straight arrow and so devoted to the children and, yes, to our happy family image. So, even though we're not having sex, I would bet he's not having it with anyone else, either. I am the obvious villain in this story.

Every day, I entertain at least two or three escape fantasies. Standing in the take-out line at the coffee shop, waiting to order my cappuccino, I think about making a caffeine-fueled all-night trip west, and then catch myself: Not tonight. It's Tuesday, my turn to carpool my older son and his friends to swim team practice. And when I voice my opinion about the Israeli–Palestinian conflict or the Iran-Contra hearings, and Jack tells me all the reasons why my ideas are regurgitated from unsubstantiated sources, I will myself to the place where Peter thought everything that came out of my mouth was brilliant, and clever and original. But I don't know if he'd think that today. Maybe he'd also tell me I'm trite. Maybe I am.

No one except me ever notices the smudgy circles under my eyes. It's been years since I appeared at the breakfast table with a naked face. My husband, like some 1950s comic-strip denizen, eats his breakfast behind the *Times*, and then leaves for the train after depositing a perfunctory peck on my foundation-and-blush-covered cheek. The children are always embroiled in early morning squabbles, frantic searches for lost library books—"But it's due *today*, Mom, and I'll get detention if I have one more overdue book!"—stray sneakers—"They won't let me play dodge ball without my sneakers!"—and matching socks and, finally, the twenty-five-meter dash to the school bus. Sometimes I catch my youngest, Caleb, eyeing me curiously. Sometimes I think he knows, though he never says anything but "I love you, Mommy," as he gives me a quick, hard hug before he, too, is out the door.

It wasn't even any one thing that had brought me to this place, even before my phone call to Ernesto. It was more like the slow drip, drip of the everyday misery, like water on stone over the millennia, that has eroded the bedrock of our marriage. I knew I needed to leave before I became as insignificant as the way I felt, like a grain of sand. But I stayed. There was nothing to leave for, no place to go—until I learned that Peter was still alone. And then I couldn't *not* leave.

The children would be in camp for July and August, and the idea of spending a silent summer in this house with a man I hardly knew anymore, and without the buffer of the kids, seemed too awful to contemplate.

In the end, I was afforded the perfect opportunity for my getaway, and I grabbed it.

Some days the thought of it feels brave and exhilarating, like jumping out of a plane and being 99.9 percent sure that the people who packed the parachute knew what they were doing. But on other days, I am so terrified I can hardly catch my breath. Those are the days when the to-do list plays itself out in my brain, with no let up, like the news scroll that circles Times Square: 1. Find a lawyer (someone who doesn't play golf with Jack); 2. Find new schools for the kids in North Dakota (Better, right? They need to grow up in a simpler, less entitled place. They're getting so spoiled); 3. Figure out child support and see if I can get alimony; and then, 4. The "C" word, *custody*, and I can't get beyond that. North Dakota is awfully far away from Connecticut. When would they ever see their father? Maybe once I reconnect with Peter, we can find an apartment in Brooklyn and Jack and I can share custody . . . So much healthier than raising the kids within the confines of a loveless marriage. They pick up on that, no matter how you try to conceal it by being polite to each other. That would fuck them up way more than my leaving to find true happiness and fulfillment . . . right? And Peter will be a wonderful stepfather. Maybe we'll buy the kids a dog, one of those little ones they recommend for apartments, like a Yorkie or a Shih Tzu. Maybe we'll all get together for Thanksgiving, one big happy family.

As if, as if. As if Jack would let them go without a fight.

Sometimes, though, another thought flits around the edges of my consciousness, but I can't allow it to become fully realized. Surely, I am engaged in some sort of magical thinking. If I were completely rational, I would have been stopped short by the call to Ernesto, not seduced by it. Suicide attempt, mood-stabilizing drugs—what kind of scene would I be walking my children into? If these flags were any redder, they would have been dipped in blood. But my obsession with Peter subsumes all of this. Better to focus on Shih Tzus and Norman Rockwell Thanksgivings.

Anyway, I have two months to figure all this out.

I am up at six. I brush my teeth and take a shower in the downstairs bathroom so I won't wake the others. The troops will be up soon enough, and I need an hour to myself. I pack an overnight bag with the essentials I had stashed in the guest room last night: A few layers of clothing to cope with mercurial weather, my toothbrush, contact lens solution, make-up case, black lace underwear so new the tags are still on, and my diaphragm, and set it down by the front door where the kids' duffle bags, Sarah's riding boots, and the boys' baseball gloves have been lined up the night before. With all the camp paraphernalia being loaded into the station wagon, the children will never notice an extra bag, and Jack won't even look.

I really had had little time to plan the nuts and bolts of this escape (even though it has occupied my mind for the past six months), what with camp physicals, orthodontist appointments, sneaker buying, name-tape ironing, and trunk packing; and with that nagging worry that Caleb, at eight, is too young to be sent off to sleep-away camp all summer. I hadn't wanted him to go, but Jack had other ideas.

"Best thing in the world would be for him to get away for a while. It'll help him stand on his own two feet," Jack insisted on one of the rare nights last winter when we were up talking, instead of reading on our respective sides of the king-size bed, with Jack's legal briefs piled like a bundling board between us. It was a couple of months after I'd had the nightmare about Peter, that last time Jack and I had made love. "You baby him too much, Caro."

"But he *is* a baby, Jack. He's only eight. Greg and Sarah were ten when they first went. And two months is such a long time . . ."

"Look, I was exactly the same age as Caleb when I got sent off to camp. And, yeah, I was a little scared at first, but then there was so much to do, so many new things to try, that I never even missed my parents. That was the summer I learned to sail, and it opened up a whole new world for me. Don't you think we should give him that chance?"

"Why don't we let him decide?"

I am pretty sure that Caleb would choose to stay home. He is the child who is most like I was. I think I would have found summer camp excruciating. One more place to be the weird kid, the one chosen last, the one without friends.

"Let *him* decide? He's a baby, Caro."

Exactly. Isn't that what I just said? But coming out of Jack's mouth, it sounds so negative. He's shifted the argument, using his lawyerly skills to play into my tendency to second-guess myself.

I cave. Jack has won again. I feel like shit. And then, the light bulb goes on: Caleb's possibly premature first camp experience affords me the means to leave my marriage and buys me some time. I am giddy. And that makes me feel even shittier.

"Guess what, Caleb? You get to go to Camp Willoway with Greg and Sarah this year! Isn't that super? Daddy and I decided that it wasn't fair that they got to have all the fun and you had to stay home all summer. So, all three of you are going. Won't that be neat?"

Jack turns to Caleb. "You're the same age I was when I spent my first summer at camp. It was great!"

I bite my lip and glance across the dinner table at my youngest child. Caleb, too, is biting his lip, and tears are threatening to spill over. Even Greg and Sarah are quiet for once. Jack continues to eat his dinner. The rest of us seem to have developed a sudden swallowing problem, and four portions of pasta primavera get scraped into the garbage. I wish our dog was still alive: I hate wasting food.

So today's the day. My bag is waiting at the door and I proceed to the next step: blueberry pancakes for our farewell breakfast. I retrieve the second-to-last bag of last summer's berry harvest from the freezer and set the can of maple syrup in a saucepan of simmering water, keeping my mind on the tasks at hand.

I know that pre-camp jitters will have my oldest ricocheting off the wall like a Bouncy Ball, my tween daughter hypercritical, and my little guy positively morose. Three kids in the back of a station wagon under normal circumstances is chaotic. First day of camp? I don't even want to think about it. First day of camp when their mother is leaving their father? Oh, dear God.

Greg, Mr. Reliable, does not fail me: "You know what the guys in my bunk call cherry pie?" he asks, his mouth full of pancake.

"Not at the table, Greg."

"Menstrual pudding," he guffaws, throwing out his arms, snorting milk up his nose, knocking off his glasses, and spilling Sarah's orange juice in the process. He seems all huge hands and feet lately, almost like they're gallivanting free from the rest of his body, and he has no command over them. This is not the first breakfast (or lunch, or dinner) mishap we've had lately. It's like having a giant toddler with poor impulse control, oscillating hormones, and incipient acne.

"Ewww, gross!" Sarah makes gagging noises.

"Mop up the juice, son," comes the disembodied voice from behind the sports section.

"And cooked carrots are sliced baby legs," Greg chortles as I hand him the paper towels.

"Mom, tell him to stop. I can't eat my breakfast. God, boys are so disgusting! Except you, Caleb, you're sweet."

Sarah tends to mother her little brother. I guess she thinks I'm not doing such a hot job. Either that or she's trying to enlist him on her side against Greg. But Caleb seldom takes sides or enters into the fray, choosing, instead, to just tune out.

Like now. My baby is twirling a piece of pancake around and around in a puddle of syrup. He hasn't eaten anything.

"Caleb, I made those pancakes especially for you. They're your favorite."

He gives me a baleful look. Does he know?

"I'm sorry, Mommy. I'm not very hungry." A hopeful note creeps into his voice. "Maybe I'm coming down with something."

"No, sweetie, I don't think so. Look, I'm sure you'll have a great time at camp. There'll be lots of kids your age and you'll get to swim every day and play baseball . . ."

"I could swim with you at the club every day and you could play catch with me." He is starting to whine.

"Aw, c'mon baby snot, grow up!" Greg rarely misses a torture opportunity lately. How could he have turned into such a little monster? Was it bile he was imbibing as I suckled him? Had I been so unhappy, even then? But he'd been such a sunny little boy. What happened? I wonder if he senses that everything he's known is about to change. *All my fault, all my fault,* goes the broken record in my head. And then I remind myself: he's fourteen, and no doubt adolescence in and of itself should have its own diagnostic axis in the DSM-III, right up there with borderline personality disorder. I give myself—but not him—a pass.

"Greg, enough! Apologize to your brother. Remember what it was like your first day of camp? You were so antsy you couldn't sit still for a week before, and you were ten!"

"Sorry, Caleb." But he doesn't sound one bit like he means it.

"Finish up, kids, and kiss Daddy goodbye. I've got a golf game in ten minutes. Gotta hustle." Jack gulps the last of his coffee.

"Aw, Daddy, aren't you going to come with us?" Sarah is his little princess, but neither snow nor sleet nor first day of camp will keep him from his appointed rounds on the links.

"I'm sorry, Princess, but you know I can't miss my game. Other people are depending on me."

"Yeah, I know, Daddy. See you at parents' weekend." She sighs and shrugs her shoulders, just like Jack does when I have done something to irk him, like wearing my old huarache sandals to the grocery store instead of the handmade driving moccasins he bought me. The boys take after me, but Sarah is her father's daughter, down to the blonde hair and hazel eyes, as well as the aped gestures that today seem like a reproach of me, rather than of the one who has disappointed her.

"Right, Princess. I'll be there. Wouldn't miss it. Behave yourself, guys." He kisses the younger two and claps Greg on the back.

"Take care of your brother and sister, Greg . . . and Caleb, make me proud of you, okay son?"

"Yes, Daddy," Caleb barely squeaks. And he tugs on his left ear lobe, a nervous tic he's developed lately. Jack doesn't notice.

"Atta boy. Caro, we have reservations at the club for 7:30 tonight, with George and Elaine. Wear the yellow dress, would you?" And he is off.

I hate the yellow dress. Jack picked it out. It's cut too low in front. I think he gets off on parading me in front of George Frampton, his boss and a senior partner at the firm, like he's pimping me or something. Whenever we have dinner together,

George spends the evening pretending he's not staring at my breasts while his wife, after three too many whiskey sours, doesn't give a crap that everyone can see her glancing yearningly at my husband. But then, who wouldn't stare? Even graying at the temples, Jack is still Peter Fonda-handsome (although no longer the *Easy Rider* look-alike I fell in love with).

There's a lot Jack doesn't notice anymore, like how much weight I've lost lately. I doubt if I can even fill that dress, let alone show any cleavage. In any case, I'm never going to wear it again. I make a mental note to throw it into the Goodwill bag tomorrow and then remember: I'm not going to be here tomorrow.

"Okay, kidderoonies, your chariot awaits you. Grab your gear and load it up."

Greg takes three bags (mine included) and his baseball glove and heads for the car. He can't wait to get away. I can't say that I blame him.

Sarah and Caleb hang back, conferring. His little brow is furrowed and he is tugging on his earlobe again.

"I'll tell her, Caleb. I know it'll be okay." She gives him a hug.

"Mom, Caleb told me he has a problem. He wants to take Snoopy to camp because he'll feel real bad if he's left at home, but he's afraid the other kids will laugh at him. I told him they wouldn't, but he's still worried, you know?" This is delivered with the unselfconscious egotism that only a preteen can get away with.

"Oh, honey, thanks for helping him. That's really sweet of you. I'm so proud of my growing-up daughter."

She flashes a grin, flicks her long blonde ponytail (which I would have given anything to have when I was her age) and is off to make sure Greg hasn't put his bag in the space she's reserved for hers.

Wait! Is that lip gloss she's wearing? And her eyelashes look suspiciously black. She's only twelve, for God's sake. Oh, please, baby girl, don't be in such a hurry to grow up.

But I know if I say something, she'll bristle, and then we'll get into it, and I don't want her to go off for the summer hating me. She'll have time enough for that.

Poor Caleb. Snoopy has been his companion since infancy. The dog is missing one eye, and I keep having to sew his tail back on, but my son has never slept without him. How could I have forgotten? Have my mothering skills slipped that much? Is that why he went to Sarah instead of coming to me?

"Sweetie, I'll bet most of the kids in your bunk will bring their stuffed animals to sleep with, but if you're worried, why don't you keep him in your duffle bag under your bed?"

"But Mommy, if he's in the duffle bag, he won't be able to breathe."

My boy looks so earnest. He's a young eight, on that cusp between babyhood and youth and not quite ready to let go of Santa Claus, the Easter Bunny, or his fervent hope that Snoopy could actually turn into a living, breathing confidant, even though he knows better.

"Oh, don't zip it all the way up and he'll be fine. And if he's under your bed, and you're feeling lonely at night, you can just reach down and touch him, and no one will know, okay?

He nods.

"Okay, then, why don't you run up and get him. But hurry, we don't want to miss the bus."

I don't know if I'll miss this house. It never really felt like mine. I never wanted to live in the suburbs. I was pretty happy being an Upper-West-Side mom, but Lois, my mother-in-law, was horrified that we could even *think* of raising children there, so she found us the "perfect" five bedroom, three-and-a-half bath, center-hall Colonial on this "perfect" little cul-de-sac, just a few miles from my in-laws' house.

She also gave us the services of her interior decorator as a housewarming present, and I suppose I was too afraid of hurting her feelings (Lois was the nearest thing I had to a mother) and too unsure of myself to demur when the model-thin, Diane von

Furstenberg-wrapped, platinum-blonde, British-accented decorator gushed, "Oh my dear, this fabric (or color or pattern or sofa) is *really you*!" After all, how did I know it *wasn't* me? I didn't have any idea who I was, and if the decorator thought an ecru velvet sofa was me, maybe she knew something I didn't. And when I timidly volunteered that perhaps, just perhaps mind you, ecru wasn't such a great idea, given that one member of the household was a toddler and I was six months pregnant , she reacted with mock (or maybe not so mock) horror: "Surely you're not going to allow *children* in the living room!"

I bought slipcovers, which never fit very well, and the children had the crawl and later the run of the house. They and the dog did a number (a couple of numbers, actually) on the (also) ecru Karastan carpeting. I had the whole damn wall-to-wall removed and sent to Goodwill. Lois, bless her, never said a word.

When the hell did I become *ecru*?

The house is a constant reminder of all the years I have been without a voice, all the years I have tried to please others instead of myself, all the years I have fashioned myself into what a good wife is supposed to act like and look like. I'm an imposter here.

And then, one day, in the midst of putting Greg's socks away and, as usual, wishing I were somewhere else, I catch myself remembering a conversation we had when he was five and about to lose his first baby tooth.

"Greggy, it's been years since the Tooth Fairy visited anyone in our family, and she doesn't remember how much money to leave under your pillow. Can you help her out?"

"Of course, Mommy. Tell her a penny, a nickel, a dime, a quarter, a dollar, and a credit card!"

And how, when Sarah was about four, she named all her dolls (even the boys) and stuffed animals "Elizabeth" (except she had a slight lisp, so it came out "Elithabeth" and I thought it was adorable, but Jack wanted her to have speech therapy) and she identified them by size and/or color of their costume and/or taxonomy: Big Elizabeth, Baby Elizabeth, Red Elizabeth, Yellow Elizabeth, Cowboy Elizabeth, Elizabeth the Bear, Elizabeth the Duck (not to be confused with Yellow Elizabeth, a baby doll with a gingham dress, who was not to be confused with Baby Elizabeth, who had lost her clothes).

And this cul-de-sac, my road to nowhere, is where Caleb, at six, insisted that we remove the training wheels from his bike, and in less than fifteen minutes had gone from a terrified "Don't let go, Daddy. Don't let go!" to "Mommy, look at me! Look at me!" as he flew up the street.

And the backyard, where all three of them hung upside down from the swing set and where we buried the ashes of our beloved chocolate lab. Where the children collaborated on constructing his plywood tombstone and writing his epitaph: Here Lies Bruno, A Dog. We Thank Him For The Happiness He Gave Us When He Was Young.

This is my children's home. This is the keep of all their childhood memories. I almost lose my resolve, but then shake my head to send those lovely pictures back to my heart where they belong. The children will be all right. They have to be.

I take one last look around my white-on-white kitchen. The gleaming copper pots hanging from the ceiling are lovely. I reach up to touch one, but then remember what a pain in the ass it is to keep them shiny. I think I'm ready for take-out pizza eaten in a furnished room. Or better still, in a crash pad in the East Village. Whatever happened to crash pads? They've all gone condo, I guess.

I promise myself that I will devote my full attention to the kids: no daydreaming, no thinking about where I am going or who I hope to find, until after they're on the bus. I will pay attention to every word, precious or otherwise, make a mental note of each request, and store up enough memories of that last morning, when my children's world was still intact, to get me through the summer.

That flies out the window as soon as I hand out the gum. I'm a "no junk food" mom, and Greg and Sarah aren't supposed to be chewing gum, per orders from the orthodontist, but today I'm breaking all the rules.

I'm giving the kids gum this morning because if I leave for good and if, somehow, Jack keeps me from getting custody of my babies, I don't want them to remember me as the witch who not only had the nerve to abandon them, but never let them chew gum, buy crap cereal, or stay up late to watch *Miami Vice* ("Hey, she was okay. I remember she let us have gum once.").

I hand each of them a pack of Juicy Fruit.

"Why are you giving us gum?" Sarah sounds suspicious.

"Yuk, Juicy Fruit. I hate Juicy Fruit. Why didn't you get Bubble Yum?" Greg demands, his voice cracking on "Bubble." Even though he's being snotty, I feel for him. Puberty sucks.

"Yeah, the purple kind," Sarah adds.

Caleb says nothing. He unwraps a piece of gum, carefully folds it into his mouth, and then remembers his manners: "Thanks, Mommy."

Despite the protests, two more pieces are hurriedly unwrapped and stuffed between two sets of wire-encased teeth, lest mean, stupid Mom have second thoughts and take back the not-quite-right offering.

An unmistakably artificial fruity odor fills the car, and my resolve disappears. I can't help it. It brings me back to Peter, and that time we both tried to quit smoking by chewing packs and packs of the stuff until our jaws ached and our tongues were coated white and our teeth were set on edge. And it didn't work: it sent us right back to our Marlboros.

I can barely remember what he looked like then, although I still have one blurry photograph. He was clean-shaven. It was taken several months before he grew the beard that made him appear so Christlike. Or was that an attribute I assigned him later? Nevertheless, the bearded image is the one I've carried all this time.

It's a mystery, my ties to this man. I don't know why I never severed the connection. I certainly did with the others from those years, but not with Peter. The thread that binds me to him has woven in and out of whatever garment happens to be my life at any given moment, sometimes out for months or years at a time. But it always wends its way back, and it has never broken.

"Mom, put your signal on! You're gonna miss the exit! Mom, I've been telling you that for the last five minutes. Mom, what's *wrong* with you? Are you *deaf*?" Greg is frantic.

"I'm sorry, honey, I guess I was thinking of everything I have to do this week."

"Yeah, like have a great time now that we're out of your hair!" Sarah loves camp, but that doesn't stop her from laying on a little guilt. As if I needed any reminders to feel guilty.

"I will miss you every single day," I reply truthfully. "All three of you. I'll probably even miss the bickering."

With Greg's timely reminder, I manage to make the exit for the Stamford shopping mall where the Willoway bus is waiting. Greg and Sarah, spotting long-lost summer friends, grab their gear and are off, forgetting all about their well-intentioned promises to look after their brother. Caleb hangs back, biting his nails.

"Honey, you'll get to know some really neat kids and by next summer, you'll be acting just like Greg and Sarah, rushing off to see your friends and forgetting all about your old Mom."

"I'd never forget you, Mommy. Please, please don't make me go," he implores hoarsely.

"C'mon Caleb, I got some guys I want you to meet," Greg has suddenly reappeared.

Reluctantly, my youngest drops my hand, squares his shoulders, and follows his brother. He is still looking at the ground as he joins Greg's meet-and-greet, and no doubt an awkward "Hi" is all he can manage in the midst of those older boys. I see him whisper something to Greg and, in a moment, all three of my offspring surround me to receive last-minute hugs and kisses, and, impatiently, last-minute instructions.

"You two, don't forget about using the Water-Pic every night. And if any wires break, don't pull on them or try to fix them yourselves. I've left instructions on your health forms for the camp to contact a local orthodontist, *don't forget*. And don't chew any more gum."

They giggle.

"And help Caleb make friends."

Greg and Sarah roll their eyes and Caleb is suddenly fascinated by his shoelaces.

"And don't let anyone touch you where you don't want to be touched. . ."

"Mom, you are so weird. That's just gross!" Sarah grimaces and shakes her head, her ponytail whipping back and forth.

Yeah, she is definitely wearing mascara.

The camp director's whistle breaks into my litany, and with quick hugs and "Love you"'s two of them are on the bus, but Caleb turns to me in one more desperate attempt to change his fate.

"Mommy, what if I lose another tooth at camp? The Tooth Fairy won't know where to find me. She'll get lost. I have to go home!" He is clinging to me and trying not to cry.

"Oh, sweetie, I'll send her your camp address this afternoon, I promise," and I shoo him up the steps.

He lingers a moment in the doorway, sensing my ambivalence, hoping for a last-minute reprieve, but when he sees that I will not relent, he, too, moves towards a seat.

In a moment, to the strains of "Camp Willoway Forever," my offspring are off to the Maine woods. I head to the car. The back seat is empty, save for some yellow gum wrappers, a forgotten *G.I. Joe* comic book, and the echoes of three children's voices.

"I love you," I mouth as I embark on my own journey to parts unknown, to a person who, after twenty years, is also an unknown. I am off to a small town in North Dakota to find Peter, who might need me as much as I need him. Never once, since my phone call to Ernesto, did I entertain the thought that Peter might not even be there. I guess I figured if inertia had kept him home for the last twenty years, it would have the decency to pin him down for another six months, give or take a few days, until my arrival. So, I am driving 1,537 miles to see if I can go back, make that other choice, and pick up that other road. Perhaps, just perhaps, it will make all the difference.

CHAPTER THREE

Long distance driving leaves a lot of time for thinking, especially in those radio dead zones where nothing but easy listening comes over the airwaves. I find myself going back to my laundry list: Where am I going to find a lawyer who doesn't know Jack or his firm? Will Jack contest the divorce? Will he try to get custody, based on the fact that I am a crazy woman who left her kids to follow . . . what? A twenty-year-old rescue fantasy? *Oh, shit, did I remember to unplug the iron this morning?* It's too painful to think about the children and what my present actions might mean for their future. *What if Peter's not interested in being a stepfather—then I'd be a single parent. Do I even know any? Oh, yeah, Tricia, back in Tucson . . . but she, at least, could depend on her mother for help. And she only had one kid. How would I raise three?* It's too guilt-inducing to think about Jack. *I wonder if he'll miss me.* To be absolutely fair, he does have some very admirable qualities, not the least of which is that he really does love our children, and if I were in his shoes, and he left for another woman, would I move heaven and earth to make sure I got the kids? I'd like to think I would. No, I *know* I would . . .

Oh, God, I was so cavalier with Caleb about the Tooth Fairy this morning. What if he does lose a tooth? He'll never believe in her again . . . or in me, either. Maybe I'd better call Jack and ask him to arrange something with the camp . . . oops, nope, can't do that.

And that gets me started thinking about him again. Jack's not a bad guy, and he still, on occasion, can make me laugh . . . and, in those rare instances when we found ourselves in the mood for sex, it was still pretty good. But it wasn't enough. Truth be told, I doubt very much that anyone looking at our marriage would have reason to believe that "I'm just not happy," should tip the scales. But I can't even find myself in this family. When I look at the picture of the Tanners of Westport, Connecticut, Jack and the children stand out in bold, bright colors. I am barely etched in bas relief. And then, of course, there's Peter. I used to be bold and bright and colorful when I was with him. Sometimes I even sparkled.

But I keep second-guessing myself. What am I doing, all alone, driving west across the country when I should be home planning the PTA fall fundraising fair, dressing for dinner at the club, doing the laundry or writing my monthly column for our local newspaper? That's where I belong, right? I am not without doubt.

About an hour into my trip, I pull into a rest stop to use the pay phone. No one answers, so I leave a message.

"Hi, this is Carolyn Tanner. Greg, Sarah and Caleb's mom? Listen, could you do me a huge favor? Caleb was pretty anxious this morning when he got on the bus. He's only eight and it's his first time. He was worried that the Tooth Fairy wouldn't be able to find him at camp. So, if he loses a tooth, could you please ask his counselor to remind him to put it under his pillow, and then could someone collect it and leave a dollar there? I'll pay it back. Thanks so much."

I am breaking so many promises to my children right now, but this one, at least, I've kept. And then, as I am tallying up all my failures, I remember this: even before I had my kids, I was determined that my mothering would be a 180 from the way I was mothered. But look what I'm doing now. Maybe this apple hasn't fallen far from that tree after all.

Yeah, about that tree. . .

A couple of years ago, waiting in the dentist's office, I started to read a magazine article about adult children of alcoholics. And I suddenly heard my mother's voice berating me: *What, you're going to blame me because you're an approval-seeker and have lost your identity? I had nothing to do with that. Because you think like a victim and are attracted by that weakness in your love relationships? So, this is what you saw in that Peter-person? So maybe you confused pity with love? Because you have a low sense of self-esteem? Don't blame me, Carolyn. Look in the mirror. You're a smart girl and you let people walk all over you. Especially that shiksa mother-in-law of yours. And that stuck-up husband? Please! You weren't good enough for him the way you were? I'm ashamed that any daughter of mine turned into such a doormat.*

Guilt is exhausting. After mustering all my energy to create a normal going-off-to-camp morning, to not give myself away, and then that whole Tooth Fairy scenario, and picturing my mother's disapproval, I already need another cup of coffee. I linger at the rest stop and try to focus on the details of the trip ahead. I'm an hour into the twenty-three hours from Westport to Peter's home in western North Dakota. I figure I can drive about seven hours a day, with coffee and pee breaks, so a little over three days, maybe four at the most, and I should be there. The nearness of it excites me but then terrifies me, and then I start to think about Jack and home and a kind of clipped-wing safety that I am defying with my flight.

Once I was going to be a writer, a playwright, to be specific. But now, once a month, I write a newspaper column called "Running in Place," in which I voice my opinion on school budgets, extoll the virtues of our local library, and come up with tricks to get your kids to eat their vegetables. Jack calls these efforts my "little hobby," an acceptable outlet for my trickling creative juices and naive politics. Sometimes I wonder if he, too, is disappointed in me, that I didn't become the next Jean Kerr or Lillian Hellman, and that Wendy Wasserstein *did*. But if I try to reach into my brain and find the words that once flowed to paper, I come up empty. Maybe I was just kidding myself. Maybe I wasn't that good in the first place.

But no, I *was*, and when I find Peter, it will all come back. I know it will. At least, I think it will.

And then I start doubting again and suddenly my gutsy flight seems pointless and ill-conceived.

It's not too late, I can turn around now, stop at the mall, pick up a few things, and when I get home, Jack will ask how the leave-taking went and I will tell him about Caleb and the Tooth Fairy and he'll say he wished he could have been there but, I needed to understand, the golf game had been with an important potential client and they really wanted to represent him and then he'll give me a swing by putt by chip description of the game, blah, blah, blah, and I'll pretend to listen, and somewhere in there he might actually ask me what I did after I dropped off the kids.

"Oh, nothing all that interesting, just stopped at the mall and bought some new tablecloths, then picked up the dry cleaning."

If I used this as material for my column, I'd call it "Fear of Flying."

And then I think about the whole empty summer spooling out in front of me, and I press on.

Back when I used to hang onto his every word, Jack told me this sweet story: When he was little, maybe six or seven, his mother used to park him and his brothers (two at the time, with three more to join them in a few years) in front of the TV so she could get a couple of hours of peace and quiet. Jack loved the old films from the 1930s and '40s on Million Dollar Movie, and since he was the oldest, he usually got to decide what they watched, even though his younger brothers would have chosen cartoons. All those Busby Berkeley extravaganzas had him convinced that in those bygone eras, in real life, everyone tap-danced and rode around in Packards with running boards, and they all lived in a black-and-white world.

I saw my parents' 1940s, though, in glorious Technicolor, like the Emerald City. Their story began in 1943. Manhattan was teeming with young soldiers and sailors, ready to embark for hostile shores. My mother and her best friend, both from Orthodox Jewish families in Borough Park, Brooklyn, decided to sneak into "the city," each telling their parents that they were spending the night at the other's house. My grandparents did not own a telephone, and not in their wildest dreams could they imagine that their pious eldest daughter would disobey them and behave like some kind of *hoor*, so there was little chance that she would be found out. The girls were going to a USO dance for some harmless flirtation, to do their part for the war effort by providing our brave young men a few hours' distraction from the horrors they would be facing overseas. I can see those two—they were barely nineteen—on the Brooklyn Manhattan Transit train, applying forbidden red lipstick and the blackest mascara, both exhilarated and terrified at what they were about to do.

And it was there, at that dance, on an evening she recalled years later as the most exciting night of her life, that she met my father, a Methodist farm boy from Vermont who was studying to become a large-animal vet.

"He was so handsome, Carolyn," she would tell me on those infrequent afternoons when I dragged out the old leather suitcase full of photographs and we both sat cross-legged on my parents' chenille-covered bed.

"Look . . . so tall and blond and dashing, just like Prince Charming . . ."

Yes, I could see them, the dazzling second lieutenant, Charlie Mills, and the kosher butcher's knock-out beautiful daughter, Shulamith Goldstone, the lights of Broadway behind them, falling in love while dancing the Lindy Hop to Kay Kyser's music. I wish I could have met those two.

Then her voice would turn bitter as she recited the familiar litany: "How was I to know that Prince Charming would spend most of his days with his arm up a cow's *tuchus* and come home smelling like the barn floor? And we'd live in this godforsaken place where they think the height of culture is talent night at the Grange?" She'd spew this out while lighting one cigarette after another.

I always knew what was coming next.

"I could've had a career on Broadway if it hadn't been for *him*. I could have kept my family . . ."

I was too afraid of her wrath to point out, with a twelve-year-old's unfailing logic, that a family that disowned a daughter for marrying a gentile would surely do the same to a daughter who opted for a life of sin on the wicked and un-kosher Broadway stage.

"What did you expect?" I wanted to yell at her. (I was feeling a little protective of my dad). "That it would be like all *White Christmas*-y, and Bing Crosby and Rosemary Clooney would come over for dinner?"

But I didn't. The furthest Shulamith had ever been from Borough Park was Jones Beach.

Why she stayed married to my father, why she stayed in a community that never made her feel welcome, was beyond me, but, even at twelve, I thought it must have had something to do with the magical night of the USO dance (and maybe that her family would refuse to take back damaged goods?). It never even entered my mind that they may have been staying together because of me. In any case, when my own marriage started unraveling some twenty-five years later, I had no paradigm for how to work things out. Two weeks after they met, four days before my father shipped overseas, they were married at City Hall. No one from either family was there. Two city employees were enlisted as witnesses, as Shulamith Goldstone became Shelly Mills.

And then, I think, she had the best time of her life. True, she missed my father, but there she was, on her own, living in a boarding house with other young military wives near midtown Manhattan, within walking distance of her job at Macy's, which, with Charlie's Army pay, afforded her the occasional balcony ticket to the latest Broadway show. A dream life.

When my dad came home two years later, a stranger without the spiffy uniform and gold lieutenant's bars, and took her to Vermont, she must have felt like Dorothy. Only instead of the cyclone whisking her from Kansas to Oz, this one went in reverse—from the Emerald City to *Yenemsvelt* (the ends of the earth, in Yiddish, her mother tongue).

Cows and sheep and pigs, oh my!

She was stunning, my mother. I could see why my father fell for her. Nothing that exotic had ever grown on the farm where he was raised. She had dark, curly hair, huge brown eyes (eyes I see every time Caleb looks up at me), straight, even teeth (unfortunately not inherited by Greg and Sarah), a full, sensuous mouth, and a knock-out figure. She probably could have been a movie star, or, at the very least, the first Jewish Miss America, but she was a married woman by the time Bess Myerson broke that barrier in 1945.

Unfortunately, the only physical attribute I seem to have inherited from her is her hair. On her, it was stunning. On me, it's just . . . Jewish. Ditto my nose, which my mother says I got from her father. It was the only thing I got from him, and I wish I hadn't. To the day he died, my grandfather never acknowledged my existence, even though my mother sent him a picture of me every year. Maybe that's why he never claimed me as his flesh and blood.

I wasn't such a looker, but I was smart, Mom assured me. Too smart for the kids in the local school. Too brainy and too . . . Jewish. The only real friend I had in high school was another self-styled beatnik and fellow outcast and both of us were determined to blow that town as soon as we came of age.

To Dad's great sorrow, I was not ever going to follow in his footsteps through the manure; would never join 4-H; never go to his alma mater, Cornell; never be his partner in veterinary practice. I was their only child, and I was a disappointment to them both. I wasn't a beauty for my mother, and I didn't share my father's unconditional love for all creatures great and small.

It didn't really matter, though. By the time I was in high school, Mom was spending most afternoons in her room with a bottle of gin for a bedmate, and Dad spent more and more time at his office or driving from farm to farm, so neither of them cared what I looked like or whose footsteps I wasn't following in.

I discovered teenage angst (or maybe it discovered me). I affected a completely black wardrobe to project an air of indifference, intellectual depth, and mystery (and, it goes without saying, slenderness), and found solace in books, specifically books with tragic heroines. It wasn't a huge leap from *Wuthering Heights* to *Madame Bovary* to *Anna Karenina,* and then, theater wannabe that I was, I discovered Chekhov and became obsessed with *The Three Sisters.* They all needed to escape their stultifying lives, just like me! Like Olga, Masha, and Irina, I wanted to get as far away as possible from my little provincial town, so my life could begin. Unlike the Prozorova girls, however, I would *get* to Moscow. Okay, not the real Russian capital, as the Cold War was still out there, but *my* Moscow, where I could find work, and love, and a meaningful life. I would get there, even if I had to go to the ends of the earth.

I didn't even make it to the end of the country. One afternoon, I spread out a map of the US, closed my eyes, and put my finger on what I hoped would be San Francisco, (or at least LA).

The self-imposed rule of this little game was that I had to apply to the nearest college to where my finger landed. I missed northern California by 869 miles, and that's how I ended up at the University of Arizona, in the middle of a desert with breath-sucking dry heat and rattlesnakes. "To Tucson! To Tucson! To Tucson!" didn't exactly have the same cachet as "To Moscow! To Moscow! To Moscow!" but the unknown of it was kind of cool, it wasn't Glenbury, and no one there knew my mother was a lush.

I head west across the Tappan Zee Bridge, once more looking forward to the long drive ahead of me. Like most suburban mothers, my station wagon is my second home. I love my little red Subaru with all its gadgets and light-up dials on the dashboard . . . even the funny little ding-dong when I forget to fasten my seatbelt. Jack wanted to get me a Volvo, citing its safety features (but really because it was the "right" car for us upwardly-mobile types) but, for once, I put my foot down. I just couldn't do it. Jack didn't understand why I was so adamant. I was not about to tell him that in 1965, at the age of eighteen, I'd lost my virginity to a poly-sci major in the cramped back seat of his baby-shit (aka, mustard) colored Volvo. I could just see the promotional ads (you know, the kind they used to have in *The New Yorker*: "Mr. and Mrs. Kerry Whitmore IV on their seventeenth visit to Bermuda. . ."); "Carolyn Tanner: In 1965 she got screwed in the back seat, and now, twenty years later, she's moving up to the driver's seat of her very own Volvo . . ."

Jack looked at me quizzically, but in the interest of avoiding an argument in the car dealership, he got me the Subaru, even though it didn't quite work with the image thing.

Traffic is backed up. I pull the visor down and examine myself in the mirror, then wrinkle my too-perfect nose at what I see. It isn't even my nose, it's Dr. Cederbaum's. The perfect nose had been Jack's doing. I wish now I'd had the guts to stand up to him when he suggested that we take some of our wedding present money to buy me a new nose because "You'll be so much happier, sweetheart."

In one sense, though, he was right. It tapped into all those "ugly girl" feelings I'd had in high school, and back then I *would* have been so much happier with a movie star nose. Later, I didn't really mind it, but since I would have walked over hot coals for my sexy new husband, I acquiesced. And when I was recovering from the surgery, he brought me chicken soup from Fine and Schapiro and library books and made me laugh (even though it hurt) and I felt like the luckiest girl in the world.

The next thing Jack thought I'd be happier with was straight hair. Oh, yeah, that kinky-haired "Jew girl" (as I'd been called more than once on the school bus) bought right into that one. After the swelling around my nose went down, I was off to Harlem every three months to have some harsh-smelling goo spread over my kinky locks. Then, naturally, he decided I'd be happier as a blonde. Okay, also partly my doing. I'd once confessed to him that I wished I had been one of those blonde, turned-up-nose cheerleaders in high school, and now that we had the money for a makeover, maybe he was trying to grant me my wish, but I always thought he was doing it as much for himself as for me.

Funny, in all that time, I never once suggested that he fix the slight overlap of his two front teeth, his early rebelliousness made visible. Twelve-year-old Jack refused to wear a retainer, and, in fact, lost several of them before his parents threw up their hands and resigned themselves to having a son with a less-than-perfect smile. It never stopped him from grinning broadly, though.

And I could have said something about the small flesh-colored mole below his lower lip, if I were being nit-picky, but to me, those imperfections had only made him more adorable—and desirable.

Right now, I want to turn off the air conditioner and open the window. I ache to feel my hair blowing in the wind, like in the old days in the back of Ernesto's truck, but if I do, some tiny speck of the universe is sure to fly into my eye and under my contact lens, and then my eyes will water and my mascara will run all over my face, and even though it's days before I will see Peter, on the off chance I might run into someone I know who's also driving west on I-80, I keep the car hermetically sealed and my make-up intact.

I wonder how Peter will react when he sees me. He used to love the way I looked, he would reassure me, kinky hair, ample body, and all: Earth Mother in jeans, work shirt, and sandals, adorned with Mexican silver earrings and love beads. I was always good enough for Peter, just the way I was. I glance again, through lavender-tinted sunglasses, at the mirror, and am jolted by a sudden thought: Peter won't react at all when he sees me. He won't even recognize me. Almost nothing about me resembles that girl from twenty years ago. I'm glad I left when I did. I turned forty last year, and lately I've been having the feeling that the next thing Jack thinks I'd be "so much happier" with is a face lift.

I make a vow to the woman I see in the mirror: I will let my hair grow back to its natural color and kinkiness and never step on a bathroom scale again. I wish I could get my old nose back.

After the cacophony of the morning, the car is too quiet. I miss the backseat noises already. I switch on the radio: Heavy metal, "Material Girl," "Rock Me Amadeus" (who thinks of these titles, anyway?), and old hymns. Ahh, here we are: Saturday Morning Sixties—perfect. The sounds of Simon and Garfunkel waft me across the Hudson River and back across many years.

Will the waters be untroubled when I get there? Will there even be any water?

CHAPTER FOUR

It was 1965, several years before Joan Baez would exhort us to "say yes to men who say no," but I was about to, anyway. I was in lust with a senior from St. Louis who would go to Canada if he was ever drafted, and, anyway, my virginity had become a burden.

My two big literary influences that year were Simone de Beauvoir's *The Second Sex* and Gael Greene's *Sex and the College Girl,* which made it sound like everyone was having sex but me. I read de Beauvoir and made myself a pro/con list.

Pro: I can't really be a woman until I lose it.
Con: If my mother finds out she'll kill me.
Pro: As a playwright, I have to experience all I can to help me create real characters.
Con: . . . here, I was stumped. The threat of pregnancy or venereal disease never entered my mind (only bad girls got the clap, and herpes and AIDS were decades away). I decided there was no reason to resist.

Ted, my future draft-dodger and soon-to-be deflowerer was someone I had met at a mixer. He was majoring in political science, had dreams of being in the forefront of the revolution, and was kind of a hunk. He was also on the varsity wrestling team.

So I decided to lay my burden down. I think both of us knew what was going to happen that moonlit night when he drove out to the desert after the movie and parked next to a giant saguaro cactus. Years later I cringed whenever I thought about "doing it" with an enormous spiny green phallus as backdrop, in the backseat of a small foreign car whose name was awfully close to the portion of my anatomy my boyfriend was about to pass through.

Mostly what I recall about the experience was steamy windows and a lot of fumbling with clothes. I had not yet affected my jeans-and-work shirt uniform. I was actually dressed for a date: blouse, skirt, stockings and, because I was so self-conscious about being overweight, a girdle.

I was aware of his wrestler's body on top of me, and one of my legs, the one thrown over the front seat, had a cramp in it. The noises he was making sounded very much like those he made when he was pinning an opponent to the mat. I wondered if he was having fun. As for me, I was just counting the tiny holes in the car's patterned headliner, waiting for the whole thing to be over. At twenty-seven holes, it was.

I guess I wasn't too much of a klutz, though. He told me afterwards how good I made him feel. All I felt was wet.

Back in my dorm, I put on a Kotex and belt, rinsed out my bloody underpants, and looked in the mirror to see if anything had changed. Nothing. Except I was getting a new zit on my chin. I guess I was relieved that the deed had been done, but I couldn't help wondering if there shouldn't have been something more to it.

Two weeks and two more backseat assignations later, Ted and I broke up. We had nothing in common and all that backseat grunting just reminded me of the pigs on Grandpa Mills's farm back in Glenbury.

I was sitting in Tim O'Shaugnessy's kitchen. It smelled of incense and spilled Chianti and bacon. We were trying to rehearse a scene for acting class, but what with the couple balling in the bedroom and the guys watching TV in the living room, it was really hard to concentrate.

"God, this is such a drag, Caro. I don't even *get* Pinter, do you? Why don't we go out and score us a lid?"

Hanging around with Tim and his pals for the past couple of weeks had made me familiar with the lingo, but I hadn't actually had the privilege . . . although I was dying to turn on. The closest I'd gotten was my first date with Ted the Deflowerer. We had walked into a party, he smelled something funny, and we left. For a revolutionary, he was awfully uptight.

"Hey, man, wha's happenin'?"

Tim and I were about to walk out the door when this guy I'd never seen before appeared and pulled a tan deerskin pouch from his pocket.

"I owe you, man . . . and this here's the best damn boo I could score north of the border."

"Mari-juana," Tim affected a pseudo-Mexican accent. "Ah, señorita, we will fly tonight." He nodded towards me and addressed our benefactor: "She's cool."

"She's cool." To the outcast of Glenbury, Vermont, those were the two most beautiful words in the English language.

Tim's friend (whose name I never did learn) plopped himself down on the Salvation Army couch next to the two sleeping forms. The TV watchers had passed out. He emptied the contents of his pouch onto some newspapers. It looked like . . . nothing . . . like a pile of earth and weeds. He whipped out his comb and expertly strained the seeds from the unassuming mass. Next, the rolling papers, and, voilà, a joint. And then another, and another.

"In case they wake up," he jerked his thumb at the couch sleepers. Hippies were very generous, I was learning.

"Okay, Caro, take a big drag and hold your breath for as long as you can."

"Hey, man, I thought you said she was cool," the benefactor protested.

"She is," Tim's eyes twinkled, "And she's gonna get a whole lot cooler in about thirty seconds."

When we hippies and hangers-on were not crashing at Tim's, you could find us at Erewhon, Tucson's answer to New York's Bitter End and Café Figaro. The coffee house on East Sixth Street was one long, dark, purple-painted room with fourteen tables, a counter, and a tiny stage made out of stacked and nailed sheets of plywood. It would become a footnote in musical history as the place where Linda Ronstadt and the Stone Poneys had one of their first gigs. I was in love with its ambiance, the cappuccino, and the proprietor, a Norman Mailer look-alike named Artie. Aside from my mother, he was probably the first Jew I'd ever met.

In fact, my Jewishness was the first thing he latched onto, followed closely by my tits and ass.

Tim and I stopped in one evening after scene study class. Although we had had one roll in the hay, so to speak, I was pretty sure that Tim preferred men. There just didn't happen to be any around the night we sat cross-legged on his bed, passing a bottle of Chianti back and forth until it was empty, so he settled on me, no big deal.

Artie came over to our table to take our order.

"Hey, Tim, what's happenin'? And who is this Semitic beauty you've brought with you?"

I gasped and my hand flew automatically to my nose. *"Jew girl, Jew girl. . ."*

"Relax, babe, I'm not the Gestapo. Don't you recognize a fellow M.O.T?"

"M.O.T.?"

"Member of the Tribe. I'm Artie Frankel, from Brooklyn. You *are* Jewish, aren't you?"

"Well, sort of . . . I mean, half. My mother's Jewish, but I wasn't really raised as anything."

"You were obviously raised as gorgeous, chick. Great tits. Is the rest of you as good?"

He didn't wait for an answer, even if I had had one to give him. I was dumbfounded. I'd never met anyone who came on that way.

Tim was cracking up. "Don't mind Artie, that's just the way he is. He's really cool, Caro, and I can tell he likes you. He'll probably put the make on you before too long . . ."

He got up from the table. "I'm gonna tell him we're not balling or anything, so if he wants to make a move . . ."

My protests were lost in the coffee house din, and, not surprisingly, I found myself going home with Artie that night.

He had his hand on my thigh before we even got to his apartment. I tried to push it away, at the same time trying to banish my mother's voice from my head: *What are you doing Carolyn? And with a nice Jewish boy? Don't you know he'll never buy the cow when he can get the milk for free? Who would want to marry a hoor like you?*

"Um, Artie, I have a thing about making it in cars, so could you just drive?"

"Hey, you're not one of those *nice* girls, are you?"

"Nice girls? Oh, no, I'm not a virgin, if that's what you mean. It's just that . . . well, I lost it in the back seat of a car, and I wouldn't exactly call it a peak sexual experience, that's all."

"Oh, you're definitely not a nice girl if you had your cherry busted in the back seat of a car. Good. I hate nice girls. I'm glad you're not."

His hand was back on the steering wheel, but there was a gleam in his eye.

"So, how many guys have you made it with?"

"What difference does it make?"

"Just curious. It doesn't matter, though, because after tonight, you'll forget you ever made it with anyone else. And I'm afraid I'm going to spoil you for anyone else in the future. After all, why eat hamburger when you can get steak?"

I couldn't believe how cocky he was, but an hour later, I had to admit he was right in one respect. The guy was Superman in bed.

"See, I told you," he whispered, and then stuck his tongue in my ear.

"Artie, no more, or I won't be able to walk tomorrow. And I have to be back in the dorm in fifteen minutes. Can you drop me off?"

He groaned. "Shit, Tim didn't tell me you were a dormie. Okay, just let me get my pants on and I'll take you."

He got up and put a record on the stereo: Tom Paxton. It was the first time I'd ever heard him.

(Many years later, Paxton was giving a concert in Stamford. I took the kids. "Every time I sing this song," said this balding middle-aged man by way of an introduction to *Ramblin' Boy*, "People come up to me and say 'Hey, I learned to play guitar with that song,' or 'I heard you play that song at my first hootenanny.'" And I remember where I was when I first heard that song: crawling out of Artie's bed, trying to find my underwear. "Hey, Mom, what's a hootenanny," asked Greg).

The Love House. It was a name Peter later coined for the place, and it's true, I did fall in love with him there, but the Love House was the setting for a lot more . . . a lot of unloving couplings, a lot of subterfuge, a lot of pain, deceit, and lying. And, after Peter's graduation night, the "Love" could only be an ironic appellation. It was where he betrayed me.

Artie lived there. His was the first apartment in a rickety wooden one-story attached row house divided into five separate dwellings, whose inhabitants passed freely from one space to another, as if there were no doors. The doors were seldom locked, unless the inhabitants were doing drugs or balling (especially if those doing the balling were supposed to be doing it with someone else).

I soon became a regular at the house on Seventh Street. Artie's looked pretty much like any other hippie pad in Tucson, circa

1966, except Artie was particularly slovenly, which was kind of weird because he was so fastidious at Erewhon. We always had to kick away a pile of dirty laundry before making our way to the mattress on the floor, which was sometimes covered by a sheet, but often not. There was also the obligatory purloined telephone cable spool/coffee table topped with wax-adorned Chianti bottle candle holders and the over-flowing ashtrays, which Artie never emptied and which I always did, the dirty, oversized pillows (I couldn't even bear to think about the origins of those stains), the posters of Che and Ho Chi Minh, and the one that said, "Make Love, Not War." But I suspected, with Artie, it was all for effect. He didn't really love humankind, and his social conscience seemed virtually nil: Artie loved only his prick. And I did, too, hence my willingness to bed down in his pigsty.

But long after he had tired of me and was balling someone else, I continued to hang out with his neighbors, who had taken me under their collective wing.

Brad Washburn and Miranda Lombardi occupied the next two apartments. Actually, they were on-again-off-again lovers, currently living in Brad's place.

"But I need to keep my own space," said Miranda, who was twenty-five and a grad student, and who, a few years later, would emerge as one of the most radical feminists in the Second Wave. She was a filmmaker and my role model, not just for her avocation, but because she was as thin as a reed and looked like a wraith, my idea of beauty in those days, and maybe because she had once run away with that notorious comedian, Benny Roth. Brad of the Buddy Holly glasses was a grad student in philosophy and managed Le Cine (pseudo-French, no accent, so pronounced "Le Scene"), Tucson's only art movie house. Frankly, I thought he was a little full of himself. But maybe that was because Miranda had just shot a twenty-minute film of his penis. Le Cine wouldn't show it though, so we held a mini film fest with a Super 8 projector and a roll-down screen in Brad's apartment. I wanted to be part of the in-crowd that was sucking up to Miranda, raving about how brilliant she was and comparing her to Kenneth Anger and Andy Warhol—but frankly, the film was a snooze. Maybe I wasn't hip enough to get it. And Artie was pissed that he hadn't been asked to try out for the role.

Next to Brad and Miranda lived Ulla, a Swedish exchange student with an unpronounceable last name who danced naked in the yard whenever there was a full moon. No one paid attention. She didn't speak much English, just enough to run a flourishing drug dealership from her kitchen.

Scott and Ernesto were my favorites, because they were such fun, and always up for an adventure, like the time they decided we should ditch classes and drive to the movie set at Old Tucson, to see if we could get a part in the new TV series they'd just started filming.

Scott was slight, blonde, blue-eyed and looked like the choirboy he once was, like butter wouldn't melt in his mouth (but, oh, it *would*. It was his idea to leave Kool Aid, cookies, and a note that said: "Dear Tucson Cops. Help yourself," the night we heard rumors they were conducting raids. We flushed some perfectly great pot down the toilet, got the hell out of there, and then they never showed. We ate the cookies and mourned our lost stash). Ernesto was his physical opposite. He had olive-toned skin, a bushy mustache, and dark hair that was always falling over one eye, like a patch. All he needed was a sword and a peg leg and he would have made a perfect pirate. Ernesto was the only one of us they cast that day (no parts for choir boys or fat girls). He had a couple of lines as a Mexican bandit who had it out for one of the Cartwright brothers, and thought the casting was perfect: "Just like my father!"(Yeah, in his dreams: Ernesto's dad, whom he professed to hate, was Mexico's military attaché to Washington and his mother came from one of Phoenix's most prominent families, so maybe they *were* bandits in the global sense of the word). Years later, I used to watch reruns of *Bonanza* to see if I could catch a glimpse of Ernesto. I never did.

Anyway, they lived in the last, and largest, apartment in the row. In addition to the aforementioned features of the hippie school of interior design, but in place of the revolutionary posters, the home of Scott Allen and Ernesto Sanchez featured art nouveau posters by Mucha and Beardsley and a magnificent stone fireplace with inlays of polished, multi-colored geodes. Many a night, those geodes, with candlelight shooting off their surfaces, became the focus of my stoned-out-of-my mind "oh, wows." And I loved their kitchen the best, even though I could barely boil an egg. It was full of color and looked as if someone had woken up one morning, poured a cup of coffee, and said, "Hey, I have a great idea! Let's paint the refrigerator turquoise!" Or maybe they were just stoned.

Scott and Ernesto were the first gay couple I had ever met. They were nothing like the case histories in my abnormal psych book, though, and I didn't have any problem with the fact that they shared a bed.

Hey, love was love, man.

CHAPTER FIVE

Most of my friends were guys, except for Miranda, who wasn't really a friend, more like an idol. Tricia Laurence was the first female friend I made that year. I wasn't jealous of her because she was sleeping with Artie. I had no proprietary interest in him. But I was afraid for her: She had been fucked over so badly and wanted so much for one guy to just love her and stay. Artie was definitely not that guy, though. Most of the women I knew had slept with him at one time or another. His affairs didn't last long, once we realized they were often simultaneous. We were all pretty incestuous in those days, and the fact that we'd both fucked Artie made Tricia and me closer, I think.

We had been in the same scene study class since the beginning of the semester, but I never really got to know her until we were paired up in a scene from *The Glass Menagerie*, with me playing Amanda to her Laura. Rehearsal space was scarce, what with twenty pairs of fledgling actors vying for practice rooms, so Tricia suggested we go to her apartment.

"I have to stop at my mother's to pick up Annie on the way home. I hope you don't mind. It'll only take a minute."

"Annie?"

"My daughter. She's three. You knew I was married, didn't you?"

"No. Who's your husband?

"I said *was*. Terry split right after Annie was born. Couldn't handle the scene, I guess. He lives in Frisco." She said this without obvious regret, just reporting the facts, ma'am.

I was shocked. Who could have ever wanted to leave Tricia? She was beautiful . . . and thin. She had the complexion of a porcelain doll, and her curly white-blonde hair fell almost to her waist. Her clear blue eyes, delicate features and high cheekbones suggested a royal ancestry . . . a pre-Raphaelite princess in her past, I mused. At any rate, she looked just like all the fairy tale princesses of my childhood, and it didn't make any sense. It wasn't written anywhere that the prince leaves the princess. Princesses didn't *get* left. Fat girls with kinky hair and big noses got dumped all the time, but I couldn't believe Tricia had suffered the same fate.

It was love at first sight with Annie and me. She was a cherub. Her hair was the same color as her mother's and pulled into a messy ponytail. Her eyes were also Tricia's, as was her fine-boned physique. She was so like her mother that I wondered about her father. When he split for San Francisco, did his genes go with him? What part of him was left with his daughter?

Annie was wearing a red cowboy hat, fringed suede vest, and a tiny pair of turquoise hand-tooled cowboy boots.

"Pow! Pow! Fall down! You dead."

Tricia shrugged. "Her dad calls her Annie Oakley."

I did a mock faint, and the little girl giggled.

"Annie, this is my friend, Caro. Caro, this cowgirl is my daughter."

There was such obvious love and pride in those two words, "my daughter," that I couldn't help but envy her for more than her beauty.

Annie scowled. "She not your friend. She outlaw. She dead. I shoot her."

Tricia grinned apologetically. "Sorry, her dad sent her all that cowgirl stuff last week and I can't get it off of her. She even wants to sleep with her boots on."

"Oh, don't be sorry—she's adorable." I squatted down to the child's level. "Annie, I'd like to be your friend. And I'll let you shoot me any time you want. Okay, pardner?"

She was not quite sure what to make of me, I saw, and suddenly her bravado was gone. She retreated behind Tricia, clutching at her mom's jeans, and putting two fingers into her baby mouth.

Tricia reached behind and scooped her up in her arms. Annie's Tweety Bird tee shirt had crept up, and Tricia's lips were all over her little belly, blowing air and making noises that tickled her into submission.

"Mama, tickles. Do more, Mama. More!" The child was insatiable, and the two were lost to their intimate little game. I almost felt like I shouldn't be watching.

I want one . . . or two . . . or three or maybe four of those. And when my first play is wowing them on Broadway, people will marvel: "Isn't she amazing? And she wrote it at night while her kids were sleeping!" Of course, I will have a supportive husband, who would never dream of walking out on me.

The phone was insistent, and Tricia was struggling with her key. Opening the door was made even more difficult by the burden she was shouldering. Annie had fallen asleep in the car and she was trying to carry her in without waking her.

"Here, give her to me." I put the grocery bags down and reached for her. Tricia had finally gotten the door open and rushed to the kitchen to grab the phone. Annie was now half-awake, but it was late. Perhaps if I stayed outside and rocked her in my arms, she would fall asleep again and Tricia and I could study for tomorrow's theater history exam. Annie didn't seem to mind that I was rocking her: Tricia and I had been friends for several months by then, and Annie had begun to treat me like a second mother, or at least a favorite aunt.

It was a long time before Tricia came outside. She had been crying. She motioned me to be quiet and I followed her through the living room and into Annie's bedroom. She pulled back the covers from the mattress on the floor and I gingerly lowered the sleeping child to her pillow, holding my breath while Tricia removed her precious boots. A sob caught in Tricia's throat, and Annie stirred. Clutching the boots to her chest, my friend hurried from the room.

"Trish, what is it, what's happened?"

She shook her head and stifled another sob. "That was Terry's father calling from New York . . . said he'd been trying to reach me all day. Terry's *dead*. The police in Frisco said he'd OD'd. They found him in the bathroom, with the needle still stuck in his arm. Oh, God, I can't believe it! That son of a bitch . . . that goddamned son of a bitch! He told me he was clean . . . that he was through with smack . . . that mother-fucking son of a bitch! What am I gonna tell my baby?"

She was sobbing out loud. I rushed to close Annie's door.

"Shhh, Trish, you'll wake her up. You can't tell her 'til you've calmed down. She'll really freak if she sees you like this. Here." I handed her a box of Kleenex. She blew her nose, took a deep breath, and nodded.

"You're right. It's going to be hard enough without me being hysterical. You know, Terry wasn't here for her, but he called her every week and sent presents and funny little poems and drawings in the mail. Annie has them up all over her wall. I know she doesn't even remember him, but she kisses his photo. The last time she saw him in the flesh, she was only two. Terry was here for two days. He took her to the Desert Museum to see the animals and out for ice cream. 'Daddy for a day,' you know? But I know he cared about her, even though his child support checks were always late . . . sometimes three months late, and I had to keep bugging him. Oh, that bastard, how could he do something like this to that baby?"

I put my arms around her. I wasn't very good at comforting. I didn't have the words, so I just let her cry on my shoulder for a while, wishing I could find something to say.

"Mama, don't cry. Why you cry?"

Neither of us had noticed the barefoot girl standing in the doorway. How long had she been there? What had she heard?

"Oh, God, Annie-baby . . . I'm sorry we woke you. Come to Mama, cowgirl. Mama wants to talk to you." She held out her arms to her. Annie tiptoed over, fingers in mouth and eyes wide.

Tricia threw me a panicked look and mouthed: "Help. What do I tell her?"

I shook my head. What did I understand of this death?

"Annie," she began bravely, "Remember last month when we found that box turtle next to the road, and it didn't move, and I told you it was dead, and we had a funeral . . ."

Annie nodded, and continued the story: "And we pick flowers and sing 'Jesus Love Me' and you say my turtle go to heaven to live with God and God take care of him and we can't never see him again and we put him in a box and dig a hole and I never see my turtle. I remember. Did my turtle come back? Did God send him back?"

"No, sweetie, God doesn't send turtles back after they die . . . or anyone else, either. Baby, I have to tell you something very sad now. You have to be Mama's big brave Annie Oakley now, okay?"

Annie nodded solemnly, and Tricia continued: "Grandpa just called to tell me that your Daddy died. Daddy went to heaven to live with God, Annie."

The baby blue eyes widened. "And he never come back?"

"I'm sorry, baby. No, he's not coming back."

"He write letters for me?"

Tricia shook her head.

"But Mama," she wailed, "he say he send me Mr. Potato Head. For my birthday. I want my Mr. Potato Head . . ."

"Oh, Annie, I'm so sorry . . ."

Tricia grabbed a tissue and went to wipe the tears and snot, but Annie pulled away and wiped her face on the sleeve of her tiny Bugs Bunny shirt. A sob caught in her throat and she started to hiccup.

"Is Daddy at God's house?"

"Yes, I'm sure God is taking care of Daddy now."

"Okay," she sniffled. "Can I have cake?"

CHAPTER SIX

No doubt, Jack has found my note by now. It was brief, with no accusations, recriminations, or regrets:

> *I need to get away for awhile, and this seemed an opportune time. It's something I have to do before it's too late. I will write to the kids and tell them I'm taking a little vacation. I trust you will not do or say anything to alarm them.*
> *C.*

And that, I think, is that.

It's my second day on the road, and reality is starting to encroach on my reverie. Aided by the soundtrack of my youth, I am smack dab in the middle of my upcoming reunion, focusing on the unfulfilled promise of my last time with Peter. I am rewriting that ending and can't wait for us to read the new script.

But then, the children come banging on the door, demanding to be let in, demanding and, yes, deserving my attention.

Go back to camp, kiddos. Mama's busy right now, I can't think about you.

But that's like telling someone not to think about a polar bear for five minutes. Try it. It's impossible. You spend the next three hundred seconds focused on arctic scenes, ice floes, white, white, white . . . and that enormous bear.

What are you doing? Are you out of your mind? You're about to wreck your children's future! And what about yours? You think being a single mother is a piece of cake? Remember your friend Tricia? She didn't have a choice. She did what she had to do. She was brave and strong in the face of a situation she never wished for. You're not brave, you're just being selfish and childish and lazy and you're a damn coward. You should be thinking about how to fix your marriage, not this cockamamie exercise in futility. How are you going to support those kids? You haven't even had a job since before Greg was born. Do you even know how to make a living? Who's going to pay for their braces? What about college tuition? And what about all those things Jack is happy to do around the house? That is, if you can even afford a house. So, is that going to be you under the sink with a screwdriver and a wrench fixing the leaky faucet? And who's going to hang the pictures? Who's going to make it feel like home? Where's the money going to come from? And what are you going to tell Greg and Sarah and that precious little Caleb? That you traded their happiness and security for some impossible life you think you're going to be making? I can just see their tear-stained little faces when their father isn't there to kiss them goodnight. That will be your doing, Carolyn. And what makes you think Peter's going to want you, even if he could? You're not twenty anymore, you know.

That doesn't even sound like my voice in my head. Shit! Who invited *her* on this road trip?

Come back, Peter. Please come back. That was such a lovely embrace we were locked in. Pay no attention to that woman behind the curtain.

But then all I can think of is my three babies, alone and scared on an ice floe. And that damned polar bear has my mother's eyes, and I am depleted.

It's only three in the afternoon, but I've done all the driving I can for the day. I had hoped to get to Chicago, but can't make it farther than the northwest corner of Indiana, so I pull into the next rest stop and grab a couple of pre-wrapped sandwiches for dinner (pimento cheese and tuna salad and hope that I won't get food poisoning), an armful of magazines, and brochures for nearby motels. I'll make up the time tomorrow.

CHAPTER SEVEN

I had become obsessed with French cinema. *Jules et Jim* was playing at Le Cine and I was dying to go, but everyone was either studying or rehearsing, so I found myself buying my own ticket and my own popcorn, and wishing I had a boyfriend (or two) to share this experience with me.

I *loved* this movie! I was especially smitten with the idea of a woman being the love interest of two men (two sexy men, to boot!). I loved that it was French (I tried not to read the subtitles, but my high school français could only take me so far). Yes! This could work out, this is what I wanted my life to look like. Two men absolutely adoring me in a cottage in the irreplaceable French countryside . . . oh, yeah, until the end. That didn't work out very well, did it? Okay, I wanted my life to be like *Jules et Jim,* until the part where Catherine drives with Jim off that bridge. *My* ménage à trois would be happily ever after.

Years later, I dragged my reluctant husband to an art house revival.

"But it's in French. And it's in black and white."

"Yes, and there are subtitles. . .and of course it's in black and white, it's deep."

On second viewing, fifteen years after my first, it was obvious that the naive, nineteen-year-old Franco-cinephile missed so many psychological and psychosexual nuances of Truffaut's masterpiece. Was it possible that Jules and Jim were unrequitedly hot for each other, and that Catherine, although worshipped and adored by both men, was a beard? That hit way too close to home.

But after my first viewing, I was completely caught up in the story. Even the ending was so tragically romantic. I was enchanted—and I would have settled for Oskar Werner any day.

I left Le Cine with Catherine's song, *Le Tourbillon*—about ex-lovers finding each other again and questioning why they had separated in the first place when they had had such great sex (although in French it's *s'est réchauffé*, or "warming each other")—echoing in my head.

I needed to talk to someone about this, someone older and worldly and knowledgeable and deep and brilliant . . . and a woman. Miranda!

I knocked on her door, but there was no answer. Maybe she was at Brad's. I knew he wasn't there because I had caught a glimpse of him at Le Cine. She wasn't at Brad's either, but her car was. Artie's lights were on, so I took a chance that I wouldn't catch him *in flagrante delicto*, and knocked on his door.

"Who's there?"

"It's me. Caro. Have you seen Miranda anywhere?"

He flung open the door. "Oh, Jesus, thank God you're here. Miranda's flipping out!"

Miranda, flipping out? My paragon of sophistication, of daring, of seductiveness . . . my Jeanne Moreau doppelganger? The woman who left her rich husband for that potty-mouthed comedian? She was cool enough to be *Catherine* and practically famous, for God's sake.

I entered the house, but I didn't see *that* Miranda anywhere. What I did see was a weeping child, curled into a fetal position in the corner of the living room.

"Oh, my God, Miranda, what happened?"

"I'm next . . . I'm next," she moaned. "I know I'm next."

Her face was streaked with mascara-tinted tears. Her hair was a snarled-up mess.

I should have gone to her, to comfort her, but she'd been so high on that pedestal, I didn't feel worthy.

I turned to Artie. "Huh? Next for what? What is she talking about?"

He beckoned me to the kitchen. "She thinks she's going to die. She just found out Benny Roth bought it today. They found him in the bathroom, with the needle still in his arm, just like Terry. You know Miranda and Terry had a thing a while back, and they used to shoot smack together. And you know before that, she left her husband to run away with Benny . . ."

"Oh, shit! But Miranda's clean, she hasn't used in years . . ."

"I know, but she's all superstitious about things coming in threes, and then she did that *I Ching* thing that she does, and she said it came up double pitfall, whatever the fuck that means and then she just started freaking out."

We went back into the living room. Miranda had fallen asleep with her thumb in her mouth. Artie got a blanket from his bed and gently covered her. And then, because there was nothing more to be done, we figured we might as well fuck. Not exactly the ménage à trois I envisioned.

Two hours later, Miranda woke up and insisted that we not leave her alone. I risked being kicked out of my dorm, but I stayed. The three of us played Botticelli until daybreak and never spoke of that evening again.

CHAPTER EIGHT

There might be one hundred ways to leave your lover, or your mother, or for your mother to leave you, but is there ever a right way? What about the person left behind?

I get up late the next morning—in fact, it's barely morning, 11 o'clock. Maybe I shouldn't have taken that sleeping pill last night, but after I started reading the cover story in *People* magazine ("Summer of Love: Celebrating the '60s. It's twenty years later. Do you know where your love beads are?") I couldn't stop thinking about Peter and how great it's going to be to see each other again, and then I was wide awake till after midnight.

But when I get up, my first thoughts are of Jack. I remember what "gut-wrenching" feels like, as I barely make it to the bathroom in time (the tuna sandwich, with a side order of sad). This might be what Jack is feeling now. It's how he reacted when our dog died, somatizing his grief into bouts of diarrhea so severe I almost drove him to the ER, except he couldn't stop shitting long enough to get in the car. I think, had he permitted himself, he would have fallen to his knees and wailed, he loved that dog so much. But then it was over, and he was back to his cool, calm, collected self. He is surely not calm today in that preternaturally quiet house: no dog to greet him with yips of jubilation when he comes home each night, his children off to camp, and his wife disappeared, leaving a brief note with a lie of omission for an excuse. I wonder, with no one to hear, is he keening for his lost family? I can't bear the thought.

I think about Miranda, instead. She made leaving a lover as easy and mindless as changing her clothes when it was time for that funky sweater to go to the laundromat. Bored with being married to a rich, powerful, older man, and intrigued by a politically outspoken comedian, she had said "Sure!" when Benny Roth urged "Come with me."

"I'm thinking about splitting," she declared one day when we were going over a one-act she was directing and I was stage managing. I looked around. Was there anyone else in the room? Had I become her friend? I felt emboldened. I had heard her ex had threatened to blow Benny's head off, and I was dying to know the real skinny.

"What was it like, leaving your husband?"

But I had assumed too much. She didn't look at me, then got up and walked into the bedroom. I sat for a few minutes, and then knew I had been dismissed.

So, this is how she left Brad (more than once): she'd pick up her toothbrush and move back to her apartment, entertain new lovers, and ignore his entreaties to come back to his bed.

He'd stand outside her door, sporting a sweaty wifebeater, wailing for her like some kind of third-rate Brando. As if that could recapture that prize. *Such drama*! No, when she returned, it was on her terms, not his. Sometimes months would go by, and then one night he would come home from work to find her toothbrush in his bathroom and Miranda asleep in his bed. Until the night she left him for good, and left all of us, too, running away to New York with a man she barely knew and had married on a whim.

Terry left Tricia and his baby that way, too, but he went to Frisco with a stripper when the responsibilities of fatherhood interfered with his drug habit. I don't think Tricia ever got over that: The smiling photo of her ex she kept in her living room was not just for Annie's benefit. Tricia would always love Terry, even after he died.

And then there was the way my there/not-there mother left me, so no one could accuse her of abandoning her child, because, technically, she was present. That *was* her, drunk in her bed, but there were no milk and cookies, no welcoming hugs, no "What did you learn today?" From fourth grade on, she didn't even meet me at the bus, which was a relief, because I never knew what state she'd be in when I stepped onto our lane. When I got older, I used to wish that she would really leave, but the only way I knew parents to depart was to die, and I couldn't stomach the guilt of wishing her dead.

But Jack is more than my lover, he's my legally wedded husband, and my focusing on how easy it seemed for Miranda belies the fact that I am also leaving the father of my children, and, yes, my children, too, no matter how much I deny it.

The French expression for "It's as easy as pie" is "*C'est simple comme bonjour*," literally, "It's as simple as hello."

But there's nothing simple about "Good-bye."

CHAPTER NINE

Sometimes I think there are no accidents, that everything's part of a master plan. Other times, though, like when terrible things happen to people who deserve them least, I'm convinced that there is no order to the Universe and that random is the word that most fits the scheme of things.

For a long time, I believed that fate or some unknown higher power (the jury was still out as to the existence of God) had sent Peter to me. Now I tend to think it was just one of those arbitrary occurrences that happen to have life-long repercussions. It gives me the creeps sometimes. Like, if Jack hadn't been rejected from an Ivy League law school and hadn't applied to U of A, or if he had decided to go to the library that day instead of attending the demonstration, then Greg, Sarah, and Caleb wouldn't exist. Or, if things had been different, Peter and I might have created a whole different set of progeny.

Eighties kids, '60s rock. My three think they're the first to discover the Beatles.

"Do you know what *Lucy in the Sky with Diamonds* stands for?" demands Greg. His tone implies that I have gone the way of the dinosaurs.

"Yes, Greg, as a matter of fact, I do." I say nothing more and he doesn't continue the conversation. For once, I'm glad he no longer craves long talks with me. I don't want to talk about a song that glorifies drug use. I'm frightened that the children and their friends know too much about this already, and, despite the deaths of star athletes and show-business luminaries, illicit drugs still smack of thrills within their reach.

So I don't elaborate that I know first-hand what this song means, that twenty years before, I had spent one terrifying day and night teetering on the thin line between madness and reality because I had followed Timothy Leary's call to "Turn on. Tune In. Drop Out." If it hadn't been for Peter, I might have dropped out permanently.

"Hey, hey . . . we got it, kiddo!" Ernesto greeted me as I walked through their front door that Saturday. He and Scott were grinning like twin cats that had swallowed two canaries.

"Got what?"

"The acid. And it's the real stuff. Real genuine Owsley acid, the best there is."

"You meant *today?* We're gonna trip *today?*" I felt like they were throwing me a surprise birthday party. I had been bugging the two of them for weeks to let me trip with them, only to be told that LSD was a scarce commodity in Tucson because the heat was on the dealers. I could hardly contain my excitement.

"So, where is it? What are we waiting for? Let's do it!"

"Not so fast, kid. We want it to be really special since it's your first time. So, where would you like to go?"

"Go?" This was a new wrinkle. I had assumed that where I would go would depend less on physical surroundings than on plumbing the depths of my unconscious.

"Does it matter? Why can't we just stay here?"

"Of course it matters. How about Mount Lemmon or Sabino Canyon? You want to be somewhere really far out so you can dig it. Are you hip?"

"Oh, yeah, I'm hip. I don't know . . . I guess Mount Lemmon. We haven't been there in a while. And the last time we went to the canyon, there were so many straights that I was afraid to smoke, remember?"

"Oh, yeah," recalled Scott. "You were totally paranoid. It was a real bummer.

"Alright . . . all in favor of Mount Lemmon . . ." The three of us raised our hands.

"I've got some Kool Aid to take it with." Ernesto grabbed a mason jar filled with bright orange liquid from the fridge and we raced for the truck like little kids being given an unexpected holiday from school.

We made one stop, at the 7-11, for cigarettes, potato chips, Twinkies, and M&M's.

"Don't tell me you get the munchies on acid, too?" It was the one thing I didn't like about grass. I'd put on ten pounds since I'd started smoking it.

"No, not really." Ernesto and Scott looked at each other. "But you never know, we might get hungry."

Our destination was about thirty-five miles out of town, in the Santa Catalina Mountains. It was a stunningly beautiful day, with a cloudless sky. We drove east on Speedway, a hodge-podge of billboards, fast food restaurants, bars, and used car lots, a strip favored by Tucson's teenagers who cruised up and down to banish ennui each Saturday night.

Soon, however, the vestiges of so-called civilization were left behind and we entered the Sonoran desert. There, the edifices were nature-made: massive cacti and squat desert shrubs dominated the landscape. We sang along with the radio, making up raunchy lyrics as we drove. Outside, the desert gave way to the foothills, and the vegetation changed to chaparral, manzanita, oak, pinion, juniper and cypress.

I gave a silent thank you that I was here instead of Glenbury. I had never been so happy.

"Ernesto, this is so groovy. Can't we stop right here?"

"No, c'mon, let's go to the top . . . into the woods. Those trees are even more awesome."

Awesome they were. It even smelled different up there, all piney and loamy. You'd never know the desert was just a few miles down the road. Presently we entered a dense forest of towering fir, aspen, and ponderosa pines so tall they appeared to be piercing the clouds. Ernesto was right. This was the perfect place.

We parked the truck and went the rest of the way on foot. Ernesto was in the lead and chose to ignore the well-marked trail, opting instead to find his own way to Paradise, despite the fact that being trailblazers meant we would have to ford a stream and scale some scarily sharp rocks.

Finally, Ernesto stopped. "Here." He had found a flat outcropping—mica schist, if I remembered correctly from my geology class. It was really sparkly, anyway.

We sat. The spot was perfect. From our perch, we could look over the whole mountain range.

Ernesto took a small envelope from his pocket and handed me a triangle-shaped white tablet.

"This is it?"

I guess I must have sounded disappointed because Scott countered with: "What did you expect, that it came in psychedelic colors? That comes *after* you drop it."

"Okay, then. Cheers." I took the tablet and washed it down with a swig of Kool Aid.

"Next . . ." I passed the bottle to Ernesto, who put the cap back on.

"Aren't you going to take yours?"

Ernesto cleared his throat. "So, Scott and I just dropped acid last weekend and . . . um . . . we thought it was too soon to do it again . . . but don't worry, we'll be here with you. We'll stay with you the whole time. We brought a little grass to smoke. We just want you to have a good trip."

I was nonplussed. I had not planned on making a solo voyage. I hid my disappointment, though. True to form, I was loath to express negative feelings to people I wanted desperately to like me, and short of sticking my finger down my throat, there wasn't much I could do.

"Oh, I understand. Okay, then . . . when is something going to happen?"

"Just relax. Sometimes it takes a while. It's not like grass. It might take a half hour or so. Just go with the flow, Caro, it's cool," said Scott as he pulled a joint out of his cigarette pack and lit it. He took a long toke and handed it to Ernesto. I wished I were joining them. At least I knew what to expect with grass. Instead, I pulled out a cigarette. Scott leaned over to light it.

"Stay cool, kid." His voice was strained because he was holding his breath.

An hour later, I was the coolest thing around. In fact, I was so cool, I had been crowned Queen of the Mountain. From my bejeweled throne, I overlooked the entire verdant valley where all my tiny mountain people stood ready. They lived to serve me. And I didn't even have to give them orders. They could read my mind and know my heart's desire. There they were, scurrying to do my bidding. All I had to do was think wonderful thoughts and off they went. They brought me water. They lit my cigarettes, and they sang me lullabies.

"Hey, Caro, you're awfully quiet. Are you all right?" Scott sounded worried and so far away, but I nodded regally and beneficently, as befitted my queenly status. Ernesto and Scott were merely two more of my subjects, albeit not tiny ones.

But, two hours later, coming down from their grass high and bored with the scenery, my two most loyal subjects became my betrayers.

It started with the cigarettes. The Queen had come to the realization that the only way she could breathe was through a cigarette, hence, she had smoked an entire pack.

"Give me a cigarette," I commanded. They did not comply. Perhaps they didn't hear me.

"Give me a cigarette," I demanded in my haughtiest voice.

"Caro, you can't have any more cigarettes. You've smoked a whole pack already," replied Ernesto testily.

I couldn't believe that these underlings were refusing me. Didn't they know that all I had to do was give the word, and it would be off with their heads? And who was this Caro-person they were talking about?

I lunged for Ernesto's pack, but he pulled it out of my hand. "No more cigarettes, Caro. You've had enough. Besides, it's time to go home. It's going to get dark soon."

Home? Home? What was he talking about? I *was* home. The mountain people needed me. They would die without me. I was staying.

The two of them gathered the remains of their junk food picnic. I had not touched a bite. They got to their feet and Scott offered me a hand. I refused to see it. Suddenly, I was terrified. I really *couldn't* breathe without a cigarette.

"Please," I begged "Give me a cigarette. It's the only way . . . way I can breathe. It's my breathing tube. Please . . ."

Tears were running down my cheeks. Scott finally saw that I believed what I was saying.

"Aw, give her a cigarette, Ernesto. I think she's having a bad trip."

Ernesto assessed the situation and saw that Scott was, in fact, correct. I was having a horrifying trip. I knew then they would make me leave my mountain people, and I would die.

But my power of speech had left me. I couldn't tell them what was happening. I was their prisoner. Each of them took an arm as they guided me from my happy home into oblivion.

FIRE ORANGE BRIGHT . . . converging ripe bitterness . . . NAKED ALL-POWERFUL . . . all my nameless fears retreat into madness . . . I want to stay here . . . magnificent obsession . . . my nameless ones . . . a human thing, those people, crushing my bones and I am nothing . . . but how can I tell anyone if I never get out? Rich, rubber-souled demons . . . the sun's bright MAGNIFICENCE . . . all my nameless ones riding alone . . . fire-charred into ONE . . . the red of the pure . . . my nameless ones . . . the ALL-CONSUMING . . . in that other world, babies are born . . . my mind's eye . . . melting into me . . . HELP ME . . . a souvenir from reality . . . madness.

The trip back was a nightmare. I could not speak, but I could think, if the contortions of my mind at the time could be called thinking. The above words were scrawled on the back of an envelope I found on the floor of the truck, scrawled when I thought I might never speak again. Just as we started our drive down the mountain, the sun exploded and my mountain people were lost in a fiery inferno. It was my fault. I was consumed with guilt and wracked with silent sobs. If only I hadn't left them. They were dead, all of them, even the tiny mountain babies . . . gone forever.

"Oh, forgive me, forgive me," I implored silently, but their sweet voices, too, were stilled. I was burning in a Bosch-like hell of my own making and I knew I would burn forever for my sins.

Ernesto and Scott were hungry. Again. They stopped at a Baskin-Robbins at the easternmost point of Speedway.

"Caro, do you want anything?" Scott sounded concerned.

"Oh, leave her alone. She'll be okay for a minute."

They went into the store. My captors had left me! I could escape! Back to my people. Perhaps it was not too late to save a few. Perhaps, somewhere back on the mountain, one or two of them clung tenaciously to life, and only I could save them.

My arms were paralyzed. I willed them to move, to open the door of the truck, to lead me to freedom. They were no longer my arms, though. They had turned into grotesque black snakes. If my arms were snakes, what must the rest of me be? Frantically, I maneuvered my body so that I could look in the rearview mirror. My face, too, had disappeared. In its place was a fiery skull. I was dying.

CHAPTER TEN

I had no idea how I got from the truck parked on Speedway to the apartment on Seventh Street, but I did know it was now evening, and I had been crying for hours. Ernesto and Scott had become bored with babysitting my bad trip. They wanted to party. Or, Ernesto did, anyway. I think Scott wanted to stay with me until my trip was over, but he couldn't say no to his lover. They were in the bedroom, dressing to go out.

I was sitting in the living room, surrounded by Beardsley posters that had taken on an evil life of their own. There were candles flickering all around and I was still terrified I would be consumed by fire. I tried to close my eyes, but my eyelids, like my arms, refused to obey.

They were about to leave, and I had a sudden, clear realization, the first clear thought in hours: They were *not* my friends. I had ceased to amuse them, and they had no use for me.

Scott turned to me. "Try and get some sleep, kid. You'll be all right, it just takes a while. Sleep for a couple of hours and we'll come by later to take you back to the dorm, okay?"

His eyes were pleading. I said nothing, and Ernesto was getting visibly impatient.

I was alone with the night and my demons.

Perhaps I was dreaming, or perhaps I had actually died. That was it. I was dead. The man standing before me was an angel of God (at that point, and in that state, I probably thought it prudent to be a believer). He was aglow in an aura of love. I was safe.

The angel spoke. "This is Scott's place, right? Um . . . he told me I could stop by to borrow a book, but I guess he's not home, huh? I, uh, guess I'll come back tomorrow."

Hmmm, maybe not an angel. Did my erstwhile friends send this devil to finish me off?

"Hey, are you all right?" He had drawn closer to me and he must have seen the terror in my eyes.

"I'm not going to hurt you. What's the matter?"

I could only whimper. Instantly, the vision seated himself beside me. He took my hand.

"What is it? What are you afraid of? Did you take something? Is that it?"

I nodded, tentatively at first, but then vigorously. I sensed that this angel could be my only salvation.

"What did you take? Was it acid?"

I nodded again.

"And you're having a bummer of a trip, aren't you? Oh, you poor kid. Let me stay with you. Maybe I can help. Who are you? How did you get here?"

Too many questions. I shook my head, moaning.

"It doesn't matter . . . shhh . . . shhhh. You're going to be okay. Everything will be fine very soon."

He was quiet for a moment, then he rose to his feet and pulled a record album from the nearby shelf.

"Here, this is going to make you feel just great, I know." He put the record on the turntable and placed the headphones over my ears . . . and the Beatles were in my head, singing about turning off my mind and floating downstream and not dying.

By the end of the track, the demons had fled. It was not dying. I was not dying. I was *alive.* I sighed in relief. My guardian angel was smiling down at me.

"It worked, didn't it? You look so peaceful and so beautiful now." His voice was gentle, and he was so soft-spoken I had to strain to hear him.

That voice. I've been hearing it now for so many years. No, not imagining, I mean really hearing it. When Greg was a toddler and I was pregnant with Sarah and coping with morning sickness and exhaustion, I would sit him in front of *Sesame Street* to give myself a half hour break, and then we'd play outside. One morning, I was feeling so wiped out I lay down on the couch and fell asleep for a few minutes. I was startled out of my nap by Peter's voice, coming from the den. He was telling me how special I was.

I rushed into the room. Peter was nowhere in sight, and my son was grinning at the TV, at a man in a red cardigan (which was so unfashionable it could have come right out of Peter's closet) who was now asking him to be his neighbor. It was uncanny, he sounded exactly like Peter. And Peter could have written his script, too.

Years after all three kids had outgrown Mr. Rogers, I still made periodic forays into the Neighborhood. Both Fred and Peter liked me just the way I was.

But that was something I didn't yet know on the night Peter and I met.

"Oh, yes." My voice had returned along with my sanity. I eyed him curiously. "Who are you? I think you saved my life, you know."

"I'm P-p-p-peter M-m-m-MacKinley. I'm in Scott's modern drama class. Just transferred to the department this semester. You're a drama major too, aren't you? I saw you rehearsing that scene from *M-m-mother Courage* last week. You're really good."

I blushed. I didn't quite know how to handle compliments, especially from men I'd just met. I wasn't used to them.

"I expect we'll be seeing your name in lights one of these years. What *is* your name, anyway? We really haven't been properly introduced, you know."

Hmm, he didn't sound like any of the guys I knew. He was a bit formal and polite, almost old mannish, even, and a little awkward, with that stutter, but he seemed really nice.

"I'm sorry. I'm Carolyn . . . um Caro . . . Mills, and you've just walked in on the worst day of my life. You're right, I did drop acid and it was horrible. But, thanks to you, I'm much better now."

He flashed me another grin. "I can see that. But, just to make sure you stay that way, I'm going to stick around, okay?"

"Oh, yes . . . please . . . I mean, I'm feeling a little weak. I don't know much about acid. Can you have a relapse?"

"I don't know," he answered soberly. "I've never taken it . . . and after seeing what you've been through, or part of it, anyway, I don't think I'll bother to find out. Actually," he confessed, "I've never even smoked pot."

"Really?"

"Really. We're a little backward in Hastings, North Dakota." He laughed.

North Dakota. That would fit. The light brown hair; guileless blue eyes; open, trusting face; the easy grin. No freckles, but still . . . Midwest farm boy, perhaps?

I glanced at his hands. No, not farm boy. They were not my father's hands, nor were they the hands of my high school classmates, those boys who would be up at four to help with the milking before heading off to school. No, Peter's hands had never milked a cow nor mucked a stall. They were nice hands, with long, tapering fingers. He had the hands of a pianist.

"No big deal. We're a little backward in Glenbury, Vermont, too. I never even smoked cigarettes before I came here . . . no, actually, that's not quite true. When I was twelve, my cousin

Mark and I shared a cigarette behind his father's barn, but my uncle caught us and tanned our behinds. It kind of soured me on tobacco for a while."

Peter laughed appreciatively and offered me a Marlboro.

"Oh, thanks, I've been dying for one for hours. In fact," I added soberly, "I think I've been dying for hours . . . thanks again for saving me."

"Don't mention it. It's the first time in my life I've had the chance to rescue a damsel in distress, and I'm kind of enjoying it."

"So am I. . . ." This admission was followed by an uncomfortable silence until Peter jumped in.

"Have you had dinner yet? I don't know about you, but it's way past my dinner time and I'm starving. Would you like to get something to eat? I know this terrific little Mexican restaurant downtown. They make the best guacamole tacos . . ."

"You just got here and you already know the best restaurant in town? I'll bet it's El Charro, isn't it?"

He nodded, and flashed that sweet grin again.

"It's my favorite, too. Have you tried their chimichangas? Yum! Just let me go to the bathroom and I'll be ready in a second."

I was careful not to look in the bathroom mirror, lest the fiery skull decide to make another appearance. When I came out, I found Peter examining the posters on the wall.

"Scott has rather interesting taste in art, wouldn't you say?"

"Oh, I think those posters are actually more reflective of Ernesto's taste in art. He's kind of far out."

"Ernesto?"

"That's Scott's boy . . . ummm . . . the guy he lives with. His roommate . . ."

"Gotcha. Scott told me I could b-borrow his copy of *A Doll's House* for a paper I'm writing. He said to come over anytime . . ."

"Yeah, well I think they got kind of bored with me, and besides, they had this party they wanted to go to . . ."

"That's okay. We're kind of having our own party, aren't

we? Well, m-m-m'lady, your chariot awaits thee. Shall we hie it to dinner?"

"Lead on, MacDuff."

"The name's MacKinley, m'lady." He offered me his arm as we headed out into a moonless night. "You look like you might still be a little shaky—wouldn't want you to trip down the stairs."

"Nooo, I think I've had one trip too many today."

He groaned.

"Sorry, bad pun, huh?"

He opened the car door for me. The only other man who'd ever done that was my father. My first impression was right: he was nice.

The ride downtown was quiet. I guess we had both realized that our chance encounter had materialized into a date and we were not exactly comfortable. The ice needed to be broken again.

"So, what do you do when you're not rescuing damsels in distress. I'll bet you rescue stray cats from trees, right?"

He grinned. "How did you know? As a matter of fact, that's how our cat came to live with us. We named her Juniper, because that's where we found her."

"Our cat's name is Mouser, but he doesn't live up to his moniker. He's the fattest, laziest thing you ever saw. My father says he expects his mice roasted and served on a silver platter."

Peter laughed, and for the rest of the evening, the conversation rarely lagged.

"What does your dad do?" he asked after we had pigged out on our fiery repast.

"He's a vet. He wanted me to be one too, but the only animal I like is our dog, George. How about your father?"

"He's dead—has been for quite a while. He used to sell p-p-pianos, though, and sheet music. He wanted to be a musician, but the Depression got in the way. One night he'd had one too many, and turned left where he should have turned right. The car rolled over an embankment. They say he never knew what hit him . . . or what he hit."

"Oh, Peter, I'm so sorry. How awful for you."

He shrugged. "It was, at the time. I was only ten. But it was a long time ago. . . ."

"My mother drinks," I confessed hesitantly. "I mean she drinks a lot. But she does her drinking in bed instead of on the road. She's done it just about as long as I can remember. I wish I'd known her before she started. My father said she was wonderful."

"I'm sorry, Caro, I didn't mean to get off on such an unpleasant subject—but it looks like we have some things in common, doesn't it."

"Yeah. Do you have brothers or sisters? I'm an only child. I guess they wanted more . . . I know my dad wanted a son, but all they have is me."

"Well, I had an older sister, but she died when I was two. She had rheumatic fever and she was only four when she died. I don't remember her at all. So, really, I was raised as an only child. After my dad died, Mother came to be kind of dependent on me. That's why I didn't go to college for a year, and when I did, I stayed in North Dakota for a couple more years. The university is twenty miles away from home, so I commuted. I couldn't take it anymore, though, you know? I just had to get away."

"Me, too. I had to get away as far as possible. It was pretty heavy." I had a sudden feeling of disloyalty to my mother, and I hastened to add, "But I get some nice letters from home. My mom and I have a terrific long-distance relationship. I guess she's sober when she writes. Or not."

"My mother writes, too. Lots of gossip and stuff like that. She tries not to make me feel guilty about leaving, but I can read between the lines."

There was another uncomfortable lull that I filled with the first thing that came into my mind.

"What's your favorite movie?"

"Promise you won't laugh?"

I nodded "Promise."

"*Yankee Doodle Dandy.* It's not very hip, I know, but from the time I was a little kid, it was on TV every Fourth of July. I love it."

I squealed. "I can't *believe* it! That's *my* absolute favorite, too. I used to want to be George M. Cohan so I could wear tap shoes all the time. That's who I named my dog after. I like old movies much better than the new ones."

"Same here. Hey, they're having a Bogie festival down at Le Cine. Tomorrow's a double feature, *Casablanca* and *Maltese Falcon.* Would you like to go?"

"I'd love to. Those are two of my favorites, also, especially *Casablanca*—oh, God, when Victor Laszlo leads *La Marseillaise*? I cry every time. And Ingrid Bergman is so stunning. I used to want to be her, too . . . anybody but who I was, I guess."

"I think who you are is just fine. I-I'm really glad we met, Carolyn Mills," he smiled shyly.

I, too, was shy again. "So am I . . . oh, hey, it's getting late. If I'm not back in the dorm by 11, I'll be on restriction tomorrow and we won't be able to go to the movies."

"Don't worry, we'll be back in no time." He got the check from the waitress.

I protested. "Let me pay my share. This wasn't really a date, you know."

"Of course it was a date. The best date I've had in a long time . . . in fact, the only date I've had in a long time," he mused.

We got back to the dorm with five minutes to spare. All around us, couples were making out on the steps.

He cleared his throat. "I had a really nice time tonight, Caro. I enjoyed our talk. . . ."

"So did I, Peter. Thank you."

He smiled. "Thank *you*! I was really lucky. I came after a book and found a friend."

"Some of my best friends are books."

"Ummm, mine too, but you have to admit, it's nice to have a live friend. See you tomorrow, Caro. Oh, and you do like butter on your p-popcorn, don't you?"

"Yeah, lots of it. G'night, Peter."

It had been a living hell of a day, but, oh, the ending! I was so tired I didn't even bother to brush my teeth or get undressed. I was glad I didn't have a roommate to ask where I'd been all day. Just before I fell asleep on top of the covers, I was buoyed by this thought: I have met a sweet, interesting man who seems to like me—and he didn't try to make a pass on the first date!

CHAPTER ELEVEN

And there was this, this something about him that was so familiar, like we both knew the secret handshake or something. After our movie date the next night, it seemed to me as if we'd always known each other.

And Peter said he was feeling the same thing: "Maybe in a past life?"

We had been going out for just a couple of weeks when he asked me to come to his apartment. This was a very different relationship than any I had experienced, and I treasured it for its uniqueness. But sometimes, just sometimes, I wondered.

We met every day after our last classes. Usually, we spent an hour or two in the library, studying, then had dinner at Taco Bell, where the burritos were nineteen cents (sometimes we splurged on twenty-nine cent tacos) and then went back to the drama department for rehearsal.

Both of us had been cast in the department's major spring production, Arthur Miller's *After the Fall*. I had desperately wanted the Marilyn Monroe role, had even tried out in a blonde wig. I knew I was better than the girl who got the part. Instead, I was given the role of the protagonist's ex-wife. Peter was also cast in a supporting role. I was disappointed, but he was thrilled.

"Caro, come look at the casting list! We *both* got in! I can't believe it! Oh, this is so great!" Peter was practically singing. He was, in fact, dancing, a fancy step-ball-hop worthy of George M. himself.

I didn't want to rain on his parade, but I wished that just once I would be cast as the leading lady. I wished I were beautiful.

Peter's enthusiasm was infectious, though. It was hard to feel sorry for myself when I was around him.

"C'mon, let's celebrate! Double hot fudge sundaes, okay? Ohhh, I'm so happy!" He grabbed me and twirled me around. "I'll race you to the drugstore."

"I'll have to do a lot more than race to the drugstore if you're going to ply me with hot fudge sundaes, Mister. That's probably why I'm not getting the roles I want. Nobody wants a fat leading lady . . . except maybe in the circus." He'd touched a nerve here. I loved hanging out with him, but I was embarrassed that I clearly weighed more than he did. He could eat anything and always remained his same skinny self.

"Good lord, Caro, you're not fat, you're womanly. You're what a woman *should* look like. Look at all the great art through the ages. That's what women are supposed to look like, not like this Twiggy-creature. She looks like a fourteen-year-old boy. But you, you're . . . vo-LUP-tuous!"

He grinned, and I could tell he'd never said that word aloud before and was so proud of himself, like a little kid trying to impress his parents with a big word he'd just looked up in the dictionary.

"And if I were an artist, I'd paint you in all the colors of the rainbow."

I think I fell in love with him right then and there, in front of the drama building. And then we raced each other to the drugstore and the sundaes.

Voluptuous. I'm voluptuous.

He was very casual when he called to invite me to his apartment the next night. There was no rehearsal, neither of us felt like studying, and Le Cine was having a festival of obscure pre-war German films.

"What kind of cook are you, Caro?"

"Cook? Pretty much a non-cook, sorry. I can heat up a TV dinner, and I learned how to make cinnamon toast and saltwater taffy in junior high home ec, and I can boil water and bake a potato, but other than that . . ."

"Well, I've done some cooking. Hamburgers and things. Why don't we go to the grocery store and get some stuff and take it back to my place and see what we can manage. I don't think I'm up for taffy or cinnamon toast, though."

I tucked my never-been-used, fresh-out-of-the-box diaphragm in my backpack and waited for the dorm phone to summon me downstairs.

I was so used to getting to know guys' beds or cars before I ever had a chance to get to know *them*, the past few weeks had seemed like forever. In anticipation of Peter and me someday doing it, I'd gone to see Tricia's grandfatherly gynecologist.

"Why are you young girls always coming in here and breaking my heart?" he asked from between my draped and stirrupped legs. But he fitted me anyway, since, clearly, I had already done the nasty and he was too late to save me.

When Peter picked me up, I was dressed in my usual jeans and work shirt, but I left the top button open, the better for Peter to see my voluptuous breasts when I bent over.

He had a yen for beef stew. I had my doubts, but he said there was nothing to it. We bought stew beef, potatoes, carrots, onions, celery, and peas. He insisted on paying, as usual.

His apartment was further away from campus than most of my friends'. It was in a two-story complex of tan, faux-stucco buildings that shared a common courtyard, parking lot, and swimming pool. Children's bikes, trikes, and toys were strewn everywhere. It was not your typical off-campus abode.

"Mom came down with me to help me get settled," he shrugged. "She picked out the apartment. Thought it had a wholesome atmosphere. None of those nasty hippies or dope fiends around, you know?" He winked. "And, besides, it does have that pool. You'll have to bring your suit sometime and we can swim."

As if I were going to let him see me in a bathing suit . . . Naked, yes, but bathing suit? Not on your life.

His studio apartment was furnished in early-ugly-motel style: Orange vinyl-covered chairs, blue shag rug, two twin beds with utilitarian brown bedspreads, 1950s white Formica-topped, chrome-legged table, a tiny kitchen area built into one end of the room, and a tinier bathroom at the other. No posters on the wall, no Indian bedspread. Not hip at all, but it was clean and tidy. Kind of like Peter, actually, who usually dressed in button-down short-sleeve sport shirts and neatly pressed pants. He looked like he had stepped out of a J.C. Penney catalog, but the top and the bottom of him came from different pages. The light blue shirt he was wearing would have been perfect with the khaki pants on the same page, but not with the slate blue pants from a few pages later that he paired it with. And what could I say about his hyper-clean white sneakers? But he didn't seem to notice . . . or care.

One day the week before, he had picked me up at my dorm wearing an orange polo shirt and Kelly-green pants, looking like he didn't want to alienate either side at a Saint Patrick's Day parade.

"Hey, Peter, do you mind if I ask you a personal question?"

His head jerked back, like I'd slapped him.

He took a deep breath. "I guess that would depend on how p-p-personal."

"Whoa, never mind, it's not that big a deal."

"No, it's okay . . . shoot." He sounded like I meant to aim a pistol at him.

Then I was embarrassed that I was being nosy, but I had to follow through.

"Well, it's just that . . . Peter, are you color blind?"

His laugh came like a small explosion from the back of his throat, like he'd been holding his breath, waiting for a blow that never came.

"What, you don't like my outfit? I think it's kind of spiffy."

The cool thing about Peter was that he didn't try to be cool. He didn't try to be uncool, either, like those people who want you to think they have much more important things to think about than what they put on their bodies. He just was.

"No, I love your outfit. It's so . . . you!"

The apartment was him, too. No pretensions.

"Hey, we'd better get started on dinner if we want to eat sometime tonight, huh?"

Although neither of us had ever made a stew before, he swore there was nothing to it: boil some water and put cut-up vegetables and beef into it, season with salt and pepper, and cook 'til it's done. Couldn't be simpler, right?

Right. It's just that I'd never seen beef stew that was so grey and watery.

"Are you sure we've done this right? Isn't it supposed to be brown? Shouldn't we maybe add something to it, like food coloring?"

He was dubious. "It doesn't look quite right, does it? But," he hastened to add, "I'm sure it will taste delicious."

It didn't. It tasted as bad as it looked, and it was impossible to chew. I pushed the food around on my plate until I saw that he was doing the same thing.

"Let's dump this garbage, kid . . . what do you say?" he muttered in his best Bogie voice.

"Oh, I was hoping you'd say that. I didn't want to hurt your feelings, but it really is awful, isn't it? There must be some secret ingredient we don't know about, huh?"

"Yeah . . . listen, I do have some tuna and some mayo and bread. I know how to make tuna fish sandwiches—no secret ingredients there, okay?'

"Okay. I'm starving. And, Peter, I have a confession to make . . . about that cinnamon toast? It's a family joke that my recipe goes like this: First you toast some bread, then you take it to the sink and scrape it."

And that was all that happened that night.

Years later, as a new bride armed with *The Joy of Cooking*, I found the stew's missing ingredient: flour. The meat has to be seasoned, floured, and browned in fat before it goes into the stew pot. I made many beef stews over the years and, without fail, every one of them reminded me of that first culinary disaster.

I think about Peter a lot when I prepare food. Despite an inauspicious beginning, it turns out that I'm an accomplished and innovative cook . . . wouldn't he be surprised?

"You fool," I mutter when I am preparing an onion confit to spoon over the pot roast, "I could be doing this for *you*, you idiot. Look what you're missing: my *osso buco* . . . my chicken marbella . . . my *choucroute garnie* . . . my tabbouleh . . . my lips on yours . . . my legs wrapped around you. You fool, you could have had the best."

CHAPTER TWELVE

It was Peter who convinced me to reconcile with Scott and Ernesto. If it had been up to me, I might not have spoken to them again, but Peter wore me down with this kind of turn-the-other-cheek Jesus thing, topped with erring-being-human-and-forgiving-divine, blah, blah, blah. Anyway, I was missing them something awful, and, since they were my major pot connection, I was kind of jonesing. And I was dying to turn on with Peter, convinced that if he lost some of his inhibitions, he would find his way into my bed . . . well, actually, more like invite me into *his* bed, since this was way before parietal hours in dorms.

But I was wavering. Their betrayal had really hurt, and the wound hadn't yet healed.

Funny, if I hadn't gone back that night, our story would have run a very different course, I think. But I did go back.

Scott had approached me in front of the drama building one day, a few weeks after my bad trip. I knew he felt terrible, but I was not yet ready to forgive something so unforgiveable.

"Please come back, Caro. We're so sorry. It was such a shitty thing to do, and we feel terrible about it. And we really miss you."

We, or you, Scottie? Why are you apologizing for him when it was his idea to leave? I'll bet Ernesto hasn't given it a second thought.

"Sorry, gotta go. Late for class," and I turned my back on him.

But Ernesto did turn out to be sorry, or at least he gave a good impression of being sorry, apologizing profusely when he waylaid me after class to invite us over. And he remembered that the next day was my birthday. That scored him a lot of points.

"And we've got a super special present for you, Caro. So you guys *have* to come over tomorrow."

"Hmm, not as super special as the last present, I hope. That was a gift that kept on giving, wasn't it?"

I was not quite ready to totally forgive and forget and I wanted Ernesto to know it.

"No, Caro, a different kind of super. Really, you'll like *this* one, I promise."

"You know what, let me talk to Peter and I'll let you know tonight, okay?"

I didn't want to seem too eager, wanted Ernesto to sit with his discomfort a little bit longer, but the truth was, as fond as I was of Peter, he frequently erred on the side of caution, and I missed the adrenaline rush of doing something outrageous and illegal with my former best buds.

So, after all the apologizing and convincing and forgiving shit was out of the way, Peter and I did show up at the Love House the next night, where we found an elaborate birthday dinner on the table, including one of those ready-made supermarket birthday cakes topped with blue and pink frosting roses and sugary green leaves and my name in implausibly perfect cursive.

"Oh, you guys, this is so sweet, but you shouldn't have spent all that money."

We were polishing off rare porterhouse steaks and baked potatoes and asparagus.

"You're kidding, right? Remember all those deep pockets in

my army jacket? And of course, we did the steaks-down-the-pants thing. Well, we did pay for the cake, though, because it wouldn't have fit in a pocket, and we went at two in the morning, when they're pretty short-staffed . . ." Ernesto winked.

Peter looked a little sick all of a sudden.

Oh, another adventure I wished I'd been on! I loved El Rancho, the all-night grocery out on Speedway, and, although I had never swiped anything myself, I relished playing decoy, asking the stock boys to show me where to find the tuna or the Velveeta or the Cheerios while my compatriots expertly purloined lamb chops and shrimp and frozen chimichangas. Accessory to the crime, that was me.

"So, let's save the cake for later, after your present." Ernesto presented me with an elaborately wrapped gift. He'd probably lifted the wrapping paper and ribbons, too.

"Oooh, too pretty to open. Maybe I'll bring it back to the dorm and enjoy looking at it for a while," I teased, knowing full well the package contained something I couldn't be caught dead with outside of those walls (or inside of those walls, either, come to think about it). "Just kidding, just kidding." I tore open the paper.

"Oh my God, is this what I think it is? How did you get it? You didn't stuff *this* down your pants at El Rancho, did you?"

Ernesto was grinning like the Cheshire Cat, and I was about to become Alice in Wonderland.

"Yeah, kiddo, it's exactly what you think it is. Look at the color. Isn't it far out?"

Peter, meanwhile, was trying to play hail-fellow-well-met, but I sensed his discomfort at not being in on the secret.

"Peter, it's Acapulco Gold! This is so incredible! It's the best! Supremo! You're gonna love this. Best birthday present ever, you guys. You are totally forgiven."

Ernesto rolled an extra-large blunt from the greenish-gold pile.

"Birthday girl first."

I took a toke and passed it to Peter.

He inhaled, then inhaled again. He didn't even cough. Pretty good for a newbie.

It only took about ten minutes before the four of us were draping each other in feather boas and love beads and euphorically doing our best stoned version of "Rich Man's Frug" from the *Sweet Charity* album. Peter, dancing! A lot of hip action there, but, funny, I wasn't even thinking about sex. Just loving on Peter, Ernesto, and Scott. We were family, and it all felt so right.

"Aren't we *fabulous!*" we congratulated ourselves.

"To the Fabulous Foursome," toasted Peter, lifting an imaginary wine glass and winking at me, which got me back to thinking about sex.

"To the Fabulous Foursome," we nodded in assent.

And thus we remained.

Peter's apartment was kind of out in the boonies, and my parents were making me live in the dorm for one more year, until I turned twenty-one, so our preferred hangout was Scott and Ernesto's. The Saturday after my birthday dinner, we were there again, and the two of us were rocking Botticelli. Scott and Ernesto, not so much.

"I'm thinking of someone whose name begins with G," Peter started out, as he leaned over to light my cigarette. I cupped his hand in a gesture I'd learned from watching old movies.

"Is it male?" I asked, which was kind of a throwaway question, because Peter's choices were always men.

"Yes."

I'd guessed correctly, so it was my turn to ask again.

"Is he an actor?" Also often a given when Peter was the one being questioned.

"Yes."

"John Gielgud?" And I knew this was right before he even confirmed it.

"Yes!"

"Okay, my turn. Mine starts with H."

"Is it a woman?" Scott asked.

"Nope."

"Okay, is he alive?" asked Ernesto.

"Nope.

Peter's turn. "Is he a writer?"

"Yup." I leaned back onto a paisley pillow and blew smoke rings, à la William Powell in *The Thin Man*.

"Hermann Hesse!" exulted Peter, and he didn't even frame it as a question.

"Okay, I'm up again," Peter grinned "This time I'm not going to make it so easy."

"So easy?" Ernesto complained. "Since when is John Gielgud the first 'G' actor you think of? What about Clark Gable, or Cary Grant, or James Garner, even? But John Gielgud? What would make you even guess that, Caro?"

"I don't know, I just knew that's who he was thinking of."

But Peter was on a roll and wanted to get on with the game. "I'm thinking of someone whose name begins with B."

He would never have picked that letter if he hadn't been stoned, but when he was, the stutter disappeared.

And this time, I knew Peter had chosen a woman, just to confound us.

"I know, it's a man," sighed Scott.

"No," answered Peter with a smug grin.

Ernesto's turn. "So, is she American?"

"Nope."

My turn. "Is she a writer?"

Peter nodded.

"Emily Brontë?"

"Bingo!" Peter gave me a hug.

"Wait, wait a minute. Are you two cheating? What would make you think of Emily-fucking-Brontë, Peter? When did you even read Emily-fucking-Brontë? What kind of system have you two cooked up? Are you like blinking letters at each other or something?"

No, we weren't. We just seemed to know what the other was thinking. And Emily Brontë wasn't so far-fetched: We'd just watched *Wuthering Heights* at Le Cine the night before. It kind of ruined Botticelli as a Fabulous Foursome activity, though.

CHAPTER THIRTEEN

Gradually, Peter became a little more comfortable in his own skin. Not quite like when he was onstage, and the stutter waxed and waned, but he was much more amenable to being goofy, not being such a goody-goody, trying new things, and the consequences be damned. I gave myself a pat on the back for the part I played in his metamorphosis. I was very entertaining, he said, and he told me that no one had ever made him laugh the way I did, so, of course, I made it a point to be clever and funny and adorable in his presence. I saw myself reflected in his eyes, and I liked what I saw. He refused to join the shoplifting sprees, though, and he convinced me to cease and desist, as well. I didn't mind. We were in the throes of new couplehood, and it was so much fun.

And then, two months after we first started hanging out, Peter asked me to go to church with him. I didn't quite know what to make of it. We hadn't slept together yet, but he wanted me to go to church with him? Did this mean he wanted to marry me? Oh, shit—was he expecting a virginal wife on his wedding night? That would explain why we hadn't had sex yet. He was *respecting* me. Oh, yeah, time for that talk.

"Listen, I've never done this before and it feels a little heavy. My parents weren't religious, and, anyway, my mom said it would be over her dead body if Dad ever took me to church. And there weren't any synagogues around, let alone other Jews, so . . . Seriously, this is my first time . . ."

It was Sunday morning, way earlier than I was used to being up on a Sunday morning. No one was hanging out in the dorm lobby when Peter picked me up, except the girl on the front desk. I was a little disappointed because I loved having witnesses around when my boyfriend came to get me. It didn't matter if I knew them or not, it just made our relationship that much more legit. We were on our way to St. Philip's in the Hills, a lovely little out-of-the-way sanctuary Peter had found in his wanderings. It was Episcopalian, but was designed much like the early Catholic missions which dotted this region of the country. And even though I was pretty sure there was no Divine Being, I wondered if my mother's Jewish God would strike me dead when I went inside.

"Just do what I do. Except you don't go up to the altar for communion. You don't even have to kneel if it makes you uncomfortable, or sing the hymns. You can just watch, Caro. No one will mind." He reached over and gave my hand a little squeeze, but when I squeezed back, he disengaged his fingers from mine.

"Why did you want me to come here with you? I mean, it just seems weird to me."

Truth be told, the whole scripture thing felt completely alien. I was at a distinct disadvantage in my "Bible as Literature" class, although I had to hand it to whoever wrote "Song of Songs." That stuff was *hot!*

"Weird? I don't think it's so weird. It's something I do every Sunday. It's been where I go every Sunday for as long as I can remember, and because I care about you, I want to share it with you. Just like I want to share so many things with you . . ."

He'd given me my cue: "But there are some things we haven't shared. I have to tell you this. I don't know if it's the right time or place for it, but I have to tell you . . . maybe because we're going to church, I don't know. But you have to know this about me, Peter. I'm not a virgin. I don't know what you expected . . . if it's a shock or what . . ."

He was quiet for a moment, then took a deep breath and exhaled very slowly. "You know, I kind of figured as much . . . It doesn't matter, really. Let's talk about it later . . . We're here."

We arrived just before the service began and found seats in the middle of the chapel. Peter motioned me to go ahead of him into the pew. The proprietary way he placed the flat of his hand on the small of my back filled me with such joy I wanted to laugh out loud.

Being in church made me think of weddings. I wondered what it would be like to be married to Peter. Could I spend the next fifty or sixty years with him? Could I spend the next sixty years with anyone?

I was so ill at ease. I chose not to kneel to a power I didn't think existed, but I was the only one seated, except for the arthritic old people whose joints no longer permitted them to genuflect to their God. I was one of the few who did not take communion, and I was acutely aware of the glances thrown my way as I sat in the pew by myself. I felt so . . . Jewish. I wondered what they were thinking. Were they looking at my nose? I wondered why it mattered. I distracted myself by looking past the altar, through a floor to ceiling window that looked out on the bronze- and sage-hued desert. There were two pale green lizards cavorting around a pink oleander as a cactus wren flitted by. I wished I were out there. Anywhere but here. And I worried that Peter might have second thoughts because of my lack of a hymen. Would that be a deal breaker?

I watched him make his way to the altar rail and willed him to hurry back to me. I was relieved when the service was over and I was once more outside on terra firma.

"You seemed a little uncomfortable in there. I'm sorry. I hope you'll give it another chance, though. It's a part of me that's really important . . . that I couldn't give up . . ."

"I would never want you to give it up, Peter, if it's so much a part of you. What makes you think that I would?"

"Well, it's not very hip, I admit that . . . I m-m-mean, a lot of us are so ready to give up on and put down the old values, you know? But I have a very personal relationship with God. As low as I've fallen, He's never given up on me, and I won't give up on Him."

"What do you mean, as low as you've fallen? I don't understand. You're one of the most beautiful and ethical people I know. I can't believe you could fall anywhere."

Except in love with me, please. Even if you wouldn't be my first, you'd be the only one I'd love forever and ever.

"Are you talking about smoking grass? I don't think a little weed is going to keep you out of heaven, do you?"

"Oh, no, I don't mean pot. You haven't known me long, Caro. You see, there was a period in my life when I was really in despair . . . when I even thought about . . . about . . . well . . . sui— . . . taking my life . . . ending the agony. I guess I thought of God as my last resort. He should have been my first, though. I turned to Him and He saved me."

"Wow, this is getting pretty heavy. I can't believe you could ever feel that way. You seem so at peace with yourself."

"There's a lot you don't know about m-m-me. We haven't known each other long . . ."

"I've known you long enough to know I love you."

He hesitated before he responded. I sensed he was not going to say he loved me, as well, and I was mortified.

"I believe you do, Caro. But you love the man you *think* you know . . . and you don't know all of him . . ."

"And if I did?"

"I don't know. You m-m-might hate me. You might never want to see me again, and I don't think I could stand that."

Well, he hadn't said the three magic words, but . . . close enough.

He continued: "You see, I really care about you . . ."

Be still my heart . . . he's almost said it.

". . . and I don't want to risk losing what we have . . ."

"My God, Peter, what could be so terrible? You haven't killed anyone, have you? Or bilked some little old lady out of her life's savings? Of course not! You couldn't be capable of doing *anything* terrible."

We were sitting in the car. The rest of the congregation and even the priest had left for their Sunday dinners. Peter's hands were on the steering wheel. He bowed his head. I wanted to reach over and touch him, but I didn't.

"How would you feel if I told you I'd never made love to a woman?" He didn't look up, wouldn't look up. He seemed to be addressing the steering wheel.

I laughed in relief. I would be his first!

"Since when is being a virgin a sin?"

Is not *being a virgin a sin in his book?*

"Caro, listen to me. I didn't say I was a virgin, did I?"

"Yes, you did. You just said you'd never . . ."

"Made love to a *woman* . . ."

"Oh . . . oh . . . oh my god. But you have been . . . have been with . . ."

"With men, yes . . ." He didn't raise his head.

"I don't understand, Peter . . . are you a . . . a . . ."

"A homosexual? I don't think so . . . I don't know. It . . . it only happened a few times, and I hated m-m-myself afterwards. I still hate myself. That's not what I want to be. I want to be normal, not some kind of freak. I want to get married, maybe have kids someday. I just don't know if that's in the cards for me. I just don't know."

I want it to be in the cards for you, Peter. It has to be in the cards for you—and for us. I can't bear the thought of you hating yourself when I love you so much. Isn't that enough?

He sighed. "So now that I've told you . . . now that you know what I am . . . no, not what I am . . . *I* don't even know what I am . . . but, anyway, I'd understand if you didn't want to see me anymore. I'd understand."

"Well, I wouldn't. I wouldn't understand someone who abandoned their friend because of a little confusion. We're all confused, babe. It's the age . . . the times. You're confused about sex; I'm confused about all kinds of things . . . like—Take God, for instance. I don't even know if He, She, or It exists. I'm not confused about sex, and you're pretty clear about the God-thing, so I think we make a good pair. Maybe we can help each other figure it all out. You're the best friend I've ever had, and I . . . I'd . . . I'd like to help, if I can."

"Maybe you can, but not yet, okay? I'm not ready. I can't be pushed on this, please. I can't be pushed. I need more time."

"I understand, amigo. No pushing, I promise."

"Thank you. C'mon, I want to show you something."

I followed him out of the car and back into the empty church. We walked down the aisle and I banished the thought of what it might be like to walk with him down this aisle under different circumstances. He led me down a long corridor to a heavy wooden door with worn leather straps and iron hinges.

"Are you sure we're allowed to be here?" I was still a little creeped out about being in a church under false pretenses.

"Sure, I come here a lot at night, when I can't sleep. It's never locked." He opened the door, which creaked on its hinges, and motioned me to go ahead of him.

"Look, isn't it something?"

We entered a small courtyard garden. In the center was a sandstone statue of someone I imagined to be the eponymous St. Philip. It was wildflower season in Tucson, when the desert was ablaze in color. The statue was surrounded by red Indian paintbrush, magenta prairie clover, orange cholla and milkweed, pink and white anemone, and the palest yellow mallow.

"Oh, Peter, this is so groovy. How did you find it? I didn't know anything like this existed. Look at the statue's face. Look how peaceful he is. This is a real comfort to you, isn't it?"

"Yes."

"I wish I had something like this to believe in. I wish I *could* believe. You're very lucky, you know?"

He nodded. It was time to stop talking, time for quiet contemplation and reflection. We sat together on a stone bench. We sat for a long time without speaking, then I rose to walk around the garden.

I came back to the bench and Peter looked up at me, looked up without expectation, with only acceptance in his eyes. Whatever I said would be all right, he was trying to tell me, even if I said I didn't want to see him, now that I'd processed what he'd told me today.

"I want us to stay together, Peter. I want to give us a chance."

"Oh, yes, dear girl . . . thank you."

Dear girl . . . I think that was Peter's way of putting a little distance between us, given that he'd just disclosed the most intimate thing about himself. And "dear girl" was better than "no girl," right?

He took my hand, but just my hand. This was a time to embrace, I thought. But he didn't. All right, then: A time to refrain from embracing. That was something I would have to get used to.

CHAPTER FOURTEEN

Oddly enough, Peter's revelation did not discourage me. On the contrary, I was exhilarated: Here was a real obstacle to overcome. I was in my element.

At first, I decided on a tactic of non-interference. I would be oh so careful not to make any move that would clue him in. I couldn't reveal my hand too soon, but my goal was this: Without his suspecting, I would lovingly convert Peter to heterosexuality . . . and then we'd get married. I was so convinced that this was the man with whom I could and would spend the rest of my life, that his "problem" only served to make him dearer to me.

I was adolescent, invincible, and totally unprepared for setbacks. The first came just a week after our revelatory visit to the church garden.

"Tricia, could I borrow your car for a while? I think this is an emergency. Peter wasn't in class this morning. He's never missed his acting workshop before . . . and he doesn't answer his phone. I'm really worried. This is so unlike him."

Tricia, the love, tossed me the keys to the VW. "Here, I don't need it 'til 4:30. It's parked over in the 'A' lot, on the Science Building side. But, Caro, I wouldn't worry about him. It's such a groovy day, maybe he's just out catching a few rays by the pool.

Everyone's entitled to play hooky once in a while. Aren't you over-reacting just a little bit?"

Maybe, but Peter wouldn't have skipped class unless he had a really good reason. He was so serious about school, much more so than I was. Lately he'd been talking about applying for a Schumann Fellowship to get an advanced degree in directing. He also thought it was beyond idiotic to sit around a swimming pool to change the color of your skin, especially if your skin was fair and would turn the hue of a boiled lobster after half an hour. Peter was definitely not sitting by the pool. Something was absolutely wrong.

Tricia's car was not hard to find, the only orange VW bug in the lot. I put it in gear and was off with a roar to rescue my man. I owed it to him.

I broke all speed limits and nearly ran a stop sign, but fortunately the cops were off catching other perps. I proceeded with impunity, turning into Peter's lot with a screech of tires. His car was parked in its regular space.

"Please let him be all right," I murmured in supplication to whomever or whatever might be in charge of such matters, as I rushed to his door.

My knock was not answered. My heart was pounding so hard it filled my chest and head. I knocked even louder. Still no response from within. Terrible words were recalled, words he spoke such a short time ago: "Despair . . . taking my . . . ending it all." Oh, God, he couldn't have done anything like that, not without warning me. Unless . . . unless he was determined to succeed. The thought that he might have been doing his laundry or visiting a neighbor never occurred to me. I *knew* he was in great danger.

I was frantic and began pounding on the door and calling his name. Several heads popped out from neighboring doorways, but I didn't care.

"Peter . . . oh, God . . . Peter . . . open the door. For God's sake open the door!"

"Caro," came a strained and weary voice from the other side. "Go away. . .just go away. I-I-I'll call you later. I-I have a . . . headache."

"A headache, Peter? Let me in. I'll take care of you."

"I don't need taking care of. Would you just go away, p-p-p-please? I *said* I'll call you later."

I reeled in disbelief. What could have possibly made him bar his door to me? I stumbled, as tears clouded my eyes and spilled down my cheeks. His outburst was so uncharacteristic. What could possibly have been going on?

A moment later, I had my answer. My eyes were not so clouded with tears that I didn't recognize the black Corvette with the "Timmy O" California vanity plates parked two spaces down from Peter's car. Suddenly I was running, running as fast as I could to get away from whatever had gone on, from what I knew was still going on behind that locked door.

"I'm sorry about yesterday. I really wasn't myself—I guess the strain of all my studying and worrying about the Schumann just got to me, that's all. I'm sorry I was short with you. I just needed to be alone."

"I understand."

"Do you? You sound kind of bent out of shape."

"I said I understand, Peter. Why don't we just forget it, okay?"

"Okay. Do you want to go get something to eat?"

"No thanks, I'm not very hungry. I think I'll just go back to the dorm and lie down for a while before rehearsal. I think I'm getting a cold or something . . ."

"Oh, sure, okay. I'll see you at rehearsal, then. Are you sure you're all right?"

"Yeah, I'm fine. Just a little tired. I'll see you later."

CHAPTER FIFTEEN

Tricia looked awful. The palest I'd ever seen her, like she'd been bled dry by Count Dracula. Her eyes were red-rimmed and she was shredding a Kleenex.

"Are you sure?"

"Yes, I'm sure. I saw the doctor yesterday. I'm about six weeks along. Oh, shit, Caro. What am I gonna do? I can't have another baby. I can barely manage to go to school and take care of Annie as it is."

"What does Artie say? Is he being supportive?"

She laughed. "Artie? Supportive? Gimme a break. The son of a bitch wants to know how I know it's his. He sleeps around, but I don't. I swear, Caro, I've only been with him." She started to weep.

"Shhhh . . . I know that, Trish, but obviously Artie's not going to be any help. Let me call Peter . . . he'll have some ideas."

"I thought you were mad at Peter. You two haven't seemed so together lately. Anyway, I'm not sure I want anyone else to know."

"Peter's not anybody else, he's Peter. And I'm not really mad at him. Our relationship was just getting too intense and I wanted to cool it for a while, that's all."

"Okay, call him . . . but just Peter. I can't let anyone else find out. My mother would kill me if she knew. She thinks I learned my lesson the first time."

"What do you want to do, Tricia? I take it that marriage is out of the question?" Peter had met us in a secluded alcove behind the art building.

"Hmmmph," she snorted. "Even if he *wanted* to, would *you* marry Artie?"

"I see your point," he nodded. "Okay, marriage is not an option. Then, as I see it, you either have the baby and try to raise it by yourself, have the baby and give it up for adoption, or . . .um . . . don't have it."

"I can't raise another kid by myself, and I couldn't carry one for nine months and give it up. There really is only one choice, guys. I've got to go to Agua Prieta."

"What's the going price these days?" Good old practical Peter.

"Two-hundred-fifty dollars . . . a girl in my dorm went down there last week. I only know because I found her bleeding in the bathroom." Too late, I realized what I'd said.

Tricia gasped.

"Oh, she's okay," I hastened to add. "I'm sorry, Trish. I wasn't thinking. You'll be fine. I hear there's really nothing to it."

(I'd heard no such thing).

"And Peter and I will go down with you, won't we, Peter?" I signaled him with a nod to reply in the affirmative.

"Oh, sure Tricia. We'll go down in my car. There is another matter, though, ladies. We've got to find $250 to pay for all this. I can let you borrow $100. I wish I could give you more, but that's about all I have in my savings."

"Oh, far out, man. You really are something else. I'll pay you back as soon as I can. Oh, man, are you lucky, Caro. And I get stuck with a creep like Artie." She shook her head.

"I can ask my dad for an advance on my allowance. I'll make something up. I don't know . . . tell him I want to go to Colorado to ski over Christmas vacation and I have to make plane reservations now . . . I don't know. I'll tell him something."

"*You* go skiing? Isn't that a little out of character? Don't you think he'll suspect something?" Peter looked dubious.

"Noooo . . . college is supposed to change you, isn't it? So maybe it's turned me into a jock. Anyway, he isn't the suspicious type."

"Oh, you guys are the grooviest." Tricia had brightened considerably. "I can hock my bike and maybe my typewriter . . ."

"How are you going to type your papers without a typewriter, dope?"

She winked. "Oh, I'll just borrow yours, Caro. After all, what are friends for? And speaking of friends, to use the term loosely, Artie laid some grass on me. Sort of a going away present, I guess. Shall we?"

She was already expertly rolling a joint.

Agua Prieta was about 120 miles southeast of Tucson—not nearly as easy to get to as Nogales, but a girl had died there the month before after a botched abortion, so Agua Prieta was now the destination of the desperate.

The trip down was quiet. The normally talkative Tricia was understandably subdued. Other than complain about not being able to eat breakfast, she had not said a word as we sped through the desert, the emptiness punctuated every once in a while by sleepy little one-horse towns.

"Oh, my God, I hope this isn't some kind of sign," Tricia was talking again.

"What do you mean? What sign? Everything's cool, Trish. Even the I-Ching said so." I was trying to remain calm, but there was a knot in my stomach and I felt sick when I thought about the procedure she was about to undergo.

"That sign, the one back there. It said 'Tombstone.' Oh, Jesus, Mary and Joseph . . . do you think I'm going to die?" Tricia started to cry.

After another silent hour, we reached that dusty little border town. It was not as touristy as Nogales and not as sleazy as Tijuana or Juarez. Agua Prieta shared the border with the small Arizona city of Douglas. We had no trouble getting across. I wondered if it would be as easy crossing back again.

I had the directions given me by the girl in my dorm. She probably thought I was the one having the abortion, but I didn't care.

This was Peter's first trip to Mexico, and despite the unpleasant circumstances that made the foray a necessity, he was enchanted.

"You know, I think guys who go over the border to Canada have the wrong idea. Man, it's cold up there. When it's my turn to dodge the draft, I'm going to slip over this border. Maybe go down to the beach at Guaymas . . . live off fish and coconuts and bananas. You'd have to be crazy to go to Canada—that's like going to North Dakota," he laughed.

"Yeah, but they speak English in North Dakota . . . and Canada. What about communicating?"

"Well, I'll just point to the coconut or banana I want. No, actually, I had three years of Spanish in high school. I didn't want to take Latin, and I heard Spanish was easier than French . . ." He shrugged.

We parked the car by some small shops. The instructions said to walk the rest of the way, about a quarter of a mile, but I wasn't so sure Tricia was going to be able to. She looked like she was about to faint.

"Tricia, I think we should drive you over." Peter, ever the gentleman.

She shook her head. "The instructions said to walk. We can't run the risk of being followed. God, I mean what if they get raided while I'm in there? I'd die, literally. No, I'll be fine. We have to walk."

We put on our best tourist act, looking in shop windows, exclaiming over the trinkets and souvenirs displayed within. Several merchants beckoned us into their shops and cajoled us with "the lowest prices in Agua Prieta," but Peter smiled graciously and answered them in their native tongue.

"Hey, you *do* speak Spanish. What did you say?"

"I told them maybe we'd come in later. And we will. Caro and I will buy you a get-well present, Tricia. What'll it be, maracas or an onyx donkey? Or a sombrero-shaped ash tray?"

Ewwww, maybe a little inappropriate, Peter, given what's about to happen? I know you're trying to lighten the mood, but . . . Jeez!

But Tricia was okay with it. "Probably the donkey, to remind me what an ass I've been. I don't think I'll be in the mood to shake my maracas for a while."

"I'm going to buy *you* the ashtray, Peter. Then you'll have another one to empty," I teased, getting in on the false levity. Peter was compulsive about emptying ashtrays if there was even one cigarette butt in them.

We passed a hole-in-the-wall café that advertised turtle soup, with a large poster of a terrapin, and then turned into an alley.

Tricia groaned. "It had to be an alley."

"Of course. How can you have a back-alley abortion without a back alley?"

Now who was being inappropriate? I was trying to joke, but in truth, the three of us were terrified, certain we were being followed and would be grabbed by the police at any moment. We'd all heard the horror stories about Mexican jails.

We followed the alley for three blocks and then came to a tiny adobe house with green shuttered windows. The screen door was falling off its hinges. Peter knocked on the door frame and spoke in Spanish.

"Hello, is anybody there?" He shaded his eyes and peered into the darkness within. Tricia and I hung back. She was shaking.

"Who is it?" came a woman's voice that answered him in Spanish. The voice did not sound kind. Tricia looked at me with terror in her eyes.

"We have business with you. Pablo sent us to knock on your door. He says you will sell us avocados." This was the phrase that would gain us entrance—the password. Peter had rehearsed it for days, with as much care and attention to nuance as if he were rehearsing Hamlet's soliloquy. And he didn't stutter, not once.

"Well, come in, then. Don't stand around at my door." She spoke slowly and Peter translated.

The three of us entered quickly. The light was so dim that it took a minute for us to take in our surroundings, and then, none of us liked what we saw.

"It's not very clean, is it?" Tricia whispered.

The woman flashed her a withering look. "I speak English, señorita, and I wash my hands. You have the money?"

Tricia handed her an envelope. The woman opened it and counted the bills. Satisfied that we were not cheating her, she crossed the dirt floor and hid the envelope under a bare mattress. She turned to us. Her dirtiest look was saved for Peter. Obviously, he was the cause of the señorita's unfortunate condition.

An honest mistake, Señora. Of course, the nice-looking gringo was the lover of the slim, blonde señorita with the porcelain skin. The other one, the overweight Norte Americana with the kinky hair was only a friend. A gringo like that wouldn't give her a second look.

"You leave now," she said to him in English. "You and the other señorita. You come back for your girlfriend in two hours. Make sure no one follows you."

I kissed Tricia on the cheek and held her for a moment. Peter squeezed her hand. Tricia was rigid with fear. I hesitated, and glanced from Tricia to the abortionist.

"Please, could we stay with her?"

Peter's eyes widened. This was not something he had prepared for. He shook his head.

"The señor is right. You will not be any help to your friend here." Her voice became gentle. "Believe me, I know my business."

She guided Tricia away from us. "Everything will be fine, Señorita, just fine."

They disappeared through a serape-curtained doorway. Peter and I gave each other a "now what do we do?" look.

"Let's go eat lunch. It's been hours since breakfast, and I'm starving."

"How can you think about food at a time like this?" Peter looked sick.

"It's what I do when I get nervous. Some people drink. Some people smoke. I eat."

He looked dubious, but for want of anything better to do, agreed. "All right, shall we risk Montezuma's revenge with the turtle soup?"

"Yeah, I'm game."

The soup proved to be unrecognizably reptilian and delicious, seasoned with lime and chiles and sopped up with huge flour tortillas which we folded over and over to dunk in the liquid.

"Mmmm, this is fabulous," I exclaimed with soup running down my chin. Peter cleaned me up with his napkin. "I only wish Tricia could be here."

"Yeah," Peter agreed soberly, then looked at me for a long time without speaking.

"Why are you staring at me. Did I spill soup down the front of me or something?"

When he finally spoke, his phrases were stilted and awkward.

"Caro, listen . . . p-p-p-promise me you'll be careful. I kept thinking it could be you in there instead of Tricia . . . but listen, if anything were to happen . . . I mean, if you got p-p-pregnant or anything . . . um . . . well . . . I would m-m-marry you."

I wasn't sure how to respond to this offer. That was not how I fantasized his marriage proposal. We were on shaky ground. What did this mean? Was this his way of telling me he was ready to give it a try, or what?

"What do you mean, if I got pregnant?" I had to proceed with caution, so my words were measured. "Peter, what does that mean? Are you trying to tell me something about us?"

I couldn't sound too eager or hopeful. I hoped I just sounded puzzled.

"No, it's just that . . . I think it might be hard for you sometimes . . . No, I *know* it's hard for you. I know you want more from this relationship than I can give you right now. I hope someday I can give you that, too. But in the meantime . . . um . . . if you found it . . . too hard . . . um . . . too difficult to . . . you know . . . be celibate, and you wanted to sleep with someone else . . . you know, just for sex . . . well, I just hope you'd be careful . . . but if something happened . . . I'd make an honest woman of you, m'lady." He grinned, but I saw the effort it had cost him.

"Peter, I don't know what to say. You're so dear." I took his hand. "Thanks for the offer, but I don't think it'll be necessary to take you up on it."

We had finished our meal. I wanted to leave the restaurant. There was nowhere else this conversation could go without him finding out how close I'd come to doing exactly what he said I might want to do.

"C'mon, we have to shop for Tricia's present and we have to pick her up in half an hour." I grabbed my bag and headed for the door. I didn't offer to pay for lunch, because Peter never let me. He paid the bill and followed me into the blazing heat of midday.

"It was so cool in there, I'd forgotten how hot it was outside." He was perspiring, not only from the heat, I thought, but also from the effort of the conversation we'd just had.

We took a leisurely walk to the center of town. Several barefoot children followed us for a while, begging for pesos. We ignored them: We didn't want to attract a larger crowd. We couldn't afford to have them following us when we had to pick up Tricia. Not getting a response from the gringos, they gradually fell away and we found ourselves alone in front of a tiny jewelry shop.

"Let's go in." Peter took my elbow.

"Oh, I don't think we can find anything for Tricia in here. This is good stuff. It looks expensive."

"I wasn't thinking of Tricia. C'mon, I want to get something."

We entered the shop. An old man, with skin like crinkled copper, hobbled out from behind a curtain.

"Si, may I help you, Señor?"

Peter pointed to a tray of silver and turquoise rings in the window. "Yes, we'd like to see those rings, please."

The man leaned over his merchandise to a tray at the front of the window. He turned back to Peter. "This tray, Señor?"

"Yes, that one."

The tray was placed in front of us on the counter. Peter pointed to an unusual v-shaped band with a turquoise inlay.

"Try that one on, Caro."

"Me? You want me to try on a ring?"

Peter looked around mockingly. "I don't see anyone else here named Caro. Yes, you. I want you to try on that ring. I want to buy you a ring, idiot."

First an offer of marriage if someone else knocked me up, and now he wanted to buy me a ring. My head was spinning.

"I'm sorry, it must be the heat. I thought I heard you say you wanted to buy me a ring."

"You heard right. I want to buy you a ring. Now, will you try it on to see if it fits?" Both Peter and the proprietor were looking at me.

I took the ring and put it on the third finger of my right hand. The silversmith shook his head. "It's for the other hand, Señorita. When your sweetheart buys you a ring, it goes on the other hand." He winked at Peter.

"Oh, right . . . you're right." I switched the ring to my left hand. "It fits perfectly. Thank you."

The ring did not feel right on this hand, though, and as soon as we left the store, I switched it back.

"I love the ring, Peter, but I hope you understand that I can't wear it on my left hand."

"Sure. I just hope that someday I can buy you one for that hand, too."

"You really mean it, don't you?"

"I never say anything I don't mean. I hope it's in our stars, dear."

There was that "dear" again. It made us sound like some kind of old married couple, the kind that isn't having sex anymore and call each other "Mother" and "Father." But at least that couple got to *have* sex. He could call me whatever he wanted if he'd just take me to bed.

So, like Peter said, I hoped it would be in our stars, but lately I'd begun to think that those stars were crossed. On one level, we'd become more and more involved, but I was no closer to his bed than I was on the night we met, perhaps even further away. I shuddered as I recalled the day of his "headache" and Tim's black Corvette.

"Are you all right?"

"What?"

"Are you all right? You looked like you were shivering."

"Oh, yes, I'm fine. I was just thinking about Tricia. We'd better hurry and buy that donkey." I checked my watch. "It's almost time to get her."

We selected a tiny onyx donkey and waited impatiently while the shopkeeper took an inordinate amount of time wrapping it in newspaper. But then I had second thoughts. Would Tricia really want a souvenir of this nightmare? ("Oh, that little donkey? Yeah, my best friend got it for me to celebrate my abortion.") I dropped the package in the trash can outside the shop.

Tricia was sitting on the bare mattress when we returned. She looked like death. There were dark rings under her eyes and blood was caked on her lips.

"Oh, God, Trish, was it awful?" I started to cry.

She could barely manage a whisper. "Just shut up and get me out of here."

Peter helped her to her feet and we both took an arm. The woman watched us without saying a word. We said nothing as we left the house, because there was nothing to say to her. The screen door slammed behind us.

We had taken six slow steps, steps that were obviously sheer agony for Tricia.

"Damn it, I don't care if that hag told us not to bring the car. You're not going to make it walking a quarter of a mile, Tricia. You don't look like you could walk a quarter of a block. I'm going to get the car. Stay here with her, Caro."

Tricia flashed Peter's retreating back a grateful look and then gasped. All of a sudden, she vomited uncontrollably, first bile, and then, when there was nothing left, the dry heaves. I took a tissue from my pocket and wiped her face, then dropped the sullied paper on the ground.

Peter drove up, and together we helped her into the back seat. Peter had taken a pillow and a light blanket out of the trunk. He settled her in and gently tucked the blanket around her.

"Thanks, guys," she whispered, and then closed her eyes.

I looked at Peter with love and amazement. This was some terrific guy. How like him to think of the pillow and blanket. God, I was so lucky. I stole a look at my new ring. At that moment in time, I loved Peter so much that I thought I could spend the rest of my life with him even if we never slept together.

But, of course, we would, I hastened to reassure myself. It would only be a matter of time. Or would it? It had been a day of such mixed messages I wasn't sure what to think. The ring— what did he mean by the ring? A ring conveys a serious message, a message of love and intention. What in the world was Peter's intention?

I began to get a glimmer of an idea as we crossed the border back into Arizona. I needn't have worried about being detained: A disinterested guard waved us through the checkpoint after his perfunctory "Anything to declare?" He wasn't interested in the ring, nor in the groggy girl in the back seat. No double-crossing drug dealer had sold us contraband and then informed on us to the border patrol, so the guard would have had no reason to tear the car apart looking for dope. It was too hot and too much trouble, anyway. We breathed a collective sigh of relief when we were back in the states.

But I was feeling unsettled. I stole a look at my heart's desire. God, I loved that familiar, guileless face, but now there was something more written on his visage. Today he looked . . . self-assured? I could see it, even behind those dorky old-man sunglasses. Wait. Peter, self-assured? That seemed to be a new veneer, but he was wearing it well. Peter, the self-assured. Peter the buyer of rings. Peter the protector of my good name . . .

Peter, the actor! *Of course*! This was a role, and Peter was preparing.

There are two ways an actor prepares for a role. One way, proposed by Stanislavski and espoused by a group calling themselves "method" actors, works from the inside out. An actor works on feeling the emotions his character might feel. These emotions in turn evoke mannerisms, speech patterns, actions and reactions of the character, and thereby the role is created.

The other way an actor can prepare is from the outside in, taking on the mannerisms, speech patterns, actions, reactions, even the clothing and physical attributes of a character to evoke that character's inner life. The trappings are the scaffolding to build the character, like the actor who affects Richard III's hunchback from day one of rehearsal.

That's what Peter was doing, I thought. He couldn't evoke the feelings from within, so he was using outside trappings to become . . . the boyfriend!

And I was aiding and abetting this ruse. Not even Tricia, as close as we were, or as close as I thought we were, knew that Peter and I are were not balling. She asked me once what he was like in bed. I smiled inscrutably and blushed.

"That good, huh?" she responded. "I thought so. He's so devoted to you. Say no more, you lucky girl!"

Lucky, right. And now I had a ring to prove it.

CHAPTER SIXTEEN

I still have that ring. All these years it's been tucked away in the bottom of my underwear drawer. I just couldn't throw it away, even after Jack placed that shiny gold band on the third finger of my left hand and I promised to love and to cherish 'til death do us part.

No longer hidden: I am wearing Peter's ring on a silver chain around my neck. I put it on when I stopped that first night, in Pennsylvania, just short of Ohio, just after I had phoned Jack.

"Jesus Christ! Where the hell are you? What the fuck do you think you're trying to pull?"

I knew he'd react this way, but all the same, I am crying. I don't know anyone in Pennsylvania, or in Ohio, for God's sake. I've never even been in Ohio. Even with my memories of Peter, I'm so lonely . . . and scared. Jack's right. What the fuck am I doing?

"Jack, I'm sorry. I just needed to get away for a while. I was going crazy at home . . . it's all coming apart. I just need some time, please . . . Just let me have some time to work it out in my own head."

"I can find out where you are, you know. There are ways to trace the call. I can send the police after you, tell them you're mentally ill . . ."

I know he's bluffing, that this is the way he reacts when he's wounded, but still, it frightens me. I wonder if he's been drinking.

"Jack, I'll call you in a couple of days. I'm all right, but I have to do this. Please don't call anyone, especially not the children . . . or my father. Please?"

He says nothing, but I can hear him breathing, so I know he hasn't hung up.

"All right," he says finally. "I won't call anyone . . . yet. Maybe you just need to get this—whatever it is—out of your system . . ."

He hangs up. I cradle the receiver for a moment, not at all sure why. I am tempted to call him back, just to fill this cold, impersonal motel room with a familiar voice, even a voice that's yelling at me, but I don't. Instead, I haul my suitcase onto the bed and unzip it. My hand searches the corners of the bag for my jewelry case. I extract Peter's ring and a thin, silver chain. I slip the ring on the chain and fasten it around my neck.

The ring falls right between my breasts, and I am comforted. I crawl beneath the covers of this unfamiliar bed and fall into a deep, dreamless sleep. I have many more miles to cover tomorrow.

CHAPTER SEVENTEEN

I couldn't believe I was missing the audition. Not that I was going to try out or anything. First of all, I never would have been cast as Roxanne; second of all, the only roles the director would have chosen me for were Roxanne's chaperone with about eight lines, or a nun who only appeared in the last act and had maybe two lines, and at twenty, I was tired of playing fat, middle-aged women; and third of all, I had a major rewrite due for my playwriting class, so no time for rehearsals, even though it was Edmond Rostand's *Cyrano de Bergerac*, one of my favorite plays in the whole world. But Peter was going to read for the comedic role of Ragueneau, the baker who fancies himself a poet, and I'd promised to be there for moral support.

It wasn't my fault. It was totally Andy Cathcart's for kissing me. Andy was a senior who was always being cast in the handsome guy roles and I was pretty sure he'd be cast as the handsome Christian de Neuvillette in this production. But anyway, he was married and had just found out his wife was pregnant, and he was so psyched that he went a little wild in the lobby of the theater and just started kissing everyone around and planted a big fat one right on my lips. At least I wasn't the only one who caught mono from him.

The day of the audition, I was still contagious, still confined to the infirmary. Mostly I slept, and I didn't even know what day it was when Scott started banging on my window.

"Caro, Caro, wake up! Open this window, I have to tell you something. You are not going to believe this!"

I blinked and tried to focus. They'd been giving me Tylenol with codeine for my sore throat and I was only half awake, still puzzling over the hallucinatory half dream-half drug daze of the books on the bedside table coming to life as a little singing and dancing trio with eyes and mouths and feet, serenading me with Dylan's *Rainy Day Woman 12 and 35*, but sounding more like Alvin and the Chipmunks.

At first, I thought I was hallucinating Scott outside the window, but he kept banging and yelling until I was awake and somewhat lucid.

"I can't," I croaked. "I think I'm still catching."

"I'm not going to catch mono just by talking to you through an open window. You'd have to kiss me, and we know that's not going to happen. C'mon, it's *fabulous* news."

I was fully awake by then. The mono might not have been contagious but Scott's excitement was.

"What, what? Tell me."

"Peter got the part! The reading was just amazing. I mean the whole theater was quiet after he'd finished and then everyone, except Dr. Romano, who of course didn't want to seem partial, jumped to their feet and started applauding and screaming. I've never seen anything like it. God, I wish you could have been there."

Then I felt like I was back under a codeine haze. I couldn't imagine a reading of Ragueneau the baker eliciting that kind of response. Seriously, would *"Over the coppers of my kitchen flows the frosted silver dawn. Silence awhile the god who sings within thee, Ragueneau! Lay down the lute—the oven calls for thee,"* earn a standing ovation from our peers?

I shook my head, but the cobwebs wouldn't go away.

"Oh, okay, that's good. That probably means he got Ragueneau, right?"

"Ragueneau? You're kidding, right? No, Caro, he fucking read for Cyrano and if he hadn't gotten it, Romano would have had a rebellion on his hands."

I stuck my head out the window, the better to process what I thought he'd just said. Scott quickly backed away.

"Sorry, maybe the penicillin is affecting my hearing. Or you're just plain mixed up, Scottie. Ragueneau is who he was reading for, not Cyrano. That's what he and I practiced. I had to read the parts of all five pastry cooks and the apprentice and the child who comes into the shop. Trust me, that scene, funny as it is, would not earn an ovation."

"You mean you didn't know? Oops, maybe he meant it to be a surprise. Shit! Do me a favor. Pretend you never heard me. Act surprised when he tells you, okay? Please? And, oh, yeah, hope you feel better."

"She's very attractive, isn't she?"

"Who?"

"Serena. You sure have been hanging out with her a lot lately. I've seen the way you look at her."

Peter looked at me like I'd lost my mind. "Of course I've been hanging out with her. We're running lines. And how do you *want* me to look at her? I'm supposed to be madly in *love* with her. You think that's easy?"

I wasn't ready to let go of my jealousy. It's what I'd been living on ever since Peter had gotten the part. Of course, I was thrilled for him, but since I was just on the lowly costume crew, it meant that we were hardly ever hanging out anymore. And Serena Randall, his Roxanne, was, in fact, outrageously attractive, and I was not.

That's what really tormented me: Her beauty. What if that was the secret? What if, by accident of good genes, she was the one with the power to change him, and then he would be hers?

"Where were you going Saturday? I saw you on the back of her motorcycle. That wasn't running lines. You looked pretty psyched."

"Oh, it was such a spectacular day, we decided to practice our lines out at the canyon. Too nice to stay inside."

And he delivered that with nary a stutter. What if she were to have cured him of that, too?

At least I got to be backstage each night. The costume crew thing was a joke, as my sewing skills were rudimentary and I'd had to rip out as many stitches as I'd put in, but I was Peter's dresser for the quick backstage changes and to wipe his brow, and to make sure that Cyrano's prosthetic nose was still carefully spirit-gummed on.

I'd practically memorized the whole play, the story of a gallant soldier and incurable romantic with a brilliant wit and the face of a clown who is in love with Roxanne, the beautiful woman who loves Christian, the handsome but not-too-smart, tongue-tied guy. Through some convoluted twist of plot, ugly guy agrees to help handsome guy woo beautiful woman, and they marry. Long story short, handsome guy is killed in battle before the marriage can be consummated, beautiful woman joins a convent, where she is visited each week for many years by her faithful but still ugly cousin, Cyrano. On the day Cyrano suffers a mortal wound (swordplay, as this is 1655), he comes to her for the last time. She asks him to read her one of Christian's love letters (which, of course, he, Cyrano, had composed back in the day) and when she hears Christian's words read in Cyrano's voice, she realizes, way, way too late, that it was actually Cyrano who was wooing her, and with whom she was in love, all along. So, beguiled by a handsome face, Roxanne missed out on passionate love and great sex with the guy with the big nose and now she's too old and he's on his deathbed. Stupid, vacuous woman.

Each night (and twice on matinee days) there I was offstage, just a few feet away as Peter delivered dazzling performance after dazzling performance. I tried to tame the butterflies in my stomach as he stood, unlit, under Roxanne's balcony, declaiming his love, while Christian stood in the spotlight and mouthed the words.

"Can you feel my soul, there in the darkness, breathe on you . . . In my most sweet, unreasonable dreams, I have not hoped for this! Now, let me die, having lived."

Okay, you'd think that Roxanne would have recognized Cyrano's voice (he was, after all, her cousin and they had been adoring companions since childhood), but this was theater, where one had to suspend disbelief in order to be part of the magic. And I so wanted to be part of the magic. If that had been me up on the balcony, I would have lost my heart to Cyrano (as I already had to his portrayer), not to that vapid Christian (played by the guy I caught mono from).

After the last curtain call, Peter was always surrounded by groupies, both male and female, and he basked in all that adulation. I waited outside, by his car. I could see the illusion slide off him like a cloak. It never lasted more than a few steps beyond the stage door. The clock struck midnight, the horsemen turned back into mice, the footmen into lizards, and the coach into a pumpkin.

I was glad, because then he was mine again.

CHAPTER EIGHTEEN

It was the night of the baked banana peels that I realized there was no way in the world I could have survived in a platonic marriage, even one—no, especially one—with Peter. I wasn't even sure I could survive our friendship for much longer.

As much as I tried to sublimate, sex was rearing its lovely head. Would that I could have reared Peter's. I used our good night kiss outside my dorm as a bellwether: One or two seconds longer and our bodies a few centimeters closer than the night before, and I ran up the stairs with hope in my heart; a quick peck on the lips with his lower half tilted even further away from me, and my hopes were dashed. My dorm mates never noticed, so busy were they grinding pelvises and tonguing their boyfriends.

We were mangling the lyrics to *Mellow Yellow* as if we were already stoned.

"La, la, la, la banana . . . Donovan says it's a craze . . . La, la, la, la banana . . . if it works, we might be amazed . . ."

"We're making yellow Jell-O. . ." I added, slightly off-key.

"To-nightly," Peter chimed in. We giggled as he fished out the key to his apartment.

"Shhh, someone will hear us," I hissed. But, actually, there was no danger. We were after a perfectly legal high: no one was going to bust us for the two bunches of bananas in our grocery bag.

Everyone we knew was convinced that Donovan's new song was about getting high by smoking banana peels. Of course, they had to be dried out first, and the quickest way, we decided, was by baking them in the oven.

We peeled the first bunch and spread the peels on a cookie sheet.

"An hour at four hundred degrees should do it, don't you think?" he queried as he set the oven.

"Don't look at me. I'm the one who burns cinnamon toast, remember?"

"Yeah, I think four hundred degrees. There is one problem, though. What are we going to do with all these bananas?"

"We could eat them for dinner."

"What, me Tarzan, you Jane? Who eats bananas for dinner?"

"I do. When I was a little girl, my mom used to give me bananas and sour cream for dinner. I know it was because she hated to cook, but it turned out to be my favorite meal. Is there any sour cream left from the container we bought the other day for the tacos?" I rummaged through the refrigerator. "Oh, good, here it is. Hey, even I can fix bananas and sour cream . . . and I'm really craving it now. It's like my comfort food, you know?"

"Okay, I like bananas and I like sour cream. So how bad could it be? And the frugal Scotsman in me hates the idea of wasting food . . ."

We each ended up having two bowls full, then he got up to check the peels. "Nothing's happening yet. I guess it'll be a while. Do you want to listen to some records?"

No, I didn't want to listen to his records. They were all full of love and sexual innuendo. What I really wanted was for Peter to fuck me 'til his eyes bugged out of his head. That's what I wanted, but, of course, I didn't say it.

"No, I'm tired of those records . . . you need to get some new ones. Why don't we go out and see if we can catch the Wolfman?"

Wolfman Jack was our favorite DJ. He broadcast late at night, from a megawatt tower in Del Rio, Texas. For some reason, we couldn't get him on the radio in the apartment, but he came in loud and clear in the car.

Peter checked the peels one more time. "They're starting to brown. Maybe another half hour . . . Okay, the Wolfman it is."

The Wolfman was really howling that night, but the music was not soothing the savage anything inside me. I fidgeted through *Gloria* and *Good Lovin'*. By the time the Stones were lamenting their lack of satisfaction, I'd had enough. I switched off the radio.

"I think it's time to check them again."

Our banana peels were nicely dry and shriveled. We crumbled them into a bowl and then, because neither of us had mastered the art of rolling a joint, Peter emptied the tobacco out of a cigarette and packed it with mellow yellow, which by then was an earthy brown, but no matter.

He lit it and handed it to me. I inhaled and held my breath and passed the ersatz joint back to him. He took a toke and passed it back to me. We smoked the whole thing that way and waited to get high.

"Do you feel anything yet?" It'd been ten minutes since we'd finished smoking.

I shook my head. "Maybe we need to do another one. Maybe it's not as strong as grass."

"Yeah, you're probably right." He was already packing another one. We shared it and waited.

"Anything?"

"I don't think so. Let's just try one more." Neither of us could believe that the song was a hype.

A third cigarette was emptied, filled, and smoked.

"Anything?"

"Yeah, I think so . . . maybe a little. I think I'm feeling something."

"Me, too. But what I'm feeling is sick to my stomach. I think we've been had, Peter. Or maybe we just bought the wrong kind of bananas, I don't know."

It was only 8 and we had the whole sober evening ahead of us. What to do? Too late for the movies, we'd already had dinner, and Scott and Ernesto were out of town. I'd made it clear that I didn't want to listen to his records and we'd already done the Wolfman Jack thing, and Peter didn't own a TV. If we had been any other couple, we would have started making out and ended up in bed, if only by default. But we were not any other couple.

Peter read my mind. He cleared his throat. "I'm sorry, Caro. I'm sorry I can't be that man. I care so deeply for you, more than any other person I've ever met. It's like, I'm romantically attracted to you, but I'm sexually attracted to men," he shook his head. "There seems to be this wire that's disconnected . . ."

I stared at him. That was the closest we'd gotten to the intimacy I craved, and I was almost afraid to breathe, lest it had proven as ephemeral and as impotent as the smoke from those stupid banana peels.

"Only connect," I sighed.

"*Only connect the prose and the passion, and both will be exalted, and human love will be seen at its height. Live in fragments no longer.*"

He took my hand and looked into my eyes.

"That's why I love you so much, Peter. You get me. We're on the same wavelength. I don't think I could have this with anyone else. We're so right together . . . I want to be loved and I want to be understood, and from you I have both. I have given you my truth, and I know you won't misuse it. You don't judge me. We have love and understanding, and with patience, the other will come, if we want it to."

But this was more intimacy than he could handle, even if he *had* initiated it. He disengaged his hand from mine.

"You know, I think E.M. Forster was a homosexual."

This was news to me, but I got it: way too heavy for him and there was nowhere this conversation could have gone, so I threw a pillow at him.

He laughed, and ducked, then grabbed the pillow and tossed it back at me. I picked up a chair cushion and heaved it at him, but he was too quick. I was hit from behind with the pillow. I whirled around to catch him hurling a throw pillow right at my face. I grabbed it and threw it at him, but, once again, he ducked.

And this is what was going through my mind, my poor deluded, can't-take-no-for-an-answer, couldn't-see-reality-if it-stood-up-and-slapped-it-in-the-face-mind: a pillow fight could evolve into arm wrestling, and arm wrestling could turn into you-know-what in just the wink of an eye.

But that pillow fight evolved into . . . nothing. It was just a pillow fight, and then it wasn't fun anymore.

Thank God for single dorm rooms. I was alone in my bed. I pretended my finger was Peter's cock. I came, but there was no relief. My night was filled with crazy, unresolved dreams about bananas, fish, howling wolves, tunnels, and trains.

Put that in your cigar and smoke it, Dr. Freud. I know what it all meant.

CHAPTER NINETEEN

It had been so long since I'd worn make-up (except theatrical make-up, and then one of the make-up crew did my face), that I kept screwing up the eyeliner. I'd smudged it so many times that I looked like a panda. Nothing to do but wash it off and start over again. Tonight I wanted to look just right. Peter was taking me to the theater.

Well, not exactly the theater. We were going to Erewhon for "An Evening of Experimental Theater," as it had been billed, an evening of plays the drama department wouldn't be caught dead presenting, because, you never know, there could be a four-letter word in those experimental scripts.

The event was Artie's idea, and he was director, producer, and, if I knew Artie (and I did), he was probably running the lights, handing out programs, and screwing the leading lady, as well. I hadn't seen him in months. I wanted him to think I looked ravishing (Why?), so I struggled once more with the eyeliner, blinking as I lined the inside of my lower lid and, once again, smudged black onto the white of my eye.

Why did it matter what I looked like? I hated Artie for the way he treated Tricia. He was a schmuck. Did I want to attract him to make Peter jealous? Did I want Peter to know that *someone* desired me? Yes, I think that was it. If he thought someone else wanted me, would he want me? I was desperate enough to try anything, even blind myself with eye make-up.

None of the drama department faculty would show up, I sensed. There was an unofficial boycott of the program. No, I take that back. Dr. Steinman, my playwriting professor, would probably be there. He and his wife were old lefties from New York . . . well, not old, really, but they were in their thirties. They were into Pete Seeger and The Weavers and stuff like that, instead of Dylan and the Stones, but they were pretty cool. At least Steinman didn't go along with all that department bullshit, and he was all for innovation: he actually had us reading some Off-Off-Broadway stuff. I mean, not that I understood most of it or anything.

Anyway, Erewhon was the closest thing we had to Greenwich Village and I was dressed for the occasion: black turtleneck, foot-less black tights, long wrap-around red-and-black Indian-print skirt, sandals, gypsy hoops in my ears, and finally, perfectly lined-in-black eyes.

The program had been kept a secret. Those drama students Artie had enlisted had been told not to reveal even the names of the plays, on pain of death, or worse.

I saw why.

"Oh, God, leave it to Artie to produce a play called *Balls*. No wonder he didn't want anyone to know what he was doing. It's a good thing he's not a drama student, or he'd be out on his ass. I wonder about the kids who are performing."

"They can't do anything to them, no matter how much Dr. Romano would like to. Of course, he'll probably find reason not to cast them for a while, just to let them know they've transgressed."

Peter was probably right. Their punishment for betraying the high standards of the department would be subtle. Although some of them were fairly competent actors, I'd bet they'd be relegated to prop crew for the next production or two.

"Hey, I knew Steinman would show." I nudged Peter and waved to Nate Steinman and his wife, Muriel. Steinman threw us several theatrical kisses.

"Did I tell you he asked me to babysit for his kids next Saturday? Oh, sorry, I forgot. It's their anniversary and they want to go out to dinner. He said you could come, too, if you wanted. I told him I'd tell him tomorrow. Do you want to?"

Peter shrugged. "It's okay with me as long as you're in charge. The only little kids I've had contact with are my cousin Lou Ann's brats, and they're horrible. I hope Steinman's are not of that ilk."

"Oh, no, I met them. They're little . . . two girls, three and five, I think. And they're cute . . . and smart. C'mon, Peter, it'll be fun."

I had an ulterior motive. Since I spent my high school years as practically the only girl in town with free Saturday nights, I was called upon to babysit more often than I care to remember. But kids really liked me, and I wanted the opportunity to show Peter what a wonderful mama I would make for his babies.

"Sure, okay, if that's what you want. I can always stuff cotton in my ears and read a book. Let me see the program. What else is on it besides *Balls*?"

I handed him the mimeographed program. "Since this evening is a product of Artie's sick and fertile mind, it's probably *Tits*," I snorted.

He laughed. "No, it's a one-act by Lanford Wilson called *The Madness of Lady Bright*. Sounds like an English drawing room comedy. Lanford Wilson . . . Lanford Wilson . . . the name's familiar."

"The reading list . . . Steinman's reading list. A play called *Balm in Gilead*, I think. Yeah, that's it. They haven't gotten any of those plays in at the bookstore yet, so I have no idea what it's about."

Artie ascended the miniscule stage and held up his hand for quiet. "Erewhon is proud to present 'An Evening of Experimental

Theater,' a first for Tucson . . . and maybe a last." He chuckled. "We may be out on our asses tomorrow, but tonight we're going to give you the kind of theater you won't find anywhere else in town—and we're proud to do it."

"Our first play is called *Balls,* and it's by Paul Foster . . ."

He was interrupted by hoots and laughter, mostly, I noticed, from the female members of the audience. I looked around to see who else had shared Artie's bed—probably every woman in the room except Muriel Steinman.

"All right, that's enough," he continued. "These are plays you should take seriously. *Balls* stars Joseph Barnes as Commodore Wilkinson, Chet Lester as Beau Beau, Leslie Klein as the Bus Driver, Sandra Orton as Miss McCutcheon, Tony LoMello as the Nasty Brat, Carol Johnson and John Porter as the Young Lovers, Sally Stang as the Woman Who Had No Shadow, and Mack Langdon as the Military Commander. And I'm the director and stage manager. I'm also running the lights, so as soon as I can get to the light board, we will present *Balls.*"

"The real high point of the evening will be seeing how he gets that cast of thousands onto the stage without having the actors kill each other," I whispered to Peter.

"Maybe that's what they're going to do."

"What?"

"Maybe that's what they're going to do: kill each other. After all, this is experimental theater." He chuckled.

"No, if they were going to kill each other, the play would be called *Kill.* Since it's called *Balls,* maybe they're going to do *that* to each other. A first for Tucson, group sex on the six by eight stage of Erewhon . . ."

It turned out that the actors didn't do anything to each other. In fact, the actors didn't appear on stage at all. The only things in the spotlight were two white ping pong balls hung above the stage. Only the actors' voices were heard from offstage—from a tape recorder offstage. The play ended with the sounds of the sea. There was dead silence as the lights faded to black. The audience was in shock, I think. At least I was. What the hell was that about?

"Now, tell me that wasn't the weirdest thing you ever saw, or rather, didn't see. Do you have any idea what it was? Was it even theater?" I queried.

Someone obviously thought so. "Bravo, bravo!" came the unmistakable Brooklyn-inflected voice of Nate Steinman from the farthest reaches of the room.

"Uh, oh, Steinman liked it, so maybe it really *is* a play. At least we found out how Artie was going to get all those actors onstage without any casualties. I dunno, maybe there's something there that can't be grasped at first. I guess I have to think about it . . ." Peter looked pensive.

"Oh, c'mon, Peter, it was gar-*bage*. Most of the time I had no idea what they were talking about, did you?"

"No. But that doesn't necessarily mean it's not worth thinking about. I need to go out and get some air . . . stretch my legs. Wanna come?"

"No, I think I'll stay here and save our seats, although if the next one is anything like this one, there really is no point in sitting at the best table in the house, is there? Do you want me to order you anything?"

"Yeah, just coffee . . . and a Danish, I guess. I'll be back in a minute."

I ordered the coffee and Danish for Peter and a cappuccino for me from the chippie who was probably Artie's latest lay. I could tell by the way she looked at him. He was living dangerously here. This one looked like jailbait, no more than sixteen or seventeen . . . and she was a lousy waitress. Peter's coffee was sloshed all over the saucer. I poured it back into the cup and mopped up the mess with a napkin.

Peter slipped back into his seat just as the lights dimmed for *Lady Bright*. I hoped this one was not as enigmatic.

Lady Bright was anything but enigmatic, and it was not a drawing room comedy. It was about an aging drag queen, and I felt like I was going to faint. There was no way I could get out of there without causing a scene. I had to sit there next to Peter and watch as this queen paraded around the stage draped in a pink and white bed sheet while mourning aloud that he wasn't attractive enough for some guy named Adam to want to fuck him, and then he called himself a faggot and said he'd been one since he was a little kid.

I glanced at Peter without turning my head. He was white and looked like he was going to be sick. The two of us sat through the rest of the play in a daze, immobile until the end, when Lady Bright kind of channeled Blanche Dubois and hallucinated that the men in white coats were coming to get him.

This time, the dimming of the lights brought a wave of applause. The actor's performance was a knock-out, I guess. Unfortunately, I was in no shape to appreciate it. Neither was Peter.

I had to look at him. I couldn't avoid it, but what could I say?

"Heavy . . ." is what I managed to force through my lips.

Peter nodded. "Yeah . . ." I saw that there were tears in his eyes.

"Hey, let's get out of here, okay? It's so smoky . . . it's just oppressive . . . c'mon, let's just drive for a while." I grabbed his hand.

We made our exit through the crush of bodies converging on a beaming Artie.

Peter exhaled in a long, low whistle as we fought our way out the back door and into the parking lot.

We drove all the way out of town and into the foothills before either of us spoke. He parked the car and turned off the motor. The lights of the city were winking below us.

"I want to tell you something, Caro. I need to tell someone. It's something I've never told anyone . . ."

"Peter, you don't have to . . . it's all right . . . I . . ."

"Please, please listen to me, I *need* to tell you. Please, please, you're the only one I could possibly say this to . . . You say you love me, then p-p-please, for God's sake, listen."

The urgency in his voice rattled me. I would have to hear him out, but I had a sickening feeling I was not ready to hear what he had to say, would probably never be ready to hear what was coming.

He was gripping the steering wheel so tightly, that even in the moonlight I could see that his knuckles were white.

"I'm going to tell you about m-m-m-my first time, Caro . . ." His voice was barely a whisper, and I had to strain to hear him.

"I was eleven, and I was raped."

I gasped, and he turned to me.

"Oh, not that way . . . not what you think. It was my . . . mouth . . . but I was violated, just the same.

"It was at church, believe it or not," he said with a bitter laugh. Or was it a sob? "It was the choir director. My voice hadn't changed yet. I was the star boy soprano. He asked me to stay after rehearsal one night. Church was two blocks from my house, so I always walked home alone after choir practice. Everyone else lived in the other direction, so I didn't mind staying after, and I liked Mr. Nelson. He paid attention to me. I was so quiet, most people ignored me. I don't think some of my teachers even remembered my name, but Mr. Nelson was different. He treated me like someone special, always praising my singing and stuff. I was so lonely. My father had been dead less than a year, and I was pretty lost. Mr. Nelson made me feel like *somebody*, you know?"

Yes, I knew . . . and I shuddered, thinking of that poor, lonely, vulnerable little boy . . . a little boy whose need to be noticed and loved made him easy prey for such a monster.

"Everybody else had left the church," Peter continued in a monotone. "And Mr. Nelson told me to go up to the organ loft with him, that he wanted to show me something. So, I went. I had no reason not to," he protested, sensing perhaps that I was about to ask him what could have possibly possessed him. But I was not about to say anything. I was mute with horror.

"I went to school with his kids. I'd known him practically since I was born. And," he repeated, "it made me feel so . . . warm and happy that he had singled me out to stay after with him."

I was terrified for what was to come next, and, of course, powerless to go back in time and change the course of Peter's life.

"I followed him up the stairs into the loft. It was a very narrow space, with just enough room for the organ and the two of us. He was facing the organ and I was right behind him. I was practically touching him, the space was so tight. If I had taken one step backwards, I would have fallen down the stairs.

"'Kneel down,' he said to me."

Oh, don't, Peter . . . don't. I'm going to be sick.

But I said nothing, and he went on.

"'Kneel down, Mr. Nelson?' 'Yes, son, kneel down and pray.' Puzzled, I did as he said . . .and then . . . and then he turned around and . . ."

He stopped, took a deep breath, and looked up at the dark ceiling of the car, seeing, perhaps, his monster before him. He let all of his breath out.

"He turned around," he repeated, "And there was his . . . his . . . thing . . . his penis . . . right by my face. It was so big, Caro . . . and so ugly. I gasped, and then he . . . he . . . did it!"

Peter was sobbing, but the words were coming through in torrents. He could not keep them back.

"He thrust into my mouth . . . he made me take his penis into my mouth and then he moved it in and out. I was crying in terror, but he stroked my hair. 'Hush, son,' he said. 'It's all right. I'm doing this because I love you. This means I love you . . . and it will be our secret, only for us. No one will know. Now, just take your tongue and lick it. Take your little pink tongue and lick it up and down. Doesn't that taste good? Isn't that the sweetest meat you ever tasted? That a boy. You're doing it just right.' I was powerless not to obey. I licked him and licked him and sucked him until his penis got bigger and bigger. It was a hideous kind of magic, and I was the magician. I thought I was going to die, and suddenly, thick, hot liquid spurted into my mouth and down my throat. I gagged, but he held my head . . . held my mouth around his cock. 'Swallow it, boy . . . you swallow that sweet juice right down. Now you have some of me inside you. Now you are my special boy. Ohhh, that feels so good, so good, son.' He stroked my head and withdrew his limp cock from my mouth. But it wasn't over, not yet.

"'You made me feel so good, son, and now I'm going to make you feel good.' He had his hand on my crotch and he started rubbing me. I was mesmerized. I knew there must be something terribly, terribly wrong about what we were doing. It must, in fact, be a mortal sin. But if it was a sin, why was Mr. Nelson doing it to me? And why did it feel so good?

"He undid my belt and unbuttoned my pants and pulled down the zipper. He pulled down my pants and my briefs and knelt in front of me. 'Oh, look at your sweet little white cock, son. Look how it likes me!' I glanced down in horror to see that it did, in fact, like him. It must have liked him, because it was standing right up at attention as he took me in his mouth. And who was that moaning with pleasure? There was no one else around, and Mr. Nelson's mouth was full, so it must have been me. He held me close to him, his hands kneading my bony little behind. Then he covered my face with kisses and told me again that I was his special little boy.

"I stayed after choir practice with him twice a week for two months, until one night he didn't show up for practice . . . because that night, instead of my little cock, he stuck his granddaddy's p-p-p-pistol in his m-m-mouth and pulled the trigger. I always felt like I killed him . . . and I never told a living soul . . . I never told anyone until tonight."

I was moaning. "Oh, Peter . . . oh Peter" over and over again. It was more terrifying than anything I could have imagined. I needed to comfort that little boy. If only he would have let me help him, let me embrace him, let me drive that wretched memory from his heart and mind. But he wouldn't. Instead, he ended up comforting me for not being able to ease his pain.

He reached over and patted my shoulder. "It's okay, dear. It was a long, long time ago . . . another lifetime ago. That little boy doesn't even exist anymore. I just had to tell someone about him." He sighed. "And I feel so much better for the telling . . . whew, we've gotten that over with."

He sighed again and then we were both quiet for a very long time. And then he turned to me.

"Now, why don't you tell me about your first time?" He was grinning, but there was something so very sad in his eyes. Why hadn't I noticed it before?

CHAPTER TWENTY

Mama's drinking finally caught up to her. I knew she'd been feeling poorly, but Mama was always "feeling poorly" when I was growing up. I tried to get her to go see a doctor when I was home for vacation last summer, even called Peter in North Dakota to get his advice (he being my nonresident expert on mothers), but he, too, was stymied.

My mother didn't believe in doctors (I think it was because they were always trying to help her with the drinking problem she insisted she didn't have), and when her condition grew so bad that Daddy finally noticed this was more than her usual hangover, the cancer had spread to her liver. They were going to tell me when I came home again for Christmas vacation, but she never made it.

The phone rang just before my alarm was set to go off at seven. Groggily, I reached out to stifle the clock's shrill call, but it wouldn't turn off. Awake now, I grabbed the phone.

"Carolyn, it's your . . . it's Daddy, Honey. I'm so sorry to wake you, but I'm afraid I have some bad news."

"Daddy! What is it?" But I knew what it was. My father had never phoned me at school.

"It's your mother, honey . . . she passed away a few minutes ago . . . I'm sorry, we didn't know it would happen this fast . . ."

Here, he broke down. To this day, I puzzle over his next statement: "Carolyn, I just don't know what I'm going to do without her . . ."

Were we talking about the same woman? The one who was too hung over five days out of seven to get up and fix his breakfast? The one who retired early most nights with a headache. The one who refused to accompany him on any social engagements? My mother, the recluse? What had happened for *him* that magic night in Manhattan, circa 1943? Whatever it was, it had lasted a lifetime, even though those delicate blossoms—my mother, their marriage—slowly withered and died on the vine.

I assured my father that I'd make travel arrangements and not miss any finals by coming home for semester break a few days early ("Your mother didn't want to worry you when you were taking all those exams, honey.") and hung up the phone. I hugged my knees to my chest and rested my head on them. My knees, even covered as they were with Daddy's old Cornell nightshirt, were no comfort, and neither was my ragged, one-eyed panda, my companion since infancy. I needed human comfort . . . I needed loving arms around me . . . I needed my mother, as imperfect as she was . . . Oh, Mama . . .

I got the next best thing. Peter arrived at my dorm twelve minutes after I summoned him, even though his apartment was ten minutes away. I knew my call had awakened him, but he gave no indication of minding.

"Hold on, I'll be right there." I pictured him pulling on his jeans even as we spoke.

Peter held me together those next few days. He insisted on accompanying me back east, even through my protests that it would empty his bank account.

"You're in no shape to handle this alone, baby."

Baby. My heart sang, even though it had been wrenched from my chest.

Baby. Even now, twenty years later, the promise of that endearment causes that familiar tightening between my legs.

I don't remember much about the funeral. Flowers filled the chapel, not as a tribute to my mother, I know, but out of respect for my long-suffering father. But Mama hated gladiolas . . . wouldn't have them in the house. It didn't seem quite fair to have them surrounding her closed coffin.

The service was mercifully brief and as nonsectarian as the local minister could make it. No Father, Son, or Holy Ghost, anyway. There was no eulogy. We recited the twenty-third Psalm, I think, and then there was an announcement that "Interment will be at the convenience of the family," meaning, in that cold Vermont winter, the ground was too frozen to dig, and Mama would be kept in storage 'til the April thaw.

What I do remember to this day, what is making my panties wet at this very moment, as I travel west through Ohio, is the feel of Peter's firm grip on my arm—and the yearning to have that grip evolve into something else: firm arms around me, firm legs between mine, and his firm cock lost and then found inside me.

Sex became one of Peter's favorite subjects, as if something in him were freed the night he made his confession to me.

Although we never did it, it was the subject of endless discussions, innuendos, and jokes. Not so much discussion, actually, but recitations on my part. Peter loved to listen to my sexual peccadillos.

A couple of months after my mother's death, we were sitting in his apartment, the remains of our Taco Bell take-out dinner on the table. We had smoked a little weed and the Doors were holding forth with *Light my Fire.*

Once again, he wanted to hear about my lovers, and like Scheherazade, I tried to weave enchantment with my tales— not to stave off death, but perhaps to strike a spark of life, to find the magic spell that would make him unable to resist me any longer.

But this night proved no different from any other night.

"So, who else did you make it with?" his voice cajoled.

I was running out of lovers. Soon I would have to start making them up.

"Well," I admitted rather sheepishly, "Once I made it with O'Shaughnessy."

"O'Shaughnessy?" He chortled. "God, O'Shaughnessy? *Everyone's* been to bed with O'Shaughnessy . . . even *I've* made it with him!"

I blanched and was suddenly dead sober as I recalled two things: the day I spotted Tim's Corvette at Peter's place, and the night Tim and I shared a bottle of Chianti and had fallen drunkenly into his bed.

"Always make love to your friends, Caro," Tim instructed as he proceeded to do just that. What I remember most about that night were the bruises bony Tim O'Shaughnessy left on my inner thighs. I fleetingly wondered if he had managed to bruise my beloved Peter.

All my talk about lovers seemed to be having no effect whatsoever on Peter, but my frustrations were reaching their limit.

We were lying on his bed, something we often did when we were high and listening to music. I willed him to touch me. He didn't.

He would like something to happen, I thought. He would like to touch me, but he can't. He would like to be my lover, but he isn't. I don't understand what is stopping him. It would be so simple, really. Doesn't he know how much I love him?

I had never really touched him, either. Not in that way. It was an unspoken boundary I dared not cross. The chaste kiss he gave me each night on the steps of my dorm before curfew was strictly for show, and we both knew it.

But I was horny beyond belief that night and ready to overstep the bounds. Suddenly, I ripped my tee shirt over my head, unhooked my bra, and flung both garments across the room.

He looked at me quizzically. Quizzically was not the way I wanted him to look at me. I was mortified. What could I have had in mind?

At that moment, the record we had been half-listening to clicked off. Gracefully, I rose from the bed, sauntered over to the stereo, and, with as much cool as a topless woman whose toplessness had been utterly ignored by the man lying next to her could muster, picked up several albums, turned to him and casually asked, "What should I put on?"

"Why don't you start with your shirt?"

Like a sleepwalker, I crossed the room to retrieve my clothes. I couldn't face him, couldn't bear to have my body exposed to his disinterested eyes. I felt dirty in a way no one-night stand had ever made me feel, and, ridiculously at a moment like that, I was embarrassed that I'd never been able to fasten my bra in the back. Awkwardly, I fastened it in the front, twisted it around, and slipped my arms into the straps.

"I guess I'd better take you home." He was already putting on his sandals.

"Yeah, it's getting late." Neither of us could acknowledge what had just happened. Or rather, what hadn't.

The ride to the dorm was a silent one. He walked me up the steps to our usual spot, delivered his usual dry kiss on my lips, being oh-so-careful that our lower bodies never so much as touched (didn't he ever wonder what that might feel like?), waited until I walked through the door, and, hands in pockets, took the steps two at a time, free of the ritual for another night.

I never wanted to see him again.

CHAPTER
TWENTY-ONE

Peter was not in directing class the next morning, the only Friday class we shared. I was grateful for that.

After classes, I dropped in at the coffee house. True, Artie was a prick, but at least he knew what to do with it.

"Caro Mills, long time no see. Where have you been keeping yourself, girl?" He was alone in the place, drying glasses behind the counter.

"I need to get laid, Artie. What are you doing tonight?"

"That's what I like about you, Caro. You don't play games . . . and you know quality when you see it—or rather, when you feel it." Artie had once characterized himself as a man who looked at life "through a glass penis." He was exactly what I needed after last night.

"The gig here is over at 11. What time do you have to be in the dorm?"

"It's Friday . . . not 'til one."

"Groovy. C'mon by at nine and sit in on the second set. Don't come before . . . I don't think I can keep my hands off you through two sets. It'll be hard enough through one. And I mean *hard!*"

I leaned over the counter and thrust my breasts in his face.

"On second thought, who can wait 'til tonight?" He came out from behind the counter, goosed me, and walked over to the front door. He turned the sign from "OPEN" to "CLOSED," and bolted the door.

"C'mere, Verbal Whore." It was a name he coined for me when we were first lovers. He told me I was the smartest girl he had ever balled. "I'm going to fuck you so hard, not only are you going to come, you're going to *foam*!"

God bless Artie! The tension was broken. This was our private joke, and he still remembered, even after all this time: We had just made love and were sharing a cigarette. My head was in the crook of his arm and he was holding a Gauloises to my lips.

"I've never made love to a woman like you, Caro. You're incredible. I was talking about you to one of the cats at the coffee house . . ."

I gasped, choking on smoke that I had swallowed.

"Don't worry, I didn't mention your name or anything . . . I just told him what a hot number I was fucking . . . a girl so hot that her cunt actually foamed when I went down on her . . ."

His finger traced a circle on my thigh and found its way into the aforementioned cunt. I was laughing too hard to respond to his caresses.

"Artie, you jerk, that's my contraceptive . . . it's foam. It comes in an aerosol can."

He looked wounded. I kissed him. "But, honestly, you're fantastic, and if I could foam, I'd certainly do it for you."

There were no hidden agendas here. I got over being "in love" with Artie (if, in fact, I ever was) a long time ago. Our affair had been short-lived, but he knew just what I needed, and he was giving it to me. It had been months since I'd been laid.

He pinned me against the counter and rubbed his blue denim crotch against my blue denim crotch. "Ohhhh," he moaned.

"God, you feel so good." His tongue was in my mouth and he was undoing the fly of my jeans.

"Artie, the windows! We can't do this here!"

He grinned sheepishly. "See the effect you have on me, you brazen hussy." He led me behind the counter. "Don't worry, no one can see us back here."

He pulled me down to the floor and placed a sack of coffee beans beneath my head for a pillow. He tugged off my jeans, and then his own. My legs were spread and his hand was underneath the elastic of my panties. Carefully, he parted the hair and gently caressed my clit. I moaned. Slowly, slowly his finger found its way inside me and then I was hovering right there.

"Wait for me, baby." He tore off my panties and thrust himself into me. "Now, baby, oh yes, oh YES . . ."

I smelled of coffee and of cum. I wished it had been Peter instead of Artie, but at least I wasn't horny anymore.

CHAPTER
TWENTY-TWO

Artie and I met at the coffeehouse every afternoon for a week, and when I had had a surfeit of loveless sex, I opted once again for sexless love.

"I've missed you, Peter." It was the first time I'd spoken to him since the night of my unsuccessful striptease. I found him in the library, so we were whispering.

He looked up from his book. There were tears in his eyes. "I've missed you, too."

It was just like a love story, but not quite. We could not live happily ever after.

"C'mon," I urged. "I'll take you to lunch. I owe you one."

"Okay, I've had just about all I can take of Aeschylus on an empty stomach. Let's go."

He gathered his books and ran his fingers through his hair, a decidedly Peter gesture. Oh, God, how I'd missed him!

We were back in a familiar haunt, a small luncheonette a block from the drama building.

"Hey, where you two been all week? Mama and me, we was worried about you. Whatsa matter, you have a little lovers' quarrel? See Mama, I told you they'd be back!" Guido beamed and we grinned back at him. "So, what'll it be? No don't tell me: patty melts and hold the onions, right?" He winked at Peter and Peter winked back. Even Guido thought we were lovers.

It was almost as if that night had never happened. We slipped back into our regular routine. Peter never asked where I was during that week, and I didn't offer the information. There was one change, though: We no longer talked about sex. We studied together, went to the movies, smoked a little dope and cooked dinners in his apartment. But, after dinner, we remained at the table to talk. And the talk often confused me.

"I want someone to know that I was here," he said, "That it matters. Do you think any of this matters?"

"Well, of course it matters. It has to matter. It matters to me, you know. I feel like I'm at my best with you, Peter . . . that you've found something in me that no one else has even bothered to look for."

He gave me a wistful smile. "Caro, you must always stay the wonderful person that you are, no matter what or who may come into your life. Because, in so many ways, you're the personification of love itself."

And so it went. We never lay together on his bed. We were always together. We were never together.

The ritual continued for several weeks. Every night culminated in the same farewell at the dorm. Every night was maddeningly the same, until the night I tried to drown myself in Peter's swimming pool.

We were smoking the weed that I had copped earlier in the day from Artie. Perhaps it was particularly potent, or perhaps I would have been driven to it anyway. I don't know. I do know that the unspoken became the spoken that night, and once I had said the words, "Peter, please, please make love to me," and he refused me, I had no other choice.

"I'm so sorry, I can't. I wish I could. I don't know what's wrong with me. I don't know if I'm a homosexual. . .maybe I'm asexual. I just know I don't have those kind of feelings about you. I love you, but I can't make love to you. I'm not capable of it . . ."

"How do you know if you won't even try?"

He shook his head, "No, Caro . . . no . . ."

"Then why do you even want to be with me, Peter?"

And then I couldn't catch my breath. I had to get out. I didn't want to breathe. I wanted to die. I ran out of the apartment and onto the lawn. I continued to run until I came to the pool. I jumped in and willed myself to sink.

I didn't. I wished I could have filled my pockets with rocks, like Virginia Woolf, but, of course, there were none to be found around the swimming pool. There was only artificial turf, and all those years of swimming lessons at Lark Lake paid off. I would have to take another tack. I decided to swim laps until I got a cramp or exhausted myself and just fell asleep in the water . . . and would never wake up.

I swam forty laps with no sign of exhaustion, but with the growing realization that I probably wouldn't have gone through with it anyway, and that I was no doubt trying to guilt trip him into submission, and then I was ashamed. Suddenly, I was aware of another presence at the pool. I couldn't see him, could only see the end of his cigarette glowing crimson in the black, but I knew it was him. He didn't try to stop me, so I think he knew, but I also knew he would have saved me if I were really suicidal. Which, I guess, I wasn't.

I gave up and pulled myself up the ladder.

"I guess I'll have to lend you my bathrobe while we throw your clothes in the dryer," he said matter-of-factly, as if fully-clothed women threw themselves into his pool every day. He handed me a towel. "Wrap it around your head, or you'll catch your death of cold."

I wished. But my teeth were chattering in the cool desert night. The temperature had dropped 30 degrees since sundown. Obediently, I wrapped my hair and followed him back to the apartment. He flipped off the air conditioner and handed me his brown terry robe.

"Go in the bathroom and take off your clothes and put this on like a good girl. I'll throw the wet stuff in the dryer and it'll be good as new in no time."

I did as I was told. I hadn't said a word. I handed him the pile of clothes, not even caring that my bra and panties were on top.

Suddenly, I was burning up. "Peter, Peter, help me . . . oh my God, I think I'm going to die!"

I ripped off the robe. "Oh, God, Peter, what's happening to me? I'm dying . . . God is punishing me . . . please, please . . . do something!"

I could see that he, too, was horrified, and that the horror had nothing to do with the fact that I was standing naked before him.

I looked down at my breasts, my belly, my arms, my legs, and could only shriek. This was not my body. This body was covered with huge, angry red welts. This was a monster's body.

I ran to the mirror. My face was swollen to twice its normal size. My eyes were piggy slits atop my puffed-out cheeks.

"Caro," Peter had found his voice. It was take-charge, reliable Peter. "I'm going to get a doctor. There's one who lives in this building. Just calm down. Everything's going to be all right."

I wailed.

"You are not dying," he said firmly. "Come now, lie down on the bed and cover yourself."

In short order, he went after the doctor, fixed me a cup of tea, and threw my clothes in the dryer. Peter's upstairs neighbor, a young resident at the local hospital, arrived five minutes later.

He diagnosed me immediately. "Hives. Have you eaten something you're allergic to? Strawberries? Tomatoes?" He looked at me accusingly. I shook my head.

"She just went swimming, and I think they throw a lot of chemicals in the water after hours," said my knight in shining armor.

"That's probably it." They were discussing me as if I weren't there. "I'll give her a shot that will take care of it. It will also make her sleepy. Does she live here?"

"No, but I can get her home."

The doctor filled the syringe and jabbed the needle into my arm. "There now, you'll be all right in a few minutes, but the next time you decide on a midnight swim . . ."

The hives receded quickly, as the doctor had promised, and I was asleep by the time we reached the dorm. Peter half carried, half dragged me up the steps. No one batted an eye: they were used to girls coming in drunk.

He pushed me through the door and beckoned to a girl who was bidding her date goodnight. "Can you get her upstairs? She's not feeling too well."

"Right. She doesn't look too well." The girl put her arm around me. "C'mon. You're going to be really hung over tomorrow."

"I'm not drunk," I protested, but only feebly. I didn't have the strength to argue.

CHAPTER
TWENTY-THREE

After that, I didn't hang out with Peter as much as before. We never spoke about the swimming pool debacle, so sometimes our conversations were stilted and awkward. We still studied together, though, and grabbed a meal once in a while. But some nights, I was "busy." If I didn't show up to meet him after my last class, he knew I was otherwise occupied. Sometimes I was otherwise occupied with Artie, who was always accommodating unless he was busy balling someone else; other times I was fucking Ollie Durand, an easy-on-the-eyes umber-skinned music student I had met several months before.

I'd gone to the cast party with Peter. The play was Eugene O'Neill's *The Emperor Jones*, chosen as a vehicle for Colton Roberts, the department's phenomenal—and sole—Black actor. There was only one role for a white man, so other cast members had been recruited from all over campus—the football team, the basketball team, even the separatist Black Student Union. Peter was doing the lighting and I was assistant stage manager.

There were no women in the play, and I got to shepherd all those good-looking half-naked guys around every night. I had flirted shamelessly with a fair number of them, especially Ollie, whose mesmerizing green eyes made me go weak in the knees.

Anyone who witnessed Peter on the dance floor that night would have been surprised to learn he wasn't bedding me. All the moves were there, vertically: the thrusts, the grinds, the grimace, the biting of the lower lip, and then I needed a break from all that arousal. Like our goodnight kiss outside my dorm each night, this was Peter's public persona. When he went into the kitchen to grab a beer, Ollie moved toward me and nodded his head toward the bodies gyrating in the middle of the room. I nodded back.

Ollie and I only danced once. He was uncomfortable, I sensed, but I wasn't sure why until I realized that the Brothers and Sisters on the sidelines seemed to be doing a slow burn. The Black Power movement had finally reached Arizona, and separation seemed to be the order of the day.

There was time enough before we parted, however, for Ollie to proposition me.

"I'd like to get it on with you, girl," he whispered above *Sugar Pie, Honey Bunch.*

I glanced over at Peter and then replied, "I'm flattered, Ollie, but I can't. Peter and I . . ."

"No way in the world is that white boy doing you, girl. I know that . . . I can read the signals. He's trying *way* too hard."

"I don't care what you *think* you know, man . . ." I turned back to Peter.

"Well, give me a call if you ever change your mind. I'm in the book . . ."

I changed my mind. Ollie said he knew all along I would. He just wondered what took me so long. The arrangement was strictly for sex, and that suited us both. He never took me out for a hamburger or to a movie. He never took me out of the apartment, period. The pressure from the Brothers and Sisters was too great. But that was fine with me: I didn't want Peter to know who I was sleeping with—even though I was sure he'd guessed by now that

I was with someone. And Ollie didn't want anyone to know he was balling a white chick.

All the rumors I'd heard about the sexual prowess of Black men to the contrary notwithstanding, Ollie was actually a bit of a prude when it came to our lovemaking. For one thing, we always did it in the dark. Maybe that way he didn't have to admit to himself that I was white, at least while we were doing it, I don't know. And he wouldn't go down on me or let me go down on him. He said it was "nasty." And we always did it in the missionary position. Given these constraints, however, Ollie wasn't bad in bed, and I was sort of getting off on the idea of balling a Black man. Okay, I secretly wished I could have flaunted it.

The arrangement lasted for two months until Ollie told me he'd gotten back with his ex-girlfriend and they were getting married and I'd better not come around anymore. Just like that. We fucked one last time, for the hell of it. Afterwards, I went into the bathroom to dress. When I came out, he was stripping the sheets and stuffing them into a denim laundry bag.

"Well, I'll see you around, I guess." He seemed too embarrassed to look at me.

"Yeah, man, I'll see you around . . . and congratulations, she's a lucky lady."

My pride was hurt a bit, but I was starting to get tired of the "back street girl" number. The novelty had worn off, and Black men could be just as limited as white ones. I was bored by Ollie and Artie, and Peter was driving me crazy, but I didn't know how to untie the knot that bound the two of us together.

What was it that kept drawing me back to him? He believed in me, he said, and I could make him laugh, and there was his kindness, I suppose, and safety, and inspiration and acceptance, and tenderness, and, love, and, of course, hope, dear Miss Emily Dickinson's thing with feathers.

But what did he see in me, if I couldn't even accept him as he seemed to be? Maybe he was putting too much stock in my magical powers to seduce, like with Artie or Ollie, when really, all that was nothing more than a mutual recognition that we were ripe for fucking. Maybe these powers were strong enough to grant him his wish to be "normal?" Once again, I think it came down to the feathers.

Perching precariously in both our souls. We were running out of time.

CHAPTER
TWENTY-FOUR

O n again, off again, but the default was always the on position. We were back together, but Peter said we absolutely could not see each other that weekend. That was okay with me. He was one of six semi-finalists for the graduate directing fellowship, and his final essay was due the following Wednesday. The six would be winnowed down to three, and then each of them would direct a play as a final project. He was uncharacteristically but understandably irritable, so not all that pleasant to be around. Anyway, I had to do my laundry and, besides, I was hungry.

I had discovered this Buddhist diet book called *Zen Macrobiotics* that promised to cure diseases, prolong life, but more importantly as far as I was concerned, promote a spiritual awakening. That kind of hooked me. Did Peter think it would help me believe in God or at least some higher power? He wouldn't commit, but agreed to try it with me to provide moral support, as he was already spiritually awake, and we embarked on a not-so-gradual elimination of everything good to eat. We were down to a few veggies and a lot of brown rice, which had to be chewed into a disgusting maceration before we could swallow it. We had been on this regimen for a week, and I didn't feel any more spiritually aware than before. Peter said we probably needed to try it a little while longer. I was ready to kill for a taco.

So, I was in the dorm that Saturday, scrounging in all my pockets for quarters to feed the washer and dryer in the basement, and hoping there would be enough left over to indulge in my secret vice, vending machine pimento cheese sandwiches. I trusted that Peter would have so much on his mind he would forget to ask me on Monday if I'd stuck to the diet over the weekend. And, anyway, I would never tell him about the cheese. *So* not Zen.

I had just finished my second illicit sandwich, late that afternoon, when some freshman from down the hall said I had a call from Peter on the pay phone. I had volunteered to read his essay for grammar and syntax, but I didn't think he'd be finished that soon.

"Done already? Wow! That was fast."

I didn't even recognize the voice on the other end of the phone. No, actually, I recognized the voice. It was Peter's. But the tone and speed at which he was talking, no, more like babbling, were completely foreign.

"Done-duh-done-done," he was singing the theme from *Dragnet.* "The story you are about to hear is true. The names have been changed to protect the innocent," he recited, sounding uncannily like Jack Webb playing Sgt. Joe Friday.

"Huh?"

"Yes, I'm done. And it's magnificent . . . a masterpiece. Best thing I ever wrote. And we're going out to celebrate. Will you go out with me tonight, beautiful Caro? Will you? Will you? Say that you will. There's a full moon . . . like June. And it will be reflected in your beautiful eyes up in the skies, just like moon pies."

The sentiment was nice, but . . .

"Peter, what the fuck? Are you on drugs? What did you take? Are you speeding?"

After a few more minutes of his nonsensical rhyming, I finally got out of him that yes, in fact, he had popped some dexies the night before, had never gone to bed, had spent the last twenty hours writing the essay, popping a few more pills and drinking black coffee as the day wore on, and had not eaten a thing—not a carrot stick, not a mouthful of brown rice—since the afternoon before. And, as he said, his masterpiece was complete.

Every college freshman knew the myth of the underclassman who went into his final exam high on pills and proceeded to fill the entire bluebook with one sentence, "I am the big blue Easter Bunny" over and over again . . . or maybe the bunny had become the walrus or the egg man, Kookookachoo. Maybe not such a myth. Based on his rantings, I could surmise that Peter's essay had been written in the same vein.

"Shit, Peter. Don't take any more pills, promise me. And for god's sake, don't drink any coffee. Make yourself a cup of chamomile tea and go to sleep. Pick me up in the morning and we'll go over the essay, okay?"

More babbling about "coffee and tea and you and me," a chorus of *Tea for Two*, and finally, a promise to see me in the morning, but not before he had sung all three verses of *Oh, What a Beautiful Morning*. In a very nice tenor, I might add.

I was getting ready for bed at about nine when my intercom buzzed and the girl at the front desk said there was a man there to see me.

"Who?" But I knew.

"She wants to know who you are," the girl said to my gentleman caller.

"It's your knight in shining armor, Caro, my sweet." He was loud enough so that the whole lobby had probably heard him.

Oh, crap.

"Tell him I'll be right down."

I pulled on a pair of not-so-dirty jeans and a sweatshirt and ran down the stairs.

"I told you on the phone we'd be going out," he said, before I could even begin to form the words that threatened to spill out of my mouth.

"What the . . ."

He looked abashed. "I'm not speeding now, and I'm not crashing, either. Just nice and mellow."

"Yeah, speaking of crashing . . . I can't believe you drove over here. Do you know how dangerous that is?"

"Don't be mad, Caro. I needed to see you. I have something I want to show you. Please come with me. It's really, really important."

Ugh, he probably wants to take me up to St. Philip's again, to sit in the garden in the moonlight. That's where he goes after he drops me off at the dorm and he can't sleep. It's not a place I want to revisit on account of that first revelation, but still . . . He says it's important.

"I'll go with you, Peter, but only if I drive. I am *not* going to be the passenger with you on dexies."

"But then it won't be a surprise."

"You arriving here in one piece is surprise enough, thank you very much."

He finally agreed to let me drive, but told me I was not allowed to ask any questions about where we were going or what would happen when we got there.

"What's all that in the backseat?" It was dark, but it looked to me like a pile of velvet drapes.

"No questions, remember?"

"Can you at least give me a hint?"

"Nope. But it's going to be very special, trust me."

Oh my God, could this be the night I've been hoping for all these many months? And my diaphragm sitting in my top drawer? Not a problem, though. Peter said he'd marry me.

I followed his directions to turn right on Kolb Road and then right again on Craycroft. This was the way to his apartment. Why was he being so mysterious? But then he had me turn onto North

Swan, which was past his house. Crap, we were heading right out to the desert. If we were going to make love for the first time, I sure as hell didn't want it to be in the backseat of his car—déjà vu my virginity loss all over again—and if he had any romantic notions of doing it under a full moon on velvet drapes spread on the desert sand, he had another thing coming. My fear of rattlesnakes was greater than my desire for Peter. I didn't know if they hunted at night or not, but I was not about to find out.

"Turn in here. Look, isn't it something?"

I'd heard about the Mission in the Sun, an adobe chapel built by an Italian artist on the outskirts of the city, but I'd never been there. It was one of several buildings that comprised the artist's gallery, and that night, it was completely dark and deserted. Frankly, it creeped me out a little. In addition to the rattlesnake phobia, I had developed a distaste for churches and was afraid that Peter might have something even more revelatory to disclose if we went inside.

"Here, put this on." He handed me one of the velvet things, which turned out to be a robe, trimmed with fake ermine—not drapery, as I had guessed—and wrapped himself in the other one. Thoughtful of him. It did get chilly in the desert at night. So, we would not be making love on drapes, with our passionate panting serving as rattlesnake bait, and we had gotten out of the car, so no backseat assignation. But what?

"Where did you get these?"

"Costume storage room. I filched the key. No one's going to miss them, though. They were tucked away in the back, probably haven't been worn in years."

"You filched the key? Are you crazy?"

"No, I'll return it in the morning. And the robes, too. We only need them for tonight."

I looked around. So, if we weren't going to make love on the sand or in the car, where? Surely not the chapel. Even *I* knew that would be sacrilegious.

But Peter was holding out his hand to me.

"Come my love, let us enter the sanctuary. It is our time."

Are those lines from a play? Not one that I can recall. I hope it wasn't "Murder in the Cathedral."

I started to shiver.

"Don't be afraid, Caro. This will be a magical night. Just wait, you'll see."

What role is he playing? Is he on something else besides the dexies? Shit, did he drop acid without telling me?

But his face was calm, almost beatific, as we entered the chapel, which was lit only by the moonlight coming through the roofless edifice.

He dropped my hand and walked over to the altar and lit six votive candles. Then he returned to me.

"Tonight, your soul and mine will be joined as one."

Yeah, he's on acid. What's he going to do now?

I soon found out. It was not the union I would have planned.

"God spoke to me last night, dear. He said you and I were to be soulmates forever and tonight we will seal our union. And now we can start the ceremony."

Can't we just skip all this pomp and circumstance and go right to the sex?

But Peter was so earnest as he gave me my instructions.

"We will become one, Caro, and we don't even have to touch each other. We have transcended our bodies. Our souls will meet when we look deeply into each other's eyes. Look into my eyes, Caro, my dearest. This is love in its purest form."

Shit, shit, shit! Why couldn't he have dropped the acid that made him want to have sex?

"God's love is speaking through me, dearest Caro. We are alive in love and it is radiating into infinity. You are within me and I am within you. Nothing could interfere with the vibrations flowing between us. We are strong and confident. Mankind will survive and will learn to love. People will make mistakes, but will eventually find the way, the way of truth and love."

He beamed at me, expectantly. Shit, it must have been my turn to talk, but I didn't have a script. This was like the scariest actor's nightmare ever, where you're standing on stage naked, the audience is waiting, and you can't remember your lines, only I wasn't naked. I wished we both were.

I'd have to revert to artifice to convey what Peter wanted from me. Tears. Tears could work. Peter would have thought I was so overcome with rapture that I could not speak. Actors use the technique of summoning up the saddest or most joyful experiences of their lives onstage, depending on the emotion they want to convey, and memory-driven tears flow from their eyes. Unfortunately, I couldn't think of a damn thing, sad or happy, at that inexplicable moment. Shit, where were those glycerin eye drops or chopped onions when you really needed them? So I reverted to that old trick for crocodile tears, staring without blinking. Peter was too far into his own world to notice that I was practicing that technique. Within thirty silent seconds, my tears were spilling over.

After the silent part of the ceremony, where we stared into each other's eyes and our souls ostensibly became one—and I kept thinking of the game where you try to get the other person to blink, but I dared not laugh—we climbed a rough-hewn wooden ladder to the roof of one of the galleries and gazed at the moon. We were both silent, but for very different reasons. Peter had had a religious experience, that was clear. His eyes were shining, and he looked so at peace. I, on the other hand, had no words because I was stupefied.

So, whose bride was I? God's? Get me to a nunnery? Sorry, I don't think Jewish girls pass muster. And what kind of wedding was this, anyway? Where were my bridesmaids, my flower girl, my something borrowed and blue?

Well, those moth-eaten velvet robes were borrowed, or rather, purloined. And the something blue? Well, that would be me.

Days later, he swore to me that he hadn't taken anything. That his heart was just filled with love for me because:

"It's with you that I'm able to share the greater part of my life."
And I felt so unworthy. Because I still wanted that other part.

Could I have even imagined those vows coming out of Jack's mouth, let alone entering his head and residing in his heart? Well, not without both of us collapsing with laughter, with Jack gasping for breath and me peeing myself. We cracked each other up a lot in those early days. I never shared the story of that desert ceremony with Jack, though. I couldn't bear the thought of Peter being the object of our ridicule.

In contrast to my dark soul of the night union to Peter, my wedding with Jack took place on a radiant June afternoon. It had all the Kodak moments: Blue sky, puffy cumulus clouds, Lohengrin played by a string quartet, Jack's youngest brother, who was eight, walking next to my cousin Mark's tiny daughter, who stole the show by dumping all the rose petals from her beribboned basket in a heap in the middle of the aisle, to the accompanying "Awww," from family and friends gathered to witness our union. My father gave me away and we both teared up when he kissed my cheek and whispered, "I wish your mother were here to see how beautiful you are."

And under the flower bedecked trellis arch in my in-laws' backyard, Jack, with a tear escaping from the corner of his eye, read me the John Ciardi poem that has since become a time-worn wedding staple, but on that June day it was new and meaningful, and ours:

Most Like an Arch This Marriage

Most like an arch—an entrance which upholds
and shores the stone-crush up the air like lace.
Mass made idea, and idea held in place.
A lock in time. Inside half-heaven unfolds.

Most like an arch—two weaknesses that lean
into a strength. Two fallings become firm.

Two joined abeyances become a term
naming the fact that teaches fact to mean.

Not quite that? Not much less. World as it is,
what's strong and separate falters. All I do
at piling stone on stone apart from you
is roofless around nothing. Till we kiss

I am no more than upright and unset.
It is by falling in and in we make
the all-bearing point, for one another's sake,
in faultless failing, raised by our own weight.

At that moment, in that place, I believed it all, as he poured his heart into mine until it was overflowing with gratitude—he chose *me*—for my new life and for growing old together and for happily ever after. But I guess everyone thinks that. Otherwise, what would be the point?

I wanted to read my favorite poem, by my favorite Beat poet, but as much as he loved it when I recited it to him in our bed, Jack didn't think Lenore Kandel's *Love-Lust Poem* would have wowed our parents. Yeah, I was only kidding, but wouldn't it have been so cool to read:

I want to fuck you
I want to fuck you all the parts and places
I want you all of me

all of me

I want this, I want our bodies sleek with sweat
whispering, biting, sucking
I want the goodness of it, the way it wraps around us

and pulls us incredibly together
I want to come and come and come
with your arms holding me tight against you
I want you to explode that hot spurt of pleasure inside me
and I want to lie there with you
smelling the good smell of fuck that's all over us
and you kiss me with that aching sweetness
and there is no end to love.

I settled for Lenore's *Love in the Middle of the Air,* instead. It conveyed what I wanted to say to my groom, albeit not in such a graphic way:

CATCH ME!
    I love you, I trust you,
    I love you
CATCH ME!
    Catch my left foot, my right
    foot, my hand!
    here I am hanging by my teeth
    300 feet up in the air and
CATCH ME!
    here I come, flying without wings,
    no parachute, doing a double triple
    super flip-flop somersault
    RIGHT UP HERE WITHOUT A
    SAFETY NET AND
CATCH ME!
    You caught me!
    I love you!

Now it's your turn

And unlike my ersatz desert wedding night of two years before, which I spent alone in my single bed in the dorm, Jack and I had a weekend honeymoon in the Plaza's bridal suite, a gift from his parents, who knew we'd been sleeping together for two years, but pretended otherwise.

My virginal white silk wedding nightgown and peignoir (also a gift from my mother-in-law) clothed me for exactly twenty-seven seconds. Jack and I were *so* hot for each other. It had been *days* since we'd made love, ensconced as it were in separate wings of the Tanner manse, under Lois's watchful eye, until I walked down the aisle. So hot, we couldn't even wait to pull the covers down, but consummated our marriage atop the shimmery gold, rose-petal-strewn matelassé bedspread. We never even left the suite, ordering burgers and fries and champagne and chocolate-dipped strawberries from room service, soaking in bubbles in the oversized tub until we shriveled, and then I got to unshrivel my groom all over again. We never removed the "Do Not Disturb" sign from the door, and when we checked out, we tipped the maid fifty dollars from our wedding money, because we felt so guilty about the disarray and the good smell of fuck we'd left as a result of our insatiable carnal appetites.

CHAPTER
TWENTY-FIVE

The weird thing was, I really did feel closer to Peter after that night in the desert. And he clearly felt closer to me. It was the way he looked at me, and the gentle tone he always used with me, except, of course, when we were arguing over the direction of the play.

Miracle of miracles, Peter's Dexedrine-fueled essay was spot-on, and he was chosen as a semi-finalist for the Schumann. The final round was an even bigger challenge, however, and one that needed to be taken on completely sober.

I was waiting with bated breath to learn which play Peter had been assigned. I used to think it was "baited breath" which made no sense at all to me (if I had been able to "bait my breath," maybe I would have been able to snare Peter with a kiss?). Now that I knew it was "bated" from "abate," it made perfect sense. Sometimes I felt like I'd been waiting with bated breath for the past sixteen months.

But, anyway, Peter was in the department head's office, along with the other two candidates. Each of them had to pull the name of a play out of a hat, and that would be his final directing project. The candidate who directed the best production, based on a jury vote, would win the Schumann. No one knew which three plays were in the running.

I was waiting outside the office, silently reciting Peter's wishes into my mantra:

"Please no Pirandello, please no Pinter, please no Shakespeare, and please, pretty please, no Greek tragedies . . ." I repeated over and over again.

All of a sudden, Peter burst into the anteroom and threw his arms around me. He had the biggest grin on his face.

"Guess!"

"Well, obviously not Aeschylus or Euripides. I don't know . . . Arthur Miller? William Inge? Tennessee Williams?"

"Nope, right century, wrong continent."

"Okay, so . . . twentieth century . . . and knowing you, I'm going to guess early to mid-twentieth century, probably nothing after 1950? And not Asia or Africa or Antarctica."

"Good answers."

"Oh, c'mon, give me a hint. The suspense is killing me."

"Okay, *you're* gonna love it."

"*I'm* gonna love it? Hmmm, that rules out T.S Eliot and Genet and Gorky . . ."

"You're getting warmer . . ."

"What, Russian?"

His grin was even wider, and I was screaming: "Peter! Chekhov? Please, tell me, did you get *Three Sisters*???"

That had been my dream play since high school, and Masha, the middle sister was my dream role. And Peter knew it.

"See the power of prayer?" he teased.

Tryouts were to be held in two days, the bare bones (minimally costumed and no sets) production was to be mounted in five weeks, and my whole life seemed to depend on Peter winning this prize. If he weren't coming back to Tucson for graduate school, when would I ever see him again?

But, first things first. Would he even cast me? True, he had looked into my eyes and told me our souls were joined, but that didn't mean he saw Masha in there. And what if he did cast me, and I did a shitty job and ruined the play and lost him the fellowship?

I had to try out just like everyone else, but after a day of (more) bated breath, the role was mine.

"I had to cast you," he said. "Not because of us, but because you're so strong and earnest and truthful and hopeful, and vulnerable, just like Masha. I see her strength in you. She will live and survive, even though she doesn't get her wish."

It was almost as if he'd said it out loud: "Because you will never get your wish, either, Caro."

"Oh, and because you gave a damn good reading."

He also wanted me to assist with the direction. Why?

"Because it's *Three Sisters*, not *Three Brothers*, and I want to make sure it's informed by a female sensibility."

Could anyone have blamed me for loving this man?

But that didn't stop me from standing my ground when I thought he was wrong.

Far be it for me to criticize my fellow actors, but I couldn't stand the way Jeannette Spencer was portraying Natasha, the sister-in-law of Olga, Masha, and Irina, the eponymous sisters.

"And you're letting her get away with it, Peter. Natasha isn't a villain. Chekhov doesn't *write* villains. We have to have *some* sympathy for her, she's been so woefully put down by the ladies in the first act, who are so *very* clear that she is so *very* far beneath them."

And then Peter admitted that he didn't have much sympathy for her at all, and that it drove him crazy that she had all those trees on the property cut down in Act 4 and he ridiculed her for her bourgeois airs.

"Whoa, the sisters can make fun of her, but you can't, Peter. You need to have some sympathy for her. You can't let Jeannette just play the vanity and selfishness. It's so one-dimensional."

"But that's what she is, vain and selfish and ruthless . . ."

"No, at first she's insecure and lonely and she lives in that hostile environment. And when Olga puts her down in her first scene, when Natasha wants so much to make such a good impression: *'The green belt you're wearing! My dear, it's just not right!'* Well, that's just cruel. She deserves a fairer portrayal. I know you're an aesthete, Peter, and she's a destroyer of beauty in the end, but she has feelings, too. You owe her some compassion, don't you think?"

I was pretty much on my high horse, but, after all, Peter wanted female sensibility, and he was getting it.

He wasn't ready to back down, though.

"What about all that striving, and that fawning over her children? It's so off-putting. She makes Irina move out of her room, just so her *precious* little Bobik can have it. It's so manipulative. That's just her plotting to take over the household."

"No, it could also be Natasha's maternal instinct: *'I am afraid little Bobby is quite ill. Why is he so cold? . . . I am so frightened . . . I am afraid his room is too cold for him. It would be nice to put him into another room till the warm weather comes. Irina's room, for instance, is just right for a child: it's dry and has the sun all day . . .'*

"Peter, *really*? Give her the benefit of the doubt. Think about the times and conditions people were living in. A lot of children died before they turned five. She was being a good mother, protecting her child. You have to give her credit for that! And, yes, she was manipulative, too, but that could have come out of her protectiveness."

Oh, Jesus, even that Natasha Ivanovna, as shallow and social-climbing as she was, proved to be a better mother than I am. Where have my maternal instincts gone? Am I still searching for goddamn fucking Moscow, and willing to sacrifice my children to find it?

Peter said he'd think about it, and to his credit, he did. The next day, he came to rehearsal with a changed attitude and coaxed a decidedly different and much more honest and effective performance out of our Natasha. And out of all of us, actually. I know

I'm biased, but Peter turned out to be a remarkably intuitive director (with a little help from his friend, when his intuition failed him).

I conjured up our future. We were destined to become the next First Couple of the American Theater, like Alfred Lunt and Lynn Fontanne or Hume Cronyn and Jessica Tandy, and then the founders of a theater dynasty, like the Redgraves or the Barrymores. And Peter's conjuring matched mine: If he won the Schumann, his graduate year would overlap with my senior year, and then we would both move to New York and share an East Village walk-up with a bathtub in the kitchen. Of course, we would have to get day jobs, he said. He'd drive a taxi, I'd wait tables, and we'd buy *Backstage* each week and go to casting calls and eat rice and beans for a while and I'd write a play that would debut off-Broadway, and he'd direct it, and that would be the lucky break for both of us. He was so convincing, I almost believed him.

But sometimes, not quite. As much as I was reveling in playing my role, watching characters evolve, marveling as Peter shaped the play into something whole and significant, and imagining our tomorrows, I was uneasy.

He's unattainable. Masha will never get to Moscow. I will never have Peter, not in the way I want him. My life imitating art.

"Listen, how the music is playing! They are going away from us, one of them has already gone, gone forever, and we are left here alone to start our lives again. We must go on living . . . we must go on living . . ."

I recited Masha's final lines. No, not recited: I was living those lines. Was this *my* existential cry, or my character's? I wanted to go on living with Peter. I wasn't ready to accept life without him.

Those Russians, they were such fatalists.

CHAPTER
TWENTY-SIX

It was the end of May, and Peter would be graduating in two weeks. His mother was flying down from North Dakota for the occasion. I was finally going to meet her, and I wanted to make a good impression. A good impression did not mean work shirt and jeans, and the love beads and braids would have to go. The last time I wore a dress offstage was to my mother's funeral. It was time to go shopping.

I enlisted Ernesto and Scott in the project. They had impeccable taste, and Peter definitely did not. No, I couldn't rely on Peter. He would just look at me and say "You look nice," even if I were dressed in overalls with a scarecrow hat on my head, and chewing on a piece of straw.

"What sort of thing did you have in mind, kiddo?" It was a gloriously sunny day, and Scott and I were catching rays in the back of the pick-up. Ernesto was driving. We were on our way out Broadway to the El Con Mall.

"God, I don't know. Mrs. MacKinley is pretty straight, from Peter's description of her. I don't want her to think her baby boy has been hanging out with the Queen of the Hippies, you know? Oh, shit, Scottie, I just want something that won't make me look like Mama Cass."

Scott was reassuring. "Nothing could make you look like Mama Cass, Caro. She's fat . . . but you, you are *buxom*. How about something low-cut? I've got it! Why don't you just wear your *Sweet Charity* costume?" He cracked up. The electric blue costume in question was one I had worn as a dance hall hostess in the department's annual musical, and in a line from one of the show's numbers, it was "cut up to here and down to there." It was so "down to there" that during one performance, as I leaned over, my right nipple was slightly exposed. I only found out when I saw a photo someone had snapped. Funny, I wasn't embarrassed. I was kind of proud, actually. It seemed such a subversive act.

"Nooo, I don't think so. She would probably just flip out. I think I need to buy something a little more . . . you should pardon the expression . . . conservative."

Scott guffawed. "You, Caro, are anything but conservative . . . but don't worry, kiddo, we'll find you something."

We were a rather unconventional triumvirate, Scott, Ernesto, and I. The salespeople did not seem terribly eager to help us. They kept their distance, as if whatever we were might be catching, but then one of them came rushing over and tried to block the entrance to the dressing room when it became obvious that the two of them intended to accompany me inside.

"You can't do that, that's the *ladies* dressing room!"

Ernesto looked her right in the eye. "So?"

"Well . . . well . . . *you* can't go in there."

"Oh, no?" He twirled his moustache, like the villain in an old Western. "Well, did it ever occur to you that *we* might be ladies?"

I couldn't believe his chutzpah. Scott was laughing so hard he was choking, and I wiped tears from my eyes.

"I'm calling the manager . . . I'm calling the manager!" the woman was shrieking as she ran off.

"Cheese it, the cops!" On cue, the three of us dropped the dresses in a heap and sprinted for the exit. We made it to the truck as the manager and a cadre of salespeople rushed out the door.

"Damn commie hippies! They ought to throw you all in a concentration camp and shave your heads! Damn faggot hippies!"

We crowded into the cab of the truck. Ernesto gunned the motor, backed out, and drove like mad through the parking lot in case the manager really had called the cops.

I noticed that he was holding on to the steering wheel with his pinkies sticking out, and as soon as we were safely down Broadway, he and Scott started dishing everyone outside our own little intimate circle of friends. And I was reminded that, as much fun as I found them, I couldn't really be part of their world. They were a two-person in-crowd and I was still on the outside. Story of my life.

"Listen, you guys, I don't think I'm really in the mood for any more shopping today. Would you mind just dropping me at the library? I've got a Modern Drama paper due next week, and, as usual, I haven't started it yet, so I'd better get on the stick."

"Okay, kiddo, maybe another time. Why don't you and Peter come over tonight? We just got the new Beatles album and it's outasight . . . got some hash, too, if you want. It's pretty heavy stuff."

Ernesto never let his studies interfere with his dope. I knew for a fact that he had an exam in his Shakespeare class the next morning.

"No thanks. If I don't hit the books tonight, I'm going to be in deep shit. We're probably going to just grab a couple of tacos for dinner and go back to the library. Too many distractions everywhere else."

Lately, I had been avoiding situations where the four of us would be together, especially when dope was part of the evening's entertainment. Maybe I was getting paranoid, but there seemed to be strange vibes at the Love House. I hadn't been able to figure it out. It wasn't anything that was happening between Peter and me, and I was never aware of it when I was alone with Scott and Ernesto, but when the four of us were sprawled out on the Love House floor, stoned out of our minds, with The Beatles echoing in our heads, I had the strangest feeling that Ernesto had gotten Peter on a wavelength I didn't even know existed.

CHAPTER
TWENTY-SEVEN

She didn't like me . . . hated me, in fact. I could tell. First of all, my dress was all wrong. It was an orange and black paisley tent, bought in desperation two days before. It made me look like Mama Cass on Halloween. I was wearing sandals because I couldn't get my feet into anything else, and my attempt at securing my long, frizzy locks into a French twist had not succeeded.

In honor of Peter's graduation, Mrs. MacKinley was taking us both out to dinner. Just before Peter went out to the airport to meet her flight, I tried to uninvite myself.

"Really, Peter, she hasn't seen you in so long. It might be better if just the two of you had dinner. Um, I'll be there for commencement, and I'll see you afterwards, but I'm not so sure this dinner thing is such a great idea."

"Don't be silly, everything will be cool. I want you two to get to know each other. I've told her so much about you and she can't wait to meet you. She knows how special you are to me. Please don't be uptight. I know she's going to love you, just like I do."

He'd said it in such a matter-of-fact way, I knew he hadn't meant it the way I'd hoped.

The dinner was a disaster. I was on my best behavior, but it was not good enough. I sat in the back seat of the car, already looking daggers into the back of her grey permed head. She was in my seat, and at the restaurant, she urged him to slide into the booth next to her. Could she have been more obvious? I was a fifth wheel here, too.

She was full of stories about people "back home."

"Well, Billy got out again—got to little Ivy right behind that old apple tree. Serves that Letty right, always going on about what a sweet, perfect little girl Ivy is. I'm sick of hearing that woman brag about her . . ."

Peter chuckled. "What is it, the fifth time he's done it? Good for old Billy. He sure is persistent."

Where did Peter live, Peyton Place? Child molestation and they were laughing about it? Did I really know this man I'd spent the past year and a half loving? What's more, did I want to?

Peter noticed the expression on my face. "Ivy is a miniature French poodle, Caro . . . and Billy's the mutt across the street. Ivy's owner thinks the sun rises and sets on that dog, but she keeps forgetting to keep her in when she's in heat. And Billy's just doing what comes naturally, so . . ."

I flashed Peter a look which he chose to ignore. He didn't finish the sentence, but, instead, turned back to his mother.

"How about Gerald? How's his diabetes? Is he sticking to his diet?"

"Oh, didn't I write you about Gerald? Poor man had to have four toes amputated off his left foot—gangrene set in, you know. And did I tell you about his nephew, Carl, who lives over to Bismarck? I don't think you know him. No? Well, I can't tell what I've been thinking lately, not writing you about that. It was in all the papers and even on TV. Bunch of kids got drunk after a basketball game, piled into a pick-up and tried to outrun a freight train. Six of 'em were killed . . . all but Carl. He was driving, and he's going to be paralyzed for life. Such a waste." She shook her head, tsk-tsking, but I could tell she relished reporting these events.

Between the gangrene, the dog in heat, and the body parts strewn across the railroad tracks, I was having difficulty swallowing my dinner. True, I'm the daughter of a veterinarian, and my father had some pretty gory stories to tell, but he had the good sense not to bring them to the dinner table. Suddenly, the rare steak I'd ordered (she insisted we get steak, because "After all, we're celebrating.") was the last thing I wanted to put in my mouth. I was seriously thinking of becoming vegetarian at that moment.

I tried to change the subject. "Mrs. MacKinley, you must be so proud of Peter winning the Schumann Fellowship. It's such an honor . . . I mean, of all the directing students in the country, they only chose twenty. Did Peter tell you that? He's so modest, he probably didn't."

"Oh, yes, he told me. He's very capable when he sets his mind to it. Son, as soon as we get home, we have to go out to visit Daddy and Sissy. I don't know if anyone's been watering the rose bushes I planted there. There's been a drought, you know, and I've been going out every other day. The roses will probably be dead by the time we get home. And they haven't been doing a very good job at cutting the grass around the graves. I don't know why I'm paying for upkeep if they're not doing anything about it . . ."

He soothed her. "I promise we'll go as soon as we get back . . . and I'll cut the grass myself if I have to. Aren't you going to finish your steak, Caro?" He finally noticed I was around.

"No, do you want it? If not, I'll get a doggie bag and have it for a midnight snack. I guess I'm too excited about the graduation ceremonies to eat."

I burned my tongue on black coffee while the two of them topped their meal with strawberry shortcake.

"Only coffee? Are you dieting, my dear?" Her tone implied that if I wasn't, I should have been.

"Well . . . sort of . . . I've gained a couple of pounds I'd like to take off . . ."

"I've always been lucky that way, I guess . . . never had to worry about my weight. And Peter takes after me . . ." She pulled a lipstick out of her purse and reapplied the slasher red that was so inappropriate for a woman her age, but so right for the role she was playing. She blotted her lips on a napkin and then flashed me a victorious grin.

Okay, that was it. Now I hated her just as much as she seemed to hate me. I congratulated myself on not being so obvious, though.

The waitress brought the check and Peter automatically reached for it, but his mother was quicker. "No, son, this is my treat. It isn't every day I get to take you out for graduation dinner—and your friend, too, of course." She kept puzzling over the check until Peter finally took it from her hands. "I'll figure out the tip, Mom, okay?"

She was flustered, and suddenly, I almost felt sorry for her.

That feeling was fleeting, though. She took Peter's arm as we left the restaurant, and I was left to tag along behind. *Bitch!*

It took forever to get rid of her after commencement. For one horrifying moment, it looked like she was going to convince Peter to take her along to Ernesto and Scott's graduation/farewell-to-the-Love House party.

"A graduation party, Peter? How nice. And all of your friends are going to be there. You know, you haven't introduced me to any of your friends, son . . . oh, except Cassie here, of course, but it would be nice to meet the others. . .and their parents, too, of course. I feel like you live in a whole different world here. What are your friends' names, the ones who are giving the party?"

"Ernesto and Scott, Mother . . ."

"Ernesto . . . Is that an Eye-talian name?"

Peter looked at me. I rolled my eyes. He said nothing.

"Well, do you think Er-*nest*-o and Scott would have any objection if you brought your old mother to the party, just for a little while? It would be so nice to go to a party," she sighed wistfully. "It's been such a long time . . ."

Don't be taken in, Peter. There's a witch behind that helpless façade. There's no way you can take her to that party. God damn it! You have to stand up to her.

"Now, Mother, none of the other parents are going to be there. It really isn't that kind of party. It's just some friends, um, getting together and . . ."

Smoking grass, getting high, making out, getting the munchies, dancing to the Stones, getting stoned out of our fucking minds, fucking. . .I hope. . .painting the soon-to-be-torn-down walls with Day-Glo, going 3/5 of a mile in ten seconds while we groove to the Airplane . . . Not your kind of scene, Mrs. MacKinley, not really. You'd be a real downer at that party . . . a real mind-fuck, lady. And I don't think the refreshments would suit you one bit. They don't serve Alice B. Toklas brownies at church suppers, do they, Mrs. M?

"Look, Mother, I don't have to go to this party. It's all right. We can go back to the apartment and turn in. We do have to get an early start in the morning. But Caro really wants to go . . . it's . . . um, the last time she'll see some of her friends who are graduating. We could drop her off and . . ."

You drop me off and you are dead to me, Peter.

Angry tears welled up in my eyes, but she was sitting in the catbird seat and, of course, couldn't see me . . . didn't want to see me . . . didn't even want me to exist, I see now, despite what Peter said about her being so eager to meet me. Eager, my ass.

"Oh, no, Peter, I wouldn't hear of you missing your party. I . . . I'm sorry. I didn't realize I wouldn't be welcome there . . ."

"Mother, it's not that you wouldn't be welcome, it's just that . . ."

She wouldn't be welcome, idiot! No one wants to see your mother spying in the shadows. She wouldn't be welcome.

"Don't worry about me, dear. If you don't mind taking me back to the apartment, I think I'm a little tired. Perhaps it's jet lag. It's an hour later back home, you know. You and . . . um . . .

your friend go to your party. I want you to have a good time, son. It *is* your last night in college, after all . . ."

No, it isn't, Mrs. M. Haven't you forgotten about the Schumann prize? He'll be back here for at least another year. Long enough for me to finish school. Long enough for him to realize he can't live without me, and he can live very well, thank you, without you.

I waited in the car while Peter walked her back to his apartment.

"So nice to meet you. . .um. . .Karen."

I didn't bother to correct her. "It was nice meeting you, too, Mrs. MacKinley," and I stuck out my tongue. She couldn't see it, but it made me feel a little better.

It was ten minutes before Peter returned to the car.

"I'm sorry. I know you didn't have a very good time tonight . . ."

"Why, Peter, how can you say that? I had a wonderful time tonight. It was almost as much fun as my mother's funeral."

He gasped. "Oh, God, I am really, truly sorry. She can be very difficult sometimes . . . but you have to understand: I'm really all she's got."

"Forget it. Can we just forget it? I want to have a good time tonight, so let's go, okay?"

No lights were blazing at the Love House, but we had to park down the block because there were so many Harleys, VW Bugs, and Day-Glo painted campers in the empty lot by the house. It looked like all of Tucson's heads had come to say good-bye. The following week, the house would be razed to make way for a high-rise dorm.

Peter took my hand. "It won't be the same without the Love House, will it?"

"No, it won't . . . but we'll still be the same . . . all of us. We'll carry the Love House wherever we go. I know you and I will . . . and Ernesto and Scott, and Brad and Miranda, and Tricia. . .and anyone else who has ever felt its vibes. It can't die . . . it won't."

"You know what I really want to do?" he asked suddenly, eagerly. "I want to build a dome—you know, a geodesic dome like Buckminster Fuller's—a dome in the desert, big enough for all of us . . . all of us who have felt love in this house."

"A dome? Oh, wow, I can dig that. And it could be like a commune. We could become self-sufficient and everything . . . oh, it would be really groovy. Who would we invite?"

"Whoever wants to come. And there wouldn't be any hang-ups like possessions . . . and . . . and, you know, no owning other people. It would be so free, Caro . . . no one would belong to just one other person . . . we would like all belong to each other. It would be family."

Wait, wait! What about New York and sharing an apartment and you directing my play and living on love and rice and beans?

I wasn't liking this new fantasy of his one bit.

The party was a bummer. Too many bodies. Too many bad memories, not good ones were evoked: The time Ernesto and Scott left me alone to wallow in my bad trip . . . The time I saw Tim's car in Peter's parking lot . . . The many, many times Peter refused to make love to me.

Ernesto and Scott were dancing, cheek to cheek and crotch to crotch. Scott had his arms around Ernesto's neck, and Ernesto's hands were in Scott's back pockets.

"Shall we dance?" Peter took me in his arms in a clumsy imitation of Ernesto and Scott, cheek to cheek, but definitely not crotch to crotch. We were awkward on the dance floor, but it didn't matter. There were so many people dancing, the light was so dim, no one could see that our lower bodies tilted away from each other instead of toward.

No, someone had seen: Artie of the bedroom eyes. He must have seen us through his glass penis. He cornered me in the kitchen where I'd gone in search of Alice B. Toklas's brownies.

"Why don't you dump that faggot and come back to me, babe? I know he's not balling you, so I can't figure out what's in it for you. What is it, you feel like his mother or something? You're not going to change him, you know, no matter what you do. That kind doesn't change, baby. He'd rather be fucked in the ass by Ernesto. Haven't you ever seen the way he looks at him? He'd give anything to be in Scott's place."

I raised my hand to slap his face, but marijuana had slowed my reflexes. Artie grabbed me before I could make contact.

"Hey, make love, not war, baby. And that's what I want to do to you right now. Did you bring your foamy stuff? C'mon Caro, let's blow this scene and then you can blow me. I know what you like, baby . . ."

Before I could protest, his lips were on mine and his tongue was trying to force open my clenched teeth. I grabbed the only part of him I could, his ponytail, and pulled, hard.

"Ow, you bitch! All right, go back to your faggot, cunt! Who needs you?" He stalked off. I sank down to the floor and began to weep.

"Caro, what's the matter, dear?"

I hurriedly wiped my eyes with the back of the hand that failed to slap Artie. "Oh, I don't know, Peter. I'm just sad, I guess. Everybody leaving, and the Love House being torn down and . . . just everything, you know?"

He nodded. "Yeah, it's kind of depressing. Everybody trying to have fun getting stoned out of their minds so they won't have to think about tomorrow or next week. Do you want to leave?"

"I'm sorry, I just can't deal with it tonight. Could you take me back to the dorm? I'm starting to get a headache."

"Sure, I need to get home, too. I want to get started by seven tomorrow morning."

That made me weep anew. "Oh, no, so early? I thought I'd at least get to see you. That means we have to say goodbye tonight. Oh, I wish it were September. How am I gonna get through the whole damn summer without you?"

"It'll be okay. It'll pass in no time. Here," he handed me his red bandana. "Once again, your tear ducts are leaking and you're without a handkerchief."

I grinned through my tears, "Yeah, me and Scarlett O'Hara."

"Except that, frankly my dear, I *do* give a damn," he said softly. "Hey, I've got a great idea! Why don't you fly out and spend a week with me before school starts? I'd like to show you around Hastings. Then we can drive down here together . . . that would be great!"

"Really?" I was suddenly beside myself with joy, until I remembered that a week in Peter's house would be a week with the Spider Woman, too.

He read my mind. "It would give her a chance to get to know you . . . and for you to get to know her. She's not always like this, really. I think she just felt out of place . . . uncomfortable . . . so she got really possessive and . . . oh, please come, Caro. Give her another chance."

There was a parking spot right in front of the dorm. Most of my dormmates were still out celebrating. No one was making out on the steps. I didn't want to go through the motions tonight. "Let's just say goodbye here in the car. It'll be too depressing . . ."

He put his arm around me and we kissed. Was he a little too eager to comply with my wishes for a quick farewell? Afraid I'd make one last attempt at a pass?

"The summer will pass quickly, dear, you'll see. We'll write. And I'll pick you up at the Fargo airport right after Labor Day. Is it a date?"

"It's a date. I'll be there . . . see you."

I ran up the stairs before my tear ducts sprang another leak.

CHAPTER
TWENTY-EIGHT

"Scott, are you home?" My arms were full, so I pushed the door open with my foot. Dylan was on the stereo, but I didn't see anyone.

"Caro?" Ernesto's voice came from the bathroom. "Scott had to go to work early, everybody's trying to re-sell their textbooks. Bummer, huh? C'mon in. Pour yourself a cup of coffee. I'm just gonna take a shower . . . got really grubby cleaning the place up this morning. Be right out."

I had come to return the books and records I'd borrowed from Scott. I didn't really want to stay. Artie's voice was still echoing in this room. I didn't want to be rude, though, and I needed some coffee. I chose a bright yellow mug and poured myself a cup. I loved that sunny kitchen, with its lemon yellow walls, turquoise-painted refrigerator, and foreign movie posters. Farewell Truffaut . . . Au revoir, Jean-Luc Godard. I sat in one of the unmatched chairs at the kitchen table.

There were fresh wildflowers in the Mexican pitcher. I wondered who picked them? There was also an open envelope. I looked more closely. The hand was familiar . . . too familiar. Oh, God, could Artie have been right? This letter was addressed to Ernesto, and it was from . . . it was from Peter.

My hand reached, involuntarily. Shower sounds were coming from the bathroom and Ernesto was humming the theme from *A Man and a Woman*. I grabbed the letter and tore it from the envelope.

"If I'd known you were coming over this morning, I would have burned that." Ernesto, a towel wrapped around his waist, was standing in the doorway.

So appalled was I at the contents of the letter, that I hadn't even noticed that Ernesto had finished his ablutions. Said letter was balled up in my hand. I didn't even remember doing that. I felt totally disembodied. Someone else was sitting at that table. Someone else had just read Peter's declaration of love and desire.

"He didn't mean for you to see that, Caro. I'm not even sure he wanted *me* to see it. It took a lot of guts for him to write it. He brought it over early this morning, around two. The party was still going on. He asked me if he could talk to me for a minute. We went outside to his car, and he gave me the letter. He asked me not to read it until after he'd left town this morning, that he just had to let me know how he felt, and then he left. I put the letter in my pocket and kind of forgot about it. I guess I was pretty stoned, anyway. Scott and I fell asleep in our clothes around four, and then he was up at eight to get to work. I didn't remember about Peter coming over until I started to undress and the letter fell out of my pocket. I just read it myself and I haven't really had time to digest it. But I want you to know that I never did anything to lead him on. All that is in *his* head. It's *his* fantasy. There was never anything between us, and I'm sure Peter knows that. That's why he didn't want me to read it until he was on his way back home.

"I don't think it takes away from what the two of you have. That's very special, Caro, and this doesn't change it. He's confused about his sexuality and it's causing him such pain. He wants to come out, but he can't. I know what that's like, but you can't possibly know what he's feeling. Scott and I really love you, kid, but we've watched you and known what was going on with you and Peter for over a year now. Look, nobody wants to see you hurt, especially not him. Anyone who read that letter, anyone who knows the two of you could see that. All he said about me in that letter . . ."

"All he said was that he cares for you deeply and that he's wanted you to make love to him from the day he first set eyes on you, from the first day I introduced you! Isn't that enough? And you knew! How *could* you, Ernesto? How could you keep that from me?" My fury was unleashed, I was shrieking. "How could you humiliate me like this?"

My inclination was to pound my fists on his bare, hairless chest, but I wouldn't touch him. I pounded the table, instead.

Ernesto stepped towards me, his arms outstretched to comfort me, but I ducked out of his embrace.

"Don't touch me! I hate you! I hate you and Scott . . . and especially Peter! I guess the three of you must have had some good laughs over the last year . . ."

"Caro, we never talked about it with Peter . . ."

"Oh, but you and Scott did, didn't you? So, what am I to you, huh? A fag hag? A jerk?"

"A friend, Caro, a best friend to all of us."

"I don't want to be a friend; I want to be Peter's . . ."

"Lover, wife, mother of his children. I know, I know."

"I'm sorry. It's not your fault, I know. I guess I just have lousy taste in men . . ."

"On the contrary, kiddo. Peter is a wonderful person, and if he were straight, you two would be a match made in heaven. You're great together. You really care about each other. But Peter needs to accept himself and right now he doesn't know how. You could tell by what he said in the letter. He hates himself for the way he feels. He'd give anything to not feel that way. He doesn't really love me, Caro . . . he loves *you*."

"But he wants to sleep with you."

"Yes, he wants to sleep with me," he nodded soberly. "But I don't want to sleep with him. I've never wanted to sleep with him. It's very sad, you know. Peter can never be happy until he accepts who he is, and I don't know if he'll ever be able to do that."

"But why does that necessarily have to be what he is? People do change, you know."

"Yes, people can change some things, but changing your sexual orientation is not something you have any control over. It's like you can't change the color of your skin, you know? I always knew what I was. I think people are born that way."

"That's not true! Peter wasn't born that way! He was sexually abused by a man when he was a child . . . by a man he knew and trusted . . ."

"That's not what makes someone gay, Caro. None of us believe that."

This was something new.

"Ernesto, how . . . when . . . how did you know that you were . . ."

"A faggot?"

"Oh, c'mon, you know what I mean."

"I don't mind. I guess I knew from the time I started school. I mean, it wasn't like I wanted to dress up in my mother's clothes or anything. It's just from a very early age I was attracted to boys."

"But all little boys want to play with other boys and don't want to have anything to do with girls . . ."

"No, this was different. It had nothing to do with latency. I knew that the way I was attracted to others of my sex was different . . . that it wasn't 'normal.' No one told me that, at least I can't remember anyone telling me that, since I never told anyone how I felt. It's just something I knew all along, and it was confirmed when I got to high school and met someone who had the same inclination."

"Oh."

Would anyone meeting Ernesto be able to tell? I tried to see him as if for the first time. He was very masculine-looking, I thought: Dark brown hair that fell rakishly over one eye; deep, piercing brown eyes, dark, bushy moustache, broad shoulders . . . and a round, jagged scar in the middle of his chest.

"Ernesto, where did that scar come from? I've always been curious about it . . . but I didn't want to be rude . . ."

"And today you have license to be rude?" He laughed. "It's no secret. It's an occupational hazard. I was in New York, in the backroom of a bar making it with a gorgeous hunk from Sweden, when my boyfriend walked in and decided to tattoo my chest with a broken bottle."

I gasped. "*Scott* did that to you?"

"*Scott*? Good Lord, no! Can you imagine Scott doing anything like *that*? No, before I met Scott and decided I liked my men gentle and sensitive, I had a thing for rough, macho types. Raymond was a little too rough and macho, though. Twenty-seven stitches cured me of Raymond and his ilk. I'll live much longer with someone like Scott . . . which doesn't mean I don't sometimes have the hots for a Raymond . . . or a Xavier . . . or a Sven . . ." he mused dreamily.

Oh, Peter, is this what's in your future? A Sven? A Xavier— one-night stands with guys whose names you don't even know? Anonymous, impersonal sex in the backrooms of bars? Don't you know that I can give you so much better?

"Ernesto, how could you tell about Peter? Was there a way I could have known . . . I mean, from the beginning, before he told me? By then, it was too late . . . I was in love with him . . ."

"Radar, babe. We have a special kind of radar. I told you, we know our own . . ."

"But *I* introduced him. . . we were going out together . . . wasn't it obvious to anyone else besides me that we were a couple?"

"Let me tell you something. When I was a senior in high school, I decided that I was going to try to go straight. My parents were starting to look at me strangely. My mother kept reassuring my father that I was a late bloomer, but I don't think he was buying it. I was afraid they were going to find out about my secret life—I'd been meeting boys on the sly for three years. So, I asked this girl, Barbara Alejandro, to go out. She was quiet and shy, and pretty much non-threatening, I thought. But we went to the movies and I guess she expected me to, you know, make a move. I tried . . . I mean, I held her hand when we walked home. But I was really in a cold sweat. She said she thought it was sweet that I was so shy, that she appreciated my not trying to paw her on our first date. We went out a few more times, but then I couldn't hack it. So, one day at school, I told her we just couldn't go out anymore. I never told her why. I know she was hurt, and I hated to do that to her. I'd been using her, but I hadn't meant to, you know? She was a really nice girl, too. I heard she got married after her freshman year of college. She has a couple of kids . . . one of them is named Ernesto . . ."

"I wonder if she ever got over you . . ."

I tore the letter into dozens of tiny pieces and flushed them down the toilet. Ernesto didn't try to stop me.

CHAPTER

TWENTY-NINE

This is a mistake. I just need to go home. Last night I dreamt that Caleb was falling into a gorge and that Jack and I were scuffling at the bottom, each of us trying to be the one to catch him. Then I woke up at 3 a.m., sweating and terrified, fearing that my pounding heart would burst my ribs wide open. Hours later, I fell back asleep and awoke just before check-out time. And then I kept getting lost and driving in circles, trying to find my way from the motel to the interstate.

It's been four days since I left home. I've been making terrible time. I should have been there by now. I was so focused on Peter, my prize at the end of the rainbow, I hadn't bargained for the crushing exhaustion and ennui of the actual trip. I've only been able to drive for four or five hours each day, and then I pull into a motel before sundown, and then I can't get to sleep so I pop a Librium and don't get up till almost noon the next day. I planned on traveling at least six hours today, but my dream has me in such a state I don't know if I'm capable of getting to the next stop I've plotted on the AAA Triptik.

I have to find out if my children are okay. They're supposed to write postcards home the day after they get to camp. Those cards might be sitting on the hall table right now, below the mirror. But I don't want to call Jack.

Wait, today's Wednesday. Marya will be there cleaning 'til 4. I can just about catch her and ask her to read me the cards. She'll leave before Jack gets home, so no risk of him finding out . . .

I pull off into a rest stop to use the pay phone. But it's not Marya who picks up at the other end.

"Jack . . . what . . . what are you doing home?"

"Caro." He sounds a little relieved. Wary, but not angry this time. "Why are you calling?"

"I had a dream—and I was worried about the children . . ."

"That was no doubt your guilty conscience . . ."

"Jack, please. I told you, I just need to get away to think about things, about us . . . Please, I want to know that the children are okay. Did you get postcards?"

"What about me? Do you want to know if I'm okay?"

"Yes, of course I do . . . but I know you can't be. I'm sorry . . ."

"Yeah, you're right. I'm not okay. My wife is gone, I don't know where. I don't know when or even *if* she'll be back. So, yeah, not okay . . ."

"Please—I can't talk about this right now. Please, please just tell me if you got the postcards."

"Yeah, I did."

There is a long pause, and then: "Do you want me to read them to you?"

"Oh, please, Jack, yes . . ."

"Okay. Sarah writes 'Dear Mom and Dad, The food here is gross (Three exclamation points with little smiley faces where the dots should be). Good thing I like peanut butter (one exclamation point, no smiley face). My horse's name is Dolly. I made advanced swimmer, YAY (All caps and three more exclamation points with smiley faces). Love you guys.'"

I can tell from his voice that Jack is smiling. I am, too.

"And here's Caleb's: 'Dear Mommy and Daddy, Two boys threw up on the bus. I didn't. I like tetherball. xxxooo.'"

This morning's nightmare fades from memory. He likes tetherball!

"And Greg's is best of all. No salutation, just: 'A guy in my bunk has his ear pierced and has a gold stud. It is sooo cool! He said it didn't hurt. Can I have one? He says you have to get your parents' permission. Oh, yeah, I almost forgot. We got here safe but the bus smelled like barf.'"

This last missive breaks through the frost. We are both laughing.

"I miss you, Caro."

But that's more than I can say back.

"I know you do, Jack. And I'm sorry. That was so good and generous of you to share the cards. I know you didn't have to. Please, I need to go. I'll call soon. I will."

"Wait, wait—I need to know . . . are you with someone else?"

My stomach begins to churn, and I'm afraid I'm going to vomit. I speak through clenched teeth.

"No, Jack, I'm alone."

And I hang up the phone.

I'm jolted awake by a noise in the middle of the night. I reach across the bed for Jack. I know he'll tell me it's just the house creaking or the automatic ice machine in the fridge doing its job, but I'm scared, and I want his reassurance. And, I realize, I want *him*. The clock radio by the side of the bed says 4 a.m., but we don't have a clock radio. And then I remember where I am and that I'm alone. And I'm not supposed to be wanting Jack, I'm supposed to be wanting Peter. Isn't that the point?

I get up to pee. I know I won't be getting any more sleep this morning.

CHAPTER THIRTY

The summer after Peter's graduation, I worked in my father's office. I hated it, but not as much as I hated the evenings in that big old, empty house. My mother's presence was palpable, and Daddy and I were both very careful with each other. Too careful. He was always relieved when the phone rang and he was called out on an emergency. A night spent in a dimly lit barn performing a C-section on a cow was infinitely preferable to the interminable evening at home with so much to say and no way to say it.

I spent those nights rereading all my old Nancy Drew and Cherry Ames books. My father had not been able to bring himself to go through my mother's things. It was unspoken, but I think he expected me to do it. Whenever I opened her closet and smelled her perfume, though, I couldn't touch a single garment, even the ones she let me dress up in when I was little.

Finally, out of sheer boredom, on the third night in a row that my dad had been called out on an emergency (a horse had gotten tangled up in some barbed wire), I walked over to my mother's dressing table, sat in front of the mirror, and opened a drawer. It was full of half-empty jars of cleansing cream, Q-tips, bobby pins, and breath mints. I popped a mint in my mouth. I was looking for my mother in this detritus, but I couldn't find her. I rummaged further. More of the same. And then I felt a small wooden box in the back of the drawer. It was painted blue, with a yellow decoupage rose. There were only three items in the blue velvet-lined box: a tiny, red, flat cardboard container of Maybelline mascara, with a teensy red brush and a crumbling cake of black, the box imprinted with the come-on "Harmless, tear-proof, and will not smart the eyes"; a tarnished silver-plated tube of Elizabeth Arden Victory Red Lipstick; and a small gold Jewish star on a delicate gold chain.

I knew their significance immediately, even though I had never seen them before. Surely, this was the illicit make-up my mother had applied on her way to the USO dance. She probably spat onto the cake of mascara to wet it. And was she an expert at applying lipstick, or did she need to wipe it off and start again, having never had the practice? And the Mogen David? I wonder if she wore it hidden under her dress to protect her from the gentile world that would swoop her up that night.

I slipped the necklace over my head. The Victory Red had a tiny bit left at the bottom of the tube. I stuck my pinkie in and applied it to my lips. But the Maybelline tag-line was a lie. Even without application, the mascara brought tears.

I think my dad and I were both regretful but relieved when he drove me to Boston to catch the plane to Fargo. I was looking forward to spending a week at Peter's before we returned to Tucson. I'd managed to convince myself that the letter to Ernesto was a fluke, that Peter was stoned out of his mind when he wrote it. How could I have believed otherwise? I knew things would be different for us now. A summer away from me had had to bring him to his senses. I really believed that old saw about absence making the heart grow fonder.

I boarded the plane with hope renewed, settled into my seat, and, after take-off, lit the first of many cigarettes. I had the bad luck to be seated next to a talker. She went on and on about how she had once smuggled mushrooms from Tuscany and cheese from Paris (or was it cheese from Tuscany and mushrooms from Paris?), blah, blah, blah, and I was completely not interested but kept nodding and saying "Uh, huh" to be polite, until finally she fell asleep. Then I proceeded to wallow in a cross-country X-rated fantasy, starring Peter and me.

By the time the plane landed, I was in a real state of arousal, but my hopes for at least a passionate necking session in the parking lot were dashed as soon as I entered the terminal. Ubiquitous Mother had accompanied my love.

My greeting was less than enthusiastic, and he hadn't a clue that he was to blame. I gave him a quick hug and held my hand out to his mother, who dropped it quickly.

Edna knew I didn't like her. She hated me. I didn't understand how Peter could be even remotely related to her.

She was exercising her prerogative as *numero uno* woman in his life, as Peter helped her into the front seat. Was that a triumphal grin she flashed me, or was it my imagination?

I found out that evening that *nothing* would be left to my imagination.

"May I help you with dinner, Mrs. MacKinley?

Peter had been dispatched to corral the cat, who had been spotted roaming the neighborhood.

"Well, I suppose." She was anything but gracious. She acted as if I were planning to steal the family jewels. I was.

She handed me three plates and three glasses. "The silverware's in that drawer."

I'm not sure why she chose to drop the bombshell at that moment. Maybe she needed an excuse to buy a new set of china. More likely, though, it had been timed for when Peter was out of the picture.

"Peter wrote to you that he won't be going to graduate school after all, didn't he?" she queried, knowing full well he had done nothing of the sort.

I had been wounded, perhaps mortally, but I said nothing. My face betrayed me though, and she continued, victorious.

"No? Well he should have told you. Peter's decided that his place is at home. He's going to stay home and take care of me."

Bile rose in my throat and I clamped my jaw to keep from throwing up all over her spotless black and white linoleum (made that way by Peter, no doubt, who would have made someone an excellent wife . . . I was beginning to hate him . . . again), but I couldn't let her know that she had won, that her pronouncement had done more to dash my hopes than all of my chaste encounters with her son, than all my unfulfilled longings. With the brash self-confidence reserved only for youth, I had been convinced that if I were a good girl, ate all my vegetables, and played my cards right, I could eventually make Peter straight . . . and mine.

But even *I* knew that I was no match for Edna. I walked woodenly to the table and set three places. My left eye was beginning to twitch. I knew before the evening was out, I would have a whopper of a migraine.

Peter returned shortly with the errant cat, did not notice my distress, and went to wash up for dinner.

Edna sat at the head of the table. Her son and I took seats across from each other. Peter, perhaps in response to my tic, winked at me. I looked away.

"Son, will you say grace for us?" This was not a question, but a command.

"Bless, oh Lord, this food to our use and us to Thy love and service and make us ever mindful of the needs of others. We ask it in Thy holy name. Amen."

"Amen," she echoed, and proceeded to serve the meal. She had not outdone herself: Grey roast beef, mashed potatoes with thick, floury gravy, canned peas, and, my least favorite food in the world, green Jell-O salad (seriously, who ever thought celery in Jell-O was a good idea?). Of course, even if she had been Julia Child, I would have choked on her dinner.

"Excuse me . . . I'm terribly sorry, but I'm not feeling well. If you don't mind, I think I'll just go lie down for a while."

Edna was uncharacteristically solicitous. She could afford to be. "Oh, what a shame. Perhaps you're just tired from your flight. I hope you'll be able to join us for dessert. It's Peter's favorite, banana pudding."

"Perhaps." I couldn't look at him. I knew he was anguishing over my refusal to break bread at his table. I knew he would get to the root of my malaise, but I wasn't sure I cared any more. The Judas had once more betrayed me, and I never even got the kiss.

From my bed in the guest room, I could hear the conversation escalate from "I hope she's not sick" to "You *told* her? Mother, I told you I was going to talk to her about it tomorrow . . . that wasn't fair."

I fell asleep. I dreamed about my mother. We were talking on the phone and she was dying. She made horrible, gasping sounds. I tried to resuscitate her through the phone, but I knew I couldn't save her. I must have cried out. The next thing I knew, Peter was knocking at the door.

"Caro, are you all right? May I come in?"

"What . . . oh, Peter . . . yes, all right."

He didn't turn on the lamp, but I could see his face in the light that entered from the hall. He looked worried.

"Caro, dear, what was it, a bad dream?"

I gave him a baleful look. He had the grace to look away.

"Mother told me what she said to you, about my not going to grad school. I'm sorry, I should have written you about it, but I was afraid you wouldn't come if you knew . . . and I wanted so much to see you . . . to tell you in person so you would understand. I guess I was being selfish. I know we were going to drive together, but I'll pay for your plane ticket. I really feel terrible about this. I'm sorry Mother told you that way. She's sorry, too, and wants to make it up to you. She suggested I take you to the movies . . ."

He rattled on, afraid of my silence.

"Do you want to go to the movies? I'm afraid there's only one in town, a drive-in," he said apologetically. "Um, I'm not sure what's playing . . . I think it's *The Dirty Dozen*."

I shook my head, which by then was throbbing. I wanted to go back to sleep, but I had to get out of the house. The walls were closing in on me.

"Could we just go for a ride? I could use some air."

The kitchen had been tidied. My unused place setting had been removed from the table. Edna had retired for the evening, secure in the knowledge that I was no longer a threat to her boy. She had thrown an invisible but iron-clad net around him. It was impenetrable.

We drove around town. Peter pointed out his old elementary and high schools, the drug store where he'd had his first after-school job, the church he and Edna attended faithfully each Sunday, and finally, the cemetery where his father had rested for the past dozen years.

I burst into tears.

"Oh, my God, Caro . . . I'm sorry . . . I wasn't thinking . . . your mother . . . it's too soon. I guess I just wanted you to know more about my life here . . ."

"Why bother? We don't have a future together, only a past. You won't be going back to school with me. I probably won't ever see you again after this week."

"Don't say that, please. This is only temporary. We just felt it would be better for me to be home at this time. She has these spells, you see, and she needs me . . ."

She had spells, all right, but they weren't the kind Peter thought they were. She had magic spells . . . the kind you read about in fairy tales . . . the kind that put people to sleep for a hundred years. I knew all about those kinds of spells. He was already asleep.

He wouldn't have listened to me, anyway—wouldn't have heard me. I knew the arrangement wouldn't be temporary. Peter's fate was sealed: there would be no magic kiss to free him. He'd be with her 'til death did them part, and I didn't anticipate that that would happen any time in the near future. She was too spiteful.

"I promise you, it's just temporary. Honestly, dear, we'll still build our dome in the desert . . . you, me, and all our friends from the Love House, all together again. But this is something I have to do for now."

For the first time since June, I allowed myself to think about the Love House. I was sure that by "all our friends" first and foremost he meant Ernesto.

I didn't want to think about that anymore. I had successfully banished Peter's graduation night missive from my mind after I had read it, as if, in destroying it, the letter had never existed.

Suddenly, I was ravenous. It had been twelve hours since breakfast on the plane.

"Peter, I'm starving. Could we just forget all about this tonight and get something to eat?"

Relief flooded his face. I had let him off the hook, and, as far as he could make out, I had forgiven him.

I hadn't, but hunger won out. We drove to an A&W Root Beer stand, where I devoured two hamburgers and a side of onion rings. Peter ordered coffee.

Upon our return to the house, I had heartburn as well as a headache. I knew I would have to cut short my visit and get back to Tucson ASAP. I couldn't stand staying in a house with a woman who put fake fur on her toilet seats and made Snow White's stepmother look like Pollyanna.

I slept in the next morning. There was still-warm coffee on the stove, store-bought cinnamon rolls on the counter, and a note from Peter on the table: "Didn't want to wake you. Today is Mom's volunteer day at the hospital gift shop. Be back as soon as I drop her off and pick up some cat food at the store. Peter."

Not even "Love, Peter." Well, he could just take his cat food and shove it. His stupid cat gave me itchy eyes, and its owner had broken my heart . . . bad karma all around. But, masochist that I was, I decided to give it one more chance.

By the time Peter returned with a bag full of cat food cans, I had had my coffee and hatched my plot. I was going to sever that umbilical cord once and for all . . . make him forget that Edna even existed . . . at least for a little while, and by then, he'd be mine.

"Hi. Mom's going to be working at the hospital 'til 5. What would you like to do today?"

No one mentioned last night. Our whole relationship consisted of not mentioning last nights.

"You know, I'd like to see your cottage. You promised one day you'd take me there. We could bring a picnic . . ." (We could also bring the really great grass I'd copped from my friend Jocelyn the night before I left home . . . but I didn't mention it to Peter. It was part of my secret plan).

It felt like old times, making sandwiches in Peter's kitchen. Old times? Was it really only three months ago? What had happened to him since?

Sandwiches, pickles, Cokes, and cookies were soon stowed in the car, along with our bathing suits and towels. I had also packed two carefully rolled joints and my diaphragm.

The cottage, a lakefront bungalow set on a couple of acres with a half-dozen others, could have been indigenous to anywhere. It was in good repair, but the white paint was peeling and the red trim had faded to a dusty rose. And the lawn needed mowing.

Peter was apologetic. "I haven't gotten around to the painting . . . it's on my list for this fall. We really haven't used the place at all this summer . . . just Fourth of July with my cousins and their families. It's been so rainy that we haven't gotten much swimming in."

Because I was trying so hard to ignore the proprietary "we" sprinkled throughout the recitation, I guess I missed the red flag word, "rainy," which should have alerted me at once.

Hardly used cottage by the lake plus lots of rain equaled . . . mold. I smelled it as soon as Peter shouldered open the front door ("Sorry, it sticks."), but, fool that I was, I walked in anyway. The screen door slammed behind us. It sounded like summer.

Peter bustled about, getting glasses for our Cokes, dusting off some chairs, emptying a trap of a rotting mouse carcass. I stood around, willing my throat not to constrict, but to no avail.

"Sorry," I rasped "This isn't going to work . . . I can't breathe." I rushed out, inadvertently banging the screen door behind me. That time, it sounded like an ending.

"I have to get back to Tucson." By then, I was wheezing. "This whole thing is a bad scene . . . bad karma, man. If I stick around much longer, she'll probably poison me."

The look he gave me was one of pity, but . . . what else? Probably disgust. I know how I must have looked and sounded: A swollen-eyed, gasping shrew. I wouldn't have wanted to go to bed with me either.

"That's not true, Caro! How can you say something like that? She likes you . . . it's just that . . ."

"It's just that what? That she's afraid of losing you? That having a gay son is infinitely preferable to having a straight one who might love another woman more than he loves her? That's really sick, you know?" By then I was sobbing, and, what's more, dripping. I didn't even have a Kleenex.

Peter, ever the gentleman, even when I was crucifying him, offered me his handkerchief. There were tears in his eyes, too.

"Oh, Caro, how can I make you understand? I guess it's wrong of me to expect you to. She doesn't even know about me. It's just that there is a need here . . . an obligation I have to fulfill. I admit there's not much of a future in it, but for now, I have to stay."

"But what about me? What am I going to do without you? What about our apartment in New York and you directing my play and breaking into the big time . . ."

He looked so defeated, I almost wished I could have taken it back, but then he shook his head and set his jaw.

"Well, first of all, let's get you some pills or something so you can breathe . . ." He guided me gently into the car. "The druggist's an old family friend. He'll give us something."

Peter was at his best coping with small, tangible emergencies. I certainly think he welcomed this one . . . he didn't have to answer my question.

The next day, he drove me back to the airport. Edna was so pleased by my early departure, she baked oatmeal cookies for me to take on my journey. I dumped them in the trash near the entrance to the terminal. Peter raised one eyebrow, but said nothing. Edna had not accompanied us this time . . . she knew she didn't need to.

"Well, I guess this is it, Peter . . . it's been real." My flight had been announced. I could only speak in platitudes.

"I'll write to you, dear . . . don't ever forget me. I know we'll see each other again soon." He squeezed my hand and kissed me on the cheek before I could pull away from him. He was crying, but my eyes were dry. I seemed to have cried all my tears already.

CHAPTER THIRTY-ONE

Everything had changed. Three months away and I hardly recognized the place. Ernesto and Scott had broken up and Ernesto had split for New York (back to the bar scene?). No one knew where Scott was. Someone said he'd gone back home to Chicago, but someone else reported that he was seen in Guadalajara with an older man. Artie, too, had left for greener pastures, and Erewhon was nowhere. It had been replaced with a health food bar called the Bean Sprout Café. The specialties were carrot juice and avocado smoothies. Tricia had found a new man, dropped out of school and she and Annie had moved with him to Phoenix. The Love House existed only in memory now. I felt Peter's absence most acutely, of course.

"You're planning on graduating in June, Carolyn?" Dr. Romano, my academic advisor, had my records spread out on his desk.

"Yes, I hope to. Why? Isn't everything in order?"

"Well, everything except in one little area. Will you be so kind as to tell me how you managed to get out of taking physical education for the past six semesters? They won't let you graduate without three credits! How could you overlook this?"

"I didn't overlook it. It's just that there was always a schedule conflict. They never had anything I wanted to take at the times I could take them. The only courses that didn't conflict with my other classes were things like golf and field hockey. A real bummer, you know?"

"Yes, well it's going to be a 'real bummer' if you don't graduate this year, particularly since Dr. Steinman informs me that you are his most gifted playwriting student and he wants to recommend you for a graduate assistantship next year. So, I would strongly advise you to get the hell over there and sign up for tiddlywinks if you have to!"

An hour and a half later, I had signed up for tennis, fencing, and intermediate swimming (I neglected to inform the phys ed department that I was already Red Cross Water Safety Instructor certified—it was the only way I could fit three credits into my gym schedule). Unofficially, I was signed up for running: The gym was way across campus from the drama building, and we only had four minutes between classes. The unexpected dividend, of course, was that by the end of the semester, I had lost thirty pounds. And, for the first time since I was a little girl, I liked what I saw when I looked in the mirror. Sometimes, I even caught a glimpse of the beautiful Shulamith looking back at me.

I had responded to a bulletin board posting for a house share a few blocks from campus, so I was living with two geological engineering grad students who carried their slide rules and ball point pens in pocket protectors. I had trouble telling them apart, but they were nice enough, and they pretty much lived at the library, so I hardly ever saw them. Anyway, I had a place to lay my head, my own bathroom and no curfew (not that I had anywhere to go).

Peter and I wrote chatty, newsy letters, letters that touched base, but just barely. I wrote about my studies and the play I had written for Steinman's class, which he was submitting to a national playwriting contest. He wrote back about painting the living room, the cat's escapades, and acting with a community theater group. He never mentioned his mother, and I never asked. My soulmate seemed to have vanished into thin air, replaced by some pen pal I hardly recognized.

I slept with Jack the first day I met him, moved in with him two months later, and finally, mercifully, Peter was gone.

CHAPTER THIRTY-TWO

S ex and politics filled those early days with my new man. We didn't really know about sexual politics yet. I never minded making the coffee at the anti-war meetings while the guys haggled over strategy, because, afterwards, I bedded down with the sexiest guy there.

Jack, the burner of draft cards, the leader of sit-ins, a man who was surely on the FBI's surveillance list, was also an incurable romantic: he recited Khalil Gibran to me when we made love.

"To melt and be like a running brook that sings its melody to the night . . ." he moaned as he thrust.

Half the battle was won: There was no doubt that he was hetero. All I had to do was keep him interested in me.

To that end, I planned my life around his. Jack had one more year of law school after this one, but this was my senior year. I hadn't really considered graduate school, but Steinman was definitely recommending me for the assistantship in playwriting.

"C'mon, baby," Jack urged. "Take it. You don't have to complete the program. Just stay for the year it takes me to finish. I don't think I could stand being away from you. Then we can travel, drive around the country in the van . . . maybe join a commune . . ."

This sounds vaguely familiar. Where have I heard this before? Oh, yeah, Peter's dome in the desert. Nope, no dome. No commune. No van. No thank you.

"What're a lawyer and a playwright going to do in a commune, Jack, milk goats and chop wood?"

"No, baby, we'll join a lawyers' and playwrights' commune . . . c'mon, it doesn't matter where we go, does it? As long as we're together. And, since we're together, why don't you just take off your clothes, woman. I'm tired of talking. All I've done all night is talk and try to convince those assholes that protesting at Fort Huachuca is an inalienable right guaranteed us by the Constitution. What chickenshits! I don't want to talk, babe. I want to fuck you and suck you and I don't ever want to stop."

Oh, my God, I was mad about this man! I felt like I'd hit the boyfriend trifecta: smart, great in bed, and behind that scruffy beard, a real looker, as my mother would have said. And, he loved me! But at the same time, there was something about him that I couldn't put my finger on. Something that seemed to be lurking behind the radical politics, the long hair, and the clothes he wore like a manifesto, but he wasn't telling, and I was afraid to ask.

What was the deal with my karma? Was it my fate to fall in love with men with secrets? Well, at least this one loved fucking me as much as I loved fucking him. I decided to let it be.

Of course, it was much more difficult to keep that secret after we'd moved in together, and one night it became self-evident after I'd overheard him arguing with his father on the phone:

Jack came from money! Old money. WASP money. It was his biggest shame, and everything he did was meant to be antithetical to his upbringing.

Did that everything include falling in love with me?

"So, now you know." Jack was red-faced and breathing heavily after the telephone shouting match. It wasn't clear who had hung up on whom.

"My father is one of those capitalist pigs who are destroying this country. I hate his politics, I hate his beliefs, I hate that the money he pays for my tuition and the rent on this place comes from the same pot of money he sends to the God-damned Republican Party. He fucking loves Nixon's ass and the whole God-damned military–industrial complex war machine that's getting our compadres killed in Vietnam. But he's still my father. . . ."

He looked so miserable. I could see through the man he had become to the little boy he once was, the one who rode on his dad's shoulders and begged for one more bedtime story, and I knew what he was afraid of. I felt his pain, I really did. Despite the complicated relationship I had had with my mother, despite my life's purpose to not turn out anything like her, the little girl in me still loved and missed her terribly.

"Oh, baby, oh baby. You're not your father. You never could be." And I covered his face with kisses.

I wasn't clear if I was reassuring Jack, or myself. At that point, it all seemed one and the same.

In April, they shot Martin. We had barely recovered when, two months later, Bobby was dead, too. And the war was escalating. I was numb: Too many dead boys (how dare they call them "casualties"), too many grieving widows and uncomprehending children and Vietnamese babies ("collateral damage") who would never grow up. But Jack was enraged.

"We'll take this to the streets. Fucking bastards! If anyone's blood is going to flow, it's going to be theirs. No more peace, love and flowers. It doesn't work, baby. They're killing the best of us. Oh, Jesus Christ, they want war, all right, they'll get war. But this one won't be in Khe Sanh or in the DMZ. This one's going to be right at home on the streets of Amerika."

He strode across the room and threw back the lid of the trunk at the foot of the bed.

"Here, pack this." He tossed me an item from the trunk.

I caught it, and then looked, stupefied, at the gas mask in my hand.

"Jack?"

"And here's another, for you. Start packing, babe, we're going to Chicago."

Far be it for me to remind him that we'd be flying to the convention on his father's dime.

By the end of those days of rage that August, kids had been teargassed, beaten, and incarcerated. The Democratic Party was in shambles. And Jack and I were engaged.

Every once in a while now, I catch a fleeting glimpse of that Jack-of-the-past, and it makes my heart happy, like some rare bird sighting. Well, maybe not totally rare, not like an emu running around in our yard in Connecticut, but more like a bird you didn't even know you were looking for, like the indigo bunting that landed on the lilac outside our back door last spring.

Yes, that kind of delight.

"How do you feel about contributing to the NAACP Legal Defense Fund this year? I'd like us to write them a big fat check. What do you think?"

This is our year-end sit down to figure out which heart-tugging annual appeal letters we will respond to: Salvation Army, no; UNICEF, yes; ASPCA, no; our local animal shelter, yes. Of course, it's not all altruistic: our accountant is pushing us to up our contributions this year as a way to reduce our tax burden come April.

So, what do I think? I think Brown vs. Board of Education. I think Montgomery Bus Boycott. I think the Little Rock Nine. I think Martin Luther King and all the hundreds of freedom fighters this fund has supported over the years. Mostly, I think that revolutionary iconoclastic boyfriend of mine is still in there somewhere, and it gives me a thrill.

I see a flicker of a smile play around Jack's lips as if he, too, has seen that bird, but also, I think, that he wants me to be proud of him. And I am.

"Of *course* let's send them a big fat check, the fatter the better." He winks. "Oh, and don't mention it to my parents, okay?"

And then Jack-of-the-present, the one who's under the thumb of his father and "the firm," is back.

Like I said, fleeting.

It wasn't the rough flight that terrified me: I had absolute confidence in the pilot's ability to get us through the storm intact. It was the anticipation of what would happen once we got on the ground.

"Babe, relax. She'll love you. I guarantee it. She's been waiting for you all her life, Caro. I mean, the woman has six sons. She couldn't wait for one of us to get married and provide her with a daughter. She's gonna love you as much as I do."

Déjà vu. They even used the same words: Peter about Edna, Jack about Lois. I would have felt safer playing out on the wing, lightning or no.

But she did. Love me, I mean. And I liked her the moment she threw her arms around me and laughed: "Thank God, at last!"

Lois was tall, almost as tall as Jack. When she said she was going to take me under her wing, she meant it, literally. Her arm was around me as she escorted me from the car to the house. "Come and meet the rest of my men, Caro," she said, giving me another hug.

Jack's father was as cool as his mother was warm, but he didn't frighten me. Jack had warned me about his gruff exterior, and, anyway, he wasn't the one I needed to win over.

It was Lois I had to impress, and I did that by virtue of being female and in love with her firstborn. If she had had any reservations about Jack marrying a half-Jew who wouldn't know the Social Register if it conked her on the head, she (and Jack Sr.) hid it well. It also helped that I didn't have a mother to plan my wedding: Lois had the caterer lined up before Jack and I even got there.

"Ma," my husband-to-be protested, "No caterer. We're gonna get married in the backyard, and everyone will bring food. It's not that kind of wedding . . ." He looked at me, helplessly.

"I hope the bride doesn't plan on going barefoot," Jack Sr. harrumphed.

"You should be glad she's not pregnant, Dad."

"Jack!" My face reddened.

"Your bride is right, son. That was really out of order."

"Sorry, but Jesus Christ, whose wedding is this, anyway?"

"Honey, could I talk to you for a minute?" I beckoned him to Lois's squeaky-clean, straight out of *House and Garden* kitchen. "Honey, really, I don't mind. Let her do the wedding. She's so happy. And if my mother were alive, she'd be doing the same thing. I don't see any point in turning this wedding into a family feud. Let's let her. I mean, God, Jack, she likes me. I was so scared she wouldn't. And it'll make my father happy, too.

"Look, after we're married, we can live any way we want. It's just one day, Jack. Can't we give in just a little, so they'll feel comfortable?"

"You really don't mind that she's taken over, do you?"

"No. In fact, I'm kind of relieved. I have no experience planning something like this. If it were up to me, I'd elope. I just want to be your wife. I don't care how we do it. So, if doing it this way makes everyone else happy . . ." I shrugged.

"You're sure?"

"I'm sure."

And that's how, the next day, I found myself in the city with Lois. We were going to pick out my wedding dress.

"We'll try Bergdorf's first, dear. The bridal consultant's an old friend."

But I knew Bergdorf's was not for me as soon as we walked in the door. I wasn't dressed right for Bergdorf's. I wasn't born into the right class for Bergdorf's. How was I going to tell Lois that my knees were shaking so badly that I wasn't going to make it to the bridal department?

I didn't need to tell her. She took one look at my face, took me by the hand, and walked me out the door.

"On second thought, I don't think there's a dress in that store that will do you justice, Caro. All those exotic dark curls and those dark eyes. You don't want pearls and lace and organdy, do you, dear?"

I shook my head . . . but I would have worn them if she'd wanted me to.

"No, they really wouldn't suit you. I know the perfect place, though—Taxi!"

An hour later, I had my dress, the second one I tried on at Fred Leighton's funky West Village boutique: a Mexican wedding dress that I could have gotten for a fifth of the price in Nogales, but Lois was pleased as punch to be writing the check and I loved her for it. The dress was beautiful, and I was beautiful in it. This was the next best thing to having my mother here. Not the drinking mother, of course, but the idealized mother I still dreamed about.

"Now, don't lose any weight between now and June," she cautioned. "I know brides get nervous and sometimes don't eat, but that dress fits you perfectly. Let's see, we don't even need a veil with it . . . fresh flowers in your hair, I think. Yes, gardenias, or maybe camellias . . ."

"I can't wait to show Jack how I look in this dress."

"What?"

"I can't wait to get to your house so Jack can see me in my dress."

"Oh, my dear, out of the question! Out of the question!" Lois was horrified. "It just isn't done. Your groom can't see you in your wedding dress until you walk down the aisle."

My groom had seen me naked, had seen every crevice, every orifice. He'd sucked my tits, licked my cunt, slid my diaphragm into my eager vagina, and plunged his cock as far into me as it could go. But see me in my wedding dress before the ceremony?

That was a taboo we dared not break.

The dress was safe from harm in Lois's closet. Jack and I were back in Tucson. He was cramming for his last law school exam, and I was directing a production of a one-act I wrote under Steinman's tutelage. Our protesting ended with Chicago.

Lois called once a week to fill us in on wedding plans. Jack always handed me the phone: "Hi, Mom, here's Caro." This was woman talk. His head was full of torts and writs and habeas corpus and corpus delicti . . . there was no room for brides-maids and champagne punch and orange blossoms. That was my department.

CHAPTER

THIRTY-THREE

"Caro, I'm cured!" was the way Peter announced his presence when I answered a knock at our door that evening in May, two years after I'd seen him last. Jack was out at a meeting and I was in the midst of packing up the house for our trip east.

"What?"

"I'm cured . . . I'm straight . . . we can get married!" His eyes were sparkling as he threw his arms around my neck and pressed his body (all of it) against mine.

I felt like I would faint . . . or worse, throw up. My tongue cleaved to the roof of my mouth.

"Didn't you hear me?" he exulted. "We have our future!"

Oh, Peter, you always had such an impeccable sense of timing on stage, but in real life . . .

"No."

"What?"

"No, Peter. No future." I had finally found my voice.

He recoiled, much the way he did that night years before, when I'd stripped to the waist in his apartment.

"What do you mean? All this time . . ."

"Oh, my God, Peter, I wrote to you last year about Jack . . ."

"I didn't think you were serious . . . I thought he'd be like the others . . . you always came back to me before . . ."

"But I never answered your last letter. Surely that must have told you something."

"I was going to write to you, baby, to tell you what was happening . . . about the therapy . . . but I didn't want to get your hopes up, in case it didn't work. But it did work, it *did*. And I'm here now. Nothing else matters." He was insistent.

So was I.

"Peter, something else does matter. I've been living with Jack in this house. We're getting married next month."

"Oh . . ." He straightened his shoulders. "Oh, well . . . then . . . um. Oh, hell, do we have to discuss this in the doorway. I mean, can you ask me in, or is your . . . boyfriend home?"

My heart ached for him . . . ached in more ways than one, and I was suddenly terrified. I, who once would have given my right arm, my right breast, all my worldly goods and anything else asked of me if I could just get Peter willingly and eagerly into my bed, was terrified of the very thing I had wanted most— perhaps still wanted, if truth be told.

"No, I can't . . . Peter, I'm sorry . . ."

"Look," he said, suddenly back in control. "You don't have to decide right now. C'mon, if you won't ask me in, let's go for a ride. I think we need to talk."

I hesitated.

"C'mon, Caro, it'll be okay. Really, have you ever known me to attack you?" He laughed.

That laugh broke the tension, and for a moment we were old Peter and Caro again.

"Hold on, I just have to get my shoes on." I grabbed my sandals and followed him out to his car.

Once on the road, however, I knew I'd made a mistake. We could never be "Peter-and-Caro" again. There were too many memories in that car . . . too many nights parked in the Catalina

Foothills with the lights of Tucson sparkling beneath us . . . too many nights when I would reach out for him, only to stop myself before my hand reached its goal, knowing that there would be no response.

Now, I was to be the unresponsive one. I moved as far to the right as I could, clutching the door handle, as if poised to escape.

Peter noticed. How could he not. But he didn't comment.

We drove into the deserted parking lot of St. Philip's, but I made no move to leave the car.

Peter reached for his cigarettes and offered one to me.

"No, thank you. I quit last summer."

A quizzical eyebrow: "A lot of changes, Caro."

"Yes—I've changed."

He eyed me curiously: "Still smoking anything else?"

"Nope. I quit that, too."

"And you've lost weight." For the first time, perhaps ever, he was looking at me, eyeing me up and down. "He must be quite a guy . . ."

Here, a note of bitterness crept into his voice. He, too, was regretting the invitation to drive over our memories.

"He is. I love him. I have a future with him."

"You've sold out, Caro. It didn't used to be that way. It didn't used to be the future that mattered, only the moment we were living in." It was the first time he had ever raised his voice to me. "You loved me, too, remember?"

We were both close to tears. It would have taken a leap of blind faith to follow Peter at that point . . . faith I no longer had, perhaps never had. The future with Jack was certain, I believed, and stable, and now I wanted stability more than anything. I no longer wanted the emotional roller coaster ride that was, and no doubt would be, life with Peter. I was getting too old for roller coasters.

"I did . . . I do . . . I can't. Peter, please take me home. I don't know what to say to you."

Wordlessly, he started the car. The trip back continued in silence. I was acutely aware of the whir of the air conditioner and of the sweat dripping down my back. Only once did I allow myself to look at him. His jaw was clenched and his eyes were focused straight ahead.

He had the good sense not to walk me to my door. I didn't think either one of us could have managed that scene.

"Peter, I'm sorry we couldn't . . ."

"Yeah, so am I . . ." All at once, he flashed me the old familiar peace sign and, as quickly as he'd appeared, he was gone.

For some time after that night, I thought I had dreamed the whole thing, but a month later, two days before Jack and I were to fly back east for the wedding, I received my last missive from Peter.

"Dear Caro,
Our being together again was rather discomfiting, wasn't it? I am trying to understand how it happened, but I don't know if I'll ever be able to accept it. I look for permanence . . . perhaps this is unrealistic. But I didn't expect our relationship to be quite so transitory, either. But that's where we're at, I guess. I thought you would be happy to see me, but it seems I was wrong.

"I guess we really have changed, haven't we? What once seemed so permanent will now be only a memory. In spite of the way it all ended, though, I will always remember you . . . and us.

"I wish you happiness with Jack, because I love you . . . because you have been such a vital part of my life.

"Even though it was painful, I was glad we could see each other one more time . . . it helps me put things into perspective . . . to distinguish reality from a dream.

"I guess we just live the best we can . . . and I will try to live the best I can without you . . . I will never forget you, Caro.
"As I am now,
Peter"

But wasn't he the one who had left me? I was the one who wanted permanence. The letter made no sense in my reality and I couldn't allow myself to explore whatever reality Peter was living in. Besides, in four days, I'd be married.

CHAPTER THIRTY-FOUR

May 4, 1970: The news was terrifying that day. Suddenly, a place no one had ever heard of was on the minds and lips of everyone—like My Lai two years earlier, only these two syllables were in America. Kent State. Four kids were dead, ten others seriously wounded. On a college campus in a little Ohio town in the United States of America. Shot dead by the National Guard of the State of Ohio, in the United States of America.

We were both horrified. By evening, I was still weepy, but Jack was subdued.

I was ready to leave the country, but, instead, red-eyed and spent with crying, I was dressing to go to dinner at Jack's parents. It was taking me forever. Jack was impatient.

"What are you putting on your arm?"

"It's a black armband. I'm in mourning, and I'm protesting." I struggled to tie the armband I had cut from the hem of an old black skirt. I was not adept at one-handed tying, so I was holding one end of the strip in my teeth.

An expression of something I couldn't quite pin down flitted across his face. Was it regret? Resignation? But it only lasted a moment.

"Don't you think you're carrying this a bit too far, Caro? You look like . . . like you're about to shoot smack . . . and I hardly think that's an appropriate addition to your outfit, under the circumstances."

In spite of his words, I could see longing in his eyes.

The circumstances of which he spoke were that he had cut his hair, shaved his beard, and was now working in his father's firm. I had envisioned him defending the Black Panthers and war resisters. He had envisioned a roof over our heads and dinner out a couple of times a month. The circumstances were also that my father-in-law was still Nixon's biggest cheerleader, and I knew that wearing my politics on my sleeve would be rubbing his nose in it. But the circumstances were also that four of our comrades were dead.

"Appropriate? Appropriate? You know who you sound like, don't you? Except for an accident of time and place, that could have been *us*, Jack! Us and all of our friends. They weren't doing anything we didn't do. Don't you understand in some ways it *was* us?" I was sobbing again, but I had succeeded in tying the armband.

"Oh, come off it, baby. It wasn't us. We never would have been that stupid. Those guys had loaded guns, for Christ's sake. Now take it off and let's get going."

"I'm not taking it off. I can't believe you're asking me to do that." But he wasn't asking me, he was ordering. We had purposely deleted the word "obey" from our marriage vows. What was he doing?

"My God, Jack. Wasn't it only two years ago that we were willing to get tear-gassed and who knows what else in Chicago? You were right beside me then, remember? The last time I looked, this was a free country. The armband stays on."

My arrows had hit home, I saw. He looked wounded, but I was standing my ground, even though I knew what it would cost him to show up at his parents' house wearing his radical persona.

It was the first time I had stood up to him, and he didn't know what to make of it. Given a few moments to see the folly of my ways, would I give in? I could see him weighing the alternatives. He turned to leave the bedroom.

"I'm going to call my folks and try to bow out of this evening as gracefully as possible. I'll tell them you're not feeling well . . ." He paused to see if this threat would sway me. It would not.

"No, on second thought, if you persist in being so stubborn, I'm just going to go myself. Well . . . ?"

"You'd better hurry, then. You don't want to keep your parents waiting."

He gave me an incredulous look. I stared right back at him, unwilling, unable to give in. We were both stuck, and neither one of us knew how to come unstuck. Without another word, he left the room. The apartment door slammed behind him. I held my breath. He couldn't be doing this. In a minute, he'd cool off. He'd be back. But then I heard the elevator door open, and he was gone. I waited by the door for a few minutes, imagining him getting into the car and maybe debating with himself about moving it from the miraculous right-in-front-of-our-building-alternate-side-of-the-street parking space I had found that morning, the one that would be good for the whole weekend. But after ten minutes, I knew he was heading north on the Henry Hudson Parkway. I took off the armband, threw it in the trash, and got into my nightgown.

We had had our first fight, and I couldn't help but feel a little proud for not caving. But Jack had gone off without me, and I began to spar with myself. Would it have been such a big deal to take the armband off? Why did I have to be so stubborn? Would it have been so awful if I had commiserated with my husband's no-win situation and played my part as supportive wife? Now I had something else to cry about.

I spent the evening in bed with my transistor tuned to the all-news station. Every twenty-two minutes, the events of the day were replayed . . . sixty-seven shots fired . . . four dead . . . fourteen wounded . . . Allison Krause, Jeffrey Miller, William Schroeder, Sandra Scheuer . . . by 11 p.m., the names were as familiar to me as my own . . . and every twenty-two minutes I couldn't help wishing that the old Jack was here beside me, vowing to take it to the streets. Eleven p.m . . . My husband had still not returned. Had he left me? We hadn't even been married a year yet. The tears wouldn't stop, but I wasn't sure if they were tears of anger or chagrin. Did I even want him in my bed that night? For the first time in our relationship, I would feign sleep.

CHAPTER
THIRTY-FIVE

Fortunately, the fight didn't last long. Jack came back that night full of sorrow and remorse, and affirmations of love, and regret that he had wasted a whole evening keeping his tongue while his father ranted on about our fucked-up generation, so, half-asleep, I pulled my nightgown up to my waist and welcomed him home.

Every morning when I woke up by his side, I realized anew how very, very lucky I was. The only template I'd had was my parents' sad excuse for a marriage, and I was determined that mine would look nothing like theirs. I was the good wife. That's why I got up before he stirred. I'd put on the coffee, and by the time he was showered and dressed, breakfast was on the table (yes, I'd learned to cook, so the toast was never burnt). I was so happy I wasn't my mother.

"Write something brilliant today, sweetheart." He kissed me goodbye at the door. I waited there until he got into the elevator.

But I didn't write anything, let alone anything brilliant. It was the same every day. I'd sit down at the kitchen table after Jack left for work, load a sheet of paper into the typewriter, and then stare at the blank page. I'd type a little, then rip the paper out, crumple it, and throw it on the floor. Then I'd start over with a fresh sheet.

After four or five false starts, I'd find any excuse not to continue. I read (telling myself that it was research for my next play), I did a lot of laundry, I made myself a sandwich to take to my afternoon job at the bookstore around the corner.

Our marriage had a downside, I'd discovered. Apparently, I was too happy to write.

"How can you be too happy to write? That's ridiculous."

It was Sunday morning, and we were on our way uptown to buy bagels. Our arms were entwined and we were walking in lockstep.

"No, it's not ridiculous at all. Look at O'Neill, look at Tennessee Williams—depressed, even suicidal, both of them. Even Shakespeare was not a happy camper. You are making me way too happy, darling. I can't find my creative spark."

"So, what are you saying? You'd rather be unhappy?"

"Of course not! You're the best thing that ever happened to me . . ."

"Then what?"

"I don't know . . ."

"Well, I think I do. You have no place to write. When you're sitting at the kitchen table, there's so much to distract you—the breakfast dishes, planning dinner, all the trappings of our domesticity. It's quotidian, not inspiring. You need a dedicated writing space, babe. Let me think about what we can do about this. I'm sure we can solve it. You're such a good writer, sweetheart. Far be it from me to be the impediment to your Tony Award."

Maybe that was it. He was so sure of himself, and I was so the opposite. Damned if *I* had the solution to my writer's block.

Two weeks later, after many mysterious after-work trips to our building's basement, Jack came upstairs with a professionally refinished antique desk that he installed under the window in our bedroom, the former site of his exercise bike, which was exiled to his parents' basement in Connecticut.

And the icing on the cake? An early birthday present: an electric typewriter to replace my second-hand Remington. But that just made me happier than ever.

Years later, when I was the mother of three, when we had long since left the city and were entrenched in suburbia, I would give it another try.

I didn't have any real friends in Westport. The other women on the PTA Fall Fling Committee were also stay-at-home moms, so we had that in common. No one was divorced and none of them seemed to have marriages that needed work. Yes, they complained about kids who talked back, and having to fire the maid whom they suspected of stealing, and husbands who spent every Monday night watching football. But they did it with a knowing camaraderie. They sported diamond-encrusted anniversary rings and tennis bracelets that came in Tiffany-blue boxes, and they shared stories of romantic weekends on St. Barts or Bermuda or Martinique. They gave the impression that they wouldn't have traded their lives for anything. It was weird, because some of them were truly smart. And funny.

I was both repelled and fascinated by them. Sometimes I joined the group for coffee, because I really wanted to figure them out. How did they keep this up, day in and day out? Did they ever have dreams of doing something more meaningful, more creative, more fulfilling than wiping snotty noses and picking out paint colors for the living room? Afterwards, I rushed home to fill notebook after notebook with my observations, like some eager anthropologist studying a heretofore undiscovered tribe. And, before I knew it, I was writing a play about the vacuous lives of women who have squandered their creativity and their intelligence and consoled themselves with expensive gifts from their husbands, the giftedness of their children, and the status of their unearned positions in life, not even recognizing their own miserable stasis. But what if they had secret lives and desires?

What if they dreamt about doing something bigger than organizing PTA fundraisers? And what if they were stuck? What happened when their dreams and their hopes collided with the utter meaninglessness of their lives? What if they were mired there forever?

This was the first thing longer than a grocery list I'd written in years and it was *so* heady. It was like falling in love or great sex or the best chocolate mousse ever, eaten in a tiny outdoor café on the banks of the Seine.

And then I remembered Moscow. Chekhov had already written this story, in an opus that would forever soar high above my miserable, derivative little scribblings. I would never be a brilliant playwright. Who was I kidding? I sucked. So one day, I just burned it all and went back to grocery lists.

CHAPTER

THIRTY-SIX

W e were trying to make a baby. It wasn't as easy as I thought it would be: Three months had gone by, and my period still came regularly. I was oblivious to anything else. The world was transfixed by the drama playing out around the Watergate break-in, but I was fixated on the viability of my eggs. Jack did not take kindly to my suggestion that he get his sperm tested.

The first month, nay, the first night we tried, I started writing naive little notes to the baby: "We have decided that we want you now, and tonight I think you were conceived . . . Read books about you and how to make you perfect . . . Bought all the things at the organic food store to make you healthy . . . even drank milk! After eating tons of good, wholesome food all day, I can hardly move . . . all the things to make you a superior baby . . ."

I took Adelle Davis as my guru, the result of which was, after three months, I had gained five pounds—but I wasn't pregnant.

"Let me take you away from all this." For the third time in as many months, Jack had found me weeping over a box of Tampax.

"Where away?" I sniffled.

"Oh, I don't know, but I think it's about time we took that honeymoon I promised you a few years ago—the one we couldn't take because I was cramming for the Bar." Jack pulled an envelope from his pocket.

"Two tickets to Zurich, my love. I have some work to do there for three days, but then the next three weeks are ours, to go wherever we want . . . Italy, France . . . you name it, honey. But there are conditions, of course: I don't want to hear the words 'ovulate', 'ovary', 'uterus', 'conceive', 'sperm', 'cycle', 'embryo,' 'fetus,' or 'baby,' the whole time. All you need to do is relax and forget about it. It'll happen, sweetheart, just give us a chance."

He held the tickets above my head. "Promise you won't say those words, and the tickets are yours, Mrs. Tanner."

"Oh, Jack, you darling. Yes, I promise. Could we go to Paris? And Florence? And the Mediterranean?"

"Anywhere your little heart desires." He handed me his credit card. "And you'd better start shopping—you only have two months to get ready."

"Two months? Sweetie, I could be ready in two hours!"

I had a momentary pang of guilt as I pocketed the card: *Oh, crap, I've sold out, haven't I?*

Our long-range plan was for Jack to make partner, and then he'd be freer to do the pro bono work of representing indigent clients and radical activists. But just then, I was enjoying the perks of having a husband who was practicing corporate law. And besides, I rationalized, if my fate was to be infertile, at least Jack and I would always have Paris.

Jack's "relax and forget about it" prescription worked. By the time we embarked for Europe, I was allowed to say 'baby' again: I was carrying one.

It was late. Peter and I had been drinking, and we were both very tired. I was lying on the couch. He was sitting on the floor, his back resting against the seat of the couch, his head only inches from mine.

All I had to do to kiss the back of his neck was to turn my head ever so slightly, but I didn't.

Abruptly, he interrupted his monologue, the story of his life for the past six years, the six years we had been apart, to pose this question:

"Do you still want me?"

My breath caught in my throat and it was a long time before I could answer.

"If I say yes, will you run away from me again?"

"No, not this time . . . not any time. I never want to be away from you again."

"Then yes," I breathed joyfully, truthfully. "Yes . . . yes . . . I do . . . I . . ."

And then, Peter's mouth was on mine and he pressed himself against me.

"Oh, yes . . . oh YES . . . OH NO! No, no, no . . ."

Oh God, something's happened to the baby. What have I done to my baby? I awakened to find my uterus a hard lump in my lower abdomen. *Oh God, have I killed the baby?*

"Honey, what was it? Were you having a nightmare? You were saying 'yes, yes, yes' and then shouting 'no, no, no.' Having trouble making up your mind there. What were you doing, trying to decide between two sweaters at Bloomingdale's?" Jack teased.

"What? Oh . . . no, I'm sorry." Flustered, I glanced around. Had anyone besides Jack heard me cry out? But no, everyone around me was occupied, and the noise of the plane's engines had drowned out my cries. Two of the people across the aisle were engrossed in the movie, another was reading, and still another was napping.

"No, darling, it wasn't Bloomie's. But I guess I was dreaming, and suddenly, my uterus contracted. It frightened me. I thought the baby would be crushed. Oh, Jack, I was so scared."

I put my head on his shoulder so he couldn't see my face and catch me in my betrayal. I hadn't thought of Peter for years. Why had he surfaced now? I didn't need him, and I didn't want him. I loved Jack, I loved our unborn baby, and I'd never been happier.

Jack laughed gently, tolerantly. He was going to humor the pregnant lady. "Honey, the baby isn't even a baby yet. It isn't even as big as a tadpole. It probably still has gills. Relax . . . Hey, remember the book said it was normal for you to feel your uterus contracting when you had an orgasm? Hmmm, what were you doing, babe? Dreaming about me?"

And then we got to eat the best chocolate mousse ever, feeding each other from tiny dessert spoons, and groaning orgasmically in a little outdoor café on the banks of the Seine. I loved my life.

CHAPTER

THIRTY-SEVEN

Eight years after our last, painful reunion, I wrote Peter a letter. It was to be the first of many long, introspective, self-indulgent missives, none of which were ever mailed. Each time I wrote, I hoped to have the strength, guts or pure folly to ignore all vestiges of good sense and drop the letter in the mailbox. I never did—which makes my leaving Jack for Peter even stranger, I know.

"Dear Peter," began that first non-letter, written in March of 1976 . . .

"Listening to the Beatles . . . feeling nostalgic about Tucson . . . the time, not necessarily the place . . . I used to think I wanted to spend my whole life there in the desert . . . I haven't communicated with you for many years, but I've thought about you more times than I care to acknowledge . . . I guess that's why I'm writing this . . . I may not send it . . . I may just have to get it all down on paper.

"We were so close, it's hard to accept the idea that we'll probably never see each other again . . . maybe it's just curiosity, but I don't think so . . . I guess I just can't stand the idea of not knowing what's happened to someone who, at an important juncture of my life, was probably my very, very best friend."

And my oh so elusive soulmate.

"This may a terrible thing I am doing . . . I know I really hurt you (not something I could help, given the situation) and this letter may be a real intrusion . . . wish I had a crystal ball and could look into your head without imposing my presence . . . I may be writing to absolve myself of some of that residual guilt . . . it's an awfully long time to be carrying it around . . . that's what comes from being Jewish, ha ha . . . Actually, I'm not even sure why I should be feeling guilty . . . but I don't want to cleanse my soul at your expense . . . On the other hand, you just might have some of those feelings about me, regrets that a deep and nurturing friendship has been lost . . . What I hope you would tell me is that you have found someone . . ."

Not true, not true—I want you to love me forever.

". . . that you are happy . . ."

But how could you be really happy without me?

". . . really in touch with yourself, and using your extraordinary creative gifts . . . Look, I know it's been forever and so many things have changed, but there must be something left of the people we were . . . I realize now that some of my dreams were not only unrealistic, but got in the way of achieving 'person-hood' . . . certain expectations I had (for one, that marriage was the be-all and end-all of everything, that I could depend on my husband to meet all my needs) really stood in my way for quite a few years . . .

"It's a very scary and exciting time to be female . . . so many traditional values being questioned, so many options being made available . . . and so many women's lives are in turmoil (which is not to say that men's lives aren't in turmoil, but I can only speak from my own experiences) . . . I mean, it was so easy in the '60s . . . we were all against the war, and that was that. I don't think anything will ever be that black-and-white again. I agree in principal with the tenets of the Women's Movement. I join my sisters in fighting for the right to control our own bodies, for equal pay, for community day care centers, but I admit to feeling pressured, too. Right now, I don't want to go out and be a brain surgeon, or an airline pilot, a Supreme Court justice . . . or even a playwright! I'm not ready to travel along all those great avenues that are being opened up right now . . . The most important fact of my life right now is that I am a mother! My son is almost two years old. It is most extraordinary what changes can be wrought by such a small being . . . the love I feel for him is overwhelming. I know now what it is like to feel that I could die for someone. I would do anything for him . . . not for anything he's done—although what he's done for me, what he's contributed to making me a more complete person, cannot be measured—but simply because he exists . . .

"I haven't done any writing in years (grocery lists and to-do lists don't count). Perhaps I'm too complacent in my domesticity . . . I have a good marriage . . ."

Okay, that's a stretch. On a scale of one to ten, I'd say we're a five, maybe a six on a good day. Truth be told, this is no doubt the reason I am trying to conjure you up, Peter: I have, in fact, a pretty mediocre marriage.

". . . an incredibly unique, brilliant, remarkable, wonderful child, and I'm learning more and more to draw on my own resources . . . someday, perhaps, the writing will come back . . . meanwhile, I tend to

the needs of my family and my home . . . God, who would have thought eight or nine years ago that this sort of life would suit me . . . I thought it was all so dull and ordinary, then. Remember the girl in *The Fantasticks,* the one who said *'Oh, God, please don't let me be normal'?* Was anyone ever as young and naive as we were? And what was it we were looking for? Have you found it? Have I?
"Not as you once knew me, but still
Caro"

By the time I attempted another letter, three months later, I had dug myself even deeper into the trench of domesticity. Jack and I had decided it was time to add to our family. I think we both hoped another baby could fix whatever it was we weren't talking about. By June, I was six weeks pregnant with Sarah.

Most of those early weeks were spent with my head in the toilet, followed by long sessions comforting a terrified Greg, who thought the toilet was going to swallow his mommy up. Needless to say, this put a crimp in our toilet-training. I gave up and just let him wear his diapers, pretty sure that he'd be trained by the time he started kindergarten, and if not, we'd worry about it then.

I did manage to find a moment between bouts of vomiting to compose one letter to Peter, again, unsent, and similar in content to the first one. I didn't mention my pregnancy. I didn't want him to picture me this way. I know the old saw about pregnant women glowing, but that was definitely not me. I had zits on my chin, my hair was oily, and my breath smelled of puke, even after I brushed. I couldn't abide the smell of cooking meat, so had become a quasi-vegetarian.

"I guess you'll think it's rather strange for me to be getting in touch after all these years," I wrote. "But I ache to know what is happening in the lives of all who were connected with the Love House . . ."

Not true, I haven't given the others a thought. I ache to know what's happened to you, Peter . . . mostly because, babies or no babies, I still want you . . . and this both exhilarates and frightens me.

"And I miss those warm friendships . . ."

Correction, I miss that crazy, unconsummated love affair.

". . . that developed in those glory days of Flower Power.

"As you once knew me, perhaps . . ."

Hardly!

"Caro"

CHAPTER

THIRTY-EIGHT

I was a motherless daughter and I was afraid to be the mother of a girl child. I'd fuck her up, for sure, and that's why, even though I answered "I just want a healthy baby," when people asked me whether I'd hoped this next one was a boy or a girl, I was praying for another son. My little guy so clearly adored me, and the feeling was mutual. It was so uncomplicated. Could I ever feel that way about a daughter, knowing what had happened to my mother, knowing what was happening to me? Nope, it just seemed safer to be the mother of sons.

And yet, when Sarah slid out of me, all purple and slick and slippery, I laughed out loud. Jack said that proved I had wanted a girl all along. I didn't think so. I heard that girl child's fierce, angry first wail, and laughed in relief. This one would be her own person, a force to be reckoned with. And I saw my mother in her, the brave, rebellious, dazzling young girl I never knew but wished I had, not the embittered woman I grew up with. So I called her Sarah, following the Jewish tradition of naming a child for a dead relative. I couldn't justify "Shulamith," but it was okay to give her another name starting with "S." It was to honor my mother. I wish she could have known. I never told Jack. He had heard such sad stories of my childhood, that he would never condone placing such a burden on our baby girl. He liked the name, liked that it meant "Princess," and that's what he calls her, but I always think of her as Sarah the Strong.

Having two children was not twice as much but ten times more work than having one. Being the mother of two left little time for thoughts of an earlier love, but sometimes, late at night, Peter seemed to appear by my bed—unsummoned, but usually welcome.

I did have one steadfast rule, though: When I was in physical contact with Jack, Greg, or Sarah, Peter could not penetrate our family circle. If I was nestled up against Jack for warmth or comfort (and his sleeping body did provide me that), Peter was banished. And if I was snuggling Greg back to sleep after a bad dream, Peter had to wait until the monsters were dispatched and my boy was slumbering once more. If I was in the rocking chair, nursing baby Sarah, Peter had to sit quietly and patiently in the dark until that last snuffling signified her 2 a.m. feeding was over. I would quietly ease my nipple from her not-quite slack baby mouth and hold my breath as I lowered her into her crib. Then, still not daring to breathe, chilled in my damp, milk-spotted nightgown, I padded silently back to bed. If I managed to slip between the covers without waking Jack, then Peter was welcome there, too. But if Jack reached out to me, the spell was broken: Peter had to retreat.

Almost two years went by before I wrote the next letter to Peter. By that time, my dissatisfaction and ambivalence were no longer opaque, even to me:

> "This is the seventh day I've been cooped up in my house. The weather is awful and both my kids have been sick since last Tuesday. Aside from two visits to my shrink . . ."

Jack and I are floundering, Peter. Characteristically, he calls this my problem and refuses to seek help for our shaky marriage. He treats my visits to Dr. Hirsch as an unnecessary indulgence and bitches every time he has to pay the bill.

". . . and one to the grocery store, I haven't set foot outside.

"I write this by way of introduction because you're probably wondering why, after all this time, I'm communicating with you. I don't know, put it down to temporary insanity brought on by cabin fever . . . I just have to be in contact with someone who knew me before my name was changed to Mommy.

"No, actually, I've been wanting to do this for years and years, and this isn't the first letter I've written to you. None of the others has been mailed, but I'm hoping I have the courage to mail this one."

Because, Peter, I seem to have lost my voice, my courage, and my autonomy here at home. Remember that strong, independent girl? I've folded into myself. You'd hardly recognize the person I've become.

"I feel like so much of my life has changed since we were together in Tucson . . . not only the outward trappings, but the inner me, too. I've just about lost touch with that flower child who was Caro Mills. I guess that's where you come in. I have this fantasy that you're living in some sort of time warp . . . that somewhere in this little town in North Dakota is Peter MacKinley as he was in 1967, and that, despite all the upheaval in my life, a part of me, the young, idealistic, hopeful part, is preserved, intact, with you. Maybe your life has changed, too, and you long for those more innocent days?

"Do you remember you used to say 'Pray for the hippies,' Peter? Do you still say it? Do you still pray?

"I don't know, maybe this is just my midlife crisis, or whatever people have when they turn thirty-ish . . . but I seem to remember all of us being so special, so unique. Where are the inhabitants of the Love House now? I'd like to think somebody's living in that dome you envisioned way back when, but it's not me. And in those ensuing years since last we met, I have had this uneasy feeling that I've gradually turned from an "us" to a "them," and it feels so weird, Peter. Sometimes I don't recognize myself.

"So, the reason for this rambling letter is . . . I'm not sure. Do I really want you to destroy my illusions? Do I really want to hear that you have a) a nine-to-five job, b) a wife . . ."

No, no, no, anything but that!

"c) three kids, d) a mortgage, e) life insurance, f) a station wagon, g) a paunch, h) creeping baldness, i) money anxieties, or j) all of the above?

"Somehow, I hope you've managed to hold on to the idealist I knew then . . . or at least a part of him . . .

"Yes, I *do* want to hear from you as you are now.

"As I am now,
Caro"

This letter, too, went into my bottom drawer, accompanied by a profound sadness. What if I'd chosen the wrong guy on that very last day when I could have had either?

CHAPTER
THIRTY-NINE

This is what I loved about being in therapy: Taking the train into the city by myself, without having to pack apple juice, snacks, diapers, wipes and toys; having a whole hour (well, fifty minutes, anyway) when the focus was on me, just me; and getting to eat a post-session cream cheese and walnut on date nut bread sandwich (without having to share it) at Chock full o'Nuts before taking the train home.

This is what I hated: Having the doorman of 26 East 63rd Street ask who I was coming to see when I entered the building every single damn week—you'd think he would have known by then; and I really hated those long pauses when I couldn't think of anything to say and Dr. Hirsch was quiet, except for an occasional "hmm mmm." Did they teach them that in psychiatrist school?

"What did you find attractive about Peter?"

"Um, I don't know . . . he was kind and gentle and he heard me . . ."

Kind of like you, Dr. H.

Another one of those interminable pauses which I guessed had gone on too long, because Dr. H. prompted: "And . . ."

I was stuck. What was so attractive about Peter? He wasn't handsome, like Jack. In fact, he was pretty ordinary looking. He was my intellectual equal, but Jack was also no slouch in that department. He had a spiritual life, for which I envied him, but not enough to take on Jesus as my savior. He liked the same books and music as me, but so did pretty much everyone else in our crowd. He was a brilliant director, but so were Orson Welles and Elia Kazan, and I didn't want to jump *their* bones. And we often knew what the other was thinking, although I wasn't always happy with what I had intuited.

"Caro?" Dr. H. was looking over his bifocals and staring right at me.

And then it dawned on me, and I couldn't say it. I couldn't fucking say it. I looked away.

More silence, but the doc was on to me. He knew that I knew. "Caro?"

"All right, all right! He was broken! Peter was broken and maybe I could fix him?" I reached for a Kleenex.

Okay, I've answered your $64,000 question. Can I go home now?

"Umm hum." And he was writing something down in that intrusive little black notebook of his. He was beginning to piss me off. But my fifty minutes weren't up yet.

"How was he broken, Caro?"

"Well," I sniffled, "I guess I thought because he was gay . . . But that wasn't it, was it?"

Maddeningly, he answered my question with one of his own.

"And was there anyone else you've ever tried to fix?"

"Anyone else? Not Jack, that's for sure. Oh . . . I get it. I get it. This is the part where if it's not one thing it's your mother, right?"

I wanted Dr. Hirsch to like me. I wanted him to laugh. Half the time, I felt myself trying to entertain him, so he'd think I was cute, and funny and smart and clever and endearing. So he'd love me? Oy, an approval seeker even with my shrink.

But he didn't laugh.

"Could you fix your mother, Caro?"

And suddenly I am six again: I am putting on a show for my parents. I have donned a tutu and my new pink ballet slippers, and my father has pushed the living room furniture back, rolled up the rug, and put the Mantovani record on the turntable (I'm not allowed to touch it) and I am leaping and twirling to *Swedish Rhapsody* and dancing my little heart out, but at the end, only my father is still in the room.

No, I couldn't make sad, broken Shulamith/Shelly whole again, although God knows I tried. I couldn't make her love me, either.

I started to sob.

"Caro," Dr. H. said gently, "it wasn't your job to fix your mother."

CHAPTER FORTY

"I think it started when the kids came along. Caro just didn't seem to have time for me anymore . . ."

"Talk to Caro, Jack," Dr. Hirsch interrupted. "Address Caro. Tell her how you feel."

Jack's chair was facing mine, but he had not looked at me once during the first forty minutes of our session. And then he did, though, flashing me one of his "now see what you've gotten us into" looks.

I felt for him. I really did. I knew it was my fault our marriage was deteriorating. I'd been talking to Dr. Hirsch about it once a week for the past six months, but this was Jack's first time. He finally agreed to this joint session when I hinted that Dr. Hirsch thought it might help our waning sex life.

"Jack?" Dr. Hirsch prompted.

Poor Jack. Now the lawyer had to take the stand. He loosened his tie and cleared his throat. This was not a man who was comfortable airing dirty linen or baring his soul.

"Um . . . Caro, I feel like when the babies were born, you spent all your time with them . . . I felt like you didn't need me anymore . . . that I was superfluous."

I could feel my face redden. Actually, Jack was right. After holding and touching and nursing those tiny beings all day, after giving and giving, being the sole source of life and comfort for those demanding baby mouths, hands, bodies, and psyches, I didn't want to be touched by anyone, especially not Jack. I needed time and space to myself, and Jack needed to get laid.

"Caro?"

"Well, yes, I can see why Jack . . . I mean why you would feel that way, Jack. I *was* busy with the kids. I still am. Sometimes they take so much out of me, that I just don't feel like there's anything left . . . not for you, not even for me . . ."

"Well, it looks like you need to make a conscious effort to make time for yourselves. You mentioned something about an anniversary, Caro, didn't you?"

"Yes, next Wednesday . . ."

"Well, that's perfect. This is what I suggest: Caro, you see if you can make arrangements for the children to spend the night somewhere else—with your in-laws, perhaps. And Jack, see if you can get home from the office a little early. Perhaps a bottle of champagne and a new negligee wouldn't be a bad idea, either.

"Ah, I see we've come to the end of the hour. I'll see you both next Friday. I'm sure you'll have a lot to talk about then."

Tears of rage filled my eyes. The good doctor had betrayed me. All those months of spilling my guts, revealing how my life was in shambles around my feet, and he was talking negligees and champagne and everything would be all right. Shit!

Jack was whistling and there was a bounce to his walk as we went down the hall to the elevator.

"You know, maybe there's something to this therapy after all. Dr. H. was pretty right-on in there."

I said nothing. Dr. H. sucked. This was band-aid bullshit. I vowed to find a woman therapist.

"What time did you tell the sitter we'd be home?"

"6:30. She's going to feed the kids and give them their baths."

"Great, then we have time."

"Time for what?"

"For you to go to Bloomingdale's and find that new negligee." He winked.

My outrage could no longer be contained.

"Oh, fuck, you don't honestly think that crap about the champagne and negligee is going to solve all our problems, do you? I mean, how simplistic can you get?"

He looked wounded.

"I thought it might be worth a try, sweetheart. I know you don't believe me, but I really do love you and the kids. I don't want to lose you. I'm willing to do anything to hold on to what we've got . . . to make it better. Look, you got me here today, didn't you? Let's try it, huh? I mean," he grinned wryly, "what have we got to lose—anything's better than this once-in-awhile-wham-bam-thank-you-ma'am that we call a sex life, isn't it?"

I sighed. "All right, I'll buy the negligee. But I don't think for a minute that it's going to work."

"It will if you want it to. Please, Caro?"

Dr. Hirsch's office was on 63rd and Madison. While Jack was trying to convince me of the merits of the doctor's advice, we had been walking south towards Bloomie's. Jack knew I'd give in.

"I have to get a couple of shirts. Why don't you head up to the lingerie department and find the sexiest nightie you can? I'll meet you at the Lexington Avenue entrance in a half hour, okay?"

I hadn't bought a sexy nightgown since the European honeymoon. Both of us used to sleep nude, but when the kids came along, I graduated to flannel granny gowns in the winter and oversize T-shirts in the summer. I didn't feel sexy enough to be buying a negligee. I was ten pounds overweight, and I had stretch marks. My thighs were a study in cellulite. What the fuck was I doing there?

Bloomie's lingerie department had certainly changed in the years since I purchased my trousseau. The choices then were white, pink, baby blue, or, if you wanted to be really risqué, black. But that evening, I felt like I'd walked into a Frederick's of

Hollywood catalog: Hot pink, electric blue, mauve, chartreuse, red, shimmery, satiny, slithery, sensual. I was reminded of that low-cut dance hall hostess dress I wore in that musical so many years ago, when a costume malfunction exposed my breast, and I wasn't even embarrassed.

When I met Jack twenty-five minutes later, my yellow bag held a hot pink teddy trimmed with black lace, a matching garter belt, black silk stockings, and pink mules. *You wanted sexy, Dr. Hirsch? All right, you got it.*

"Happy Anniversary."

"Oh, God, Jack, what are you doing home so early?"

I was running way behind schedule. It had taken me forty-five minutes to tear myself away from a clinging, weeping Greg, who didn't want to be left at Gamma's house without Mommy and Daddy. And Sarah, who would have been perfectly content if I hadn't come back for weeks, as long as Grandma plied her with M&M's, took her cue from her brother and chimed in, wailing as if her heart would break.

I was completely frazzled when I walked in the door. The last thing on my mind was sex. I wondered if I could return the teddy, garter belt, et al., and get some new pj's for the kids.

"C'mere baby, you look beat."

Jack was really trying. I saw that the champagne was chilling in the ice bucket, and he had brought home a small tin of caviar, as well. All I wanted to do was crawl into bed . . . alone.

"Why don't you go upstairs, take off all your clothes . . ."

"Jack . . ."

He held up his hand. ". . . And slip into the tub I've drawn for you. Then, when you're feeling nice and relaxed, slip into something . . . sexy, and join me in a glass of champagne. And by the way, I love you."

Tears welled up in my eyes. This was a Jack I hadn't seen in years. Perhaps there was method to Dr. H.'s madness after all.

I came downstairs a half hour later to newly-opened champagne and Johnny Mathis on the stereo. I felt a little silly in my new get-up, but the look on Jack's face was worth every penny of the $209 (therapy session included) it had cost me.

"Ooooh, c'mere you gorgeous lady, you. Where have you been hiding yourself, baby . . . and may I have this dance?"

Jack crooned along with Johnny as he took me in his arms. The dance didn't last very long, though. It had been so long since we'd made love to each other, really made love and meant it, that neither of us could bear to linger over the preliminaries. Jack followed me up the stairs. One of his hands clutched the champagne bottle; the other was stroking my garter-belted behind.

"God, woman, you have a gorgeous ass, you know that?"

We barely made it to the bed. It used to be like this . . . so hungry for each other that we made love on the floor, on chairs, in the shower, in his parents' swimming pool one midnight. This was the way it was supposed to be. How had we let it get away from us?

"God, you were wonderful tonight."

"No, my darling husband, *we* were wonderful tonight."

"Yeah," he giggled. "I'd like to propose a toast: To Dr. Hirsch."

He raised his full glass. Champagne sloshed over the rim onto the pillow. "Oops, made a mess." He giggled again.

I was not much of a drinker and had nursed one glass of champagne during the evening. Jack was about to finish the bottle.

"Fuck Dr. Hirsch. I propose a toast to *us*," I corrected him.

"I don't want you to fuck Dr. Hirsch—I only want you to fuck me, baby."

"And I only want you, darling. From the first day I met you, I've only wanted you. I don't know what's happened to me the last few years. I'm sorry I've made it so awful for you."

"No, I've made it awful for you, baby. I've made it awful for you. God, I'm such a shit . . ." All at once, Jack was weeping.

I knew he was drunk, but even so, it scared me. I'd never seen him like that.

"Jack, darling, you haven't done anything. It was me . . . but it's going to be better, you'll see."

He pulled away from me. He would not be consoled.

"No, no . . . look what my life has turned into . . . I've turned into some kind of money-grubbing power freak . . . I don't have any ideals left . . . I can't even remember the things I used to care about. Those things that were so important to us . . . what were they? Who was I? Who am I? How could you love someone like me?"

I was starting to feel a little dizzy. Jack was the one who was so sure of himself. I was supposed to be the one filled with self-doubt. He'd gotten the parts all mixed up.

I held his face in my hands. "Jack, for God's sake, listen. You're still the same man I fell in love with and married. The day I met you I thought you were the bravest, most principled man I'd ever seen. Do you remember that day? Do you remember the rally? Do you remember what you did?"

He pulled away again. "You don't know what I did . . ."

"Of course, I know. It was the most incredible thing. Joan Baez's husband—what was his name? Oh, yeah—David Harris—he was talking about taking a stand, going to jail if he had to, and the next thing anybody knew, you had pulled out your draft card and set it on fire. Then *all* the guys followed you and burned theirs. I think I fell in love with you right then and there. And when I found out later that you were a law student, and that act could have jeopardized your whole future, I was hooked. I could *never* stop loving that man."

He was very quiet for an uncomfortably long time, and when he finally spoke, I could barely hear him.

"You don't know the half of it."

"What?"

"I said, you don't know the half of it."

"What's that supposed to mean?"

"It means, goddammit, that I'm not that brave man you fell in love with . . . there was nothing brave about what I did . . ."

"How can you say that? The consequences . . ."

"There *were* no fucking consequences, Caro. My ass was covered . . . I put my fucking career above my principles. It was one big fat fucking lie. That was my fucking library card I burned."

"Oh, Jack, no . . . Honey, I think the champagne is getting to you. You're not used to drinking so much. You're not thinking very clearly . . ."

"I didn't burn my draft card, Caro. Shit, I was so fucking afraid of my old man and of breaking the law that I probably would have gone to 'Nam if they'd sent me. I was just lucky my number never came up, that's all."

He was shaking his head. "There's nothing brave about me. You married a fucking coward." He laughed bitterly.

"No I didn't. I love you, darling. It doesn't matter what you did or didn't do. It's all right," I lied. "I love you and everything's going to be all right."

I covered his face with kisses and then held him in my arms. I held him until I felt the tension leave his body. In a moment, he was snoring.

It was only then that I remembered the step I had left out of my pre-coital preparations, so taken was I with the new outfit and the anticipation of real intimacy, not to mention great sex. Caleb was born nine months and three days later.

CHAPTER
FORTY-ONE

It had been snowing for three Saturdays in a row, but that day it had warmed up considerably and was merely raining. Jack was away clinching a major real estate deal for a client in Denver. Greg had been home with a cold all week, but he was better. The four of us just had to get out of the house.

The afternoon before, the radio was on while I was ironing. I had just gotten the baby to sleep, Sarah was napping after preschool, Greg was in his room engrossed in building a Lego tower, and fifty-two American hostages had just been freed from Iran. Greg came downstairs just as the newscaster started to talk about deprivation and torture.

"What's that about?" I quickly flipped the dial, but he'd heard enough. "Mommy, what's that about? What are hostages?"

I explained, in language I hoped wouldn't be too frightening for a seven-year-old and said that everyone was glad they were safe and were tying yellow ribbons on trees to welcome them home.

Next thing I knew, Greg was running through the house, his arms full of ribbons (none of them yellow), strings and anything else that could be tied—the belt to my bathrobe and the dog's leash, for instance—yelling in his loudest outside voice, "Welcome to the hostages! Welcome to the hostages!"

Of course, he woke up Sarah, who never wanted to be left out of anything:

"Welcome to the hospital! Welcome to the hospital!" Also very, very loud.

And that, in turn, woke the baby from his abbreviated nap, he couldn't be consoled no matter what I tried, and that was my afternoon: welcome to my (mental) hospital.

So, that Saturday we were going out, lousy weather be damned.

When we lived in the city, before Sarah was born, rainy days never fazed me. If we couldn't go to the park, I just packed up my toddler, folded up his umbrella stroller, and took the bus to the Museum of Natural History. He loved it, and other New York mommies and I found this enclave a welcome change from the "don't touch" edict of most New York institutions.

"Greggy, do you remember when you were little and it rained in the city? I always used to take you to the museum with the dinosaurs? How would you guys like to do that today? We could drive in and have lunch in the cafeteria and see the whale and the animals and the pretty rocks . . ."

Sarah gasped. "*Real* dinosaurs, Mommy?"

"No, dummy head. There aren't any dinosaurs, everybody knows that. They just have their bones there, stupid." Greg, at seven, was the authority on everything.

"Greg, that's not nice. Sarah's only four. She hasn't learned about things like that, yet. Sarah, honey, the museum is a wonderful place. There are statues of animals and all kinds of things. And you can get a hot dog and chocolate milk in the cafeteria, if you like . . ."

"Can I have a straw?"

"Sure, you can have *two* straws. Why don't you go and get dressed? You can wear that new sweat suit Grandma and Grandpa bought you for Christmas." (Even though I knew the pink outfit would come home from our foray with chocolate milk—dribbled from two straws—down its front).

"Will they let Caleb in, too? Do they let babies go there?"

"Didn't you hear what Mom said? *I* used to go there when *I* was a baby." Greg turned to me. "Was I that dumb when I was four?"

"I'm four and three-quarters and I'm not dumb!" Sarah was dissolving into tears, and I was starting to talk through clenched teeth.

"Greg, Sarah is a very smart little girl. Sometimes I think she's smarter than you because she knows when to keep her mouth shut. Now, go get dressed while I change the baby. I want to be ready to go in 15 minutes so we can spend the whole day in the city."

"But I'll miss *Sesame Street* . . ." Sarah pouted.

"You can see *Sesame Street* every day, sweetie. C'mon, let's get going. You're such a big girl now, I'll bet you can get all dressed without my help, right?"

"But Mommy, it's Mr. Hooper's birthday, and Big Bird is giving him a surprise party, and I'm invited," she wailed.

"Mr. Hooper will have a birthday next year, and we can sing Happy Birthday to him when we have lunch today. Won't that be fun?"

"Can we have cake?"

"We could bring the cupcakes we made, Mom, and some candles. Then it could be a real birthday, Sarah, okay?"

"Oh, Greg, that's a wonderful idea. A birthday party at the museum. What a special day! You're such a good kid when you're not teasing your sister, you know? And I love you very much."

My firstborn beamed, but he wriggled out of my hug. "I saved my allowance, and I'm going to buy a magnifying glass at the museum store."

He knew the lay of the land: his class had taken a field trip to the museum last year.

"Okay, and yes, you can buy something, too, Sarah. Now, c'mon you two. If you dawdle much longer, the place will close before we have a chance to see anything."

"Uh, oh, Mom, look at Caleb!"

The baby, ignored up until now, had decided to grab the spotlight. It said on the package that the thing was baby-proof, but somehow, my one-year-old had managed to pry the spouted lid off his Tommee-Tippee cup and had given the dog a milk bath. Bruno's thick brown coat was spotted with white droplets. The children were shrieking with laughter. Caleb was banging the empty cup on the high chair, thrilled to be entertaining his siblings. The dog looked so surprised that I couldn't help but join in the gayety.

Greg eyed me curiously. "Aren't you mad at him, Mom? Look at the mess he made."

I wiped my eyes. "Oh, Greg, how can I be mad at him? He's just a baby. And he's so proud of himself for learning how to open that cup."

"Boy, I wish I was still a baby."

I'd left the stroller home. Not enough hands for two kids and a stroller, so Caleb was in the backpack. The rain had let up a little, and I'd found a parking space on Columbus Avenue, only three blocks from the museum. My spirits were high, as were those of the kids. I wasn't sure why I didn't do this kind of thing more often. Lethargy, probably. Sometimes just getting up in the morning was overwhelming.

The museum was a great success, but after fifteen minutes in the cafeteria line (half the mothers in New York had had the same idea I did), forty minutes for lunch and Mr. Hooper's birthday party, a half hour in the gift shop, and, almost as an afterthought, a half hour checking out the dinosaurs, I needed some fresh air and I didn't want to push my luck that one, two, or three of them were on the precipice of a meltdown. Surely the rain had stopped by now.

It had! There were a few lingering puddles on the sidewalk, which Greg and Sarah happily splashed in. Caleb strained to get out of the confines of the backpack. It wouldn't be long before he, too, would be soaking his pants from the outside instead of the inside.

"Wow! Mom! Look at this!"

Greg's attention had been grabbed by a fabulous display of fantasy creatures in the window of a boutique called Mythology. I wasn't sure who or what the shop catered to. When Jack and I had moved from the Upper West Side to the 'burbs, the avenue was beginning to transform itself. Shoe repair shops and mom-and-pop markets were giving way to purveyors of snakeskin boots and Häagen-Dazs. And now, a store that sold myths. What next?

"Mommy, could we go in? Please? I want to see the unicorns. Pleeease, Mommy?" Sarah's eyes were wide.

Even the baby was reaching yearningly over my head toward the window.

"All right, kids, but just to look. The things in there are very expensive. This really isn't a store for children . . . more like toys for grown-ups. So, don't touch anything, okay?"

A bell chimed as we entered, but the proprietor was not so welcoming. He took one look at me and grimaced. I guess I really couldn't blame him. Greg and Sarah were so overwhelmed by their phantasmagorical surroundings that they had forgotten my warnings about not touching, and the baby was pulling my hair with one hand and batting a soft-sculpture mobile of the planets with the other. There was one other customer in the shop, a long-haired man who was looking at greeting cards. I looked at the floor, desperately trying to think of a way to get the troops out of there without a scene.

"Don't touch that, little boy!" barked the man behind the counter.

Greg, who had been shaking a plastic paperweight to see the snow come down on the scene encased within, was startled by the anger in the man's voice. He dropped the paperweight, which, fortunately, did not break. Sarah gasped, and ran to hide behind me, and even Caleb had stopped his batting game, baby fist raised in mid-air like a diminutive prize fighter.

"That's not a little boy, that's an aboriginal Pygmy! He's never been to this country before and he's never seen snow."

The store's other customer was making these pronouncements.

"What kind of welcome is that to give a first-time visitor to these shores? What kind of stories do you want him to take back to his tribesmen? They practice voodoo, you know. Do you want him to put a curse on Columbus Avenue and all its inhabitants, especially nasty shop owners? Are you crazy, man? Prostrate yourself before him and beg his forgiveness before his curses bring a reign of terror to the whole city. Beg his forgiveness, beg his forgiveness. Hurry, hurry!"

Greg and Sarah's mouths hung open in astonishment. They were not used to the Upper West Side crazies, but I remembered them. They used to dog my steps wherever I went—to the grocery store, the park, the dentist, the library. I used to think they were talking to me, but then I would see their vacant stares and realize that I didn't even exist for them.

This one sounded a little familiar. Was he perhaps one of those homeless guys who was parked on a bench on the island in the middle of Broadway? The one who used to curse me as I made my way home from D'Agostino's, pushing a stroller full of groceries, with a baby balanced on my hip?

But, no, the voice was somehow *too* familiar, and the story too outrageous. Could this be someone I knew?

Oh, my God, I knew who it was! It was the person who once tried to talk his way into the women's dressing room at the El Con mall in Tucson.

"Ernesto? I can't believe it! It *is* you, isn't it?"

Of course it was. The moustache had been shaved, the face was a little rounder and the body a little softer, and there was a diamond stud in his right ear lobe, but it was definitely, unmistakably Ernesto.

The children looked shaken. Not only did some crazy man say the strangest things about them, but Mommy actually knew this weirdo and seemed happy to see him.

"Caro? My God, I thought it might be you . . ."

"You *thought* it might be me . . . only *thought* . . . and you said those loony things anyway?"

"Sure, nobody pays attention to crazies in this town. But, wow, kiddo, you sure have changed. You look *fabulous*! I mean, not that you didn't look great before, but now . . ."

He shook his head in disbelief. "And these wonderful creatures, are they yours?"

"Mine? Don't be ridiculous. I just have this thing about carrying baby Pygmies around on my back. I especially love it when they drool in my hair."

Caleb was doing just that, and the drool was running down my cheek. I disengaged my hand from Sarah's so I could wipe my face. She gave Greg a frightened look and moved closer to her big brother. If Mom wasn't going to protect her, maybe he would.

"Of course they belong to me. Guys, I want you to meet an old friend of mine. Greg, Sarah, and Caleb, this is Ernesto. We went to school together a long time ago."

"A *very* long time ago. Greg, Sarah, and Caleb, I'm delighted to meet you. And Greg, I was only kidding about all that stuff I said before. I know you're a kid, not a Pygmy. Hey, do you little guys like ice cream? How would you like to get some? What do you say, Mom? Baskin-Robbins Jamoca Almond Fudge still your favorite?"

"God, you still remember that? No, I'm afraid not. Baskin-Robbins ain't what it used to be."

"Isn't, Mommy. You said 'ain't' wasn't a word."

"You're right, Greg. Well, I don't know about the rest of you, but I'm up for some ice cream."

"There's a Häagen-Dazs just a couple of blocks from here. Let's go, kids. Caro, I can carry the baby on my back. He looks awfully heavy for you."

"No, thanks, though. It's okay. I'm used to it. You develop a strong back this way. Anyway, he's at an age where he's not too happy about strangers."

"Hey, little fella, I'm not a stranger. I'm a friend of your mom's." He offered a finger to Caleb, but the baby turned away.

"I told you. But don't take it personally. It's the age: he's just realizing he's a separate person from me."

Ernesto shrugged. "No problem."

We set the back carrier, which turned into a seat, on the black and white tile floor of the ice cream parlor. I ordered vanilla, because I knew Caleb would consume most of mine.

"From Jamoca Almond Fudge to vanilla? That *is* a radical change, my dear," Ernesto mocked. "So tell me, what have you been doing—I mean besides having babies? Doing any writing? I heard you had the assistantship in playwriting."

"How did you know that? You were long gone by then."

He winked. "The grapevine, kiddo, the grapevine."

I sighed. "No, no writing, not unless you count grocery lists and memos headed 'Things I Have to Do Today: fold laundry, pick up cleaning, buy Cheerios, call diaper service . . . and recently, this little monthly newspaper column I write about the joys of suburban life . . . "

"That bad, huh?"

"Yeah, I haven't even written any letters to anyone the past couple of years. I've lost track of just about everyone . . ."

"Even Peter?"

I nodded toward the children and shook my head almost imperceptibly. They were oblivious, though. Ernesto, over my protests, had treated them to sundaes. Sarah's sweatshirt now had hot fudge as well as chocolate milk all over it.

"That was another lifetime ago. My world is so different now."

"Mmmm, I see that."

I had to steer the conversation in another direction.

"What about you, Ernesto? What are you doing? Any acting?"

"Yeah, well, I had a soap, but they killed off my character after the third episode. And I've done the usual. You know: trade shows, children's theater, and summer stock. Right now, I'm between jobs—going to auditions in the daytime and waiting tables at night. My mother still wants to know when I'm going to get a *real* job, like be a lawyer or something." He laughed. "So, what does your husband do?"

"He's a lawyer," I shrugged.

"Oh, that's nice. And you live . . . where? Let me guess: Scarsdale? Great Neck? Westport? Please tell me you don't live in New Jersey."

"You got it on the third try. Ugh, does it really show? Can you read 'suburban mom' all over me?"

"There, there, Caro, it's not as bad as all that. We'd have a house in the suburbs, too, if we could afford it."

I raised my eyebrows. "We?"

"Just how enlightened *are* these children?"

"Not much . . ."

"Right. Okay, yes, I have a . . . uh . . . a friend. We've been . . . friends for almost three years. My friend designs window displays for Bloomie's. You'd like my friend, kiddo . . . Hey, you want to hear something that'll blow your mind? Scott's married!"

"Married? You mean *married* married or 'married?'" I made quotation marks with my fingers.

"No, I mean *really* married. That summer after graduation, he went back to Chicago to work in his father's bookstore. His dad had had a minor stroke and needed Scott to look after things for a while. We had already decided that, you know, what we had wasn't a forever thing, and I wanted to split for New York and, well, Scott was thinking that he might be a switch hitter . . ."

That was news to me. The water I was drinking went down the wrong way and Ernesto had to pound me on the back. Greg and Sarah looked up, startled, but when they saw I was alright, went back to arguing about who had more hot fudge. The baby just demanded that I continue spooning vanilla ice cream into his waiting mouth.

"Greg, Sarah, you both got the same amount of sauce. If you can't stop bickering, I'll have to take the ice cream away."

"You okay?"

"Sure."

"Okay, so, anyway, he went home and he met this girl . . . she worked in the store. And they found they shared a passion for opera, and then they found they shared a passion for each other. They've been married for eight years, and they have two little girls. His father died a couple of years ago, so now he owns the bookshop. They came to visit last year when they were in town for a booksellers' convention."

"You mean, he told her?"

"Oh, yeah, he told her everything before they got married, and it was okay. He seems very happy . . ."

"Oh, my God, look at the time . . . and look at the kids!"

The three of them looked like they had bathed in ice cream, and the older two in chocolate sauce, as well.

"I'd love to stay longer, but I have to get these three home and into the bathtub. Jack's due home tonight and I've got so much to do . . ."

"Are you happy, little mother?"

"What? Of course I'm happy. Why?"

"I don't know. Something about the look on your face when I mentioned Peter . . . and your sudden urge to get home when I told you about Scott's marriage. There's still something there, isn't there?"

I was aghast to find tears welling up in my eyes. I had thought I had all that under control and well hidden, to be summoned up only when I knew I was truly alone.

"I got a letter from him about a year ago," he said quietly.

"A letter? From Peter? How did he know where to find you?"

"He knew I'd come to New York and I guess he just called up information for my number. Anybody could do that. Even you could have looked me up if you'd wanted to, old girl."

"I'm sorry. Actually, I did look you up one day a few years ago. And I did almost call. But something stopped me. I guess some things are better left as they were, you know?"

"Do you want to know what was in the letter?"

I'd managed to compose myself and was busy wiping the children's faces.

"I didn't want to know what was in that other letter, and I don't think I want to know about this one, either."

"But you read that first one, remember? I feel sorry for him, Caro. Remember I told you that he could never be happy until he accepted who he was?"

I nodded.

"Well, he still hasn't dealt with it. He's still living in the closet in that little town in North Dakota. No one there knows . . . Don't you think that's odd?"

"No, I don't think so. He's a very private person."

"I don't know . . . I don't think you can go through your whole life living a lie. Something's going to snap one of these days . . . he's gotta come out one of these days . . ."

"I'm sorry, I've got to get home. Kids, thank Ernesto for the ice cream and get your raincoats on."

"Yeah, well, I have to get home, too. It was nice meeting you, kids. I hope I'll see you again, Caro. This was almost like old times."

He walked us to the car and watched, bemused, as I buckled all three of them into the back seat.

"You've got it down to a science, haven't you?"

"I have to. We do what we have to do."

He kissed my cheek. "I'm glad we ran into each other, kid. See you."

"Me, too. See you."

Caleb fell asleep as soon as we hit traffic, and Sarah and Greg were quiet, too. I was almost lulled into believing that we would get home without any questions, but I was wrong.

"Mommy, was that man a boy or a girl?"

"What, Sarah?"

"I said, was that man a boy or a girl? He looked like a boy, but he was wearing earrings, Mommy."

"One earring, honey. Some men wear one earring. I'm not sure why, but it's a new style."

"Mom, who's Peter?"

That's the question I was really afraid of, but I was prepared. "Oh, Peter was someone Ernesto and I went to school with. A friend, Greg. When I went to college, there were a lot of us who were friends. We went to classes together and parties and stuff like that. You know, like you and Mikey and Jeremy and Richard. Friends."

"Oh, yeah." The answer seemed to satisfy him and I breathed a sigh of relief. But I was not yet off the hook.

"Mommy," he asked, "is Ernesto a faggot?"

CHAPTER FORTY-TWO

S omewhere roundabout the flat middle of the country—Wisconsin, maybe—I get cold feet, as my family comes unbidden into my consciousness. I try to focus on Peter, and what I hope is waiting for me in North Dakota, but there they are: Greg, Sarah, Caleb, and Jack. It's the reverse of what it used to be, when Peter would surprise me late at night while I circled the wagons to keep him at bay, but knowing, at the same time, that he would find egress, and that I wouldn't mind.

But this time, I do.

"Go away," I beg them. "I am so very, very sorry, but I have to get away and you can't come with me." But they don't listen.

It's a Saturday, and, miracle of miracles, we have nothing on the schedule, absolutely nothing. No school, no office, no Cub Scouts, no ballet lessons, no dentist or doctor's appointments, no bike-a-thons, walk-a-thons, no guests to cook dinner for. Jack has gotten up to change the baby. He brings our third-born to my breast, and then settles back in next to me. We smile at each other above Caleb's bald baby head, silently congratulating ourselves for once more creating a perfect tiny being. A cuddly little Sarah in footie pajamas crawls into our bed, and then a sweet, sleepy-eyed Greg snuggles in between Jack and me. Caleb has finished his breakfast and is safe in the crook of his father's arm. Our hasty, on-the-fly, run-out-the-door weekday hugs and kisses can be prolonged, and they are. We spend the next half-hour trying to find an un-ticklish spot on Greg (and discover two, the tip of his nose and the top of his head) and counting Sarah's freckles. And Caleb, half-asleep and sated, starts to smile. Is it gas, or is he intuiting that he has had the good sense to be born into this perfect, happy family? Whatever it is, it's delicious.

Tears are rolling down my cheeks, and I have to pull over to the side of the road. "Go away," I tell the actors in this idealized family drama. "It didn't stay that way. Maybe that's what it was like for only a day, a morning. Your Dad and I fucked it up. It's not like that anymore, and I can't bring it back. You have to let me go now."

Even so, I am tempted to turn around, but I cast a sober mind's eye on what would actually await me at home. It is so far removed from the lovely, ephemeral scene I have conjured up, that I am once more resolved. I have driven so far, and I am just a couple of days from the finish line. The car continues west.

CHAPTER
FORTY-THREE

*N*ow it is my turn to surprise Peter, my turn to show up, unannounced, on his doorstep.

*Shock, disbelief, then unalloyed delight register on his face. Oh,
how I remember that face. It has not changed much in twenty years,
although the beard is gone and the hair is thinner . . . but the eyes
are the same, and so is the boyish grin.*

*Neither of us can speak at first, but in a moment, I am folded
in his arms.*

*"Oh, my God," he murmurs into my hair, "I knew some day
you'd come back to me . . . I felt it . . ."*

*"Then you're not angry . . . I mean that I didn't call or anything?
I know this must seem so strange after all these years . . ."*

*"Well," he teases, "It took you long enough." He holds me closer.
"But strange, no. How can it be strange? We've been spiritually
linked forever, Caro, and through all the years and over all the miles,
I've still felt close to you. There were times, many times over the past
few years, when I've actually felt your physical presence here . . ."*

*He pulls back and looks at me quizzically for a moment, and
then he goes on: ". . . And I can tell by the expression on your face
that you've felt it, too, haven't you?"*

I nod, afraid to speak, afraid that if I say one word, the spell will be broken.

"Well, do we want to give the neighbors something to gossip about, or are you going to come in? And how about a suitcase? You are planning on staying a while, aren't you?" He grins again.

"Oh, yes, of course I want to stay . . ."

"Good. Let me get your bag."

He is off to the car and back in a second. I follow him into the house. It is exactly as I remember it, but I don't want to remember it . . . don't want to remember the last time I was here. I want to start fresh in new territory. The place has such rotten memories, and I am experiencing such a whirl of emotions: Joy at being with Peter, relief that Edna is not here, remorse for feeling such relief, guilt about my children, fear that Peter might once again reject my advances, for if nothing else, I am here to make advances.

"How about some coffee, love? Hey, you look as if you were a thousand miles away . . . and that's not right, is it, considering you just got here . . ."

"Oh, I'm sorry. Yes, I'd love some coffee. I'm sorry, I was just thinking . . ."

"Thinking about the people you've left? It's not just one person, is it, Caro? There are children, aren't there?"

There is such love, and understanding, and caring in his voice, I can no longer hold back the tears.

He leads me to the couch and puts his arm around me.

"It's all right, love. It's all right." He hands me his handkerchief. "For someone whose tear ducts are as leaky as yours, you'd think by now you'd learn to carry a handkerchief. There, blow your nose like a good girl and dry those tears."

I do as I'm told and suddenly, there is no one else, no one in the whole world except the two of us. Nothing outside of this room, this moment, exists.

I reach for his hand. He takes mine, raises it to his lips, and kisses the palm, then the fingertips, and then his lips are on mine . . .

not the lips I remember . . . not that dry, brief graze of flesh, not lips hardly touching. These lips are moist, insistent. His tongue is playing against my lips, gently, gently parting them and finding no resistance.

Our embrace becomes more intense. "Oh, Caro, my darling girl, oh God, how I want you. Please, please help me . . ."

"Baby, you know how much I want you . . . how much I've wanted you for so long. How can I help you? Tell me how I can help?"

He leans out of my embrace and puts his head in his hands.

Oh, dear God, I've blown it again. What have I done now to make him pull away from me?

I put a tentative hand on his shoulder. When he does not reject my touch, I begin to stroke his back . . . gently, as if he were a child who, awakening feverish in the night, needed to be soothed back to sleep.

"It's all right, darling, whatever you want me to do. I'm here for you. What do you want?"

He raises his head. His eyes are bright with tears.

"Oh, Caro, I want so much to be a good lover for you. I want so much to make you happy. You've waited so long . . . It's just . . . just that . . ."

He takes a deep breath and then blurts it out: "I still haven't made love to a woman. Isn't that a joke—a forty-three-year-old virgin? Will you help me? Will you teach me, please?"

Can anything be more sweet than this? I'm to be his first. I cannot speak . . . can only kiss his eyes, his cheeks, his lips . . . gently, oh so gently. I don't want to frighten him away, not now, now when it is all so close.

"Oh, my darling, my love. Of course, I'll teach you. And you'll teach me. We have so much to learn about each other, darling. Don't worry . . . we'll go carefully and gently and slowly. I don't want to rush anything. I just want us to be happy."

Wordlessly, he rises and takes my hand. He leads me down the hall to his bedroom. I am surprised, but not too surprised, to see a double bed instead of his single one.

"I guess I've been expecting you," he grins shyly. "It was my parents' bed, and, don't worry, I've never shared it with anyone. It's true that I've never made love to a woman, but I haven't been with men . . . not since those few times in college. Darling, I haven't been with anyone . . ."

We are facing each other, gazing into each other's eyes. I am so used to looking up to meet my husband's eyes, I have forgotten that Peter is just about my height. There is something so comfortable about that. I can't help smiling, and now Peter is smiling, too, and taking me in his arms again.

Our tongues gently explore each other's mouths, while his hands move slowly down from my neck to my breasts. He moves his hands beneath them, cupping them, then stroking, now gently squeezing.

"Oh, God, your breasts . . . they feel so wonderful. Let me see them, Caro . . . I want to see your breasts."

He unbuttons my blouse and slips it off my shoulders.

"Oh, God, what a beautiful body you have."

He fumbles briefly with my bra hook, and then my breasts are unfettered. He gasps and bends down to lovingly kiss each nipple, then buries his face between them.

"Behold, thou art fair, my love. Behold thou art fair. Thy two breasts are like two fawns that are twins of a gazelle, which feed among the lilies . . ."

"Rise up, my love, my fair one . . ."

Now I unbutton his shirt. I play with the hair on his chest and kiss his nipples, his shoulders, his neck, his ears. Then my tongue finds his again, my breasts against his bare chest.

I take momentary leave of my lover's embrace and step out of my skirt and sandals. He follows my lead, kicks off his shoes, unbuckles his belt, and takes off his jeans.

I stand before him in my panties, suddenly shy and not quite willing to part with the last bit of clothing that comes between my lover and me. But his hands find my silken behind, and he strokes me until I want nothing more than to be rid of that barrier. Gently, *and oh so slowly, he slips off my panties and then steps back to look at his prize.*

"Oh, baby, you're more beautiful than I ever dreamed you would be," he breathes, and I know he is not lying. I know he sees beyond the stretch marks and the crow's feet and the dimpled thighs. I know he loves me.

And now, he too, has removed the last of his clothes, but I see that his body does not want me . . . not quite yet. But it will.

"Are you afraid, Peter?"

He winces, "It shows, doesn't it?" and looks down at his sleeping cock.

"Don't be afraid, darling. I can't hurt you. I love you."

"I know that, Caro, and I love you. I guess I've dreamed of this moment so long, and now it's here . . ." he laughs, ruefully. "And I'm not sure what to do next . . ."

"Tell me what you've dreamed, darling."

"Tell you?"

"Yes. What did you do first?"

"Well . . . I . . . I led you over to the bed and pulled the covers down . . ."

"Show me."

He takes my hand and we cross to the bed.

"And then what?"

"We sat next to each other on the bed and I kissed you . . ."

"Show me."

He does. His tongue plays with mine and he is moaning. I sink to the pillow and reach for his penis, which responds at once to my caresses.

"And what happened next in your dream, Peter? Did this happen?"

I pull him down on top of me. I am ready . . . more than ready. I have been waiting over twenty years for this to happen.

"I am my beloved's and his desire is towards me . . ." my murmur turns into a moan.

"Yes, oh yes. . ." he moans, too, as I guide him into me, as our bodies move in tandem . . . I am so close . . . so close . . .

He is breathing hard. "Caro, oh Caro . . . I love you . . . I've always loved you . . ."

"Oh, Peter . . . oh God, yes yes YES . . . NOW . . . NOW!"

There is no reason to hold back, and soon, deep inside me, where he belongs, Peter has finally, finally found himself.

But then we are in his living room and Peter is lying on his side on a yoga mat, his chin propped on his fist, and I am standing in front of an easel and trying to paint him, but that paint-by-numbers guy is on TV, telling me I'm doing it all wrong because I don't have the right colors.

I wake up with my pillow wet with tears. I don't remember if I'm in the Holiday Inn near Youngstown or the Travel Lodge in Rockford. The rooms are all the same, and the drive ahead seems endless.

CHAPTER

FORTY-FOUR

If this were one of those "find yourself" journeys, I might be headed for Big Sur to some whacko self-actualization seminar where you sit for days on hard chairs in a room with a hundred strangers, they take away your wristwatches, give you one meal break between 9 a.m. and midnight (and who knows when they let you pee?) and some guy named Werner harangues you to free yourself from your past. Or, more likely, my find-myself-road-trip would meander over back roads and I might stop to see Iowa's Largest Frying Pan, or Wall Drug, or the World's Largest Ball of Twine (in Cawker City, Kansas). I would take time to write in a journal, or meditate, or interact with complete strangers, and the serendipitous encounters would change my life. But I think I might be afraid to find myself (what if it turns out there's no one all that interesting in there?), and the only person I want to interact with is Peter, who was never a stranger from almost the first moment I saw him. I want to get from Point A to Point B as quickly as possible. No detours, no scenic lookouts, no tourist attractions, bizarre or otherwise. Just a straight shot on the interstate into Peter's arms. And then he can find *me* and we will both be saved.

But the car has other ideas. This morning it started sounding like a jet plane about to leave the runway. I chalked it up to road noise, until I saw pristine yellow lines and smelled newly poured asphalt. I pulled off at the next rest stop to consult the owner's manual (which Jack, bless him, insisted I keep in the glove compartment, even though he schedules all the maintenance for the cars). So, based on the kind of noise it is, the manual tells me that it might be the muffler, but it also might be a wheel bearing, depending on where the noise is coming from, and I can't tell. I consult the yellow pages in the phone booth and find one garage in the town at the next exit: Walter's Fixit. Doesn't sound promising. Have they ever even seen a Subaru? But beggars can't be choosers, and I'm not going to drive any more than I have to with that unsettling roar getting louder and louder. I wish I could call Jack. He would know what to do. But it's time for me to put on my big girl panties (as I used to tell Sarah when I was trying to get her to use the potty) and do this on my own.

But I just know that Mr. Fixit is going to take one look at me, a woman traveling alone in a foreign car with out of state plates, and the cash register in his head is going to go *ka-ching, ka-ching*. I go back to the manual: Muffler seems too obvious, like the first thing the blondie who is a complete ignoramus about cars might guess. So, I'm going with wheel bearing (plus, on second hearing, it sounds like it's coming from the front passenger side and I don't think that's where the muffler lives) because it makes me sound more knowledgeable and maybe Walter Fixit won't cheat me quite as much. I pray that Jack hasn't cancelled the credit card and then make the call. The woman who answers the phone tells me to bring the car right in.

"Mom, '86 Subaru's here."

The freckled red-head at the front desk, who looks to be about sixteen, calls into the garage.

She's probably covering while her mother, the receptionist, has gone to the bathroom.

But "Mom" turns out to be a strawberry blonde, equally freckled woman about my age who is wiping her hands on a grease-stained rag.

"Hi, I'm Carolyn Tanner. I called a few minutes ago. Not sure what's wrong with my car. I think it might be a wheel bearing. Could I talk to the mechanic before he looks at it?"

She raises one eyebrow, then sighs as if she'd expected better from me.

"Well, I'm the mechanic, but don't feel bad, everyone makes that mistake at first."

I'm flustered. My kids have been raised to believe that girls can grow up to be anything. Their pediatrician is a woman, and so is their dentist. I just never pictured a mechanic.

"But Walter? Is your name Walter?"

She laughs. "No, it's Kate. Walter's my dad. This used to be his shop and when I took over, I didn't want to change the name. It's been Walter's Fixit forever, that's what everyone's used to. Plus, it makes my dad happy. Look, don't worry. I know what I'm doing. I've been hanging out in this garage since before I could walk, and fixing cars since third grade. I have a degree in mechanical engineering and spent five miserable years working in the corporate sector until I realized that what I was best at, all I really wanted to do, all that really made me happy, was sticking my head under the hood of a car, listening for what was wrong, and then making it right again. And my daughters, both of them, are following in my footsteps. So, yeah, girls can be motorheads, too. My credentials okay with you?"

I blush. Her credentials are impeccable. My feminist credentials? Not so much.

She reads my mind. "So, wheel bearing, huh? Let's take a look and see if you're right. Want to see what we're talking about?"

Now it's my turn to raise an eyebrow.

"Look, I can tell that you probably opened the manual—kudos to you for having one, though—read about what could cause a roaring noise, and took a guess. I'll bet your alternative was muffler, right? You don't even know what a wheel bearing does, do you?"

I blush again, bite my lip and shake my head.

"So, wouldn't you feel better if, every time you brought your car in, you actually knew what went on inside the engine? And didn't feel like the mechanic would take advantage of your ignorance and charge you an arm and a leg?" She says all this while looking under the hood.

"Mom, are you trying to push your classes again? She doesn't even live around here."

Turns out, Kate can not only do, she can teach, too. Once a month, she gives a free basic two-session car repair workshop, for women only, and it just so happens that the class is tonight and tomorrow night.

"Well, it sounds like that would be a really useful thing to do, but I'm in kind of a hurry to get to North Dakota and I'd like to be out of here this afternoon and . . ." I babble and then catch myself. Kate seems like a friendly, chatty person and I don't really want to start having to answer questions about why I'm in such a hurry.

Meanwhile, the car has been up on the lift, and Kate is under it.

"Hey, lucky guess, it's your right wheel bearing. I can fix it, but fortunately or unfortunately, you're gonna have to stick around a few days. We don't get many Subarus in these parts . . ."

She sees my look of alarm and clucks reassuringly. "I know how to fix it, sister. It's just that I have to order the bearing from the nearest dealer in St. Paul. It's going to take a couple of days, so, looks like you can take that workshop after all. I highly recommend it. And it has the Gloria Steinem seal of approval," she winks.

Two days later, I am on my way again. I have a new wheel bearing and I know what the fuel injection does, how to change the oil, spark plugs, and battery, replace the windshield wipers and air filter, and fix a flat. I feel changed in some way I don't have a name for, and I am inexplicably happy.

CHAPTER

FORTY-FIVE

B ut when it comes to the unknown, I'm kind of a glass half-empty girl. My elation is short-lived. It lasts about an hour after I drive off from Walter's Fixit. And then trepidation takes its place, and I can't shake it for the rest of the day.

It's late Friday afternoon but the sun is still beating down on geometrically-aligned cornfields. I'm a few hours east of Hastings, and the corn is knee-high, the way it would be back home in Glenbury. Funny, I haven't thought of Glenbury as "back home" in a long time. I'm not sure what back home is anymore—not Westport, Connecticut, that's for sure. Could I be at home in a place like this? Yes. Yes, I could. I could be at home anywhere with Peter. I know that. Will he know that, too?

Beads of perspiration stud my upper lip and sweat rolls down my back, in spite of the air conditioning. I stop at a diner to bide my time a bit, hoping the courage to make the call will be forthcoming.

There are no other customers, at this off-time between lunch and dinner. The lone, middle-aged waitress, who resembles Nancy Walker of TV-commercial fame, eyes me curiously. I half expect her to hand me a Bounty paper towel ("the quicker picker upper") to wipe my brow, but she says nothing as she escorts me to a booth toward the back. I slide onto the seat and see that the red Naugahyde banquette is ripped and the Formica table is marred by cigarette burns. I reflexively wrinkle my nose and then turn my head away from her. I hope she hasn't noticed.

She has, and slaps the menu down on the table. Maybe I'd better re-think the Nancy Walker thing.

"I'll have an iced tea, please." And then I feel bad that I've inadvertently insulted her, so I order a donut as well, even though I know I won't eat it.

I'm so tired. I lean my head back, but then sit upright when I think about the ice cream-sticky toddler fingerprints or worse that might be covering the banquette. I look out the window and spy a phonebooth outside the Texaco station across the street. Good. I don't want to use the pay phone in the diner. The waitress already hates me.

I sip the tea slowly and start to think about what might be awaiting me at the end of this pilgrimage. As I crumble the donut so it looks like I've eaten it, this movie starts to play in my head:

The door to the phone booth is closed. I open it and step into a steam bath. My hands are so wet, I can barely dial his number. I wish I'd used the ladies' room—I'm beginning to feel my old familiar symptoms of stage fright. Too late now. The phone is ringing. I pray he's home . . . I pray he isn't home. What am I going to say to him after all these years? I will my hand to hang up the receiver, but it is paralyzed.

"Hello?"

It's a male voice, not unlike a young Peter's, but it is not Peter. (I'd cast that actor who played Fredo Corleone in The Godfather, but with a mid-Western accent. I can't remember his name, but I think he and Meryl Streep were lovers).

"Umm . . . is Peter MacKinley there?" Perhaps I've dialed the wrong number.

"No, Pete's not back from work yet . . . should be back in about an hour."

Pete. No one had ever called him Pete. When had he turned into a Pete? And who was answering his phone?

"Um . . . is Mrs. MacKinley there?" *Why I asked to talk to the Spider Woman, I don't know, but in my rising panic, it was all I could think of.*

"Nooo . . ." *The voice is puzzled now.* "Edna passed on about two years ago. Are you a friend of Pete's?"

"Yes . . . an old friend . . . from college. I was passing through town and um . . . will you . . . um . . . will you be seeing him?"

The man with the Fredo Corleone actor's voice laughs. "Sure. We live together. I'm his roommate. What's your name? Are you going to be in town long?"

"Uh . . . I don't know . . . I . . ."

"Say, is this Caro? It is, isn't it? Pete's told me so much about you, I feel as if I know you. Where are you staying? I'll have him call you the minute he gets in . . . Or better still, why don't you come by the house now and surprise him? We'd love to have you stay for dinner."

That proprietary "we" has brought me to my senses. I hang up the receiver.

And now I know what I have to do and in which direction I have to go. There is one more call to be made. My hands are shaking, but I could dial this number in my sleep. It rings three times and then I hear my own voice:

"Hi, you've reached the Tanners. No one can come to the phone right now. If you have a message for Jack, Caro, Greg, Sarah, or Caleb, please leave your name and number after the beep. Thanks, and have a great day."

"Jack, I can't come home the way things are. I'm so sorry, but there was no other choice. I was drowning, Jack, I was disappearing. I don't even know who I am anymore. Jack's Wife. Greg, Sarah, and Caleb's Mom. I don't even have a name; my identity is dependent on all the rest of you. Would anyone looking at me know I was once the pride of the drama department, with an assistantship, and the author of a prize-winning play that got national attention, before

I even graduated? I know it wasn't your fault that I couldn't write anymore, but I wanted it so much, and then it just got lost, like I'd put it in a box in the back of the closet and never opened it again. And then I put all the rest of me in that box, too, and then sealed it with duct tape. That kooky free spirit that you said you fell in love with . . . And now you try to squelch that spirit whenever it comes out. Who cares if I want to wear my old sandals to the grocery store? Who cares if I have a Jewish nose and frizzy hair and I'm a pound or three or even five over my perfect weight, whatever perfect is. I can't be perfect for you. Sometimes I just want to be messy, with my emotions hanging right out there, you know? You tried to change everything about me, Jack. Not just the way I looked, but my whole identity, the way I thought and the way I behaved, like I was one of the children. And the pathetic thing is, I let you. I am complicit in my own erasure. I thought you wouldn't love me if I stayed true to myself. I want to be her again, not a perfectly put together extension of you and the kids. Why was I good enough for you then?

"*Maybe if I find Peter, I can find me again. I want away from our lifestyle, Jack. I never want to set foot in that goddamned country club again. I don't want to be a slave to those damn Jane Fonda tapes you got me. Real women don't look like Jane Fonda and what kind of anniversary present is that, anyway? I don't want to have your parents telling us everything we're doing wrong with the kids. I want to be spontaneous; I want us to have adventures and I want you to be my partner, not my Henry Higgins. I want to color outside the lines.*

"*If I come home, things have to be so, so different. I can't go back to the way it was, because, Jack, now I know how to change the spark plugs and the tires . . .*"

"Anything else?"

The waitress stands over me, poised with a pencil and my bill, and suddenly the movie spinning in my head ends, with the film flapping over and over again at the end of the reel. My cheeks are wet, and my heart is racing. I shake my head, put a $20 bill on the table and walk slowly back to my car.

So, once again, my subconscious has created a scenario, and this one, in which Peter has a lover, I suspect is probably closer to the truth. And while we're playing Truth or Dare, I don't trust that anything will change at home (Truth) and I'm relieved that the long rambling message I left on the answering machine (Dare) only played out in my head, not in real life.

I've come this far, and I just have to press on. But first I have to slow my heart rate and catch my breath.

I thought I could reach Peter's house last night, but I was so tired that, at seven, I pulled into the first decent-looking motel I spotted. I didn't even get dinner, just scribbled three quick postcards to the kids and crawled under the covers. As soon as my head hit the pillow, I fell into a blessedly dreamless sleep and woke, ten hours later, just before dawn.

Peter is not an early riser. I remember that from school: He had avoided scheduling eight o'clock classes whenever possible. It's 8:30 a.m., not a civilized hour for a lovers' reunion. I'll wait until ten. By ten o'clock on a sunny Saturday morning in July, Peter should be out washing the car, tending the garden, or loading up the car for a trip to the dump.

I drive up and down the streets of Hastings, North Dakota, trying to spot remembered landmarks. The A&W Root Beer stand of my last supper here is a casualty, I see. Across the street, however, McDonald's seems to be doing a land-office business in Egg McMuffins (no one could be eating Big Macs this early in the morning, could they?). It makes me think of the children. I decide to buy a paper and have a cup of coffee. I am too nervous to eat, even though I skipped dinner last night.

The paper, *The Hastings Reporter*, is full of items of local interest. I look carefully for Peter's name, but I don't find it under Police Blotter, Newcomers, Obituaries (thank God!), or Wedding Announcements (". . . the bride was attended by her cousin, Maryanne Johnson, who wore a gown of cocoa polyester and carried a bouquet of yellow roses and baby's breath . . ."). Nor has Peter MacKinley opened a New Business or gone camping in Canada. His name is not listed among the debtors in the Public Notices, and he is not the perpetrator of the most heinous crime to hit Hastings in half a century, the destruction of all the athletic equipment at the Boys' Club. He is not among the lame and the halt listed under Hospital Admissions, and he hasn't caught the biggest catfish, walleye, perch, or bass in the Sheyenne River Tournament, either. And he has definitely not won the paper's grand prize in the Crossword Competition.

The coffee is vile, but no one around me seems to realize it. I put the plastic cap back on the cup and dump it and the paper into the trash basket. Except for the truck drivers and farmers and Midwestern accents, this could be the McDonald's in Westport.

I kill another ten minutes in the ladies' room, combing my hair and carefully reapplying my make-up, so it looks like I'm not wearing foundation, blush, and eye shadow . . . so, perhaps, I could fool someone into thinking I'm still that fresh-faced twenty-year-old. Fat chance. I pull out two grey hairs that have appeared overnight. If I go back to my natural color, will it turn out to be grey?

Nine-thirty. Nothing to do but drive around until it's time. But what if he decided to get up early? Perhaps his inner clock has changed. Maybe he likes getting up early now. Maybe he got up at 5 a.m. to leave on a week-end fishing trip with his buddies. Have I already missed him?

South Oak Street is not hard to find. The house is about a mile and a half from the center of town. My heart leaps when I see a car in the driveway—he hasn't gone fishing! Nothing to do but screw your courage to the sticking post, old girl, get out of the car, walk up the path to the porch, climb the three steps, cross the floor and knock on the door. Nothing to it, but I am sweating and wish I'd put on extra deodorant this morning.

I can't do it. Twice more I drive around the block. Twice more, I slow as I pass his house. This time, I park. No point in making headlines in *The Hastings Reporter* as the mystery woman in the car with out-of-state plates who was seen cruising the town and casing the joint.

No one answers my knock. I knock harder. Still no answer. Maybe he's in the garden. I walk around to the back of the house, but the yard is empty and the garden looks in need of weeding. I knock on the kitchen door, and this time there is a response.

Shit! It's Edna! I had been so convinced by the veracity of my dreams, both night and day, I hadn't even considered that Edna might still be on the scene.

The voice is feeble: I can barely hear her. She was old twenty years ago . . . I do some quick calculating: she must be close to eighty. She doesn't come to the door, so I knock again. This time I hear a weak "Come in."

The house is dark. The curtains have not been pulled to let in the morning light. There are dirty dishes in the sink, and the linoleum is cracked and peeling.

"Mrs. MacKinley?"

"Y-ess . . . who is that? What do you want?"

"My name is Caro Tanner . . . er . . . Caro Mills . . . I'm a friend of Peter's . . . from college? I visited here once. Do you remember?"

"A friend of Peter's, you say? Where is Peter? Where is my son? Please, please come back here where I can see you. I haven't been very well. It's hard for me to get out of bed."

Where the hell *is* Peter? Has he gone off for the weekend after all, leaving his invalid mother to fend for herself? That gives me the creeps. But that doesn't sound like Peter at all. Was Ernesto right? Did something finally snap? And what would that look like? Is he holding her prisoner in her own house? Has he flipped out?

I shake my head to rid myself of such absurd thoughts. Kind, practical, level-headed Peter. He's probably gone off for the paper and the senile old bird thinks he's abandoned her.

But what I find in the bedroom is not a mother held prisoner, nor a senile bird, but a sick, fragile woman whose energy has been drained in her struggle to sit up and greet me. Nervously, she tries to smooth back a lock of white hair.

"I . . . I'm sorry . . . I haven't been well . . . one of those darned summer colds, you know." She is doing her best to be hospitable, despite the circumstances. "You say you're a friend of Peter's?"

"Yes, from school . . . remember? I stayed here for a couple of days. Oh, but it was over twenty years ago, so I wouldn't expect you to remember that. Peter's probably had lots of people visit since then . . ."

I can see by the expression on her face that Peter has not, in fact, had many visitors. There is a sudden shock of recognition, and then she looks embarrassed.

"Oh, dear, yes . . . I think I do remember you. Your name is Karen? Cassie?"

"It's Caro, Mrs. MacKinley. Short for Carolyn, but nobody but my father calls me that. I was just passing through town. I'm driving to . . . uh . . . Vancouver, and I thought I'd stop in to say hello. Um, Peter's not expecting me or anything."

She shakes her head sadly, "No, Peter couldn't be expecting you, my dear. He hasn't been here in six months. I don't know where he is. I was hoping, perhaps, that you had brought news of him . . ."

This is one scenario that had never even penetrated my subconscious, let alone colored my expectations. Peter gone? And she doesn't know where he is?

"Six months! How can you not know where he is for six months?" I accuse, forgetting, in my distress, the condition of the person I am attacking.

"Please . . . please . . . I'm feeling a little weak. I haven't had my breakfast. Please, could I trouble you for a cup of tea? I feel like my legs wouldn't hold me up this morning."

"Oh, my God, I'm sorry. Of course I can fix you a cup of tea. Would you like a little toast, too? Do you have eggs? I could fix you some eggs if you like."

"No, toast would be just fine, dear. Perhaps when I've eaten, I'll feel a little stronger and we can talk . . ."

She can only manage half a cup of tea and a few nibbles of toast before her head sinks back on the pillow. She motions for me to remove the tray.

"I'm sorry, I guess this cold has taken away my appetite. Usually I'm as healthy as a horse."

"Would you like to rest now? If so, I can come back later when you're feeling a little stronger."

"No, I'd like you to stay. I haven't had company in a few days. My next-door neighbor usually looks in on me every day, but she's visiting her daughter, over to Fargo. She has a new grandbaby. I didn't start feeling poorly until after she left. I was out in the rain the other day, trying to do some work in my flower garden. Perhaps I caught a chill . . ."

I feel her forehead. It's warm, and I don't like the way she looks.

"Mrs. MacKinley, don't you think you ought to call a doctor?"

She looks at me scornfully. "For a little chill? No, the old fool will probably tell me it's pneumonia and try to put me in the hospital. Ever since Peter left, he's been trying to get me to move into a home, you know what I mean? I'll die before I move out of my house."

I look doubtful. I think she is closer to the truth than she will let on. She probably does have pneumonia, and without medical attention, she just may die.

"Mrs. MacKinley . . ."

"Please, call me Edna."

"All right. Edna . . . you say Peter left six months ago? Haven't you heard from him? Can't you tell me where he's gone?"

Tears fill her eyes and she is seized by a wracking cough. I wipe her mouth and ease her back down to the pillow.

"Look, perhaps we've talked enough for now. Why don't you see if you can get some rest? A little nap will probably make all the difference. I'll stay here while you sleep, and I'll fix us some lunch when you wake up. Probably with a little rest and food, you'll be up and around in no time."

She flashes me a weak but grateful smile. I smooth her hair from her forehead and pull the cover up over her shoulders.

"We'll talk later, Edna. And I'll be here if you need me."

A quick tour of the kitchen shows a well-stocked larder. Someone, perhaps the good neighbor, or even a stronger Edna, has made sure there would be food on the table. It's not the pantry of one who lives alone, however. Does she keep the shelves stocked with Peter's favorites because she expects to awaken from her bad dream at any moment and find him at the table?

Peter's room is monkish: A single bed, covered by a navy and white seersucker bedspread with a matching throw rug on the floor, a Bible on the bedside table, and a few books on the shelf. I check their titles: *Growing Young* by Ashley Montagu, some tomes by R.D. Laing, and *Selected Plays of Eugene O'Neill*. Heavy, as we used to say in the old days: heavy.

For lunch, I fix egg salad and heat a can of chicken noodle soup. Edna is stirring. She needs to be helped to the bathroom. Was this fragile creature really once the object of my scorn and hatred? I'm ashamed.

She finishes the soup, but has no appetite for the sandwich. She says she'll eat it for dinner. I want to coax her to talk, but I know I'll have to leave it up to her.

Finally, she gives a sigh and begins, shakily. "Peter . . . we were talking about Peter. I thought he was happy here. All those years of living with someone and you think they're happy. At least, they never say anything to you that makes you think they're not. And one day, he just ups and leaves. I don't know where . . . and I haven't heard from him. Before he left, he transferred the money from his bank account into mine . . . so I don't need anything. Except . . . except . . . I need him . . . I need my son. You understand that, don't you?"

I nod. Of course I do.

She continues. "After my husband died, Peter became my whole life. I guess that was wrong. Children have to live their own lives. But we had a good life together," she adds, defensively. "Peter had a good job over to the arts center. We took some nice vacations. One summer, we went to Yellowstone." She smiles, recollecting. "Oh, yes, we had some good times . . ."

"Edna, does Peter have any friends who might know where he is?"

She shakes her head. "I'm afraid Peter didn't have many friends. I always said he had an old head . . . was an old soul. He seemed to prefer my friends—older people. They always remarked about how kind and polite he was . . . I mean *is* . . . how polite he *is*."

She notes the look of horror on my face.

"No," she says firmly. "You can't even think that. I know he's not dead. He left me a note. It just said he had to get away and do some thinking, but I was not to worry, he was fine and he would contact me when he could, but I was not to worry if it took a while. And he sent me signals. Every couple of weeks, the phone would ring and when I picked it up, he would hang up, before I even said 'Hello', but I knew it was him. That was his way of telling me he was alright."

I can feel the blush rising up my face. I turn away so she can't see the cringe.

"He knew Mrs. Beranski next door would look in on me, and I wasn't sick then," she says in his defense. "He told me he loved me and to please respect the need he had. That he wouldn't be able to write to me until he 'found himself' but that I was not to worry," she repeats.

And she accepted that? If I ever received a missive like that from Greg or Sarah or Caleb, wouldn't I travel to the ends of the earth to find them? But then, my compassionate side over-rules my judgmental bent: this woman can't even make it to the bathroom herself.

The soup seems to have given her a little strength. She continues. "When you said you were a friend of Peter's, I thought you were bringing a message from him. I thought you might have seen him . . ."

"I'm sorry. I wish I *had* seen him. He was my best friend then. I wish I'd kept in touch . . ."

She prompts: "But you couldn't?"

I shake my head. "No, I . . . I got married . . . and . . . I don't know . . ." I shrug.

"Do you have children, Carolyn?"

"Yes, I have three, two boys and a girl. Greg and Caleb are fourteen and eight, and Sarah is twelve."

The old woman gasps.

"What is it? Are you in pain? Should I call a doctor?"

She shakes her head no, but when she speaks, I have to strain to hear her.

"I had a little girl once. She had rheumatic fever and died when she was four. Peter was only two. He doesn't remember her. *Her* name was Sarah . . . Sarah Jane . . . we called her Sissy."

"Oh . . . oh . . . I'm so sorry, Mrs. Mac . . . Edna. That must have been so awful for you."

The fear of losing one of my children stalks me constantly. I don't know how I could bear it if one of them were to die. How did she?

She raises one shaking hand and points to a bookcase across the room.

"There's a picture album in there . . . it's white leather . . . that's it. Would you bring it here, please? I want to show you something."

I carry the album to the bed and take my place in the chair.

"I want to show you a picture of Sissy . . . of my Sarah." She turns the leaves. "There," she points. "She was beautiful, wasn't she?"

I am struck by her resemblance to Peter: the same shy smile, the same finely sculpted nose, the same long, feathery eyelashes.

"Yes, she was . . . very beautiful . . ."

She shakes her head. "You never get over that . . . never. I still dream about her. I lost one child—I couldn't lose another. Don't you see? When you came along, I could see you were going to take him away from me. I couldn't let you. I'm sure you were a nice girl . . . and I see that you've become a very nice woman, but I couldn't let him go. I guess I held on so tight, he finally had to go without telling me where . . ."

She hesitates. "I know now that I shouldn't have interfered. I should have let him go with you . . ."

"Don't . . . don't blame yourself. It wasn't the only reason. There were other things . . . things we had no control over. It . . . it wasn't just you."

She looks at me, assessing me, I think, wondering how much I know. How much does *she* know? Both of us are wary.

"I know that," she whispers. "I know you and Peter were close, but you weren't lovers, were you? Tell me, what do you know about him? How well did you really know him?"

I am careful, evasive. The woman is so ill. If I tell her what I know, will it kill her? And how can I betray Peter?

"How well can anyone really know another person?" I counter.

She eyes me, knowingly. "You're very loyal to him, aren't you? But I know his secret, and I see that you do, too. He didn't tell me, but I found out. I never, ever said anything to him about it. I wish I had. If only we'd been able to talk about it . . . but, the way I was brought up, you just didn't talk about things like that.

"Poor Peter, pretending his whole life . . . One day, about twelve years ago, I was cleaning his room . . ." She smiles apologetically, "A grown man, and I was still cleaning his room . . ." She shakes her head. "I was changing the bed linen and I turned the mattress over. There was a book in between the mattress and the springs. I'll never forget the title. It was called *City of Night . . .*"

I close my eyes and sigh.

She continues. "I read the description on the back . . . and I knew. I just knew. But I put the book back and never said a word. The whole time, we never talked about it . . ." She starts to weep, quietly.

I go to her. I want to comfort her. This woman, who was once my enemy—can I be her friend? We have the same, unspoken fears about the man we both love.

"I'm sorry," she says. "I know I have no right to ask you to help me when it was me who came between you and Peter."

I shake my head to protest, but she goes on. "Yes, it *was* me. Perhaps you could have changed him—made a man of him. Some of those kind of people do change, I know . . ."

"Edna, Peter *is* a man, a very wonderful one. He didn't need me to make him a man. Being a man has nothing to do with one's . . . with that."

"I kept wondering if it was something his father or I did. You read all kinds of things . . ."

A violent coughing spasm prevents her from finishing. She sinks back to the pillow, gasping.

"Mrs. MacKinley . . . Edna . . . please, let me call a doctor. Tell me your doctor's name and I'll call him."

I take up my vigil on a rocker on the front porch. This is the porch where Peter played, and read, and dreamed as a child. The woman who bore him and raised him and fiercely loved him is probably dying. In her dying, will Peter and I finally come together? More and more, I think not, but I know I must see him again before I am able to get on with my life.

"Edna says you're a friend of Peter's." Dr. Bolling exits the house quietly, carefully closing the screen door.

I nod.

"I've given her some antibiotics, and something for the congestion, but she's very weak. I've tended Edna and her family for forty-five years. I brought both her children into this world, and I stood by, helplessly, as one of them was taken out. It's almost Edna's time now, her heart is failing. And, I tell you, it would make her leave-taking a whole lot easier if her son were home."

"I don't know where he is, Dr. Bolling. I thought he was here."

His gaze is steady. "But you can find him, can't you?"

My returning gaze is equally steady. "Yes, Doctor, I think I can."

I use the phone outside McDonald's. It takes but one call to track him down. It's an embarrassing call, despite its urgency. Now Ernesto knows that I am not only pathetic, but a lunatic to boot.

"Caro, I can't give out his phone number. He . . . he didn't want her to find him . . . or find out about him. He's finally come out, and maybe there'll be a little happiness in his life now."

"I'm glad for him, Ernesto, but she's very, very ill."

"I promised him. I can't go back on my word. It might destroy everything he's worked so hard for these past six months . . . his stability . . ."

"Oh, for Christ's sake! The woman is *dying*. How stable do you think he'll be if she's gone before he gets to see her again? Look, I'll tell you what: Call him and tell him to call home. That way, you won't have to go back on your word and he can make the decision about coming home or not. But that decision should not be left in your hands, Ernesto. He has the right to know."

He hesitates, but then agrees. "Okay, I guess you're right. I'll call him."

"Oh, thank you." I am about to hang up, but there's one more thing I need to know. "Ernesto, could I ask you something?" I don't really want to ask, but I have to know. "Are you and Peter lovers? Did he come to New York to be with you?"

"No, we're not lovers. We're friends. I'm in a long-term relationship with someone. Peter came to New York because he was ready . . . and he thought I could help him. He knew no one else here . . ."

"He knew *me*," I interject. "Did you tell him you'd seen me?"

"Caro," he says gently, "he didn't *want* to see you."

CHAPTER
FORTY-SIX

He will have to see me. I am waiting for his plane to get in. Our conversation had been circumspect—the phone is in the hall, right outside Edna's room. I couldn't answer when he asked what I was doing at his house, could only offer "It's a long story." Today, I will have to tell him.

The flight's arrival is announced. I strain, standing on tiptoe, looking for him, but he doesn't seem to be there. One by one, two by two, disembarking passengers are greeted by loved ones. My loved one is not here.

I assess the crowd again. Not everyone has someone waiting, I see. Two or three business-types head toward the car rental desk, an elderly woman is wheeled from the area by an airline employee, and now, even the flight attendants have left the plane. Peter has decided not to come, or perhaps he has missed the flight.

It takes a few moments to realize that the slight, balding, verging on middle-aged man seated in the orange, molded plastic chair across the room is not only the object of my search, but the object of my affections, as well. He has the air of a person who is expecting someone, but he looks right through me.

I walk over and hold out my hand to the stranger in stone-washed jeans and Nike high tops whose new fashion sense has clearly been shaped by his sojourn in New York. This is not who I've channeled, or how I've dreamed it would be, but this is real, and it will have to do.

"Peter."

He looks up at me, puzzled. I wait a moment, but he gives no sign of recognition.

"Peter, it's me, Caro. . ."

He jumps to his feet. "Caro, my God, what have you done to yourself? You look like a completely different person."

"Oh," I say as nonchalantly as I can, "I always heard that blondes with small noses had more fun, so I thought I'd try it out . . ."

"And do they?"

"No, Peter, they don't."

He takes my hand. "I'm sorry."

I do most of the talking on the ninety-minute drive to the house, mostly about the children. Peter asks a few pertinent questions, but, for the most part, he is quiet until he asks again, the question he posed on the phone.

"What are you doing here, Caro?"

And, suddenly, despite everything that has driven me to this time and place, I have no answers.

"I don't know," I answer softly. "I don't know anymore. I thought I did. I left Jack because I thought I did. You were in my thoughts constantly. I dreamed about you, and I convinced myself that was a sign that you needed me. I wrote you dozens of letters . . ."

"I never got them," he says, surprised.

"I know. I never sent them. They sat in my sock drawer for years, until I burned them."

His eyebrows arch and he shakes his head.

I continue. "I was obsessed with you, Peter . . . with what we had . . . No, that's not really true. I was obsessed with what we never had."

He shakes his head again. "Oh, Caro, Caro, Caro." And then there is a rueful laugh. "I guess we always want what we can't have. You were in love with a fantasy . . . and so was I. Do you know what I went to New York for?"

"Yes, Ernesto told me. So you could finally come out and live your life as you had to . . ."

"Well, he was only half right. What I went to New York for was . . . Ernesto. I knew he had a lover, but hope springs eternal, and I haven't been able to get him out of my head for twenty years. You have no idea what that's like . . ."

"Oh, yes I do. I know very well what that's like."

"Oh, shit, of course you do . . . of course you do."

"So that makes two of us. Too bad the obsessions weren't for each other, huh?"

"Oh, but life isn't like that. There's no irony in *that*," he says.

"Yeah," I sigh. "So what happened when you got to New York? When you called Ernesto?"

"Well, he was delighted to hear from me. Invited me to have dinner with him and his lover the very next night. I knew after that evening, that he and I were never to be . . ."

"But you decided to stay in the city?"

"Yes. I told you years ago I had to leave North Dakota. It just took me longer than most people. And I know I left rather precipitously. I couldn't tell Mother where I was going. I was afraid she would find out about me. Anyway, I got a job as a copy editor—one of Ernesto's friends helped me find work. And I left her enough money to live on, but I couldn't bring myself to write to her, because it all would have been a lie. I had to make that break: I couldn't look back. I couldn't run the risk she might find out that her son was gay. I would never be able to face her . . ."

"She knows, Peter."

He gasps. "You told her? Oh dear God, how could you? Do you hate me that much . . . do you hate her that much? How could you do that to a sick woman? How could you betray me?"

"I didn't betray you, Peter. I would never betray you. She's known for years . . . for twelve years. She was very careful about telling me . . . kept trying to feel me out. She didn't want to betray you, either. When, after some rather round-about questioning, she was pretty sure I knew what she was alluding to, she told me. Said she'd found a copy of *City of Night* while she was turning your mattress."

Peter has turned white. He gives a strangled cry, which soon breaks free: "Oh, God, oh God," he keens.

I pull the car over to the side of the road and turn off the engine. I undo my seatbelt and take him in my arms, comforting him the way I comfort Caleb when he's convinced that a dropped pop fly in the last inning with bases loaded means the end of his world.

I am surprised to find that's all I'm feeling right now. Peter is one human being needing comfort from another. When his sobs die down, I release him from my arms.

"Okay?"

"Yes, I'm sorry. But . . . she knew . . . all these years she knew and she never said anything . . ."

"She didn't know how, Peter. You can't really blame her. She's a product of her times, just as we're a product of ours. She wasn't part of all that '60s openness and freedom and acceptance. And maybe, just maybe, she thought if she didn't say anything, it would just go away, it wouldn't be real. So, she had to go on pretending that she'd never seen the book, that she never had a clue. That there were other reasons you didn't go out . . . never got married . . . for her own peace of mind. She wishes now she'd said something . . ."

We pull into the driveway and he bolts from the car. The private duty nurse greets him at the door, her finger to her lips.

"She's resting comfortably now, but she's been asking for you. Just go in and sit quietly by the bed. She'll be awake soon."

Edna dies, peacefully, in her sleep, two days later. Peter is by her side. The two days have provided them both with a gift: a gift of forgiveness, forgetting, reconciliation, and loving acceptance.

CHAPTER
FORTY-SEVEN

The day of the funeral dawns hot and humid, in stark contrast to the frigid December when Peter helped me say good-bye to my mother. He has not wanted to talk much during the last couple of days. The first day, he was all efficiency, calling the undertaker, choosing her burial outfit, notifying the newspaper, and phoning out-of-town relatives. Yesterday, I stayed here while he and his uncle and a cousin held calling hours at the funeral home.

The air is so heavy, and my blouse is already sticking to me. Peter and I drive to the church in silence. After twenty years, you'd think we'd have so much to say to each other, but Peter has Edna on his mind, and that is how it should be. Later, perhaps, we will talk.

I am not family. I hesitate as we enter the church and turn to take a seat in the back of the tiny sanctuary, but Peter takes me by the elbow and guides me into the pew next to him.

"Stand by me . . . please," he whispers.

We come back to the house alone. Peter's uncle and cousins leave for Iowa right after the burial, and Edna's friends have seen to it that Peter will be taken care of. They have sent over cakes, fried chicken, breads, and salads.

"God, is it hot!" Peter takes off his tie, unbuttons his morning-crisp, now-damp shirt, and flops on the couch while I see about lunch.

"Do you want some chicken or anything?" I call from the kitchen.

"Naw, too hot. I wouldn't mind a cold beer, though. I think I put some in the fridge last night."

I have no appetite, either. I bring two Coors into the living room. Peter grins. "Hot enough for you?"

"Yeah, I thought it was supposed to be cold up here in the north."

"Don't worry, come October, November, it will be. Hey, this seems like old times, doesn't it? When was the last time we had a couple of beers together, huh?"

"The last time was never, actually. Beer was not my drug of choice in those days, as you may recall . . ."

He chuckles. "Oh, yeah . . . right."

There is an uncomfortable silence, and then he says "A lot of water under the bridge, Caro . . ."

"Yeah . . ."

"Look," he says suddenly. "I don't know what made you show up when you did. Whether it was just one of those lucky, random things, or whether there was some kind of divine intervention . . . but I want to thank you . . . I . . . it gave us time . . . time to . . ." His voice breaks.

"I know, Peter. I know. It's all right . . ."

"I wouldn't have left if I'd had any choice, but I didn't. One morning, I woke up and knew, I just knew if I didn't leave that very day, that very morning, in fact . . . I would kill myself. I . . . I tried once before, but I knew this time I would succeed. It was that simple. Nothing had happened, it was just going to be another ordinary day, but I knew if I was in the house by nightfall, I wouldn't live to see the next day.

"So, I took Mother over to visit a friend, went to the bank and transferred most of my savings from my account to hers . . ."

"Most of your money?"

He grins wryly. "Yeah, I got to New York with $800 in my pocket. I don't know, maybe I thought the streets were paved with gold or something . . ."

"Go on . . ."

"After the bank, I came home, packed, wrote a resignation letter to the theater . . . the show must go on, and all that. But if I hadn't gotten the hell out of Dodge, my show would have been over. And then I caught the 10 a.m. Greyhound to Fargo. I was able to get on the plane to New York just a few hours later. Got to the city just in time to call Ernesto before he was about to turn in."

"But how could you be so sure Ernesto would be there?"

"How could you have been sure that *I* would be *here*?"

"You weren't . . ."

"Right. But Ernesto was . . . and so, of course, was Roger."

"Ernesto's lover?"

"Yeah, he does windows for Bloomingdale's . . ."

"Good lord, Ernesto told me about him six . . . no, seven years ago when I ran into him one afternoon."

"Yeah, well they just celebrated their tenth anniversary a couple of months ago. They had a party . . ."

"Did you go?"

"Sure. On my salary, I can't afford to pass up an offer of free food and drink."

"Wasn't it hard, though, seeing Ernesto so happy with someone else?" I probe.

His eyebrows raise. "What do you think? Of course it was hard, but I had to do it. I have to live in the real world . . . can't afford to stay lost in my dreams. Anyway, I'm glad I went. I . . . I met someone."

"Oh, Peter . . . you have someone . . . someone special?"

His face begins to redden, and I remember how that blush used to start on his neck and work its way up to his ears and I'd thought it so endearing.

"Well, no, not exactly. It only lasted a couple of weeks before we realized that, other than both of us being gay, we had absolutely nothing in common."

"I'm sorry. I thought . . ."

"No, it's okay. I'll always have a very warm spot in my heart for Randy. He ended a long, dreary, self-imposed term of celibacy."

"Jesus! You mean for twenty years you didn't . . .? No wonder you wanted to kill yourself."

"Yeah. For a while, I thought I might convert to Catholicism and join the priesthood. Maybe I'd finally get lucky and get laid in seminary or something."

He disappears into the kitchen and returns with two more beers and a bowl of pretzels.

"Lunch, madame . . . unless you'd care for some heavier fare?"

"Nah, not until this heat breaks, anyway." I fan myself with the newspaper.

"Peter, Ernesto said you didn't want to see me? How come?"

He looks annoyed. "He shouldn't have said that, but it's true. I didn't. I didn't want to know anything about you. I knew you were married . . . probably had children. I had such mixed emotions about everything. I didn't feel stable enough to see you. Part of it was that self-loathing thing. You know, if only I'd been straight, I would have been your husband . . . they would be my children. I've reconciled myself to being gay, but I feel so sad that I'll never have children.

"Sometimes, years ago, I used to fantasize that we were married and had kids, the proverbial white picket fence and everything, but . . ."

"But what?"

He looks away. "But you always turned into Ernesto. I'm sorry."

"Hey, listen, we have to stop saying 'I'm sorry' to each other. Remember what 'Love means never having to say'?"

He groans, then laughs. "Oh, wasn't that an awful movie . . . even I could have done a better job dying than Ali MacGraw."

"Oh, Peter, I do love you. I miss having you as my friend."

"I love you, too, and believe me, if there had been any way, *any* way we could have made it . . ."

"Yeah, I know. But what was it? What was it when you came back for me—when you said you were straight? Sometimes I thought I'd dreamed it."

"That whole scene was kind of bizarre, wasn't it," he admits. "I guess in order to make some sense out of that, we have to go back to the beginning."

"The very beginning . . . you mean when we first met?"

"How about the sixth day, when 'God formed man in his own likeness . . . male and female he formed them both' . . ."

"C'mon," I protest. "Seriously . . ."

"Seriously. I am being serious. That part where God puts Adam to sleep and fashions Eve out of one of his ribs . . ."

"I'm beginning to see."

He nods. "Okay, now us. You know all about my early history. I think I told you that when I was still at the State U. here, I had a couple of one-night stands, but I was really fighting it. Maybe that's one reason I transferred . . . wanted to get away from my history and make a new beginning.

"You remember I was still pretty heavy into my religion at the time, which only served to make me feel more guilty, of course. The Church wasn't all that enlightened in those days. And now, not only are they ordaining women, but avowed lesbians, as well. Isn't progress amazing? But I digress. Anyway, remember when I walked into the Love House, I told you I was there to borrow a book? Well, actually, I was, but I had an ulterior motive.

"It was about a month or so after I'd gotten to Tucson. I had been going to church a lot, vowing to change, praying to change. Praying for a miracle, I guess," he adds ruefully.

I reach for his hand. "You know, you really don't have to go through all this again. I was just curious . . ."

"I know, but I want to. After twenty years, it's time all the pieces were put together. Maybe it will finally make some sense."

"In as far as life ever makes sense . . ."

"Right. So, where was I?"

"Praying for a miracle . . ."

"Yeah. So, anyway, I had met Scott in one of my classes, and . . . I don't know, I kind of just knew about him."

"Uh huh. Ernesto told me . . . radar."

"Ernesto told you I knew about Scott? He wasn't even there. When did all this come up?" He is incredulous.

"No, actually, Ernesto told me how he recognized you . . . how gay people know about each other . . ."

He looks at me in a bemused kind of way, one eyebrow raised, his mouth in a half-grin. "Is that something you want to talk about when I finish my story?"

I nod, slowly. "It's all part of the same story, isn't it? And I guess if we're putting all the puzzle pieces together . . ."

"Okay, so, anyway, I could've had Scott bring the book to class, but I asked if it was okay if I dropped by his house to get it. I kind of had it set up as a test, you see. Sort of . . . well, a sign from God, if you will."

"I don't understand. You mean a sign from God whether you should be gay or straight? You had no idea I'd be there that night . . ."

"No, but I had it set up in my own mind. Well, you know, if Scott was there alone, and if he said something to me . . . I mean, you know . . . approached me . . . Well, I know this sounds really dumb now, but remember how angelic he looked? That silky blond hair and those guileless blue eyes . . ."

"Careful, you're waxing rhapsodic."

He tosses a throw pillow in my direction. I duck and don't toss it back.

"So," he continues, "I set up this test, see? If Scott made a move, it would be like God's angel saying what I should be, that I was gay, and that it was okay, that that's what I was and what I was supposed to be, in God's eyes, despite what the Church taught."

"And if he wasn't there? Which, as you recall, he wasn't . . ."

"Well, if he hadn't been there, or if he was there with a lover . . . well, that would have been a sign that I *wasn't* supposed to be gay, and that I would just have to fight my impulses even harder, but that God would help me.

"Actually, I wasn't really sure what it was supposed to mean if he wasn't there . . . that part of it wasn't very clear. The thing was, I was so distressed, so ambivalent. I wanted Scott there . . . I didn't want him there. I wanted him. Lord, how I wanted anybody, at that point. I guess what I really wanted was a clear, irrefutable sign from God. I wanted the finger of God to come down and point. I wanted a heavenly voice to say '*This* is the way, my son, the only way . . .'"

"Jesus, it must have really blown your mind to find me there—and totally out of my mind, to boot."

"No, no . . . it was *wonderful* to find you there, that's what it was. It was my clear and irrefutable sign from God: 'I want you to be *straight*, my son, and this is the woman who will make you that way.'"

"God should have consulted me on that one, Peter. Although, if He had, He certainly would have found that our thinking followed the same lines. God knows, I tried. He certainly can't fault me for trying."

"I know you did, dear, and I love you for that. It's just that, after a while, I realized it wasn't really a sign, that there never would be that sign pointing to the one and only way, that I would have to find my own way, without divine guidance. And that wasn't the one I would have chosen, if I had had any say in the matter. But, you know, I always wanted to be normal. I hungered for normality with the same intensity I hungered for members of my own sex. I was fighting myself every step of the way, and that day I showed up on your doorstep—I guess it was just one more attempt to fight that losing battle."

"So, you wanted so much to be straight that you had yourself convinced you were?"

"No," he grimaces, "My shrink had me convinced I was. Once a week, I saw this guy in Fargo. He did a lot of behavior modification for gay 'conversion' . . . kind of like Pavlov's dogs, you know?"

I shake my head.

"Well, it's like this: They show you pictures of these hunky guys, you know? And if you respond positively, you know, if your pulse starts to race and . . . um . . . other things start to happen . . . well, they give you this electric shock."

"God, it sounds positively barbaric. Were they naked pictures?"

"Naked? Of course. Or else they were wearing these teeny little bikini pants or jock straps. Anyway, then they showed you these pictures of women, like out of *Playboy* and *Hustler* . . ."

My nose wrinkles in distaste. "Ugh . . ."

He laughs. "Yeah, that's what I thought," and ducks as I throw a pillow at his head.

"Anyway, if you responded positively to the pictures of the women, you got rewarded."

"How?"

"Would you believe Hershey's Kisses? So, anyway, after a while, I learned to respond in the 'right' way. I mean, I'll take chocolate over megavolts any day. So, the shrink said I was cured, and I guess I believed him. You know, that's the same kind of 'therapy' they use on child molesters in the state prison here . . . only they give them shocks when they see pictures of little kids. I was in great company, wasn't I?"

"So then you went back to Tucson?"

"I hopped in my car the very next day, my dear . . . and then, did you burst my bubble."

"Oh, God . . . I'm sor—"

"Hey, hey, hey. Remember what we weren't going to say?"

"Oh, right . . . sor—I mean, oh shit, forget it."

"Right. But after a while, after I wrote that last letter to you, I realized that, electric shocks or no electric shocks, I couldn't make it with a woman, that I was really and truly, irrevocably and undeniably gay. And then my real problems began."

"You mean living here?"

"Yes. My mother's family has lived in this town for generations. They were pillars of the community. How the hell could I reconcile that with being a pansy? How could my mother hold her head up if anyone knew? So, I just resigned myself to a quiet, celibate life. Mother needed me. She was too old to be transplanted somewhere else. All her friends were here. So, I made a sacrifice. Plenty of people do.

"Anyway, I lived my quiet little nowhere life until that fateful day—the day I chose between flight and hanging myself from the rafters in the attic. And the rest, as they say, is history."

The shadows have gotten longer and the oppressive heat has finally lifted. He glances out the window.

"Look, there's a breeze. What say we take some of those victuals the good church ladies have provided and make us a picnic in the backyard. I do miss having a backyard," he sighs.

"You know, I probably should have stayed with my first shrink, the one who wasn't trying to change my sexual orientation . . ."

We have polished off fried chicken, biscuits, and coleslaw and have downed another beer apiece. I am feeling rather woozy: I'm not used to drinking so much. Lying on my back in the hammock, looking up into the branches of a giant oak, I find myself getting sleepier and sleepier as I struggle to hold up my end of the conversation.

"Why? What did he say?"

"That my homosexuality was all tied up with the rest of me. That if I gave that up, provided it was possible to, I'd sacrifice something else, like my creativity. I struggled with that for a year, but I couldn't resolve it. Anyway," he says with a wave of his hand, "That doesn't matter now."

"What? What doesn't matter?"

"The question of going straight. Because it's not a question anymore . . . We also talked a lot about you."

That snaps me out of my stupor.

"About me? What about me?"

He laughs. "You needn't act so indignant. When you were in therapy, didn't you talk about me? I mean, you must have, with all those unsent letters and everything."

"Well, yes," I admit. "But that was different."

"Right. Different . . . *c'mon*. Anyway, don't you want to know what the shrink said about our relationship?"

"God, I don't know. Do I?"

"Sure. I mean," he hastens to add, "it's not anything awful or perverted or anything. He said I was looking for Sissy—for the sister I never really knew. I had completely forgotten, but it came out during the course of the therapy: When I was a little kid, I guess about seven or eight, I used to pretend she was still alive. She was like an imaginary playmate, except she had once been real. I used to get teased a lot—I was small and sickly. I'd come home from school and go to my room and shut the door and tell everything to Sissy and she always stuck up for me . . . said she'd go and beat those nasty kids up if they ever bothered me again . . ."

"You never told me that, Peter."

"I didn't remember . . . not 'til it came out in therapy. Anyway, the shrink said that when I met you, it was like, without my being aware of it, I had found my sister again. And, of course," he adds gently, "you can't go to bed with your sister."

"No . . . Why did you stop seeing him?"

"Because I couldn't reconcile myself to being gay. It was so unnatural. Everything I'd ever heard, everything I'd ever been taught, both in church and out, told me it was an abomination. God, how I hated myself . . ."

"And that's when you found Dr. Frankenstein and his megavolts?"

"No, first I tried to do it on my own. I read a lot, and then decided what I really had to do was to start asking women out and just go to bed with them, and not even think about it . . ."

I try to control myself, but I can't. Soon my muffled giggles become loud guffaws.

"I don't think it's one bit funny," says an obviously miffed Peter.

"Oh, oh," I gasp, "I'm sorry. It's just that the idea of you going to bed with women . . . treating them like objects . . . I mean, that's what Artie used to do. He had it down to an art, if you can call being a pig like that an artist. But I just can't see you doing that. God, you didn't, did you?"

"What do you think? Of course I didn't. I wouldn't have even had a clue as to how to go about it. But I thought, you know, if I could just do it once or twice . . . get it over with . . . No, I don't mean get *it* over with . . . just those first few awkward times over with, then I could go back to you and all that would be behind me, and I could be, you know, just . . . normal. I wanted that so much I fell for Dr. Megavolt and his crazy theories. And, you've heard all the rest, my dear."

"What are you going to do now?"

"Now? Well, I guess get Mom's stuff together to give away or sell, and put the house on the market. And then, I have to get back to work. Really, I need to get back to New York by the end of the week. What about you? What are you going to do now?"

"Me? I don't want to talk about me."

"Caro, dear, we have to talk about you."

"Not yet. I'm not ready to talk about me yet. Let's talk about you some more. What are you going to do when you get back to New York?"

In truth, I'm terrified to talk about me, Peter. I know I can never have you, but now I fear that I've crossed the line with Jack, that even if I went back to him, he wouldn't have me.

"When I get home . . . and I do think of it as home, now . . . I'm going to take a sublet on an apartment. One of Ernesto's friends joined a touring company of *Les Mis*. It's for six months. That'll give me time to look for my own place. The Y is not exactly conducive to the more creative aspects of my life, although I have started writing a play. I'm even thinking of dipping my toe in the water and going to a couple of casting calls. And, of course, I hope to improve my sex life," he laughs.

"Aren't you afraid sometimes?"

"Afraid? Oh, you mean of getting AIDS?

I nod. "I'd be terrified."

"Oh, my dear, don't you read the papers? All us gays practice safe sex now. Yep, I've actually turned into the all-American boy: I carry rubbers in my wallet. Isn't that a hoot?"

He sees that I am not amused.

"You're right. It's not funny. It's especially not funny in the context of the two of us. You know, even if I could have managed the mechanics—and I'm not sure I could have—I would have done you a terrible disservice by making love to you. I would have had to fantasize you were a man, and I couldn't degrade you that way. *That* would have been the *real* betrayal.

"Don't you think I knew how much you loved me? Don't you think I'd say to myself, 'My God, this girl cares about you like no one has ever cared about you besides your mother. Why can't you just go with her . . .' But I couldn't do that to you. I knew it wouldn't have worked for me . . . that sooner or later, I'd be sneaking around behind your back, meeting men on the sly. And who knows where that would have led: given what's happening out there the past few years, we could both be dead.

"I knew that as much as I loved you, or as much as I was capable of loving you, you were better off with Jack. I think I knew even as I came back that day in Tucson. . .came back to get you. But I wouldn't let myself believe it.

"Okay, Caro, we've talked about me. End of story. Look, I feel kind of responsible for you. I mean, you left your husband and children . . ."

"I did *not* leave my children. They're in camp. They don't know . . . they think I'm just taking a vacation. I left my *husband.*"

"Okay, okay," he concedes. "You left your husband, and, in some way, I must be responsible for that."

"No way! In no way are you responsible, Peter. You didn't know that one day I'd decide to chuck it all and set off after you. I mean, you want to feel guilty, fine, but don't feel guilty for my *mishegoss.*"

"Your what?"

"You've been in New York for six months and you've never heard someone use that word? All you'd have to do is spend five minutes in Zabar's and you would get some *mishegoss* along with your nova and cream cheese. It's Yiddish. My mother used to say it. It means 'craziness.' And you are definitely not responsible for mine. Yours, maybe, but not mine."

"All right, all right, so your misha . . . craziness . . . made you get in your car and drive halfway across the country to find someone you didn't even know would be there. What if you hadn't found me? And may I remind you that you almost didn't. What would you have done? You must have had a plan B?"

"Actually, I didn't."

Exasperation shows on his face. "Caro, Caro, Caro . . . You sound like you're fourteen years old or something. Grown women just don't do this sort of thing."

"On the contrary, Peter, grown women are leaving rotten marriages all the time. Don't you remember how we met? You went to Scott's house to borrow a copy of *A Doll's House*, remember? What the hell do you think Ibsen was writing about?"

"Touché. But is your marriage really that rotten? Think about it. You have those three great kids. Do you really want to raise them without a father? Is it as bad as all that?"

I don't know how to answer. I've spent the last few years convincing myself that there was no future in my marriage, but part of that was based on the premise that Peter would accept me with open arms and an erect penis.

He continues. "You and Jack share a history. That has to count for something."

"You and I share a history, too . . ."

He shakes his head. "No, dear, twenty years ago we had a shared fantasy, that's all. What is that compared to a marriage, having children, sharing the good times and the bad with one person, experiencing the heights and the depths of life . . ."

"Mostly the depths," I mutter.

He puts a finger under my chin. "Caro, look at me. Is that really true? Don't the good times outweigh the bad?"

"What good times?" I rise from the couch and walk away from him. "Peter, there was something you and I had that I never had with Jack."

"And there are so many things you have with Jack that you could never have with me. Nobody gets to have it all. I know what it's like to be obsessed. You've let it take over your life. *It can't work out.* We can't make it, but maybe if you can let go of me, you and Jack can find what you once had. I know it must have been special. You were so ready to give to that one special person. I wish it could have been me, but I think you did find that person in Jack, didn't you?"

"Well . . . yes," I admit. "The beginning was wonderful. But he's really changed . . ."

"And haven't you? Time and responsibilities change everyone."

"Yeah, but . . ."

"No buts. C'mere, sit back down next to me. I want you to think about the good times you've had with Jack. Stop thinking about what you don't like about him. Tell me about the good times."

"What're you, my shrink?"

"No, your friend, and I want to help. You've done so much for me, dear. Let me reciprocate . . . or try, anyway."

I take a deep breath and let it out slowly. "Okay, the good times . . . Where should I start?"

"Wherever you want. You said the beginning was wonderful. Why don't you start there?"

"Yeah, beginning—I do so love beginnings. You know, like from the second date on, when you have a feeling that something is really happening and you're all tingly and everything when you think about him and—God, do you want to hear about the sex and everything?"

He grins. "I think I can take it. I seem to recall some pretty lengthy discussions on that topic . . ."

"Yeah, well, okay . . . The beginning: I went back to school and everything was different. No Love House . . . No Ernesto . . . No Scott. Tricia was off in Phoenix, living with some guy. And you, of course, were sorely missed.

"So, I threw myself into my work . . . Really, I *did*." I respond to his look of bemusement. "My grade point average was terrific. And the war was escalating, and so was the protesting. There was sort of a loose group of peaceniks on campus. I mean, nothing like SDS or anything. You remember that most of the jerks at that school—not the drama department, of course—were more concerned with their suntans than with the state of the world. Vietnam was so far away . . . a half-hour show we saw on the news every night . . . You know, I've been thinking a lot about the paradox of the '60s lately. They really were the best of times, the worst of times. I mean, my mother died, for God's sake, and JFK and Bobby, and Martin Luther King . . . and Vietnam was being napalmed . . . So, how come we had such a good time? Why do I look back and think of that time as so heady, so wonderful?"

"Well, in some ways it was, wasn't it? No responsibilities, really. All we had to do was make halfway decent grades and the rest of it was a piece of cake. Neither one of us had to work to put ourselves through school. And even when I said I was worried about the draft, I really wasn't. I knew I'd be 4-F as soon as I got out of school. Life really *was* great then, wasn't it . . ." he trails off wistfully. "Despite what was happening in the rest of the world. The war never really touched us, did it?"

"No, Peter, not in the Love House . . ."

There is a lull in the conversation. Peter shakes his head as if he can't believe how we got from there to here.

"Wow, there were some incredible times in that house, weren't there?" he says finally.

"Yeah . . ."

"Yeah . . ." he shakes his head again, then starts to chuckle. "Hey, remember the milk bath? That was some night, wasn't it?"

"What milk bath?"

"You know, the milk bath . . . you and Ernesto and Scott . . ."

"What are you talking about? Ernesto and Scott and I and *what* milk bath?"

"The three of you . . . you took a milk bath. I remember it so clearly . . . the Stones on the stereo, the candlelit bathroom . . . and the three of you in the tub."

"The three of us in the *tub*? The three of us *naked* in the tub?" My voice rises.

"Of course, naked. How else do you take a bath?"

I shake my head. "But there wasn't any bodily contact, right?"

He laughs again. "Listen, there had to have been *some* bodily contact—it wasn't a very big bathtub."

"Oh, God, I don't remember that at *all*. What were you doing while all this was going on?"

"Me? I was the one pouring the milk over the three of you."

"You were . . . I can't believe this . . . Were you naked, too? No, I'll bet you weren't, were you? I *know* I wouldn't have forgotten *that*."

His grin is self-mocking. "*Moi*, naked? Surely you jest, my dear. But I can't believe you don't remember the milk bath. It was something *else*!"

"Oh, Peter, I'm sure it happened if you say so. I trust your memory. It's just that I have no recollection whatsoever of that night. I guess I've blocked it."

"Hmm . . . I wonder why you'd block something like that."

I shrug. "I don't know . . . but I guess . . . well, you know enough about psychology to know why people block things . . . about selective memory, and why some things are repressed . . . things that are too painful to remember. You know that."

"Yeah, but I don't see why you'd need to repress something like that. It was great."

"Hmmm, maybe it was . . . for you. But think about it, Peter. The four of us: Scott wanting Ernesto, Ernesto wanting Scott, me wanting you, and you wanting . . . Ernesto. Although I couldn't have known that at the time, could I? So, who wanted *me*? And what in God's name was I doing in a situation like *that*? Probably one more futile attempt at trying to be seductive with you. And you probably never even looked at *me* that night. God, I must have been an incredible masochist. Of course, you remember it as great: it was probably the closest you came to your heart's desire, wasn't it?"

He says nothing. It's clear I've hurt him.

"Shit . . . I'm sorry, Peter. There's no point in opening up old wounds . . ."

"I didn't know it was a wound. I'm sorry."

"Listen, just forget about it, okay? Just accept that it's something I had to repress, that's all. It's probably all tied up with my finding out about you and Ernesto . . . I mean, how you felt about him. And, I guess I felt like you'd betrayed me . . . used me . . . you know, to be near Ernesto. And I guess I didn't want to remember, that's all . . ."

"I never used you," he protests.

"Listen, Peter, I know there was no malice involved, but people *use* each other. People have needs, and they use each other . . ."

And how have Jack and I used each other?

"I guess that's something *I've* repressed—I mean using you. I never wanted to do that . . ." He shakes his head sadly.

"I know. So, why don't we both repress it. There are certainly enough good memories, dear. Let's just hold on to those."

But all of a sudden, I don't want to repress it at all.

This would make an amazing first scene of a play, wouldn't it?

I'm already writing the dialogue, casting the roles, and preparing for a triumphant opening night when Peter interrupts my internal monologue.

"Okay . . . no, wait, before we close that door . . . something you said . . . I'm just curious about something. How did you know about me . . . and Ernesto?"

I slip back into bitter, and hurt and guilty, and pretend I don't hear. "Listen, I'm going to make some iced tea. It's really hot out here. Do you want some tea?"

"Caro, answer my question. How did you find out? Did Ernesto tell you?"

I shake my head.

"Then how?"

I can't look at him. I start to walk away, but he grabs my hand. "How did you find out?"

I extricate my hand from his and take a deep breath. "I found the letter, Peter . . . the one you wrote to him on graduation night. Ernesto didn't tell me. I went over there the next morning. Scott was at work and Ernesto was in the shower. And the letter was on the kitchen table . . . So," I shrug, "I read it."

"Pretty nosy, aren't you? And look who's talking about *betrayal* . . ." His voice rises in a way I've never heard it.

We stare at each other for a long time, until he says gently, "I guess you were bound to find out sometime. I was just kind of hoping you wouldn't. I mean, not that it ended up making any difference or anything. I'm just . . . sorry you had to be hurt that way. I never wanted to hurt you, Caro. You must know that . . ."

I put my fingers to his lips. "Shhh . . . no more. We're supposed to be remembering the good times, right? Or have you forgotten?"

"No." He grins, "How could I ever forget?"

"So, where were we? You wanted me to tell you how I met Jack, right? Okay, I started reading more and thinking more and I marched and I protested that stinking war. I believed that we'd make a difference, and I think we did. One of the happiest days was when Johnson said he wasn't going to run again."

"Yeah, I hated that bastard."

"You know, I didn't know anyone at the U of A who was being drafted, but then I thought about those boys back home. Those farm kids who didn't have the luxury of student deferments, the ones who were all gung ho to serve their country and defend Mom, the flag, and apple pie. Three of the guys I went to high school with died there. One got blown up in a helicopter, another was a medic who died trying to save a buddy, and a third stepped on a punji stick, and that was the end of Bobby Porter. They were all good kids. You know, no malice or anything . . . just wanted to go over there and get the job done. Daddy sent me the clippings from the paper. It was horrible. So many boys from such a small town. Thank God I didn't have to worry about you. It was such a relief to get your letter about your hernia and being 4-F.

"Anyway, I started attending more rallies and marches. Would you believe some of us even occupied the dean's office?"

I grin. "I wish you had been there—No, actually, I'm glad you weren't."

He looks surprised.

"Well, that was the day I met Jack."

"Aha, the plot thickens . . ."

"Anyway, he was cute, and bright, and earnest, and politically aware . . . and sexy. And I was extremely horny . . ."

"Are you trying to tell me you slept with him on your first date?"

"God, it wasn't even a date. Well, I mean, it was, sort of. You know, I can't even remember why we were occupying the dean's office. I think we wanted him to declare a moratorium for some reason or another and cancel classes for the day in solidarity with protests at more enlightened campuses. Anyway, I think he threatened to call the police or something, and this being Arizona instead of Columbia or Berkeley, we carried our protest outside instead of standing our ground. Guys started burning their draft cards and everything. It was fabulous. And Jack and I started talking, and, well, one thing led to another . . ."

"To bed?"

"Is that a leer, Peter? Yes, bed. I mean, I'll bet it didn't take long with you and what's his face in New York before you were in his bed, did it?"

"The night I met him," he admits sheepishly.

"Anyway, Jack was everything I could have asked for in a lover . . ." And suddenly I am there, in Jack's big brass bed and it's our very first time.

"Caro? You looked like you just floated off somewhere. Where did you go?"

"Maybe back to 1967. Funny, it probably didn't occur to me at the time, but Jack kind of looked like you then. Oh, he was taller and blonder, but there was something about his eyes . . . and the beard was the same. Of course, half the guys we knew had beards then . . . but still . . . maybe, subconsciously, I thought I'd found a straight incarnation of you . . ."

"I guess I should be flattered?"

"It doesn't have anything to do with flattery. I mean, when you think about it, it's pretty logical. I had a lot invested in us, and I'd been rejected by you in a big way. My God, you even gave up the Schumann fellowship rather than come back to school with me . . ."

"That's not the only reason, Caro, but . . ."

"But what?"

"You're right, it was part of it."

"Oh, Peter, I'm sorry. I wish I'd known how to back off, but I couldn't. I loved you so much."

"And then you fell in love with Jack," he prompts.

He's right. We have been over and over it. No point in pursuing it any further: we will never be lovers.

"Yeah, I did, and he fell in love with me, which I found pretty amazing."

"I don't find anything at all amazing about that. You are one terrific woman. You were then, and you're even more so now. Although, I have to admit, I miss the long, dark curly hair, and you're a trifle on the skinny side . . ."

"Well, after what I put away today, we probably don't have to worry about the skinny part for too long. And I'm thinking about letting my hair grow back to its natural color. . .although that's probably grey by now. Nothing I can do about the nose, though."

"Oh, I like the nose, now that I'm used to it. But I liked the other one, too."

"Well, the nose was Jack's doing . . ."

"Okay, so the guy's not perfect."

"Mmm, but he wants me to be . . ."

"Whoa, this is 'The Good Things About Jack Tanner Show.' No fair switching channels. All right, Contestant Number One, can you name ten good things about Jack? You have thirty seconds . . ."

Okay, Peter, I'll play your silly game.

"One, he doesn't smoke. Two, he doesn't drink to excess. Three, he doesn't gamble. Four, he doesn't fool around with other women, at least, I don't think he does. Five, he doesn't beat up on me or the kids . . ."

"Bzzzz. Sorry, Contestant Number One, you are disqualified for not following the rules. All of your answers must be phrased in the positive, not the negative. Contestant Number Two, can you tell us ten good things about Jack Tanner? And, remember, your responses must be phrased positively."

"Okay, okay. Let's see . . . One, he's given me three terrific kids and he's a really good dad. Two, he's a good provider. Three . . . umm . . . he used to make me laugh . . . once in a while . . ."

"Careful, Contestant Number Two, you're coming awfully close to the line that separates the positive from the negative."

"Sorry. Where was I? Oh, yes. Four, he's really smart. Five, he's still in pretty good shape, although he's a little bit obsessive when it comes to his running . . ."

"Contestant Number Two, if I have to warn you again . . ."

"Sorry, sorry. Okay. Six, his mother's crazy about me. I'm the daughter she never had . . ."

Peter's eyes fill suddenly. I squeeze his hand, but I go on.

"Seven, he's a wonderful Little League coach: never yells at the kids when they make mistakes, and always finds something to praise about each kid, even the klutziest outfielders. Eight, on my 40th birthday, he and the kids fed me breakfast in bed, cleaned the whole house, ordered in my favorite Chinese food for dinner, and when the kids went to bed without being told . . ."

"Yes, Contestant Number Two?"

"Nine, he can be so loving in bed, Peter. He was from the beginning and I guess he still would be if I gave it a chance . . ."

Peter nods.

And all of a sudden, I start to laugh.

"What's so funny?"

"Sorry, I was thinking about Jack in bed."

"And that's funny?"

"No, not during, afterwards. Not too many people know this about my button-down husband, but he's got a wicked, whimsical sense of humor. Sometimes, after, he just thinks of something and it riffs into something so funny. Like that time he started whistling this old '60s song and I guessed what it was and then I whistled one and he guessed, and then it was his turn and by then we were laughing too hard to even purse our lips. 'Post-coital whistling,' he called it . . ."

"Too much information."

"Oh, sorry." But by then I am remembering other times he's cracked me up and I start to giggle.

"What now?" asks Peter. I think he is enjoying himself.

"Well, there was this time when he took me to a revival of *A Man and a Woman*. You remember how enamored I was with French movies?"

He nods.

"Well, it was a surprise. I didn't even know it was playing in town. It might have been an anniversary or something. I remember we had to get a babysitter . . . Anyway, Jack had never seen it, and I always raved about what a great love story it was . . . And I was so psyched about this wonderful romantic evening we were going to have . . ."

"And this was funny?"

"Oh, God, yes. It was clear that the film hadn't aged well. It was so '60s, you know, and by the time Jean-Louis Trintignant, who plays this race car driver, jumps in his car after participating in an all-day race, and then drives all night from Monte Carlo to Paris because he gets this telegram from Anouk Aimee, who he kind of has a crush on and she kind of has a crush on him, but they haven't done it yet, but you think they will when he gets to Paris, Jack and I are getting kind of antsy. And then Jean-Louis pulls out his electric razor and starts shaving, because, of course he didn't have time between the telegram and jumping in his car and he's shaving while the theme is playing—so you know they're going to have sex and he doesn't want to scratch her with his three-day beard—anyway, you know that theme, the one with no words, just a chorus going *Ba da da DA da da, da da DA da da da* . . . and then Jack leans over and starts singing in my ear . . ."

By now I'm laughing so hard, and Peter can't help laughing, too, even though he has no idea what I'm talking about.

"So he starts singing to the theme, in a bad French accent: 'And now I'm SHA-ving in my car, SHA-ving in my car . . .

And now I'm SHA-ving on the train, SHA-ving on the train . . . And now I'm SHA-ving at the Louvre, SHA-ving at the Louvre . . .' And by the time he gets to: 'And now I'm SHA-ving with DeGaulle, SHA-ving with DeGaulle', we can't contain ourselves, and they actually ask us to leave the theater . . . It was one of the best times we ever had."

Then my laugh catches in my throat. I am suddenly sober and quiet, and wondering where Jack and I got lost.

"And number Ten?" prompts Peter.

I sigh. "And, Ten, we've built a life together . . . and I guess he loves me, still. But I think I've been so busy being the person he wanted me to be, or maybe the person I thought he wanted me to be, that I . . ."

"But the Caro he fell in love with was *you*. What made you think you had to be someone else to make him love you?"

Peter has dropped his quiz show emcee persona. His voice is gentle and comforting.

I shake my head. "I don't know. I guess there was something wrong with the person I was, if it wasn't enough to make you love me. I know better than that now, of course, but, at the time, I guess I thought I had to make some kind of radical change to keep a man interested in me. It's like, remember Anne Conover, in our scene study class, the tall redhead you directed in that scene from *Trojan Women*?"

"Yeah, what about her?"

"Well, every time she started going out with a different guy, her taste in music changed to whatever the guy happened to like. By the time she graduated, she had the biggest, most eclectic record collection anyone had ever seen, everything from Coltrane to The Fugs, with a little Mahler left over from that suicidal philosophy major she dumped after two months of angst, but none of it was really her, because she never felt confident enough to tell them what *she* liked. Afraid they'd put her down, I guess. She liked the Beach Boys.

"So, it was like that. I was afraid Jack wouldn't love who I was, so I took on the persona that reflected whoever he was at the time—super radical anti-war protester, for instance. Did I tell you we were in Chicago in '68 for the Democratic Convention?"

"Oh, no, really? I could barely stand to watch it on the tube. You didn't get your head bashed in by those storm troopers, did you?" he asks anxiously, as if the event I am recounting happened this morning instead of twenty years ago.

"No, we were tear-gassed, but we emerged none the worse for wear—at least, physically. But that's something that always stays with you, watching the cops beat up on your comrades . . . It was pretty terrifying. It scared Jack into proposing to me."

"You mean in the middle of all that chaos, he had the presence of mind to ask you to marry him? I think I like this guy."

I giggle. "Yup. But I'm not sure it was as much presence of mind as fear of dying. He probably thought by committing himself to a future act, he'd at least guarantee himself a future.

"Anyway, that was my radical phase. Next came perfect wife and helpmate to perfect young lawyer who by then had cut his hair, shaved his beard, and joined his father's law firm. That's when I had my nose job and started coloring my hair."

Peter clicks his tongue and shakes his head.

"And it was a pretty logical progression from perfect wife to perfect mother. Well, I aspired, anyway. I'm far from perfect, but, on a good day, I'm not bad, Peter. In fact, it's a role I've really taken to. Oh, God, I miss my kids!"

"So, the mother part is a reflection of the real you, right?"

I nod vigorously. "Uh huh, and it's the part of me I like best. It's the other stuff, though . . . the social stuff . . . the suburban housewife who can't stand up to her husband shit. It's not me. Remember Caro the promising young playwright? I think she died."

"Nah, she didn't die. She's just been asleep for a hundred years. What makes you think Jack wouldn't love Caro the

Playwright as much as or more than Caro the Mad Housewife? Why don't you give yourself a chance to find out?"

"Hearing me is not one of Jack's strong suits."

"You mean you don't talk about it?"

"I tried over the years, but then I gave up. It always seemed so ungrateful. I had this successful husband, these amazing children who we were raising in the best neighborhood, going to the best schools, and if I was miserable, it was probably my own fault. So, I just gave up."

"That doesn't sound like the Caro I knew. If anything, my dear, you sure were persistent." He winks.

I sense that this will be the end of our conversation and I am not quite ready to say goodbye. As Peter said: Persistent.

"Hey, remember that time when we both agreed that if neither of us had a partner by the time we were, like, forty, we would move in together and spend our old age in twin rocking chairs on our front porch?"

"Where are you going with this?" He cocks his head and raises one eyebrow.

"I don't know . . . maybe we could all live together . . ."

And I know exactly where that came from, almost as soon as the words leave my mouth, and so does he.

"Oh, please, Carolyn Mills, tell me you're not still hell bent on living your *Jules and Jim* fantasy?"

This man knows me so well, even now. I will miss him so.

"Wait, wait, I need to tell you something and I may never have a chance to say it if I don't do it now."

I take a deep breath and then let it all out at once.

"I'm sorry, Peter, you were my best friend and you never, ever tried to change anything about me. You accepted me and loved me just the way I was, and I paid you back by trying to erase the most fundamental thing about you. I'm so ashamed."

"Oh, dear girl, you don't need to apologize. You were the best you knew how to be, and I realize now that I was culpable, too.

I kept telling you how much I wanted to be 'normal.' It's human nature to hear what you want to hear and ignore those other warning signs. You have nothing to be ashamed of. I know you did it out of love. And, in my own way, I loved you, you know. So, let's keep the best part of all that and forget about the rest, okay?"

I nod, wipe my eyes with the back of my hand and then blow him a kiss.

"Look, I have a couple of errands to run in town . . . and I think you have a decision to make. You remember that man you fell in love with, the father of your children and the one who makes you laugh just thinking about him? I think he just might be waiting for you."

And this is what I am suddenly, indelibly sure of: I love my husband. I know what Peter would say if I were to voice it: "Well, of course you do, dear girl." And I am so very grateful that not once in our twenty-year relationship has Jack ever called me that. "Sweet girl," "baby girl," "my girl," yes, and I reveled in every appellation that was not modified by that holding-me-at-arm's length "dear." But this is what I also know: I have shortchanged both the men in my life. I have made my amends to this one. I hope it's not too late with Jack. I hope Peter is right.

Peter stretches, brushes crumbs from his lap, leans over to kiss me on the forehead, and is gone.

CHAPTER

FORTY-EIGHT

For the second time in a week, I am waiting at the Fargo Airport for a man to disembark from a Northwest Orient flight from New York. But this time I know the man *wants* to see me. Can't *wait* to see me. Will be sprinting off the plane to see me, and, life is funny that way: I can't wait to see him.

It took about a half hour after Peter left me sitting on the porch before I could pick up the phone and talk to the husband I thought I was leaving forever. When I called Jack that first night, he was ready to sic the cops on me, commit me to a mental institution, and who knows what else. When I called the second time, he was wary and subdued. This time, I was prepared for just about anything. And I could not blame him in the least if he were to tell me to fuck off and stay the hell out of his life. I probably deserved it, and I was ready for that. Ready, but scared shitless. I played the anticipated conversation over and over in my mind. Jack would tell me he was through with me. I would say how sorry I was. And he would say he was going to get custody of the kids because I was crazy. And then I would be alone. My hands were shaking as I dialed our number.

I was not prepared for what happened next.

"Jack, I . . ."

"Oh, God, oh thank God, Caro . . ." and then he broke down. I could hardly understand him, he was sobbing so hard.

And then I was, too.

"Oh baby, oh baby, you don't know what it's been like here without you. I feel like my heart's been cut out of me, and there's no anesthesia that can take away the pain. I've been hurting so bad. And I know it's my fault. I know I made you leave. I've been as wrong as a man can be. I should have been paying attention. I'm so, so sorry. I can't eat, I can't sleep without you in our bed. Every corner of the house reminds me of you. Please, Caro, I know things have to change. I'll go to Dr. Hirsch with you. I'm willing to do anything. Anything. I just need my wife in my arms again."

So we are on a road trip. We are following the same route I took last week (without the car repair detour) only in reverse, and Jack is doing most of the driving.

At first, we're quiet, both of us kind of astonished that we've found ourselves so unexpectedly here. And me because I am so wary of trying to explain myself, because I said it all in that imaginary message I left on our answering machine, and because I am feeling so guilty and abashed for bolting the way I did. And I wonder if he is re-thinking his tearful phone confession from the other day.

Finally, he clears his throat.

"You know," he says hesitantly, "I missed you even before you left. Sometimes, late at night, when you thought I was in the den watching the news, I would sit there with the TV turned off, and just wonder what ever happened to that lusty free spirit I'd married. And I blamed you. I shouldn't have. I was just too dense to see the part I played in my own loneliness, too selfish to recognize my role in that lovely, kooky girl's disappearance."

"Oh, Jack . . ." I am so touched and surprised by his insight, and I am beginning to catch a glimmer of that tender, impassioned boy I'd lost my heart to, back on the steps of the University Administration Building, in the midst of protesting that hideous, illegal, unconscionable, and endless war.

We were on the same side then, and I think I've found my ally again, both of us trying to end our quiet, decade-long battle.

He now knows where I've been, and why. He's curious, but he's not angry. If anything, my revelation makes him kinder. His questions are gentle, not accusatory. Attorney Jack Tanner is not in this car.

"Babe, tell me: What was it about Peter that made you want to go back to him? What was it you needed that I couldn't . . . no, make that wouldn't . . . give you?"

"He saw me, Jack. He saw me and he heard me. He listened without arguing and he never put me down. We talked and we valued each other's ideas. And he never, ever tried to change me. As best he could, he loved me just the way I was, and then I could start loving myself. The best part of me was reflected in him. And when it wasn't, when my ignorance and arrogance got in the way, he forgave me. It was the closest I'd ever gotten to divine grace, I think."

"Then I want to be more like Peter," he says. "I'll try to be more like him."

"No, just be the Jack I fell in love with. That will be enough . . . Okay, with a little bit of Peter thrown in for good measure. And Jack, I'm going to try to be more like the Caro you fell in love with, too."

"That's my girl. My matchless girl."

Jack stops chewing and puts down his BLT. He gulps some water and then hesitates and clears his throat. His brow is furrowed. I get the impression that he's been giving a lot of thought to what he's about to say.

"What would you think about selling the house and moving back to the city? We probably can't afford a big enough place in Manhattan, but maybe . . ."

"Brooklyn," we say at the same time.

"I need off the partner track," he says. "What would you think if I went to halftime at the firm and started my own practice, and then maybe in a year or so, quit Frampton and Tanner altogether to do civil rights law full time? It would be a lot less money, but I know I'd be happier . . ."

I smile and nod. "And I have a play in me, Jack. I've already started writing it."

I was going to wait until we got home to tell him, because I was afraid he was going to try to talk me out of it. I didn't want us to raise our voices in this roadside diner in Ohio, but his confession about wanting out of the firm disarmed me. I was about to tell him how it wouldn't take away from the kids, or the house, and how we could get a babysitter for after school, and that I was done with the PTA and the country club, and that eating take-out Chinese or frozen pizza a couple of times a week never killed anyone, but it was unnecessary.

A huge grin splits his gorgeous face. "It's about time, baby. It's about time."

Somewhere on that straight-as-an-arrow endless Interstate 80 that traverses Ohio, Jack turns up the radio, pulls onto the shoulder, puts the transmission in park, and gets out of the car.

"What's the matter, babe? Do we have a flat? I could fix it, you know." I had been dozing on and off, but I am wide awake now.

But no, no flat.

He walks around to my door and opens it. He's holding out his hand.

"Dance with me."

And so, here we are, almost twenty years married, in each other's arms like moonstruck kids, dancing by the side of the road. The eighteen-wheelers hurtling past on the asphalt almost drown out the music, but we know the words by heart and sing along with Elvis about wise men and fools rushing in and falling in love.

"This is what I know now," he says later that night, as we are snuggling in a not-too-comfortable bed in a motel near the Ohio/Pennsylvania border. "I'd marry you all over again. In a heartbeat, Caro Mills. I'd marry you all over again."

And I would marry him.

CHAPTER
FORTY-NINE

Peter made it a clean break: Not even a Christmas card. I guess he thought that would be easier for me. But nearly a year after our reunion, on a sunny afternoon that finds me sitting on the kitchen floor, sorting found objects into save and discard piles in anticipation of our upcoming move to Brooklyn (Save: The plaster-of-Paris handprints all three kids made in kindergarten; Discard: Takeout menus and two-year-old telephone directories), he calls.

"Caro?"

"Peter? My God, how are you? Wow! I can't believe you're calling!"

He takes a deep breath, slowly exhales, and starts again.

"Caro . . ."

"Yes?"

"Caro . . . something awful happened . . . I . . . it's Ernesto . . . last night . . . oh, Jesus, Caro, Ernesto's dead."

Ernesto? Dead? Impossible. He's only a year older than I am.

"Dead, Peter? My God, he's been with the same guy all these years. How could he have gotten it?"

"It? You mean AIDS?" He laughs bitterly. "He didn't have AIDS, Caro. We're subject to the same twentieth century ills as the rest of you, you know. Other things kill us, too. Ernesto had a heart attack. He was jogging . . . came home and Roger says he grabbed his chest, turned grey, and keeled over. It was massive. Nothing anyone could have done."

"Oh, poor Roger . . . and poor Peter . . . and poor, poor Ernesto. Oh, Peter, I'm so, so sorry."

"Yeah, me too. But, listen, the reason I'm calling is . . . well, you know that Ernesto's family pretty much washed their hands of him years ago. Never even acknowledged his relationship with Roger . . . can you imagine, they were together for eleven years, and his parents never even met his life partner?

"When Roger called them last night, they told him to do whatever he wanted about the funeral, but they wouldn't be coming. I guess they killed him off a long time ago. Anyway, Roger and I talked about it, and he said Ernesto often spoke about having his ashes scattered in Sabino Canyon."

"Often? Who our age speaks often about having their ashes scattered?"

Sometimes I'm so dense.

Peter is patient with me: "Listen, when you're gay, and you live in New York, and it's 1989 and your friends are dropping like flies, it's practically dinner table conversation, believe me."

"Oh, of course. I'm sorry, Peter. I wasn't thinking."

"It's okay. I can't expect it to be part of your reality. Anyway, Roger and I decided that we'd take him back to Tucson, and we'd like you and Scott to be there, too, if you can. At one point in his life, in that place, we were his family. As soon as I get off the phone with you, I'm going to call Scott in Chicago. I know you're really busy with your kids and everything, but it would mean a lot to Roger—and to Ernesto, too, of course . . . wherever he is."

"Peter, of course I'll be there. Just give me the details so I can book a flight."

"Look, I know it's probably none of my business, but it feels a little weird to be carrying Ernesto in a Bloomie's bag. I'd like to maybe buy an Indian pot or something to hold the ashes. It just seems a little more . . . I don't know . . . nice?"

Roger, who's sitting in the front of the rented blue Nova next to Peter, turns to me. "Thanks, Caro, that's really sweet of you, but you didn't know Ernesto the years we were together. The Bloomie's bag is perfect. It's just the way he would have wanted to go."

I turn to Scott, who nods in agreement. I suppose they're right, come to think of it. The whimsical Ernesto who came to Greg's defense in the Upper West Side shop would probably get a kick out of being scattered to the four winds from that distinctive yellow shopping bag.

The image suddenly triggers another memory, and I am provided a way to say goodbye that is worthy of my old friend. I can almost hear Ernesto's chortle.

"Guys, there's something I want to do for him. It won't take very long. Peter, can we go out Broadway for a while before we take Speedway? I want to stop at the mall."

"Sure, but what're you gonna do?" Peter glances at Roger, seeking permission for the detour. Roger shrugs and nods his assent.

"Oh, that's between Ernesto and me." I wink at Scott, who has caught on and gives me the thumbs up sign.

We pull into the parking lot by the Broadway Store.

"Okay, give me the bag. Don't worry, I'll be right out. Scottie, you can fill them in while we're gone, huh?"

Ten minutes later, my mission is accomplished.

"He made it, folks!" I raise Ernesto-in-the-bag high in the air. "It took twenty-two years, but he finally accompanied me into the dressing room—but not before the saleswoman asked if I'd like to check my bag while I tried on the dresses."

Roger gasps.

"Oh, it was okay, Rog. I just said 'No, thank you, he's going to help me decide.'"

The four of us dissolve in laughter, and then tears.

"I don't see any dresses, Caro," says Scott, wiping his eyes.

"I know. Ernesto didn't like any of them."

CHAPTER FIFTY

It's blast-furnace hot. The air is heavy in the canyon. No wind to catch our friend and send him soaring. Sitting on a flat rock, dangling our bare feet in the water, we wait for a breeze and remember Ernesto.

"You know, the last time I was here was just before graduation. He and I drove out in the truck . . . what was that, twenty-one, twenty-two years ago? Anyway, it was a day very much like today, so hot you could barely breathe and your clothes stuck to you, and sweat rolled into your eyes. The only thing to do with a day like that was to swim, so we did—didn't even bother to strip down to our underwear. The problem was, though, Ernesto had put the keys to the truck in his pocket, and when it was time to go home, we couldn't find them. We'd been horsing around, surface diving and stuff, so they were probably on the bottom of this pool. We never found them. They're probably right down there still." Scott points.

"How did you get home?" Ernesto's last lover asks his predecessor.

"With a screwdriver. We jammed a screwdriver into the ignition and used it as a key. We never even replaced it. Ernesto just sold the truck the way it was—and used the money to fly to New York the next month."

"Where we met," sighs Roger.

"How did you meet, Rog? When I ran into him that time we were surrounded by my kids, so we really didn't have a chance to discuss much."

"Oh, he told me about that day . . . at Mythology and then the ice cream parlor? He was so pleased to have run into you, Caro, and he thought your kids were great. So, how did we meet? Well, it was in a Bloomingdale's window, actually. It was around midnight, and I was installing a display, and I noticed this guy outside was watching me. That happens a lot, and I usually ignore whoever's out there, and eventually, they get bored and go away. But he didn't go away . . . and I kept feeling his eyes on me . . . those dark, penetrating eyes . . . they sort of gave me the creeps, and he was dressed in a way that suggested what my mother used to call a hoodlum—tight black pants, sleeveless black tee-shirt, black bandana tied around his head. I decided to leave by way of the Third Avenue door, just in case he was packing a switchblade, or something. And then he pulled a notebook and a pen out of his pocket. He wrote a note and held it up to the window, and that . . . that changed my mind. He came home with me that night, and I never spent a night alone again until . . . until four days ago . . ."

His voice breaks, and Peter puts his arm around him.

I'm caught up in the story, though, and Roger has skipped the turning point.

"What was in the note, Roger?"

Peter glares at me and hisses, "Caro!"

"No, it's okay, Peter. I was coming to that. It said, 'Will you marry me?' Isn't that just like him, Caro?"

"Yeah . . . yeah . . . Jesus, it's hot. I wish it were December."

"Well, I'm sorry Ernesto didn't have the courtesy to die when it was a little cooler, Caro," Peter snaps.

I'm startled. This is so unlike Peter. Perhaps the heat has gotten to him. I guess we're all getting a little edgy.

"Well, I know what Ernesto would do if he were here," says Scott, unbuttoning his shirt. "Anybody care to join me in the water?"

"No suit . . ."

"So swim in your underwear, Caro. That's two more items of clothing than you were wearing in that milk bath we took, remember?"

I groan. "You're not the first person to remind me, Scottie. Okay, anybody else going to join us?"

Roger looks at Peter, nods, and proceeds to strip down to his boxers. For a moment, it looks like Peter will hold out for sweltering on the rock, but after making sure that the shopping bag is secure, he, too, strips down and slips into the water. I purposely don't look at him.

A half-hour later, cooled off, air-dried, and calmed down, Peter takes me aside.

"I'm sorry I snapped at you, but this has been so hard for me. You know, I never stopped loving Ernesto, and now I have to let go of him and, at the same time, comfort the man whose place I wish I'd been in." He shakes his head. "Life sure is strange, isn't it?"

We hug, silently, asexually: Two old friends at the funeral of a third.

Scott walks over and taps Peter on the shoulder. "Guys, I think it's time. There's a breeze picking up, and Roger says he's ready," he says quietly.

I give Peter a squeeze. "You okay?"

"Yeah, thanks."

Scott puts one arm around me, and the other around Peter, and the three of us walk back to the water where Roger waits with Ernesto. Peter and I each hold out an arm to Roger, and the four of us embrace until the moment we all realize we can no longer hold on to the one who has brought us together. And I'm remembering another embrace on the night Ernesto, Scott, Peter, and I became the Fabulous Foursome. That story has run its course. We are not the same four, and we are no longer fabulous. Maybe we never were.

Carefully, Roger reaches into the shopping bag and gently removes the twist-tied baggie, but his hands are shaking so much that he can't undo the tie.

"Here, let me," says Peter.

Roger reaches in and gives us each a sooty handful.

What parts of you am I holding, Ernesto? I'd like to think I've got some of your laughter and mischievousness cupped in my hands.

Scott is the first to let go. "Thanks for the memories, old boy. I won't forget."

Peter looks at me. So I am to be next. *Thank you for what, Ernesto? For abandoning me on my acid trip? For being the one Peter loved instead of me?* I shake my head. *No, for the good times.*

"Thanks for that lovely ice cream day, Ernesto." The wind takes the ashes high into the air.

Roger holds Ernesto's remains to his cheek. "Good-bye, my love . . . and my best friend," he whispers, and lets go. There is a grey smudge under his left eye.

Resolutely, Peter, too, lets go. "Good-bye, my . . . friend, and God bless."

The ride back to town is silent, until Roger says he's hungry.

"Ernesto told me about this little Mexican place. I wonder if it's still there. He said they served the best . . ."

"Guacamole tacos!" Scott and Peter exclaim.

"El Charro," I say, and Peter glances back at me. He remembers. I smile at him, as if to say, "It's okay, Peter. It's where we spent our first evening together, and there's something poetic about spending our last one there, too, I guess."

Scott's plane is leaving at ten the next morning, and mine at eleven. Peter and Roger will spend a few more days in Tucson, before they go back to lives without Ernesto.

Scott meets me in the motel coffee shop for breakfast at 7:30.

"Do you think they'll join us?" he asks me when the waitress motions us to a table for two.

"Oh, Scott, you remember Peter and mornings. He could barely open his eyes before nine, and even then, he had to have two cups of coffee before even thinking about the day ahead of him. And I have a feeling Roger hasn't gotten much sleep in the last few days. Let's leave them be. They can always grab something after they get us to the airport.

"So," I say, after we have taken care of the business of ordering coffee, eggs and toast. "Tell me about your life. I couldn't believe it when Ernesto told me you were married. In fact, I was pretty jealous."

"Of my wife?" Scott feigns surprise. "Why, Caro Mills, I never knew you had the hots for me."

"You jerk, you know what I mean. That it was you who ended up with the wife and the kids and the white picket fence instead of Peter."

"I know, I know. Look, you can tell me it's none of my business, and it probably isn't, but . . . are you still in love with him?"

"It's okay. Yeah, I am, a little. I think I'll always love Peter, but I've accepted that. And I truly love my husband. Our marriage was pretty shitty for a while, but we've been working on it. It's so much better now. Actually, better than ever. It's nice . . . comfortable, you know? Jack and I have been through a lot over the past twenty years, and I expect—well, I hope—we'll grow old together. The kids are getting more independent every day. One of these days they'll decide they don't want us in their hair anymore, so we'll have to move to Florida and play golf and shuffleboard."

Scott shakes his head. "Somehow, I just don't see you doing that. Aren't you the girl who spent three years getting out of gym?"

"Just kidding. I mean, really, can you see me playing golf? No, I'll probably revert to type, join the Grey Panthers and make trouble for the Establishment. Much more my style, don't you think?"

"Definitely. You're going to make one hell of an old lady."

Breakfast arrives and the conversation is halted until the waitress departs.

"What about you, Scott? How are things going for you?"

"Well, Mary Beth and I still own the bookstore. It's a little tough competing with the chains. A Barnes & Noble opened a few blocks away, but we have a loyal clientele. So, we're doing okay. And our girls are in school—Jenny's in fourth grade and Nikki's in second." He shakes his head. "Can't believe how time flies. And we just bought a house in Lincoln Park. It's a fixer-upper, but it's a Craftsman, so we're pretty psyched. No white picket fence, though. Wouldn't go with the architecture."

But that's not the answer I was looking for.

"Scott, did you still have some feelings for Ernesto?"

He seems nonplussed, but then answers. "No, not really. Not the kind you mean. I feel terrible that he's dead, of course, it's such a shock, but he really was a different phase of my life. I went out with girls in high school and . . . well, that stuff in college . . . that was something I went through for a while, that's all . . . just a phase."

"Scottie," I protest. "You were with Ernesto for three years. That doesn't sound like a phase . . ."

And you're here today . . .

But this is something he refuses to explore. "I want to show you pictures of my girls, Caro. And I hope you have pictures to show me, too."

He proffers his wallet. Two angelic little blondes smile up from the photo. They look just like their father. "And that's Mary Beth," he points with pride to a snapshot of a sweet-faced young woman in a bridal veil. "You know what? She looks exactly the same as she did the day I married her.

"My girls. I'm a lucky man, Caro."

EPILOGUE

July has come 'round again. It's been a year since Ernesto died, a year since I once again bid Peter farewell in an airport.

Jack has made good on his promise. He started his own practice as a civil rights attorney, and we live in Brooklyn Heights, in a brownstone that's about a third the size of our old house, but about ten times as happy. The boys share a bedroom, but it'll only be a couple more years before our oldest is off to college. The kids are back in camp. Greg is a counselor-in-training this year. Sarah writes that she has passed her junior lifesaving test (alas, she's too grown up to dot her i's with smiley faces), and Caleb's latest hastily scrawled missive announces that he was chosen camper of the week. And I am no longer a blonde.

Jack is taking two weeks off in August, and we've rented a cottage on Block Island—a second honeymoon, he says. I'm up for that: I've been teaching a playwriting course at the local community college, and that play I started writing at Peter's house will go into production at the school in the fall. Not Broadway, but so what. This year has exhausted me, but it's a happy exhaustion. I am content.

Oh, and speaking of content, I finished that sampler: "*Contentment is not the fulfillment of what you want, but the realization of how much you already have.*" It's hanging in the hall, right by our front door, just in case I need a reminder, but somehow it belies the truth. Finally, what I want and what I have are one and the same.

I almost miss the postcard in this morning's mail. It was stuck between the pages of a K-Mart flyer that was destined for the recycling bin. I fish it out when I recognize Peter's handwriting. It's an invitation to a housewarming, I see: "Roger and I would love to have you join us as we celebrate the completion of our house on Fire Island . . ."

I am tempted. Tempted to see Peter again, to hear his voice, to feel his body next to mine, even if it's in the guise of a friendly, welcoming bear hug. But that only lasts for a moment. What I'd really like is to see with my own eyes that Peter is happy and fulfilled, the best possible ending to our impossible love story. But maybe it's enough just to know.

I won't go, but I'll send flowers, a vastly extravagant, every-color-of-the-rainbow bouquet that I know will make him smile.

I doubt if Peter recalls the words he spoke that day I fell in love with him. After all, it's been almost a quarter of a century. But I'll never forget:

"If I were an artist, I'd paint you in all the colors of the rainbow."

So I'll send him yellow roses for friendship and pink ones for gratitude, white daisies for patience and orange dahlias for happiness, purple heliotrope for eternal love, and sprigs of dusty green rosemary for remembrance. And tucked right in the middle, a spray of blue sweet peas, for goodbye.

THE END

ACKNOWLEDGMENTS

So Happy Together is a project that began in 1988, took a long hiatus, and is finally a book, thirty-three years later. There are so many people to thank:

Tanya Whiton, developmental editor extraordinaire, whose ability to zero in on the emotional core of my story was truly amazing, and who put up with me, even when I whined—

Me, after presenting Tanya with what I believed was my final draft: "It's done!"

Tanya, after reading the draft: "Nope, not a novel yet. Where's your inciting incident?"

Me: "What's an inciting incident?"

Tanya patiently explains.

Me: "Well, I just read a novel where there's no inciting incident. It's just this woman going through menopause and so she goes on a road trip."

Tanya: "And you don't think menopause is an inciting incident?"

Chris Daly, copy editor, also extraordinaire, who looked up all my arcane references and made sure the words fit the times, and the margins.

Nancy Hauswald, who read the manuscript and pointed out that it doesn't take three days to drive from Connecticut to Pennsylvania, and other slips.

Left Bank Books, in Belfast, Maine—and independent bookstores everywhere. Long may you thrive.

Poet and She Writes author Elizabeth Garber for graciously answering my publication questions and quelling my anxiety about going with a hybrid press.

Maine Writers and Publishers Alliance, for supporting a state-wide writing community in myriad ways.

She Writes Press, Brooke Warner, and Samantha Strom for believing in *So Happy Together* and midwifing it from manuscript to real book that you can buy (please do!); cover designer Rebecca Lown for beautifully capturing the story in a picture; proofreader Elisabeth Kauffman for finding the errors of my ways; Krissa Lagos for her corrections and her patience; Cait Levin, my tip sheet guru; Libby Jordan, my social media consultant; book designer Tabitha Lahr; Shannon Green, for pinch-hitting; Edite Kroll, for her legal advice; Kathleen Kearns, my website administrator; Rita Swidrowski, for designing my website logo; and Caitlin Hamilton Summie, my publicist, for helping me reach readers beyond my family, friends, and neighbors.

My lovely beta readers, accomplished writers all: my cousin, Nan Goldberg, who's always had the best giggle, and who laughed in all the right places while reading my work; my high school friend Candace Savage, who found me again on Facebook these many years later, and has been unwavering in her encouragement; and Linda Dickey, my oldest and dearest friend, a second mama to my children, who read the first version of *So Happy Together* over thirty years ago, which makes her my very first reader. She says she liked it then but thinks the new version is much improved (you bet it is!).

My brother, David Elliot, best sibling ever, who gave Caro her name, and who always has my back (and I'll always have his).

My son, Jonathan Shepherd and my daughter, Dinah Shepherd, who never stopped believing in me, except when they were adolescents, but we'll let that slide. I love you to the moon and back (a zillion times!).

And to my husband, Henry Wyatt, who put up with many manuscript readings (*so* many manuscript readings) and fell just a little bit in love with Caro, but still stayed true to me. You have my heart.

ABOUT THE AUTHOR

Deborah K. Shepherd was born in Cambridge, Massachusetts, and spent much of her early life in the New York area. Before retiring in 2014, she was a social worker with a primary focus on the prevention of domestic violence and sexual assault, and provision of services to survivors. After retiring, she studied French and tried downsizing. While cleaning out a closet, she exhumed the manuscript of a novel she had written (on a word processor!) thirty years before. After numerous rewrites, that novel became *So Happy Together*.

During an earlier career as a reporter, Deborah wrote for *Show Business* in New York City and for the *Roe Jan Independent*, a weekly newspaper in Columbia County, New York, where she and her first husband raised two children, two dogs and numerous goats. She also freelanced as a travel writer.

She graduated from the Interlochen Arts Academy in Interlochen, Michigan, and holds a BFA in drama from the University of Arizona and an MSW from the Fordham University Graduate School of Social Service.

Deborah lives with her husband and two rescue dogs on the coast of Maine, where she gardens, cooks, swims, reads, entertains her grandsons, tries to speak French, volunteers in her community, and writes two blogs, deborahshepherdwrites.com and paleogram.com. She is currently at work on a memoir.

Author photo © Henry Wyatt

SELECTED TITLES FROM SHE WRITES PRESS

She Writes Press is an independent publishing company founded to serve women writers everywhere. Visit us at www.shewritespress.com.

Play for Me by Céline Keating. $16.95, 978-1-63152-972-6. Middle-aged Lily impulsively joins a touring folk-rock band, leaving her job and marriage behind in an attempt to find a second chance at life, passion, and art.

Again and Again by Ellen Bravo. $16.95, 978-1-63152-939-9. When the man who raped her roommate in college becomes a Senate candidate, women's rights leader Deborah Borenstein must make a choice—one that could determine control of the Senate, the course of a friendship, and the fate of a marriage.

Center Ring by Nicole Waggoner. $17.95, 978-1-63152-034-1. When a startling confession rattles a group of tightly knit women to its core, the friends are left analyzing their own roads not taken and the vastly different choices they've made in life and love.

The Fourteenth of September by Rita Dragonette. $16.95, 978-1-63152-453-0. In 1969, as mounting tensions over the Vietnam War are dividing America, a young woman in college on an Army scholarship risks future and family to go undercover in the anti-war counterculture when she begins to doubt her convictions—and is ultimately forced to make a life-altering choice as fateful as that of any Lottery draftee.

Fire & Water by Betsy Graziani Fasbinder. $16.95, 978-1-938314-14-8. Kate Murphy has always played by the rules—but when she meets charismatic artist Jake Bloom, she's forced to navigate the treacherous territory of passionate love, friendship, and family devotion.

The Silver Shoes by Jill G. Hall. $16.95, 978-1-63152-353-3. Distracted by a cross-country romance, San Francisco artist Anne McFarland worries that she has veered from her creative path. Almost ninety years earlier, Clair Deveraux, a sheltered 1929 New York debutante, becomes entangled in the burlesque world in an effort to save her family and herself after the stock market crash. Ultimately, these two very different women living in very different eras attain true fulfillment—with some help from the same pair of silver shoes.